Alan Williams was educated at Stowe, Grenoble and Heidelberg Universities and King's College, Cambridge. As a journalist he covered the Wars in Algeria and Vietnam as well as the revolt in Czechoslovakia and the civil war in Ulster. His novels, which include *The Beria Papers*, *Gentleman Traitor*, *Shah-Mak* and *The Widow's War*, are all topical and have strong factual backgrounds.

D1581357

Also by Alan Williams

*Alan Williams*

# Dead Secret

A PANTHER BOOK

**GRANADA**
London Toronto Sydney New York

Published by Granada Publishing Limited in 1981

ISBN 0 586 04533 3

First published in Great Britain by
Granada Publishing 1980
Copyright © Alan Williams 1980

Granada Publishing Limited
Frogmore, St. Albans, Herts AL2 2NF
and
3 Upper James Street, London W1R 4BP
866 United Nations Plaza, New York NY10017, USA
117 York Street, Sydney, NSW 2000, Australia
100 Skyway Avenue, Rexdale, Ontario, M9W 3A6, Canada
PO Box 84165, Greenside, 2034 Johannesburg, South Africa
61 Beach Road, Auckland, New Zealand

Set, printed and bound in Great Britain by
Cox and Wyman Ltd, Reading
Set in 10 on 11pt Intertype Baskerville

Granada ®
Granada Publishing ®

For Harry Dawson

My thanks are also due to Lois Rodgers and
Judy Southwell, and to my wife, Antonia

## Dead Secret

*Men occasionally stumble over the truth, but most of them pick themselves up and hurry off as though nothing had happened.*    SIR WINSTON CHURCHILL

*What is truth?*    PONTIUS PILATE

# Night Callers

There were four men in the room. At least two of them looked out of place, though they were quite at ease. Big square-shouldered men with square-cut black hair, black moustaches, each wearing a chocolate-brown suit with a broad chalk stripe, wide lapels, and a silk handkerchief sprouting from the breast-pocket like a fresh orchid. The third man was slighter, with grey cropped hair and a narrow face: he had a military bearing, with a suggestion of the scholar.

The three of them were drinking Scotch, sitting in a semi-circle facing their host, who was elderly, distinguished.

It was an exquisite room, part of a bachelor flat in Albemarle Street, behind Piccadilly.

One of the big men said, 'We'd better have some music.'

'Nothing too loud, too obvious,' the grey man said.

The other got up and strolled over to a complicated hi-fi system, selected a cassette and slotted it into the machine. A Mozart piano sonata flowed through the room. 'Quiet enough?' he said, and returned to his chair.

The grey man addressed his host, who sat stiff and upright in a Sheraton chair. 'You know why we are here. Further explanations are unnecessary. We are carrying out orders.' His English was pedantic and correct.

The first big man turned to him and said, in their own language: 'I thought the fat man was joining us?' He spoke a heavy dialect, which the elderly man opposite obviously did not understand.

The grey man said, 'He's at the hotel. We're to call him when it's finished.'

'Typical. Always keeps out of the firing-line.'

'He was in the line with poor Serge, remember.'

'I'd like to know how the hell he got out of East Germany. Those people keep you locked up for a long time.'

'You know the fat man. He's very clever. He has excellent contacts. It is a serious mistake to underestimate him. But come on – this talk is wasting time.'

The big man looked up at the stout chandelier suspended from a ring in the moulded ceiling. 'Right, let's get going.' He and the second man put down their drinks and stood up.

Their host remained where he was, staring at them, wide-eyed. He did not speak because a strip of masking tape had been stretched across his mouth, from ear to ear; he was now beginning to have difficulty breathing.

One of them had produced a length of wire from under his jacket: pulled his chair up under the chandelier and climbed on to the silk seat. He could not quite reach the top of the chandelier, so the first man lifted him by the hips and held him still, while the second swiftly knotted the wire around the ring in the ceiling. He climbed down again, and the two of them took up their positions on either side of the elderly man on the chair. The grey man lit a cigarette and watched.

The man in the chair had turned the colour of clay; his nose had begun to run, and his eyes were watering.

'Take his shoes off,' the grey man said. 'We don't want him kicking.'

'Has he emptied his bowels, do you think? We don't want that smell around either.'

'How should I know? Anyway, we shan't be around to smell it. Now get on it – it's late, but somebody might come up. We want this to be tidy.'

The two big men went about their task silently, methodically, like doctors performing a routine operation. One of them removed the elderly man's black hand-made shoes, then they hauled him up and stood him in his stockinged feet directly under the chandelier. He had begun to make a muffled, whimpering noise. One of them slapped his cheek, gently, like smacking a newborn baby. The tape had begun to come loose, and there was spittle on his chin. His wet eyes rolled round, trying to focus on the slip-knot which the second man had arranged just behind his head. He let out a gurgling sound and the first man pulled the wire tight, then slipped the loop over the man's head. The second man kicked the chair away and the body dropped sharply and went rigid for a moment, then began to jig about like a puppet, swinging slowly in the middle of the room. The throat was squeezed to the size of a man's wrist and the face became unrecognizable. From the taped mouth came a series of clicking sounds, barely audible above the music.

The grey man stood up and led the way to the door. They let themselves out, quietly, leaving the music playing, the locks undamaged. They met no one on the stairs or in the hallway. The caretaker's glass cubicle was still empty. He would probably not return until the pub closed.

The street was quiet. Here they separated – the two big men getting into a Volvo saloon, the grey man walking towards Bond Street where he caught a taxi to the Ritz. He would telephone Brown's Hotel from there.

It was too late for the morning papers, but the evening editions carried the story on the front page :

### STRANGE 'SUICIDE' OF ABCO CHIEF

Sir James Milward-Smith, aged 64, Chairman of the America-Britannic Consortium, was found hanged this morning in his Mayfair flat in Albemarle Street, W.1. No note was left, and Sir James's colleagues report that he seemed in good health yesterday. Police are not ruling out foul play . . .

# CHAPTER ONE

# Death in Venice

*Secrets are edged tools, and must be kept from children and from fools.* JOHN DRYDEN

Perhaps it was the car radio which first implanted in Tom Hawn the seed of the whole outrageous, perilous idea, on that fifty-mile stretch of autostrada between Bologna and Florence. At any rate, it laid the top soil in which the idea could find refuge, sprout, and later flourish.

It was a news flash – the first news which Hawn had heard or read since arriving from England in early summer. A Greek super-tanker, under a flag of convenience, had rammed a ferry off Ancona and spilled its cargo of oil – an estimated 200,000 tons – which was now despoiling the entire Adriatic coast, threatening Venice's Lido and its fetid canals.

The commentator spoke with a shrill note of artificial urgency and outrage: the Government, as usual, was under attack for inactivity; the ecological lobby, in holy alliance with the Communist Party and other benefit groups, was continuing to stage demonstrations 'of a serious nature' in Venice, where the owners of the spilt oil – ABCO, the America-Britannic Consortium, the largest oil company in the world – were hinted to be in corrupt confabulation with local officials within the sumptuous fastness of the Hotel Danieli Royal Excelsior, which appeared to be under some sort of siege. One policeman had been shot in the arm (apparently by mistake); and a Molotov cocktail in a Coca-Cola bottle had been thrown without effect at Quadri's, on the Piazza San Marco.

Hawn heard the news with divided enthusiasm. He was

driving to Venice to rejoin his girl, Anna, after four months' exile, alone, in a farmhouse in Tuscany where he had been working on his opus about the Medicis. His mind, like his body, felt parched : he wanted to be enlivened, exhilarated, but not just by Anna – beautiful, practical, gentle Anna who cared about seal-culling and extinct whales and the sacking of our ancient heritage by big business. (The reported state of Venice today would be leaven to her soulful bread, Hawn reflected gloomily.) But as a journalist at the end of a sterile sabbatical, he wanted to get his teeth into something – something harder than just a worthy mob of Italian Friends of the Earth, and their docile Communist comrades, shouting rude things about the abominable ABCO outside the Danieli.

Still, any story was better than none. Hawn had little empathy for eco-pneuma : by both inclination and the nature of his trade, he had a touch of the romantic about him : but a robust, destructive romanticism. An unkind observer might have called him Philistine, war-lover, *voyeur*. He liked to see history being made. Secretly, the spectacle of an ancient city, tranquil and splendid under a peaceful moon, was less to his taste than that of the same city being put to the sack by mobs of crazed fanatics, so guaranteeing Hawn – providing the telex still worked – a front-page lead in tomorrow's paper.

However, the news bulletins were not entirely without hope. He rather warmed to the idea of riot-police and bombs in San Marco. It made a difference from Ruskin and Peggy Guggenheim and all those German tourists trying to civilize themselves.

But perhaps the seed had already taken root, to be nurtured in these first hours by a circumstance that had nothing to do with the scrappy radio bulletins.

Hawn had been hidden too long on his dusty perch in the Tuscan hills to have remembered that he was beginning his holiday on the worst day for motorists in the Italian calendar – the start of the Ferragosto, when the entire middle class migrates by car from the industrial suburbs to the coast.

On this steaming first day, the country's petrol station attendants had declared one of their regular lightning strikes. Hawn had collected his hired car from Siena that morning, with a full tank, and reckoned he had just enough to make it up this last eight-mile leg of the journey to Mestre.

Just north of Bologna one filling-station was open; and already the queue of cars stretched back nearly a mile, clogging both emergency and slow lanes. The heavy traffic – mostly tankers bound for the oil refineries of Mestre and the port of Trieste – was being forced into the centre lane; and before the turning off to Mantua the traffic was moving at walking pace.

At Padua it stopped altogether. Men got out in shirt-sleeves and stared impotently ahead. Rumour passed down the queue that a Lamborghini had blown up several kilometres further on. Hawn looked anxiously at his watch. It was now past three o'clock, and he had been allowing himself four comfortable hours for the drive, arriving in Venice by five at the latest. Anna had few obvious faults, but she did not like being kept waiting; and Venice in the tourist season is not a convenient place for a foreign girl to be left on her own.

Not that Hawn had anything to fear : he accepted her loyalty without question, and had himself never given her true cause to distrust him. But their four months' separation, aggravated by the chronic Italian postal service, would have opened a distance between them; and if he was now going to be late, he imagined her keeping to that scruffy hotel she had chosen, alone, biding her impatience, quietly, imperceptibly resentful.

Hawn was going to be late, and there was nothing he could do about it. She could hardly blame him for the tantrums of Italian industrial relations. And as he sat in the hot airless car, stopping and starting every few yards, he forced him to stop fretting over this temporary fuel crisis, and began – idly at first – to consider its broader, more technical dimensions.

He remembered hearing that in England, during those bloody bank holidays, the motorways in and out of London each carried between six and seven thousand vehicles an hour. He wouldn't be surprised if this autostrada to Venice was now log-jammed with as many as ten thousand, with more piling up behind him with the afternoon traffic arriving from Milan.

He thought : if the average Italian car does twenty-five miles to the gallon, how many gallons do 10,000 cars burn over eighty kilometres, or exactly fifty miles, of autostrada? The puzzle at least passed the time.

One car burns two gallons per fifty miles, ergo, 10,000 cars an hour would burn 20,000 gallons – and at approximately 300 gallons to a tonne of crude oil, that worked out at just over 66 tonnes per hour, on the short stretch between Bologna and Venice.

For the four days of the Ferragosto, with the traffic almost as dense at night as by day, and taking a mean average of 50 tonnes per hour, the total could be as high as 4,800 tonnes. Even if he halved the figure, to account for the average day in summer, it would only cover a fraction of the thousands of miles of Italian autostrada, not including Italy's secondary roads.

As a journalist, Hawn considered statistics the necessary grist to the greater drama of things. His mind now seized on the enormity of these figures, and while bogged down on this fifty-mile stretch of shimmering concrete, he let his imagination take flight over thousands, hundreds of thousands, millions of kilometres. How many millions were there in Western Europe alone? How many million cars doing twenty-five mpg over an average twenty-four hours?

Since working on the Rhodesian sanction-busting story, Hawn had come to know quite a lot about the oil industry. It was fascinating and formidable. But until now he had never considered it in its entirety; he merely knew of what had found its way 'illegally' up from South Africa, and that had been a dribble in the ocean of the world market. If his present, rough calculations were anything like correct, the total world consumption of oil on any *one day* – let alone year – must run into millions of tonnes.

The largest super-tanker can carry a quarter of a million

tonnes of crude: and he knew that approximately four thousand tankers were at sea at any one time. An industry operating on that scale would have to be more powerful than any government – as the sanction-busting fiasco had so hilariously, miserably proved. Any one of the major oil companies would have to have the resources and organization which only the super powers, and certain Arab states, could hope to rival. Yet a handful of peasants, working a few dozen pumps in Northern Italy, had managed to bring this corner of the country to near standstill.

He thought what fun one of those Soviet subs would have off the Gulf or round the Cape.

Perhaps the story was there – though it was not a new one. Nor did it help the traffic on the autostrada. The crippled Lamborghini had been shifted; but over the last few kilometres past Padua the going was painfully slow.

It was early evening when he at last came in sight of the ugly sprawl of Mestre, with towers of burning waste-gas flapping in the thick, damp air. The oil refineries had been built up to the limit of the water where the causeway runs across to Venice. There was a smell of unrefined fuel.

Helmeted leather-caped police stood at the head of the causeway, slowly processing each car. Hawn was warned to proceed at no more than five kilometres per hour. The police carried sub-machine pistols, with the safety catches off. With the Red Brigades still at large, these lads from the peasant South were taking no chances. Nor was Hawn. He was a careful journalist who knew when to play the odds. To be shot in the back by a trigger-happy Italian policeman would be a poor epitaph.

With some difficulty, he left the Fiat in one of the multi-storey car parks behind the station; then carried his scarred leather hold-all down to the jetty. There were more police here and, at a distance, crowds of demonstrators – men with beards and slogans and pretty girls in raincoats who chanted a dismisal litany which sounded like '*ABCO fuori! La Nazione per il Popolo!*' (Shades of Mussolini here? he wondered maliciously.) Then occasionally a voice, less timid than the others, would call out, 'Death to the Imperialist Industrial Military Fascist Complex! Death to ABCO!' – like a street vendor hawking his wares to an uninterested crowd. Some of the police would spit and rock back on the heels of their boots; and a few of them would smack their rolled-up caps into the palms of their gloves.

It was small beer for Hawn, with his blasé memories of Hué and Paris and Prague and Teheran. This was not so much an event, more a tiresome Italian ritual, a demonstration of thwarted *machismo* that was almost burlesque. There was not even a whiff of CS gas to wipe away the green stench of the canals; but at least it was a change from the arid stillness of those hills, with his textbooks and sheets of foolscap curling up in the heat. He wanted Anna badly.

The police here stood in a double row, looking menacing only on account of their guns and shiny black uniforms and visored helmets, and because they were unshaven and red-eyed with exhaustion. Hawn knew at once that they didn't have the stomach for a fight, and the demonstrators were too innocent, too idealistic to give them one.

He became more concerned that there was no vaporetto, no motorscafo, to take him to his hotel. His reunion with Anna was now well overdue.

A gondolier finally sidled up beside him and negotiated an exorbitant sum. Hawn did not argue. He was too old a hand to stand on petty principles in a crisis.

The gondolier moved off with a lulling lapping pace; it began to grow dark and lights came on in the palaces along the Grand Canal. A couple of times they heard the howl of sirens from police motor launches; then, rounding the bend under the Rialto Bridge, they ran into a blockade of launches, two of which picked out the gondola in the blinding pencil-beams of their searchlights. The gondolier paddled apologetically to the shore. There was no refund.

Hawn got through the cordon by producing his Press pass, and allowing himself to be searched. The police seemed bored and irritated that he should not be an obvious troublemaker. He then cut through a couple of side-streets, the corners and bridges all guarded by pairs of riot police, several of them smoking in the dark sweating recesses of stone, of arch and alcove. He emerged on the Lagoon, close to Harry's Bar. No police here.

He felt that he had lost so much time that a few more minutes wouldn't make that much difference. He pushed through the chipped saloon doors, into the air-conditioned gloom, and was asking for a chilled beer when a voice piped up at his elbow: 'Ah, mais c'est Scaramouche! You come to see the Italians play silly buggers, huh?'

He had not seen the stranger for nearly twenty years, when Hawn had still been a young foreign correspondent and the man beside him had been one of the doyens of the Foreign Press Corps in Algiers during the slow bloody death of Algérie Française.

Prince Grotti Savoia was a very small man, noble-featured, with enormous eyes, infinitely sad, as though constantly trying to retain or impart some secret wisdom which eluded him.

He was drinking Pernod. 'Like old Algiers, huh?' His leaky stare strayed down the row of noisy tourists and a few wounded drinkers. 'But it is not the same, eh, Thomas old chap?'

In his heyday the Prince had been something of a luminary. Despite his noble origins and diminutive stature, he had been a heroic Partisan, a man of passionate liberal principles, and a courageous and resourceful journalist, though notoriously lacking in tact and subtlety, and plagued by that most disastrous and disarming journalistic trait: he could never keep a good story to himself.

At one time, back in those bad days in Algiers, the entire Italian news contingent – for the most part a craven and frivolous group – had been ordered out of the country, on pain of death, by the European Secret Army. The Principe alone had refused to go. Not only that – he had chosen the most fashionable bar in the city to announce the fact, shouting, 'I am not going to be pushed around by Fascisti!'

Hawn had been young and reckless enough in those days to have helped hide him, at clear risk to his own life, and thus won the enduring love of the Prince, together with

the somewhat mysterious epithet, 'Scaramouche'. In turn
he had always, without irony, addressed him as 'Principe'.
He had not seen him since, though he in turn had retained
a nostalgic affection for the old man, tempered now with
a grudging pity.

The Prince had not perceptibly changed, except that his
clothes did not look new, and his most patrician feature –
his miniature Bourbon nose – was vivid with broken capil-
laries. He was alone, and Hawn guessed that he was down
on his luck. The Prince asked him what he was doing in
Venice and Hawn told him.

'Bah, the Medicis! Old-fashioned gangsters. Go to the
Danieli. There you'll find the real gangsters. The big men
from ABCO. The people who spill oil all down our beaches
– vagabonds, corsairs!'

'You're covering this story, of course?'

'I cover it. I cover it for dirty little Genoese magazine
who pay few hundred lire a centimetre. That, for me – for
Grotti Savoia! And you know why? Because the big Italian
newspapers are frightened to employ me – they are frightened that if I am on the payroll, the Red Brigades will put
bombs in their offices and shoot the editors in the leg. You
see, that's what comes of being a good anti-Fascist!'

Hawn had finished his beer and wanted to leave; but
the Prince skilfully ordered two more drinks before he
could refuse.

'Principe, is there any real story here in Venice?'

'A silly story. The usual people throwing things at the
police. Even a bomb in Quadri's. And the orchestra in the
square went on playing – like on the *Titanic*. What do you
call that – good colour stuff?' He ducked his mouth to his
drink and came up refreshed, glossy-eyed. 'You want a
good story? Why don't you investigate ABCO? Don't just
go along and watch a few stupid policemen protecting them
at the Danieli. Start to dig. I give you a good story about
ABCO. A story no one will print. A story maybe you won't
print – but, you could try. You were good in Algiers.'

'What story, Principe?'

'I warn you, it's not new. So to say, it's not modern.

Nothing to do with OPEC, Iran, any nonsense like that. This is history, but good history. Something that would make the soles of every ABCO executive burn holes in the floor if it was ever printed.

'December 1944, Thomas. That was the date the Allies expected the great German armies to collapse. Why? Because in August of that year the Russians captured the oil fields at Ploesti in Rumania – Germany's only source of crude oil. Then the Ardennes offensive. Christmas 1944 – *boum!* – the old Hitler dog punches a great hole in the Allied armies, with his new Tiger tanks. You know the fuel consumption of a Tiger tank?' He was eyeing his empty glass and Hawn bought him a fresh Pernod.

The little man savoured it, peering again down the bar. 'If ABCO men hear me talk like this, I am dead before tomorrow.'

'Oh don't be so bloody silly. We're not in Algiers now. But speak in French, if you're worried. What about the consumption of a Tiger tank?'

'Fifty litres to the kilometre. Less than one mile to your ten gallons. So how the hell they do it? All sea-lanes blocked, no controls of the air, enemy fronts closing on both sides – and Rumania falling to the Russians in the summer of 1944. Yet they still kept their monstrous war machine running to that last day, defending that last Berlin street in May 1945!' He smacked his brow with excitement. 'Holy Mary, I ask you, how did they do it?'

For the moment Hawn forgot about Anna. Not only did he now have the idea, but it was beginning to take root. He had great respect for the astuteness and integrity of the Principe, even if the man might not still be one of the profession's chosen few. There was a story here. There must be. It was just a matter of digging it out. It only amazed him that no one had thought of it before.

Prince Grotti Savoia insisted on buying him another beer, but he refused. 'I need something to go on, Principe. I can't just stand outside the Danieli with a placard saying that ABCO supplied the Nazis with oil. That's what you're saying, isn't it?'

The Prince's face had become crumpled, miserable. 'I know people – I know names – things I can't write. They don't allow me to write any more. They are so frightened of these fucking Red Brigades.'

'I know about that,' Hawn said soothingly, 'but can you tell me some of these names? Somebody who might give me a lead. It doesn't have to be somebody who's necessarily involved. Those sort of people aren't going to talk anyway.'

A white flash glared in their faces and a lean dark man came over and gave a ticket to a man along the bar. The lean man was obviously a professional photographer, and his client was a fat-cheeked man with a pork-pie hat. Hawn thought that the Prince was perhaps too drunk to have noticed; but he seized Hawn by the wrist and whispered, with dramatic fury : '*Vite!* Out of here. They have their spies already on us !'

Hawn quietened him down and got him outside. A siren was wailing somewhere in the city. The Prince began to cry. 'Sounds like Algiers, *n'est-ce pas?*'

'Principe, why don't we talk about this tomorrow? I've got a date and you're drunk.'

'I am drunk. God I am drunk. I am drunk with disgust for life. For the evil things that men do while good men die challenging them.'

'Good night.'

'No, please, please, a moment !' The Prince's eyes were wandering down the empty waterfront, seeking out some friendly face, or perhaps a foe. His mind seemed to be wandering too, persistent only in refusing to let Hawn leave.

Hawn said, for good measure : 'You said you had names – somebody I could contact, who would put me on to this story?'

'Yes, there is a man. In London. Very convenient for you. A *bon-viveur*, terrific gambler, lives well – very well by the standards of you miserable English.'

'His name?'

'Shanklin. Meester Shanklin. No "Sir", no "Lord". But very important. One of ABCO's *premiers franc-tireurs*. How do you say?'

'Sharp-shooter. I may have come across him. ABCO has a lot of people like that tucked away in the background. They only bring them out when there's trouble – the kind of trouble the Government prefers not to get involved in.'

'Bastards! Brigands!' The little Prince seemed to be only half listening. 'This Meester Shanklin give you a good story. He knows a thing or two. Deep secrets, dead secrets about the ABCO organization.'

'You want me to get him into trouble?'

'You don't get him into trouble. But maybe he drop you in a big shit. Drop both of us. He knows that ABCO did big oil deals with the Nazis, on behalf of British and Americans.'

'Not officially?' said Hawn.

'Officially? What is officially? Nothing an oil company like ABCO does is ever *strictement officiel*. I tell you, they are brigands.'

'How many people have you talked to about this, Principe?'

'Oh I talk, but nobody listens. Why should they listen to an old fool like me?' He laughed, a sharp odd sound in the damp stillness. 'But you listen, eh, Scaramouche?'

'Yes, I'm listening.' Hawn could already smell, above the salty sewage, more than just a fantasy scented with aniseed. 'Do you know any other names?' he said gently.

The Prince leant as far over the parapet as he could reach, and hung squinting perilously into the dark water. 'Maybe I know. But this is business, Scaramouche. You write this story – maybe you make a big fortune. World exclusive. You smash ABCO. The biggest political scandal of the twentieth century.'

'You said nobody would print it.'

'I only say, *if* they did. Now you embarrass me. I must make business. I must live.'

'I'll make a deal with you. Tomorrow, when you're sober. In the meantime, keep this to yourself. As you said, it could get you into a lot of trouble.'

'You find me at Harry's.'

'At Harry's.'

They embraced, and as Hawn moved off in the direction of his hotel, he had the feeling that his definitive study of the Medicis, made over the last few months, might be rather dull stuff. For the Medicis had worked with poison, with pikes and swords and staves, and their sole transport problem had been horses. They hadn't had to grapple with a budget of several million tonnes of crude oil a week, and worry about where it came from.

Supposing the old Principe were right, and the Nazis *had* got their oil from the West? When he looked at it in cold logic, there was a kind of deadly reason to the theory. After Rumania had fallen, what sources did the Germans have? The Allies had been rich in Texas, the Caribbean, the Middle East. But the Germans had had nothing – besides that which they had made themselves, synthetically, which couldn't have amounted to much.

The Prince's last words sounded in his ears through the sodden air: 'Remember, even their bloody staff-cars did only one kilometre to one litre! What do you think they ran them on – French cognac, or German gin?'

Hawn reached the hotel with some difficulty – a crooked, derelict building with its own rotting charm, its waterlogged roots sunk into a side-canal well behind the Piazza San Marco. Beyond the desk was a small glass-covered patio where two dwarf palms wilted under the dark sky. It was past eight o'clock and there was no sign of Anna.

The man behind the desk handed him his key, took his passport and gave him an envelope. Inside, on hotel notepaper, was Anna's rounded convent handwriting: 'Bumped into your friend H. Logan. Have gone with him to Danieli Bar. Love A.'

Hawn crumpled it up and threw it into a spitoon. So young Anna had decided to cross the tracks, to sup with a long spoon with one of ABCO's main agents and satraps! Not that Hawn had anything against Hamish Logan: the man had his uses, if not many virtues: he was head of a big public relations firm that represented, among other clients, the America-Britannic Consortium. He had also been one of Hawn's chief unofficial sources in uncovering the Rhodesian scandal : for while being an international snob and imitator of the latest fashion – both of which roles he played admirably – Logan was relentlessly conspiratorial, providing it promised to enhance his social position and win him useful friends.

Hawn was in no hurry to join the man's party; he was only surprised that Anna should have accepted Logan's invitation in the first place. She was a principled girl, with soft but persistent left-wing leanings, who detested Logan's circle, which was mostly made up of parasitic businessmen, oil executives and drunken wives. She must be either very bored or very cross, or both.

He rode up in the creaking cage-lift, let himself into the darkened room, stripped and squeezed himself into the narrow shower cubicle, which, like everything in Venice, seemed filled with that not-quite-clean smell of salt and seaweed. The water was tepid and did not leave him refreshed. He put on a clean shirt, wondered about having a drink, and decided it was not a good idea. After four months' abstinence from bodily pleasures, his innate puritan instincts restrained him. He had lain awake on many soundless nights, imagining in exquisite detail what he would do to Anna on this first night together again. He was determined to be sober.

He checked himself in the dim speckled mirror. Eighteen years in Fleet Street had coarsened him, blurred his profile, thickened his waist, given his eyes a slightly flat look. The arid solitude of Tuscany had dried him out in all ways: even a diet of pasta and bread now left him lean, sharp-eyed, lightly tanned, without that oily bronzed look common to the sun-greedy northern holiday-maker. Hawn was not a vain man, but he left the room satisfied. He thought Anna would not be displeased.

It was a five-minute walk to the Piazza San Marco, which was deserted, except for knots of caped and helmeted Carabinieri and a couple of jeeps, their radios squawking through the silence and exciting the pigeons.

Hawn looked at them with a twinge of guilty longing. He

liked to think of himself as a moderate, liberal man. Yet he was attracted by extremes and by violence, justifying them on the grounds of his work – wars, revolution, riots and death and the odious stinking aftermath of death – all the corrupt meat of the journalist's trade.

There were no demonstrators here, little hope of some *coup* by the Red Brigades. Yet just because he had heard a rumour in a bar from a sad old goat who'd fallen from grace didn't necessarily disqualify it as a good story. Many good stories began in bars.

And a story was still a story, wherever it came from.

They were at the bar of the Danieli, at the far end of the blue-draped lobby. The place was otherwise deserted, its vast gloom lit by chandeliers high in the vaulted ceiling. Anna and Hamish Logan were seated at a table with two other men. She had her back to Hawn as he came up behind her and kissed her straight reddish hair. She jumped sideways and spilt half her drink. 'Oh God, Tom! D'you have to do that? I've been fighting off these bottom-pinching Lotharios since I got here – until Hamish rescued me.'

'Well, at least they've got good taste,' he said, taking a chair.

Logan stood up heavily and gave his practised smile. He was a large man with dark glasses and a well-covered belly under a double-breasted white suit. He effected the introductions fluently, with ease. There was an American, called Don Robak – a chunky man in a powder-blue seersucker suit, with a smooth square face under a thatch of dusty-blond hair which flopped down over his brow and was tucked untidily back behind his ears. He gave Hawn a noncommittal nod; and at the same time Hawn had the uncomfortable feeling that he had seen the man before, under not altogether pleasant circumstances.

Logan announced that Robak was one of ABCO's senior European executives. But it was the third man at the table who momentarily diverted Hawn's attention from the others – even from Anna, in whom he had already sensed a covert resistance, a proud and private determination to withhold her feelings towards him – or at least to postpone them.

The man who had distracted him was introduced as Monsieur Charles Pol, from Paris – 'Charles, Monsieur Hawn used to be one of our most distinguished journalists. Now he has fled to the groves of Academe – he has become a scholar, he writes books.'

'Eh bien, enchanté! Monsieur!'

Charles Pol was one of the fattest men that Hawn had ever seen. Not just ordinarily fat, or even extraordinarily fat : he was a man of short but gargantuan proportions, like a living relic of the Michelin man – rolls of fat squeezed into an enormously outsize tropical suit, whose seams at the elbows were already breaking, his armpits displaying damp patches, although the bar was air-conditioned. As Hawn studied him, he was aware of a sweet cloying perfume that was certainly too vulgar for Anna – or Logan, for that matter.

The barman had arrived and Logan was busily ordering fresh drinks. They were all on tall Negronis, except Robak who nursed an orange juice. Hawn chose beer. He wanted to remain sober, at all costs. He also noticed that Anna's colour was unusually high. She had a good head for drink, and he had rarely seen her the worse for it. He wondered if it was suppressed anger at the general company round her; or whether it was the uncertain tension of meeting up with him again in so public a fashion, in front of strangers. But it had been her choice, not his. He tried explaining about the traffic jam and why he was late, but she shrugged as though it didn't matter. He could see that it was not going to be an easy evening.

He turned to Hamish Logan. 'So what are you doing in Venice, Ham? Long dirty week-end under police guard?' Only the Frenchman, Pol, smiled; and Hawn glanced at him, but the image, next to Anna's neat profile, was both absurd and frightful.

Logan took a long pull at his drink. 'Strictly business, my dear boy. Pre-emptive strike, so to speak – cleaning up before the shit hits the fan. Or, as in this case, the oil hits the beaches.'

'It's an absolute disgrace,' Anna said. 'And every time it happens, they get away with it. Somebody makes a packet, while the local people are left to clean up the mess.' She glared at Logan : 'Why don't they make ABCO pay the bill, for God's sake? They're rich enough.'

'Lloyds picks up the bill, my dear – they always do.' He leant out and patted her hand, which she quickly withdrew. He seemed unabashed. 'As for the ship – Greek charter, Liberian flag – can't touch her.'

'There's not much to touch,' Anna said angrily, 'It's broken in half !'

She sat there, next to one of the princes of PR and the fat French clown – she straight-haired, no make-up, in her loose brown dress that reached below her knees, like a monk's habit without a hood, and well-worn block-heeled sandals. Hawn could not tell whether she was enjoying herself or not.

Logan turned to Hawn : ''Course it's the most frightful bore. Twelve dead, as far as we know, and the whole coast awash with valuable oil. And I'm afraid a lot of people seem to be rather cross about it. Including your dear Anna here.'

'You obviously think it's rather a joke,' she said. 'A nice excuse for a few days in Venice, living it up at ABCO's expense.'

'Not a joke, my dear. Work.'

'What work? Wining and dining a few corrupt Italian big-wigs – greasing the odd palm, and selling them all the soft-soap about ABCO's great world role in keeping the wheels of industry moving, and how Italy can't do without her, and how a few spoilt beaches really mustn't be allowed to foul up the works.' Her face, in profile to Hawn, had taken on a deeper flush.

Ham Logan chortled into his Negroni. It was clear that the others too were faintly entertained by Anna's outburst. But she only increased Hawn's discomfort by turning on him : 'Well, haven't you got anything to say?'

'Oh, don't be childish,' he said, in a half-whisper. 'You're not going to change their morality overnight – let alone over a few drinks. You know what sort of people they are. And you accepted their hospitality, not me.'

As though sensing that the conversation had gone far enough in this line, they now turned to broader subjects. More drinks arrived, and the awful bogus *bonhomie* was spread more thick, with the exception of the American, Robak, who sat quietly aloof with his orange juice.

'The Saudis are windy. Don't blame them. After Iran, they're bound to bump up the price this time.'

'The Shah was a darned fool. He paid too much, to too many people, then was dumb enough to listen to them.'

'The Americans behaved disgracefully.'

'Carter, he is a catastrophe.'

'The British are all washed up.'

'Like the Italians.'

'I'd like to see Tricky-Dicky back.'

'Who's going to guard the Gulf now? It's up for grabs, and we don't have to look far to see who's going to grab it.'

'The New Islam is pretty anti-foreign – which includes being anti-Russian.'

'You think that worries the Russians?'

'The Russians need oil. Always have. They've got plenty of it, but they can't exploit it. They need the technology. They need us. I tell you, gentlemen, if anyone is going to act as the new policeman in the Gulf, it's ABCO. The Soviets aren't going to rock the boat.'

This last opinion came from Robak. Hawn, who had been only half listening, and was waiting for a convenient moment in which to extract Anna, now broke in, recklessly, as much to keep his end up with her as to make a serious contribution.

'What about the Germans in the last war?'

'So? What about 'em?'

'They didn't have oil – or nothing to speak of.'

'They had technology – the best in the world. Anyway, they lost, didn't they?'

'It took them a damned long time to lose.'

'They had Rumania, the Russian fields, and the rest they

manufactured themselves – from shale and coal.'

'Can you run a tank or heavy armoured vehicle on synthetic fuel? And the Russian fields were lost by 1943, and after that the Rumanian ones were being bombed flat, until they were taken in 1944. But the Germans kept going.'

Robak said calmly, with a thin layer of contempt: 'As I said, the Germans were very advanced in their techniques. I mean scientific techniques. With respect, Mr Hawn, I don't think you know what you're talking about.'

Logan broke in: 'The whole of Nazi Germany was bristling with synthetic fuel plants. They were up to every trick. We don't begin to equal them for ingenuity. They even built a car that ran on wood!'

The fat Frenchman, Pol, now spoke in a high cooing voice: 'They did better than that, messieurs. They constructed a train that ran on the gases from old corpses. And corpses were about the only thing they weren't short of!' He took a deep drink, then shook his head: 'But I regret, my dear Monsieur Logan, when you talk of synthetic fuel, you mean the hydrogenation process. It is one I am familiar with. It yields a very low-grade petrol, and the Germans were only able to use it in aircraft or light vehicles. They fitted their Messerschmitts with a specially adapted engine that used water-injection – the first of its kind. Very ingenious, but with a synthetic fuel it only lasted twenty minutes before it burnt out. However, that was just enough, since their production lines could produce a new engine every fifteen minutes.'

There was a pause. Logan looked momentarily confused. But Hawn's blood was up, and when he spoke again, he had Anna's full attention: 'Speer was building a thousand of those Tiger Tanks a month – in a factory under a mountain, to protect them from Allied attacks. He kept them rolling against us and the Russians right up to zero hour – when the Führer blew his head off, and the whole pack of cards came tumbling down. Hitler maintained a mobilized army that could match both us and the Russians, and could fight us all right up to the touch-line. How did he do it? Where did he get his fuel from?'

Hamish Logan sat forward and snapped his fingers; his face was very red. 'I know, you've been talking to that ridiculous little Prince Grotti Savoia! He's been making a perishing nuisance of himself here in Venice in these last few days. Things haven't been easy for any of us, without having that wretch poking up at odd times and spouting all his nonsense about the oil companies – by which he means ABCO, of course. And he doesn't do you journalists any more good than he does us. Stories like that simply lower the tone. Somebody should shut him up.'

'Perhaps somebody will. He's jittery enough. He even got all upset when somebody took an American's photograph in the bar. He sees spies everywhere.'

'Simple case of paranoia. Probably got the DTs too. He's beyond the slippery slope, is Grotti Savoia.' Logan lit a cigar and looked at Hawn, casually, conversationally. 'I suppose he just gave you his old spiel? The Nazis didn't have any obvious sources of oil, except Rumania, so where did they get it from?'

'You tell me, Hamish. Forget about the Principe. Where *did* they get it from?'

Logan sighed. 'Reserves. Everyone has reserves. At the time of the 1973 oil crisis, it was given out that the Pentagon had reserves for five years – hidden in underground lakes.' He handed his empty glass to the waiter. 'Don't tell me that old Adolf wasn't prepared. He'd had six bloody years to prepare.'

Pol popped an olive into his mouth and said nothing.

Ham Logan seemed to have recovered his professional calm. 'I don't want to sound patronizing, my dear Tom. But I do think you've been out in the wilds too long. Too much time to think. A bit of sanction-busting in Southern Africa is one thing – but insinuating that our major Western oil company may have connived at helping the Nazis is really carrying things too far.'

'Too far for you, maybe, Ham,' Anna said, 'particularly if it's true.'

'Now, don't you start being silly too, Anna. You must excuse our two young friends,' he said, turning to Robak and Pol, 'but journalists – particularly those who have been out of action for some time – tend to get a little excited. They fantasize.'

'Au contraire,' said Pol : 'I find your friend's theories most stimulating. The war still holds many secrets. We must not simply close our ears to the possibility of them, just because the idea is inconvenient, even repugnant to our interests.'

'I'd like to make one thing quite clear,' Hawn said. 'I never once insinuated that ABCO, or any other Western oil company, traded with the Nazis. Those were your words, Ham, not mine.'

'And Anna's.'

'Leave Anna out of this.'

Robak spoke, bland, his dry grey eyes fixed unblinking on Hawn. 'It's certainly a dramatic theory, I'll grant you that, Mr Hawn. And an original one. But I don't recall – did you say you got it off that Prince fellow, Grotti-something?'

Hawn did not believe that the Prince really needed his protection : yet there was something that worried him about Robak – apart from his being sure that he had seen the man before. He and Logan and the grotesque Frenchman made an incongruous, even sinister trio. He said : 'I got it off the top of my head – stuck in a traffic jam this afternoon.'

'Huh-huh. Don't laugh, Ham – some of the best ideas come off the tops of our heads. Are you going to be around in Venice for a few days, Mr Hawn?'

'It depends on the situation.'

'I don't expect that should put you off, if you're a real journalist. Come up and see me tomorrow morning – but not too early – suite 104, the Gritti.'

Hawn glanced at Logan. 'He's not thinking of having me bumped off, is he?'

'Well, not right away,' Robak said. 'Bad for public relations.'

Logan stood grinning between them, as Hawn and Anna shook hands; and again Hawn wondered where he had seen Robak before. The memory irked him like a piece of grit in his shoe.

He was still puzzling over it, as he followed Anna through the revolving doors, when he heard the pad of feet behind him, turned and saw Pol waddling towards him, his huge body balanced on tiny black-slippered feet.

'Monsieur Hawn! I regret that I have not more time to talk with you. Because, you see, I, too, am interested in your theory – from a more impartial point of view, shall we say? I have a rather personal interest in the crimes of the Nazis. I will not detain you now, except to say that I also have my theories. May I suggest that you both join me for dinner tomorrow night – the Antico Martini, at 8.30?'

He lay beside her under the single sheet, and in the cool darkness he could just distinguish her fine-boned profile against the spear of lantern-light through the curtains. Even after eighteen months it still puzzled him how a girl of such character, intelligence and obvious good looks could have progressed no further than the dingy catacombs of the London School of Economics, where she worked as a senior researcher.

They had met not there, but in the Public Record Office in Kew, where Hawn had been hacking assiduously at the deafening wall of silence surrounding the Rhodesian oil sanctions : while Anna had been delving into the industrial history of the Suffragette Movement. Hawn had followed his well-proven experience that libraries – along with art galleries – are the most propitious places for ensnaring the opposite sex. Soon he was meeting her for a regular drink in the local pub.

She was an earnest girl, quiet, undemanding; and while she was rarely high-spirited, he never found her dull. At first this had worried him : he suspected that it might be simply because he knew so little about her – that this air of secrecy might be lethally compounded by her subtle but firm refusal in those first weeks to go to bed with him. When she finally did, her attitude was equally puzzling : a mixture of gaucheness and carnal passion that both disturbed and stimulated him.

To his dismay, he became fascinated by her. For if he

could find any real fault in her – and he had a cruel and practised eye where women were concerned – it was her complete self-possession, her lack of any need of protection.

She had moved into the roomy chaos of his flat off Notting Hill; and soon, without aggression or any trace of ulterior motive, had restored it to a place of order. She offered him stability and calm; she cooked superbly, and without complaint; entertained even his most abominable friends; and afterwards she was a luxurious, uncomplicated lover. Only two conditions did she extract from him : that he cut down his habitual drinking, and that he was faithful to her. To his surprise, Hawn found himself complying.

He could not remember exactly how or when the break, or suspension, of their relationship had come. He had been growing increasingly restless on his newspaper, where he had now risen to fill a senior desk-job : he was no longer the brave trooper in the field, but the commanding officer at base-camp. He had asked for six months' paid leave, and had been granted it, together with the option of a further six months, unpaid.

A respectable publisher had advanced him enough to carry him comfortably over this period; but a worm of puritanism had persuaded him to seek out the barren solitude of the Italian hills – to escape from his work, the clatter of typewriters, spiked stories, coming back in mid-afternoon over-fed, burping with too much Hock-and-Seltzer from the cavern of El Vino. And escape from Anna – from coming back too late from the office, to have his apologies shrugged off while she warmed up the evening's dinner which they often ate in bed.

He looked at her now, at the innocent curve of her neck in the half-darkness. 'Are you asleep, angel?'

'No.'

'What are you thinking about?'

'You.'

'Anything I should know?'

'Nothing that'll hurt you. You've lost weight. You look younger. How are the Medicis?'

'Coming along, slowly. I'm going to have to get back to

London soon – spend some time in the British Museum. I haven't got enough reading material out in Tuscany, and my Italian's not up to the local archives.'

'Tom, stop fooling yourself. You're not an academic. If you were, you'd have stayed on at Cambridge. You've got a good enough degree. But you wanted excitement – the dirt and adventure of Fleet Street and Algiers and Saigon. You're an adventurer. Or you were.'

'You make me sound as though I've just castrated myself. You want me to go back to Fleet Street?'

'Only if you want to. But you said yourself what happens to old journalists – they don't even fade away, they just finish writing up Wills and Weather, or drift into public relations – like that fool Logan, only he's a full-blooded professional who actually enjoys it. You're not that sort, Tom. What was it you once said to me? That the most exciting moments of your life have been to watch the wing of your plane dipping over a city at war? That's what you really enjoy, isn't it?'

'I've seen enough war. I've covered seven altogether, not counting two civil wars, and the only difference between them was that some were nastier than others. And the one thing they all had in common was that after the first couple of days they rarely made the front page, and sometimes didn't make the paper at all.'

She turned and moved her hand gently across his chest. 'You don't know what you want, do you?'

'Do you know what you want?'

'I think so. I want you – not all of you, just to share things with you. I can't share Fleet Street – even if I wanted to – and I can't share the Medicis, except perhaps to do some typing for you. But I could . . . ' She rolled over, full-face to him, and kissed him softly, dispassionately, on the mouth. 'I could share this theory of yours – about Nazi oil supplies. I could do the research – and there'd be one hell of a lot to do – while you did the leg-work, the interviews.'

'You're not serious?'

'I'm absolutely serious. I'm not a brilliant investigative journalist, but I can tell a good idea when I hear it.'

'If you think it's such a dazzling idea, why has no one thought of it before?'

'You tell me. Who would have thought of it? Journalists, academics? You're always saying that most journalists are a bunch of lazy hacks who prefer to follow up each other's stories rather than think up their own; and academics spend most of their time in beautiful stone quadrangles, or bitching over the port.'

They lay in silence. From outside came the short warning cry of a gondolier approaching a blind corner, like a wild bird in the night. No police sirens this time : perhaps the tension was dying down. He said, 'Did you notice anything significant this evening after I mentioned my theory at the Danieli?'

'What?'

'Logan got excited – you might almost say, rattled. Started putting words into my mouth.'

'He'd been drinking. Everybody had, except that American.'

'Logan wasn't drunk – nobody was. And the Frenchman was definitely interested – a complete stranger, with interests in the oil business, and he invites us both for dinner tomorrow night. And as for that American, Robak – another complete stranger – he invites me up to his hotel suite tomorrow morning.'

'You'll go, of course?'

'Damn right I will. I touched a raw nerve there, Anna. I either got them interested, or worried, or both.'

She nestled up against him, pressing her shallow breast into his armpit. 'You've got me interested, too, love. Four empty months, then suddenly four orgasms – it may have been five – and now the thought of all those files – the LSE, Petroleum Institute Library, Public Record Office. Am I a very boring girl, Tom? Am I very *pedestrian?*'

He kissed her casually. 'That's a pretty double-edged compliment to me, after eighteen months. But if we're really on to something, it'll be more than just files and classified documents released under the Thirty Year Rule. If there's even a grain of truth in my theory, we may well run into trouble. Could be bad trouble. The oil business is a rough business, and they play rough. They'll play even rougher if they feel they're threatened.'

'Supposing we did prove that ABCO actually helped the Nazis? Would it hurt them so much, after all this time?'

'It would blow them sky-high. For God's sake, even this oil spillage in the Adriatic has worried them enough to send Logan scuttling out here to give the local bosses the sweet talk and grease a few palms. Like every big company, they're concerned about their image. And the bigger the company the bigger the image. Giving a helping hand to old Smithy in Rhodesia is one thing – giving it to Adolf Schickelgrüber is something else. I mean, think of all those Jewish shareholders in the States. It would be years before they picked up the pieces. Watergate pales.'

She yawned. 'Tom, I'm going to help you. We're going to do this together.' She smiled in the darkness. 'You're already seeing that wing dipping over another city at war.'

The two Carabinieri had stopped in the grey of the dawn on a tiny bridge that bracketed two crooked canals somewhere between the Piazza San Marco and the Rialto Bridge. They had been on duty since evening, and were tired and hungry.

One of them had lit a cigarette. The other grabbed his wrist. There was something half-floating in the slimy water off the steps at the end of the bridge. They swore quietly, reverently. They were God-fearing boys from Calabria and new to this kind of work. But both immediately saw the endless paperwork, the explanations to their superiors, perhaps a conference with the ubiquitous Press.

The one with the cigarette said, 'Shall we just leave it?'

'It might be important – it might mean promotion.' They had both moved towards the steps. The man's face was half in the water; he was wearing a suit and decent shoes. This was what decided the two Carabinieri. They reached down and pulled the body out, until it lay dripping on the cold stone. One of them had his flashlight out. There was a little blood on the face, near the left eye. He smelt of nothing worse than the canal.

One of them, who followed the television films, felt his pulse, then bent down and smelt his breath. He looked knowingly at his companion. 'He had been drinking. Must've happened last night. Slipped – the imbecile. My God, I can think of nicer ways of dying than being drowned in one of these stinking canals!'

He felt for the man's wallet. It was still there – an expensive wallet, sodden with the black water. Not much money in it, but enough to suggest that there had been no robbery. The dead man's credentials were stained, scarcely legible.

The Carabiniere straightened up. 'Dear God, we must go at once to the Commandants. This man was not just important, he was of the aristocracy! A sacred Prince!'

He left his companion to guard the body, and hurried away in search of his superiors.

Hawn heard the news by chance, on the bedside radio in his hotel while he was shaving. The police authorities were clearly splashing the story as a sign of their efficiency, even in the teeth of riots and disorder. The Prince Grotti Savoia had drowned on his way back some time late last night. They were appealing for witnesses.

Hawn took the news with superficial calm, and a certain decent professional scepticism. The back canals of Venice late at night were not the place to go wandering and stumbling when you were one over the eight. The Principe had been very drunk. He'd probably got even drunker after Hawn had left him. But he'd also been nervous, almost scared.

Scared in his cups? Hawn knew he should have a conscience about the man – after all, he had contributed in no small measure to his drunkenness. But when Hawn saw a good story – or just a potential story – the last thing he wanted was to get involved with the labyrinthine complications of Italian officialdom.

Besides, he had his date with Robak at the Gritti Hotel. He had told Anna about his meeting with the Prince, and she now looked shocked. 'But isn't he the one who gave you the original idea about the German oil supplies?'

'Something like that. But there's probably no connection. If there is, I doubt the Italian police could prove anything – even if they wanted to.'

Hawn arrived at the Gritti Palace Hotel at 10.40. The receptionist rang Suite 104 and after a pause motioned to a uniformed youth to take him up. The door was hung with a 'Do Not Disturb' notice in four languages. After a moment it was opened by a girl with frizzy hair and a large mouth. A voice from inside shouted, 'Tell him to hang on!'

The main part of the suite was huge, with curtains still half-drawn. The girl said, with a German accent, 'Mister Robak is in the bathroom. He will not be long.' She sounded to Hawn like an *au pair* made good.

He sat down in an armchair, while the girl wandered off into the bedroom. Robak appeared a moment later; he was wearing a short brown towelling gown and bedroom slippers trodden down at the heels. His hair was even more untidy than last night and there was a lump of shaving foam under his ear. 'Hi – I forgot the name.' Hawn told him, stood up and shook hands.

'Coffee?' Robak said. 'It should still be warm. Or beer – there's some in the icebox. I'm off the booze. Damned hepatitis. I'm allowed to drink again at noon on 12 February – I got that date written down big and clear in my book.'

Hawn accepted coffee, and Robak poured two cups from a breakfast tray. He sat down and called towards the bedroom, 'Hun, would you mind trotting downstairs for a moment?' He waited until the girl had left. 'Yeah, Mr Hawn. So you're the guy who has this theory about the Nazis getting some of their oil from the West?' He paused to sip his coffee, and winced. 'God damn it, you'd think in the best hotel in Venice they'd serve better stuff than this. Tastes as though the cat pissed in it. I'll ring down for more.'

'Not on my account, please.'

Robak's bland face broke into a smile. 'That's what I like about you British – you always got good manners. Now

36

about this theory of yours, Mr Hawn. What's the true basis of it?'

Hawn sketched in the facts that he had already computed in his mind, emphasizing the extreme difficulties which the German High Command must have experienced in finding fuel supplies following the Russian capture of the Rumanian oil fields in 1944.

Robak lit a cigarette, tasted it, threw it away and lit another; then as an afterthought offered the packet to Hawn, who declined.

'Are you an expert on the oil industry, Mr Hawn?'

'I know something about it.'

'It's a hell of a complex industry – there are even some angles that I sometimes think I don't understand. And you know something about World War Two? So you'll no doubt know that in a war like that every kind of racket went on. Not just cigarettes and whisky – jeeps, trucks, even planes found themselves on to the black market. And guns, of course. Half your guerrilla wars at the moment are still being fought with the help of World War Two hardware. The Eyties here even dismantled a whole US cruiser in Naples in one night and sold it off for scrap.

'But you wanna talk about German raw materials? Well, there were plenty of rackets there, too. Mostly through the neutrals – Spain, Sweden, Switzerland.'

'I know about that,' said Hawn : 'Steel and nickel and chrome. Difficult stuff to transport, specially with a naval blockade throughout most of the world – at least, towards the end of the war. But oil's fluid. It can be carried in bulk, or in very small quantities. It can be easily transferred, even easily disguised. Pump a small tanker three-quarters full, then top it up with milk or olive-oil.'

Robak sat watching him, very still, unblinking. 'You got a darn fine imagination. But facts. Where are your facts?'

'I told you, it was only a theory – and not even twenty-four hours old, at that.'

'You say you know about the oil industry, Mr Hawn. Well, maybe you do, maybe you don't. A lot of people know how the internal combustion engine works, but not many can fix an automobile when it breaks down. Let me give you a few facts. D'you know that of all the tankers at sea at any given time, only about half have a definite destination? For instance, take a tanker with a load of heavy crude from the Middle East bound for Rotterdam. In mid-ocean we may decide to switch that oil for a low-grade product bound for some other country. We switch it in mid-ocean. We can syphon that stuff – even a couple of hundred thousand tonnes – in a matter of hours. We also keep a lot o' tankers floating around empty. It's a quick, high-powered business. And plenty o' scope for smart-arses to get in and pull a fast one – sometimes against the insurance companies, sometimes against us. Only they don't usually get away with it. We've got a darn good security system. And we don't give people a second chance.'

'How does this all tie in with my theory?' said Hawn.

'I'm just trying to fill in the background for you. Maybe give you something to chew on. You got the theory – that Nazi Germany was starved of oil and somehow got it from the West. From us, maybe? Correct?'

Hawn nodded.

'So, can you explain why the Nazis were permanently, chronically short of fuel throughout the war? Why they had to manufacture it themselves? Why they made every desperate effort to block our own – and your – oil supplies across the Atlantic and in the Med, through North Africa?'

'And can *you* explain,' said Hawn, 'how this permanently, chronically starved fighting-force – one of the largest and most sophisticated the world has ever seen – somehow managed, for nearly six years, to have enough fuel to fight to the very last inch of territory? I'll believe anything about the courage and ingenuity of the German race, but I won't believe their Panzers and armoured vehicles ran on blood. They ran on high-octane fuel, Mr Robak, and I'd like to know where it came from.'

'There's a straight answer to that. Reserves and synthetic fuel.'

'I know. I got that in the Danieli. From Logan. Only that Frenchman there, Pol, rather shot him down. Pointed out that the synthetic fuel was only suitable for aircraft, not for the heavy stuff. And I don't know about reserves – but they must have had not just millions, but billions of tonnes stashed away, to carry them right through.'

Robak put another cigarette in his mouth, without lighting it. 'They had Russia. And they captured huge reserves in France. God knows what they captured in other places.'

'The Russian oil fields, from what I know, never yielded very much – far less than Rumania, and the Rumanian fields in Ploesti were bombed to hell after 1943, when the Allies captured the air-base at Bari here in Italy.'

It was a moment before Robak answered. He took a bottle out of his dressing-gown pocket and shook out two pills which he swallowed 'Just vitamins. Keeps the metabolism going. This hepatitis is one hell of a drag. You got a pretty pat theory there, haven't you, Hawn? What I call a "negative theory". Like trying to prove a man's guilty just because he hasn't got a cast-iron alibi. Let's try and be a little more constructive. Let's just suppose – without mentioning names – that a Western oil company did supply the Germans. How would they have done it?'

'I was rather hoping you might tell me.'

'So you want me to write your lines for you, huh?'

'Let's say, just a bit of prompting.'

'Sure. Well, there might have been several ways – as I said, all dependent on the neutrals. Broken convoy across the Atlantic from the Gulf of Mexico, into Norwegian waters and down to Sweden. Bills of Lading made out to Swiss laundering syndicates. Money-laundering, that is. Switch cargoes and ship the stuff across to Kiel or Rostock. Those were the main German railheads on the Baltic. You're not writing any of this down. Why not?'

'I've got a good memory. I never forget good stuff.'

'I'm flattered. All right, take the Middle East. Bring the stuff round through the Canal and ship it up to Turkey, where every kind of dirty game was being played. The Turks swap it over into barges for the Danube. Or maybe they do better – maybe they swap it over on to neutral tankers and bring it up to Trieste or Genoa where there was the only pipeline in Europe at the time, up into Switzerland. And once in Switzerland – well, it was anybody's oil. Then there was Franco's Spain, of course. It could have gone through the Straits of Gibraltar, been transferred, shipped down to Oran or Algiers, then up to Vichy, France. But of course, that was before the Rumanian fields fell.' He paused. 'How am I doing?'

'Fine.' Hawn knew Robak was just playing, but he couldn't decide just what at. The man was handing him a whole set of plausible theories to work on. They were no doubt the sort of theories he could come up with himself, but why was Robak helping him? Hawn was a poker player and was well-versed in the art of bluffing. The bluff that Robak might be pulling was to give him a broad basis for his theory which might be highly plausible, but because it came from a senior ABCO executive, could not possibly be true. That might be the way Hawn was supposed to take it, anyway.

Since Robak was playing, Hawn decided to play, too. He would bet against Robak's hand, just to find out how strong it was. 'What about the Royal Navy, the RAF, Strategic Air Command? By 1944 they had total control of sea and air.'

'So – maybe they just got a dribble through. A dribble topped up with milk or olive-oil, as you so cutely put it. But you're maybe forgetting that milk and olive-oil sink to the bottom?'

'That's where the taps are, aren't they? In any case, there are always sealed compartments. Isn't that the usual trick?'

Don Robak allowed himself a second smile. 'You've got it all figured out, haven't you?'

'Some of it. I'm just working on it, as I go along.'

'Fine. So why don't you talk to your Royal Navy boys? Talk to the RAF chiefs, to our guys in Washington. Talk to retired chiefs of Strategic Air Command, the guys who ran the blockade, guys whose job it was to go through the Nazi archives at the end of the war. Talk to the experts. Get your facts. It's no good just walking into a bar and shooting your mouth off, accusing us of helping the Nazis. That's tantamount to accusing us of mass murder. Now I'm thick-skinned – I don't give a damn what you think personally of ABCO, or of its methods of business. But I don't like being called a murderer. I like it even less when it's done by a stranger, and in front of other people. Logan may be a buddy of yours, but that Frenchman Pol's in the business. OK, he looks like a clown, but he's got a lot of funny-money tucked away in Liechtenstein and he wants to do business with ABCO, and ABCO's business is to do business.

'So I say it again – I don't like guys come butting in and making wild accusations that can't be substantiated. I hear you're a good newspaper man? Well, that's not the kind of conduct I expect from any kind of newspaper man. So get your facts. Get all the facts, and get 'em straight.' He stood up. 'I've enjoyed talking to you, Mr Hawn. I just hope I've made myself clear?'

'Thank you. You've made yourself admirably clear, on a number of points.' Hawn stood up and was about to shake hands, when he said, 'You heard, did you, that that Prince fellow – Grotti Savoia, the one who's been making himself rather tiresome for you lot in the last few days – he was found dead early this morning, drowned in one of the canals? Pure coincidence, no doubt.'

'I'd say so. Or maybe you don't believe in coincidences, Mr Hawn?'

'Sometimes. Don't you?'

'I prefer to call them Acts of God – like the insurance companies do. Might also be a kind of moral in it all – a tragic lesson to silly people who spread lies and try to make trouble.'

'Sentimental, aren't you?'

'Good morning, Mr Hawn. It's been a pleasure talking to you.' They shook hands, and Hawn left.

The fat man ate with his fingers, with neither grace nor deference. And he talked as he ate :

'I fought in Spain as an anarchist. I am not ashamed of it. We had the most superb ideals. We wanted to burn down the banks, abolish money, run public restaurants for everyone, rich or poor. I was a happy man then. I believed. I was even happier when that water-rat, Franco, invaded. I kidnapped one of his generals and ransomed him for three hundred rifles. We asked for a thousand but they wouldn't pay. I assume he wasn't much of a general. Then they captured me near Salamanca and I only just escaped, disguised as a priest.'

'When the war came, it was not quite so easy to choose sides. I hated the Nazis, and I hated the Communists because they had a pact with the Nazis. But I also hated the French bourgeois establishment. If there hadn't been a war, I suppose I might well have become an urban terrorist. I'm quite skilled in some of their practices.'

Grease dripped from his fingers, down his chin, to become matted like succulent seaweed in his little goatee beard.

'Unhappily, the war did not end well for me. In 1944 I was caught by the Gestapo. I was rather important at that time, and they wanted to ask me some questions. I didn't want to answer them. They didn't kill me. They castrated me instead. So when the war finished, I found myself not a war hero, but a eunuch. I don't know which was the more embarrassing! I took refuge in starting a shop for women's undergarments behind the Gare St Lazare. The enterprise has been remarkably successful. It has now expanded into a supermarket!' He giggled and broke off to order another bottle of wine.

'My last reputable role was in Algeria, helping Long-Nose de Gaulle sell two million Europeans to the Arabs. Of course, I had no great sympathy with the European cause – except for one thing. It was a popular movement. I have great sympathy with popular movements – but on one condition. They must have a chance of winning. Today, for instance, if the Whites in Africa had just one chance in a million of winning, perhaps I would support them. But they don't even have that.'

He had a second helping of Ossobuco and recounted various escapades in South-East Asia – where he had hijacked a plane-load of American money to Hanoi – and in

Russia, where he had double-crossed both the KGB and the British Intelligence Service, over the disappearance of one of Britain's most notorious traitors – and later in an ill-fated attempt to assassinate the then Shah of Iran.

Hawn and Anna listened to him, neither believing nor disbelieving. Most people live dull lives, and some try to make them sound exciting by inventing outrageous escapades. A few have had remarkable lives, and are usually wary of discussing them, least of all with a stranger. But on balance Hawn inclined to the view that Pol was telling the truth. The crucial question was of motive : for one thing was sure. The fat man was not merely being sociable.

He was generous with the wine, and his choice was impeccable. They were all three in an excellent mood : though Hawn was still curious, even puzzled. Cheese, fruit and Strega arrived, and Pol finally brought his *curriculum vitae* up to date. The only gaps were ones of vagueness, and these mostly concerned his recent business affairs.

From a couple of casual remarks, Hawn gathered that Pol's place of residence was somewhat indeterminate. He had talked of a place overlooking Lac Leman in Switzerland, but it appeared that he had quarrelled with the Swiss authorities and had had to move. Hawn knew that it was difficult to quarrel with the Swiss, providing you had money, and it didn't usually matter where the money came from. The most heinous crimes one could commit in that scrupulously immoral country were espionage and bankruptcy.

It is not easy to ask effectively whether a man is a spy. If he tells you he is, he is either lying, joking, or a spy of such humble calling that the information seems hardly worth knowing. And if he says he isn't, you are none the wiser – except for the sure knowledge that he will think you an impertinent fool.

It was already evident that Pol knew quite a lot about Hawn – at least professionally – and was amused that they had shared the experience, although at very different levels, of the traumatic events in Algeria and Indo-China. Of Anna he had only made polite inquiries, and seemed well satisfied that she was a researcher, particularly in economic and political matters.

He now spread his fat little hands on the table-cloth and beamed at them both. 'As you may have gathered, mes chers, I have had many interests in life. At the moment I am dabbling in the oil business. It is not a pretty business, I admit. The people who operate it are mercenaries and scoundrels. It was the great Gulbenkian who said that oil friendships are greasy. However, it is lucrative – and at my age I must have money, in order to indulge the few pleasures that are left to me.

'But, my friends, I also have another interest – one that is rather less mundane. I hunt Nazi war criminals. There are quite a number of us – quite unofficially, you understand. And none of this must appear in print – or that will be the end of our relationship. I could add that it might even have unfortunate consequences for you.' There was an edge of menace in his voice which belied his bright smiling eyes. 'But I know that you are a man of discretion, Monsieur Hawn. No good journalist can afford not to be. So I can speak freely?'

'You've been speaking fairly freely so far. Go on.'

'This Strega is delicious. A vulgar liqueur, but one of the best ways I know with which to end a meal. Cognac is so often overrated. I was talking about war criminals. You are familiar, of course, with the Statute of Limitations? It was supposed to have expired at the end of last year. I and my colleagues, however, are not concerned with the niceties of international law. We have our own law. When we find these people, we punish them.'

'You kill them?' said Anna.

'Put like that, Mademoiselle, it sounds so indelicate! Yes, if possible, we kill them. Like rats. But that is only incidental to what I want to talk about. I listened to your theory yesterday evening, Monsieur Hawn, with very great interest. You see, I have long entertained ideas along similar lines. We all know that international big business played a leading role in the Nazi war effort. You have only got to look at the structure of German industry before the war to see how intricately involved it was with some of the leading Western

44

companies and corporations. No doubt the war came as a nasty shock to many of them, but that does not mean that all links were broken. I am thinking of the steel industry in particular. I am also thinking of oil.

'The oil industry is the dirtiest of the lot. Where there's a market they sell. There is absolutely no reason to believe that when the war came they were inhibited by morals or patriotic scruples. The Germans needed oil, and somehow they got it. I personally believe that the theory you expressed yesterday may well have more than a grain of truth in it. I do not know what oil companies were involved, but I would make an inspired guess that ABCO is the most likely candidate.

'Even before the war they were by far the biggest organization, with a world-wide network. They had the contacts, the expertise, and above all, the ruthlessness. I go further. I would say that it was immaterial to ABCO whether the Germans or the Allies won. The important thing was that ABCO showed a profit at the end. And with the Germans they'd have had an almost exclusive market.'

Hawn said : 'How would they have been paid?'

'Gold. That was one commodity the Germans had plenty of – including many tons of melted down teeth. Most of it's still sitting in Swiss vaults, gathering interest, and protected by the holy Swiss banking laws.'

'I'm flattered you think my theory's serious, Monsieur Pol. But where do we come in?'

'You will help me. You have several ideal advantages. As you can imagine, I am a rather conspicuous man – not only physically, but by reputation. I need someone competent, experienced, someone I can trust.'

'How do you know you can trust us?'

'By my nose, mon cher. I have a keen sense of smell. Besides, you would hardly be so foolish as to turn down a story like this. And if you follow me, and do exactly as I tell you, you will have a story that will shake the world. Journalists, in my experience, have very special advantages – they are almost immune to certain crises. People also expect them to be curious, to nose around, to ask awkward questions. And the authorities, however much they may fear or hate them, still grant journalists a grudging respect. Am I not correct?'

'Partially. And what about Anna here?'

Pol turned to her, with his beatific smile. 'Mademoiselle is an invaluable asset. She is a professional researcher – she knows how to dig for facts, the right facts. What is more important, she will know how to connect those facts, to bring them alive.

'Besides, in difficult situations a pretty girl can be very useful. You see, I propose that you both play two roles. You can be investigating journalists one day, a happy young couple on holiday the next. *Voilà!* – those are two things I certainly cannot do.

'Now this is what I propose. I am a generous man and I have assets. Besides your travelling expenses, it is probable that during your investigations you will interview people who will demand to be paid. Some of these people may cost a lot of money. I will provide that money. I shall not expect you to repay it, but I do make one condition. I expect you to follow my instructions without question. I shall tell you what you need to know, but no more. Is that agreeable to you?'

Hawn took his time answering. He was thinking about Anna – knowing that she would go along with him, would insist on going along with him – yet he had a sudden protective instinct towards her. 'What are the risks likely to be?'

'That is impossible to say. They are likely to be commensurate with our success. ABCO is an organization which knows how to protect itself, and its methods are not always conventional. Like most international companies, it operates above the law and beyond the law. There will be risks. But you have taken risks before. Nothing is won in life without risks.'

Hawn now described his meeting with Don Robak that morning. Pol did not look pleased. 'Mon cher, if you will permit me to say so, for a journalist that was a most indiscreet thing to do. You were virtually advertising to the enemy.'

46

'I wasn't taking the theory seriously – until now. I just wanted to see what Robak's reaction would be.'

'You say he mentioned a number of possible ways in which the Germans might have got oil from the West?'

'Very possible ways. I think he was testing me. Then he began to turn nasty, without being actually threatening. He told me to keep my mouth shut, or get the facts.'

'The facts. And when you do get the facts, Robak and his friends will be watching you. Be careful, Monsieur Hawn. Both of you. Above all, be discreet. You will not be playing with fire – you will be playing with vipers. One moment they will be coiled up asleep, the next . . . ' He sat back and patted his belly, which oozed over the edge of the table. 'What is the name and address of your bank? I will have ten thousand dollars deposited there immediately. You will receive more when you need it.' He handed Hawn an embossed card with his name, and that of an obscure bank in Annecy.

They parted five minutes later, with Pol giving them both a sweaty kiss on each cheek. He had made no arrangements to see them again, but promised to contact them at their flat in London. If they wanted to contact him they could do so through a PO number in Annecy.

As Hawn and Anna walked back through the heavy night, Anna said, 'So – what do you think? It's all so fantastic I can't take it in.'

'So fantastic that it has to be true.'

'What about the difficulties?'

'We haven't come up against any – yet. Not ourselves, anyway. Remember what Churchill said – "Do not argue the difficulties, they will argue for themselves." '

'But what about your dead prince?'

'Well he's dead.'

They walked on, listening to the thick green water slapping against the slimy wall of the canal.

# CHAPTER TWO

# *Probing*

*Oil friendships are greasy.*     NUBAR GULBENKIAN

It was the second day after they had returned to England.
Hawn said, 'I'm going to go in at the deep end, Anna –
or as deep as I can, at this stage. Man called Shanklin –
Toby Shanklin. That wretched Prince mentioned him. Ever
heard of the man?'

'I think I know the name. Something big in oil, isn't
he?'

'He used to be, though he must be getting on a bit now.
I've checked back on him. Spends most of his time on the
Mayfair circuit – champion backgammon player, member
of all the in-clubs, including Boodle's and the Athenaeum
when he wants to be respectable. He's a bit of a rogue
elephant. You can look up most of his past in *Who's Who*,
but not all of it. Nobody seems to know anything about his
origins, although his life-style implies that he's well connected. He joined ABCO before the war, as a junior
executive. Then in 1940 he turned up in Cairo as one of
the hush-hush boys in SOE – Special Operations Executive
– Section Z which specialized in the Balkans. Turkey,
Bulgaria, then Yugoslavia, where he got wounded, and
picked up an MC on the way.'

'Is this all in *Who's Who*?'

'No. But we've got a file on him at the paper. Not everything, but enough. Enough to convince me that Shanklin's
not just an ageing Berkeley Square playboy.

'Anyway, he was invalided out of SOE in 1943 – at least,
officially – and rejoined ABCO, who sent him to Venezuela
where his job seems to have been keeping an eye on the

Americans and seeing they didn't muscle in on too much of our share of the action. But as an old Intelligence man – and on the assumption that Intelligence is like the Catholic Church and the CP : they never let you go – we can assume that Shanklin had other duties. The Venezuelan oil-fields were being exploited in a big way, and a lot of the stuff was being shipped across the Atlantic from the Gulf of Mexico. Mexico was not a very stable country – nor was Venezuela. Both were crawling with Germans, mostly under diplomatic cover. Shanklin's brief might well have been to keep a close eye on those transatlantic convoys.'

'You mean, he was well placed to have done a deal with the Germans?'

'I didn't say that. For a start, Shanklin is too obvious a candidate. But he was certainly involved in some sort of racket out there – as I suspect many people were.'

'But what makes you think he'll talk to you? – always assuming he's got something to tell you?'

'I don't know, I'm just taking a chance. But Shanklin's supposed to be sociable, garrulous, a good high-class gossip, and he's also said to be on good terms with the Press. Anyway, even if he doesn't tell me anything, it'll be interesting to see his reactions.'

Anna said, 'If he was really involved in any deals with the Nazis, he'll keep his mouth shut and warn the others.'

'That's part of the chance I'll be taking. And it's always possible that what he doesn't tell me will be as useful as what he does. Ask any policeman.'

Toby Marchmont Shanklin, CBE, MC, was less accessible than Tom Hawn expected. Hawn's reputation and by-line had proved a passport to the highest, the mightiest; but not so to Toby Shanklin, erstwhile executive and chief trouble-shooter for ABCO, the world's richest and most powerful oil company.

Hawn first wrote, in a private capacity – since he was loath to involve his paper in this escapade – to Shanklin, c/o America-Britannic Consortium, at their London tower-block headquarters, where he knew Shanklin still maintained an office as 'industrial consultant'. He received no reply.

Next he wrote to one of Shanklin's most exclusive clubs, again privately, and again heard nothing. The man was ex-directory, of course, but Hawn managed to get his address from the office files : a private mews house off South Audley Street. This time Hawn wrote on office notepaper, in his reluctant capacity of senior reporter. Shanklin replied at his leisure – a scrawled message asking Hawn to meet him for lunch at an odiously expensive restaurant in Knightsbridge. But when Hawn arrived, he was informed by the head waiter that Mr Shanklin had phoned to say that he was unavoidably detained. He never turned up.

Hawn tried ringing his home address a couple of times, at respectable hours, but in vain. Finally, at around eleven one evening, he called the Clermont Club.

He was informed that Mr Shanklin was dining there. Hawn gave his name and added that it was a matter of some urgency. He hung on for ten minutes; then was told that Mr Shanklin would see him at 12.45, at his home address.

At 12.30 p.m. Hawn drove up to the entrance of the cobbled mews. It was barred with a white pole and a sentry box; the pole had a black and white sign :

PRIVATE THOROUGHFARE

ABSOLUTELY NO PARKING DAY OR NIGHT

OFFENDERS WILL BE PROSECUTED

A uniformed commissionaire came out of the box and said officiously, 'Who do you want?' At the name 'Shanklin' he became deferential and raised the pole.

Hawn edged his old grey Citroën between the double rank of Rollses, Mercedeses, the occasional Porsche.

Shanklin's front door was of pale oak in a steep narrow house at the end of the mews. There were no lights in any of the windows. The door was flanked by coaching lamps, and had a lot of brass fittings and several locks. Hawn stared through the Judas eye as he rang the bell. No answer came from within.

He had no idea what Shanklin's nocturnal habits were : how many backgammon games he played, and whether he then might move on to pursue the amorous delights of the nightclub below. He suspected that this might mean his hanging around here for some hours; and not wanting to be seen loitering, he risked leaving his car and strolled back up the mews to the austere empty streets in the backwaters of Mayfair. He was beginning to feel quite like a junior reporter again on a leg-job.

Shanklin's bell did not answer until after 2.30. His voice sounded squeaky through the intercom : 'Yes, who is it?' Hawn told him. 'Oh, yes, all right, come in.' The main bolt clicked and the door snapped ajar.

There were still no lights in the windows. Inside it was very dark. A voice called from a door to his left : 'This way!'

Hawn entered a pine-panelled room : black leather armchairs, military prints around the walls, a gas 'log'-fire in an immense mock Adam fireplace. The floor was divided by a long table on which there was a recording machine with a telephone attachment (officially allowed in Britain only under police licence), a battery of more telephones, stacks of paper. A filing cabinet reached to the ceiling. The rest of the wall-space was filled with reference books. But the oddest feature in the room was a large television set, with the sound turned off, showing what Hawn vaguely recognized as 'Sale of the Century'. It was not a programme which he voluntarily watched, but he did know that it came on early in the evening, at week-ends.

The man behind the table caught his glance. 'My new little toy – video-recorder. Wonderful things. I've got *Citizen Kane, Lavender Hill Mob, Seven Brides for Seven Brothers.* It was a present from Yamani.'

He was in his shirt-sleeves, his tie undone, and it took Hawn a moment to realize – by the light of the green-shaded desk lamp – that his host was kneeling on his chair with his feet stuck through the back. His face was a drinker's face, heavy, mottled, under a balding pate with tufts of gingery-grey hair sticking out over the temples.

'Take a pew. Hawn, isn't it? Didn't we meet at Freddy Frobisher's – Lord Danebury's son? Awfully nice boy – but a bloody bad backgammon player! Won three thou' off him last week, and he didn't bat an eyelid.' He signed some papers, shuffled them as though about to deal a hand, then signed some more. He looked up. 'Your message said it was something urgent?'

'It was a tip-off I got this afternoon. There may be nothing in it.'

'Get yourself a drink. I won't join you – I'm off the bloody stuff.' His voice was surprisingly soft, and although abrupt, there was a pervasive hint of intimacy about it that made Hawn faintly uneasy.

He gave himself a Scotch and sat down. On the TV screen the compère was presenting a hideous cocktail cabinet to a giggling woman in a purple dress. Hawn said, 'It's rather a delicate matter. I'm not sure how to begin.'

'I should try the beginning,' Shanklin said, and scribbled something in a margin.

'Mr Shanklin, everything I'm about to ask you is in the strictest confidence. I'm doing some research into the oil business during the last war. I gather that after you were wounded, you spent some time in the Caribbean?'

One of the telephones began to bleep by Shanklin's elbow. He grabbed it. 'Yes? Yes, yes I know who you are. Well, what's happened?' As he listened, his jaw muscles swelled and his face grew pink. His voice, still soft, had taken on an indefinable note of menace : 'I don't give a monkey's what's happened to him. For all I care they can hang him up and beat his feet till he never walks again. And shut up when I'm talking. You can go whimpering to the FO if you want to, and a lot of bloody good that'll do you. He's not their pigeon, and he's not mine. If Assad can spring him, the best of Jewish luck to him! Otherwise, you'll have to count him as a write-off. Now I'm busy.' He put the phone down and grinned evilly at Hawn.

'Some little sod trying to do a double-act. Takes money from us, then gets picked up by the Iraqis with his pockets stuffed with dollars and an Israeli code that was broken weeks ago. God, these bloody Zionists! They're everywhere, like lice. Or are you another Israeli-lover? Most journalists seem to be, like politicians. Israel's a gangster state, and they've got everyone on the payroll.'

Hawn now remembered other things about Shanklin. His greatest asset to ABCO had been his phenomenally close relations with the Arab leaders : he had been in Iran at the time of Mossadeq, helping to smooth the way for the Shah's return; had predicted Nuri's fall in Baghdad a month before it happened; had wheeled and dealed throughout the Middle East in the calamitous aftermath of the Yom Kippur War. Toby Shanklin was one of those vintage gentlemen-Arabists : his mentors would be Burton and Thesiger and St John Philby. To him Lawrence was a minor adventurer.

He peered at Hawn from under his pale eyebrows. 'I'm listening. Something about the Caribbean?'

'It could have been more than the Caribbean. The North Atlantic, Mediterranean, Middle East. I'm thinking of writing a book about how the big oil companies – particularly ABCO – operated during the war. Because of the U-boat blockade of America after 1941, most of the big convoys sailed from the Gulf of Mexico, didn't they?'

'Some of them.'

'And the Middle East oil came through the Canal?'
Shanklin nodded.

'Would you agree that the volume of oil, and the number of ships – even given that the average tanker was no more than 25,000 tons – would have been enormous?'

Shanklin pulled down his lower lip and revealed teeth like splinters of oyster-shell. 'I believe you've been chatting to the late Prince Marino-Petri Grotti Savoia? – the gentleman who snuffed it recently in one of the noble canals of Venice.'

'You're sure of that?'

'Of course I'm sure of it. Don't be impertinent, old son. I invited you up here, remember. I'm doing you a favour.'

'Who told you about Grotti Savoia?'

'Little bird told me.'

'Ham Logan told you.'

Shanklin shifted his knees and cupped his hairy hands round his chin. 'Let's not bother too much about who told me. For the record – as you boys say – you're supposed to have got the idea off the top of your head. But let's get to the point. I've a pretty good idea what you're on to. And you want my help. All right – let's see how far we can both get. You ask the questions – I'll answer them, if I can. But don't try to be clever. No funny ones. You start being devious, playing the sharp lawyer with me, and I'll toss you out on your neck. Fire away.'

'Very well. Would it have been possible, in your opinion, that in the confusion of war, a certain amount of our oil might have found its way to the enemy?'

'In my opinion, quite possible. But you're not talking just about the big Western oil companies – you're talking about ABCO.'

'Only that ABCO was the largest.'

'Fair enough.' He shunted his knees again. 'Only I gather that in your judgement it isn't just a question of a bit of ABCO oil going astray during the war. You've been saying that the Consortium made a *deal* with the Germans, then sold them oil. Now that's serious, that's naughty.'

'I didn't say that. I may have suggested there was a *prima facie* case for some sort of deal to have taken place, but I certainly never suggested it was proved.'

'Thank the Lord for small mercies.'

'You seem extremely well informed, Mr Shanklin, about a pretty vague conversation in Venice, at a time when your people should have been far more concerned about other events. How come?'

'Because you shot your mouth off in front of some rather important and sensitive people. I talked to an old chum of mine on the phone a couple of days ago. Name of Robak. Told me about this high-powered British journalist who had been yapping in the Danieli Bar. Not just idle gossip – sounded like high treason to me. And to him. You're not very subtle, even for a journalist, are you?'

'Let me explain, Mr Shanklin.'

'I'd be glad if you would.'

'I got the beginnings of this idea driving to Venice. Then, by chance, I bumped into Savoia at Harry's Bar. Savoia was drunk, and I'm quite sure I wasn't the first person he'd blabbed to about this theory of his. I was interested, but I wasn't taking it too seriously at the time. Then I met my girl in the Danieli, with that PR man, Logan, and a Frenchman I'd never met before, called Pol, and this American fellow, Robak. I mentioned my theory just by way of conversation. I still didn't think anything of it at the time. But Robak obviously did — enough to invite me up to his room next morning to explain it in more detail. I thought his reaction was rather odd.'

'In what way?'

'He started by giving me a rough outline on how the Germans might have siphoned off our oil. All fairly plausible and fairly friendly. Then he got just a little less friendly. He didn't actually warn me off, but he gave me a pep-talk about getting my facts, and making sure I got them right. My impression was that he was taking my theory rather more seriously than I was.'

'You mentioned a Frenchman. Charles Pol. Used to be tied up with French Intelligence, now trying to tie himself up with ABCO. Robak also said you and your girl had dinner with Pol the next night. How seriously did Pol take your theory?'

Hawn said nothing. The TV screen was now showing a black-and-white musical from the thirties. One of the telephones rang again. This time Shanklin answered it with a bored movement. 'Yes? Yes, yes. What's the trouble? Not another fuck-up the other end?' He listened for a moment. 'Well, take it out in a brief-case. You've got one, I suppose?' He allowed the sarcasm to linger on his face while he heard the other out, then said, 'And don't call me again until you get there.' He put down the receiver and looked at Hawn as though he were a total stranger. 'What were we talking about?'

'You were telling me how I'd had dinner with Pol. Your friend Robak is a damned good listening service.'

'That's part of what he's paid for. And he's paid nearly half a million dollars a year, and the tax he pays you could put in your sock. What did you talk to Pol about?'

'I'm not sure that's something I can discuss.'

Shanklin looked at him with a hard bald expression; the muscles in his big face had stiffened under their fleshy liver spots. 'So you expect me to give you information, in return for nothing? That's bad sportsmanship, Hawn. Bad tactics.'

'Well, he's interested. He's interested in the Nazi war crimes angle.'

'And he thinks you can help him?'

'Only if I come up with some facts.'

'And you think you'll get the facts from me? That I'm a soft touch, perhaps?'

'I came to you because you were originally attached to SOE in the Eastern Mediterranean and then in the Caribbean. The Nazis had a network of spies all over the world, and they were particularly strong in South and Central America. They were also desperate for oil, and no doubt went to any lengths to get it. The question I want answered is – could they have received clandestine help, either through bribery or coercion, from within the Western oil companies?'

Shanklin leaned his shirt-sleeves on the table-top. His expression was now benign and condescending. 'Listen to me, Hawn. You may be a big man in Fleet Street, but where the oil industry is concerned, you're obviously wet behind the ears. You clearly do not understand the first thing about oil – and to be fair to you, I've never met a journalist who did.

'Oil companies run their affairs like police states. They're ruthless, they're competent, and they're secure. Out in Central America we made sure we didn't have a lot of dagos and wetbacks running around the place playing messenger boys and dipping their hands in the till whenever it pleased them. Nor did we have any Abwehr brass or those SD bastards sticking their noses into our affairs. Anyway, you could sniff a Nazi agent a mile off.'

He shunted his knees forward and clumsily got his legs out of the back of the chair and stood up. His pin-striped trousers were too short and revealed several inches of sock. He came round the table with a curious bowed strutting walk, like a top-heavy puppet.

'I haven't been much help, have I? And I like helping journalists. Maybe I could drop you a name? Pretty small fry, but it might help. Ever met Norman French?'

'A few times – if it's the same man. Engineer who used to work in the oil business – flogged me a few stories about North Sea oil – how the consortiums manage to get round British tax laws, including some of the cons the Government itself has pulled on the British public. I didn't like him – though his material was usually pretty sound.'

'Oh, he's the most awful little creep. No class at all. But he is good at his job – except that he's a crook. ABCO gave him a top position in the Caribbean a couple of years ago – house, swimming pool, servants, company car – and the little turd couldn't resist trying to pull a fast one. Did a lot of share-holders out of a lot of money – though I think he was rumbled before he made much himself. But he did collect plenty of enemies – and ABCO makes a bad enemy. You might remember that.'

'Why wasn't he charged?'

'Too much shit to be thrown around, and some of it would have stuck to the wrong people. Besides, Mexican law's not exactly tuned to the finer points of our own Company Laws. But somebody'll catch up with him in the end, don't worry.' He led the way to the door. 'Get one thing straight, young man. ABCO represents the interests of Britain. And anyone who tries to damage ABCO, tries to damage this country – and when he does that, he has me to reckon with. I've killed a lot of people for this country, Hawn. I might just do it again.'

'That sounds like a pretty direct threat.'

Shanklin shook his hand. 'Just a manner of speaking. And by the way, that Frenchman, Pol – be careful of him. He's a tricky bastard. Could be dangerous.'

It was over a year since Hawn had last seen Norman French. He was an unctuous, pushy little man, always nattily turned out, fond of talking about good food and wines which he couldn't afford. Hawn had heard that he had been catapulted into the Caribbean, on a tax-free executive salary, and assumed philosophically that the Fates had at last dealt Frenchie a winning hand. Then a few months later he had received a gilt-engraved invitation to a party being given by Mr and Mrs Norman French, Cocktails and Dinner, at Beecham House, off The Avenue, North London.

Hawn had gone alone out of curiosity. It had been an imposing house, ablaze with light. Norman French had evidently returned well-endowed from his misadventures in the New World, equipped now with an expensive wife, and tastes to match.

Two Vietnamese menservants and an English butler had served drinks and canapés of caviare and smoked salmon. The guests had been the usual *galère* of contemporary fashion: young businessmen of doubtful pedigree, minor showbiz and TV personalities, photographers and their parasites, a right-wing MP, a couple of Arabs, a lacing of models and their couth companions of uncertain gender, hairdressers, obscure pop freaks. Norman French did not have friends: he had contacts.

Hawn had not stayed long. A hunk of hash was being dismembered on a coffee-table and a girl with straight dirty hair had begun to sing to a guitar, when he decided to take his leave. As he fetched his coat, he passed the open door of what he took to be the library. A dishevelled man, obviously drunk, was having a furious argument with French.

Hawn paused. At first neither of them noticed him. Norman French was speaking in his quietest, most patronizing voice; but the other kept interrupting: 'You're a slimy little ponce! You took me for a ride – you took the whole Consortium for a ride! I know a couple o' nice guys were cleaned out because o' you, Frenchie-boy!' He spoke with a slurred American drawl, his hair flopping over his eyes. 'Well, I'll tell you something for nothing. Nobody skims cream off us and gets away with it! Nobody.'

French said, 'Will you please leave. Or I shall have you thrown out.'

At that moment one of the menservants brought Hawn's

coat. Hawn had never been quite sure whether French had seen him there in the doorway or not; but thinking back on the incident had cleared up a little puzzle. The drunk dishevelled man had been Robak.

Hawn had not seen Norman French since : though he had heard, though the Grub-Street grapevine, that the mansion in North London had been sold, and that soon after, Lorna French had returned alone to her native Texas. French's upper-crust had burst.

The last Hawn had known of French's activities was that he had started his own private business, specializing in a new-fangled central heating system, with a plush office behind Piccadilly; but that soon after the place had closed up, and Norman French had vanished. The only tenuous contact which Hawn retained with him was through a slight acquaintanceship with an architect who had been a partner in French's now defunct business.

Hawn finally traced the hapless French to a service flat in Paddington, where he was registered under the name of Hudson – presumably to evade creditors. The landlady was not helpful, having evidently been briefed to keep callers at bay. Hawn left his name and waited.

All next day there was no call from Norman French. Then, the following morning, as he was going out, the phone rang. The voice was smooth, cajoling : 'Tom, how are you? Long time no see. I gather you're no longer at the paper?'

'I'm writing a book. I thought you might be able to help me with some background.'

'Any time. What's it about?'

'Not the sort of thing I can discuss over the phone. Tomorrow, lunch? L'Étoile, one o'clock?'

'Only if I'm allowed to choose the wine.'

'Agreed. One o'clock then.'

French did not arrive until 1.50. He was a soft, round man, with large hips, small hands and feet, and moist little eyes behind tinted glasses. His hair, cut short, was smooth as a cat's. There was something faintly oriental about him : when he smiled, he reminded Hawn of one of those war time cartoons of Japanese generals.

He came across the restaurant with a slightly swaying walk, like a dancer. 'Tom – great to see you !'

Hawn smiled and sat down. 'How's the Jensen doing?' he said, by way of malice.

'Old age. Had to get rid of it.' Norman French's features were immobile as he consulted the menu.

Hawn paused. 'I hear things aren't too good with you, Norman?'

'The rough with the smooth,' French said, and went on to choose two of the most expensive dishes, with an appropriately good wine. Then he shifted his chair back and smiled : 'Quite like the old days, Tom.'

'Not quite. You're rather difficult to get hold of, for a start. What happened?'

'Broke. Flat, stony, on the sticks. I can't even get credit at the newsagents.'

The wine-waiter poured French's glass a quarter full; French moistened his lips and nodded. 'Very nice, Tom. Yes, it is like the old days.'

'And like the old days you're going to give me some help. Confidential information – that's the way it used to be, right?'

Norman French sipped his wine. Hawn said : 'I want some stuff on ABCO. Nothing current – but confidential. Old stuff going back to the end of the war. Do you know anything about ABCO's operations at that time in the Caribbean?'

French put down his glass and showed his white teeth. 'This information – how much does it pay?'

'Depends on what it is. I want contacts – people I can talk to, names and facts I can check on. But I'll give you two-fifty on the nail, and two-fifty if the information checks out.'

Norman French looked at him without expression. 'What do you want to know?'

Hawn knew he would have to handle French with care.

The man was not only untrustworthy – he was shrewd, with a certain coarse cunning. The least artifice would only whet his curiosity. Hawn wanted his information cold. He decided on the direct approach.

'Before the war ABCO had fairly close contacts with the German firm, I G Farben. They're supposed to have broken all contact when the Roosevelt Administration brought pressure to bear in 1940. What do you know about ABCO's interests in the Caribbean during the rest of the war?'

'They sold oil.'

'But they had a lot of interests in Central American government. And some of those governments, in one way or another, were pro-Nazi – or at least, pro-German.'

'They were pro the US dollar,' French said.

'But if the US stayed neutral, or even lost, those regimes wouldn't have been sorry to deal with the Reichsmark?'

A sly happy look had spread over Norman French's hairless features. 'I get the drift. You're priming me, Tom, to say it wasn't just the Latin American top-class who had pro-German interests. You want me to say that ABCO did too?'

'ABCO's a big organization. It only needed a handful of people. Maybe just one person. Five hundred quid, Norman.'

French pretended to be concentrating on his food. He said at last, 'Most of ABCO's top people in the war are either dead or retired. But there are people around who had very sensitive jobs in those days. I'm not saying they were pro-Nazi.'

'Norman, I'm pursuing a line of extremely tentative inquiry. It may lead nowhere. As you say, I'm probably wasting my time – and my money. I just want a lead. Someone I can interview who might know of an Anglo-Nazi connection within ABCO in the last years of the war.'

French put down his knife and fork. 'If I tell you what I know Tom, you won't have any way of confirming it. So I shall want that whole five hundred pounds now, as a full down-payment.'

Hawn said, 'There could be more to come, if you're patient.'

'I'm sorry. I'm not banking on anything in the future. I want the money now.'

'All right. Let's hear what you've got.'

Norman French took his time dissecting the last of his chicken Kiev. 'As you know, I recently spent a year down in Central America – though I was based in Texas. It's a small part of the world – even Texas. And oil men not only gossip – they've got long memories. Tom, you've got to have worked in the oil industry to know what it's really like. Each company is a cut-throat fraternity where everyone's trying to scramble to the top and steal the apples.'

'You don't seem to have climbed down with much to show for it.'

'That was uncalled for.'

'If you want to earn that first two-fifty, you're going to have to come up with something hard. Perhaps I could start you off by jogging your memory. You've heard of Toby Shanklin?'

'I have. Gets on wonderfully with Arabs. They say he still never travels anywhere without his jar of petroleum jelly.' French laughed heartily at his little joke.

'You know he was in the Caribbean in the last two years of the war?' said Hawn.

Norman French took off his glasses and wiped them on a silk handkerchief. His naked eyes were small and lustreless. 'What do you want to know about him?'

'For a start, what he was doing out there – officially and unofficially. Then how he made his money. He came out of the war with a small fortune – which wasn't unusual if you were in munitions, or even big-time blackmarket. What about oil?'

French's face took on a closed look. 'There was one thing I heard – when I was down in Vera Cruz, in Mexico. Alan Rice, I think the name was. I remember, because he was half English, with a German passport – Austrian on his mother's side and had studied in Germany before the war. He was caught up there when war broke out, and soon became one of their top petro-chemical scientists. He appears to have been a bit of a mystery. He still had dual nationality when he turned up in Colombia in 1943, where the Germans still hoped they could sniff out some oil and get the concession.

'The next thing I heard, he'd flown up to the States and asked for political asylum. He got it – presumably partly on account of his half-British nationality, but mostly because he was known to be a first-rate scientist in the oil racket. ABCO snapped him up and he continued to work for them, officially, until the last two months of the war. Then he disappeared. There were all kinds of rumours – that he was working under an alias for a rival company, that Nazi agents had kidnapped him, that he was working under cover for US Intelligence who had always taken a close interest in him, particularly in his knowledge of Nazi synthetic fuel processes.

'Then in late 1946 his world blew up in his face. Rice – or R-E-I-S-S, as he was now known – had been a top Nazi agent all the time. The stuff he'd given the Americans was mostly phoney – except what could be checked on – while he was feeding all ABCO's secrets straight back to the Abwehr. But it appears he wasn't just a secret agent.

'The Allies in Germany were going through the archives and found that Rice had been top-dog in a petro-chemical firm employing slave-labour. The Americans wanted him as a war criminal, and the British – on account of his British passport – wanted him for treason. Quite a combination. There were plenty of war criminals around, and quite a few traitors. But there weren't many people who qualified for both, in the first degree. Alan Rice, alias Reiss, must have been practically unique.'

'What happened to him?'

'Vanished into thin air. I've heard a lot of rumours – that he went East, where his professional skills would have been well appreciated. He was a master of espionage, as well as a top scientist, remember. But there was also talk that ABCO had been using their muscle – that for some reason they weren't over-anxious to have Rice brought to trial. There were even strong suggestions that they'd had him knocked off.'

'Why?'

'If I knew that, it would be worth a lot more than five hundred pounds.'

'Not if Rice disappeared over thirty years ago. Not unless you can tie him in with someone who's around today – alive and well and working for ABCO.'

French looked up at him with a simpering smile. 'Would Toby Shanklin do?'

'He might. What was his tie-up with Rice?'

'They were in the same department – even shared the same office for a time.'

'How do you know all this, Norman?'

'I peeked at the files. I'm rather keen on files. All that dead paper. then you light on something really interesting.'

For a gruesome moment Hawn compared French's enthusiasm with that of Anna, and hastily put it out of mind. 'Presumably you thought that some of the dirt on Rice would have rubbed off on to Shanklin? But sharing the same department, the same office, with a traitor, doesn't necessarily make you a traitor yourself. Christ, I know dozens of journalists who shared offices with Philby when he worked in Fleet Street – I even know one who used to lend him a typewriter.'

'You say Shanklin had made a lot of money by the end of the war. There were lots of ways of making money in Central America in those days. One of them was selling secrets to the enemy.'

'That's speculation. I need facts. I need something definite to link Shanklin to Rice – more than just an office desk.'

Norman French took his time answering. He ordered coffee and a cigar. 'There was one incident. Or rather, a memo I spotted that caught my fancy. In late 1943 Shanklin and Rice killed the Vice-Consul in Vera Cruz.'

'Killed?'

'In a car accident. At night, just outside the city. Rice and Shanklin were in the car – it didn't say who was driving – and the Vice-Consul was knocked down and fatally injured on an empty bit of road. Funny business, really. There was talk of an inquiry, but it was hushed up. The Vice-Consul was a young chap with a posh name – de Vere Frisby, I think it was – and he hadn't been in Mexico long. But the fact that he wasn't in the Services, and the minor role of vice-consul in a strategic port like Vera Cruz, suggests that he was Intelligence.'

'And he'd found something out that Rice, or Shanklin, or both of them, didn't like? Was that all that was in the file?'

'For five hundred pounds it is. If I stretch my memory back, I might come up with something later.'

Hawn took out his cheque-book and pen. Without looking at Norman French, he said, 'I'd like more details about Rice. Where he was born, date of birth, father's name, previous jobs, universities, etc.'

French watched as he wrote; he said, as though afraid that Hawn might change his mind before signing : 'I think he was born in Wales and may have studied at Heidelberg. And I've heard that he was extremely tall, with a hunch-back.'

'Christ, he and Shanklin must have made a handsome pair.' Hawn signed the cheque and pushed it across to French. 'Thanks, Norman. That ought to make your land-lady happy. And if you get anything else, ring me.'

The entrance-hall of the Public Record Office resembles the foyer of a cheap modern hotel. A uniformed porter checked Hawn in, gave him an identification card, and showed him across to the reception desk. Here a girl handed him a form in duplicate and he filled out the details and dates which he required to check. She directed him up some shallow steps to a long corridor lined with steel drawers, like the receiving end of a crematorium.

A second girl took his names and dates, stamped them out on a card and slotted them into a computer. He was told to wait at a desk at the far end. A few minutes later a number of plastic-covered files were placed in front of him. The top one was fairly thick. Across the front was typed :

Vol 6   1943-44

The first thirty pages were mostly a mass of statistics; but on page 32 he came to a sub-section marked : CARIBBEAN : VENEZUELA, GULF OF MEXICO. COMMERCIAL OPERATIONS.

Four pages later was a photostat, headèd :

Confidential from H.M. Honorary Consul, Mr D. M. Price, Vera Cruz, Mexico. 18 May 1944. The incident reported on the night of 12 May has been fully investigated by officers Diaz and Guarez of the Vera Cruz Criminal Police. The death of R. de V. Frisby was recorded in the General Hospital, following a car accident in which two British Subjects, employees of ABCO, were concerned. Since the Mexican authorities have not involved the British, the identity of the two employees concerned need not be included in the record.

There followed a scribbled memo in the margin which Hawn had some trouble deciphering. He thought it said : '"T" (or "I") S. and R. are damned lucky. The Mexics take an extraordinarily lenient view of drunken driving. Somebody might take a note of this.' It was unsigned.

Six pages further on, he found a smaller, rather smudged photostat :

AMERICA-BRITANNIC CONSORTIUM. (UK Division, Caribbean.) Confidential Report to Sir Richard Maynard, Foreign Office, 30 June 1944. Following a fatal accident outside Vera Cruz last month, I have arranged for one of our personnel, Mr Alan Oscar Rice, to be interviewed by SOC/Division Officers, Major D. Dyson and Captain G. Simpson. Their report contained in File 237/42 ABF.

Hawn disregarded the second, slimmer file whose code was not what he wanted. He returned to the computer desk and asked for File 237/42 ABF. The woman fed the information into the machine; it hummed, then stopped. No card appeared. 'Are you sure you've got the right code?' she asked.

Hawn showed her the bulky ABCO file. She looked faintly puzzled. 'According to the computer, it should be stored.'

'What does it mean if the computer rejects it?'

'It means that the information has either been reclassified or is missing.'

Hawn then asked her if they had anything on Alan Oscar Rice, German refugee, granted asylum in the US in 1943, and worked for ABCO in the Caribbean, 1943-44.

She fed the card into the computer, and a moment later the information came back : all references to Dr Alan Oscar Rice were contained in the file he had been studying. He next asked for Shanklin, Special Operations Executive, later employee of ABCO in the Caribbean, 1943-44.

Shanklin's SOE period was little more than a detailed elaboration of his *Who's Who* entry, with the potentially useful information that he had spent five months in Istanbul between November 1942 and April 1943, where his duties were to recruit agents. His career in the Caribbean referred once again to the ABCO file that Hawn had been studying.

There wasn't much to learn about Toby Shanklin, except that he might or he might not have once been guilty of causing death through dangerous, even drunken driving on an empty road outside Vera Cruz. Hawn had made a note that there had been no mention of witnesses – except for Shanklin and Rice.

Yet HM's Vice-Consul's masters had been worried enough to send two officers all the way across the Atlantic to investigate de Vere Frisby's demise, and had drawn a blank. Either the paper-work had been scanty, or it had been suppressed.

He had just time for a pub lunch, before going on to the London Library, where he looked up the complete Foreign Office Lists for 1939-44.

Rupert de Vere Frisby was born in 1916 in Berkhampsted : graduated with First-Class Honours in PPE from Trinity College, Oxford, 1936; entered Foreign Service 1937, posted to Baghdad. 1940-42 worked at Bletchley Park. Served as Information Officer to British

Embassy, Lisbon 1942; transferred, Vice-Consul, Istanbul 1942-43; transferred, Vice-Consul, Vera Cruz, Mexico, 1943-44. Died in road accident 12 May 1944.

Not a startling wartime career; but there were several aspects of this cryptic entry which interested Hawn. De Vere Frisby had come down from university with excellent qualifications for the FO; but a top degree in Philosophy, Politics and Economics seemed incompatible with the esoteric rigours, four years later, of Bletchley Park – the top-secret decoding centre, which had handled the 'Enigma' machine.

Hawn guessed that Frisby had been employed as some kind of political evaluator – a job which would have carried enormous responsibility, as well as giving him knowledge of a wide scope of secrets. Yet two years later he was popping up as Information Officer in Lisbon – certainly a cushy capital at that time, as well as one of the most volatile nests of spies and intrigue. It was also well known, on the inside, that FO Information Officers were mere errand-boys for the Ministry of Defence, or MI6.

After Lisbon, Rupert de Vere Frisby had been given Istanbul – another neutral capital, and again hardly a dull spot for a young man still of military age : followed by the port of Vera Cruz on the other side of the world, where he had met his untimely death. Except for Bletchley, all his jobs had been Consular. Rupert de Vere Frisby had been a British secret agent.

And he had been killed either by another British agent, or by a Nazi agent who was also a war criminal – depending upon which one of them had been driving that car.

Hawn then checked on the two SOC/Division officers, Dyson and Simpson. Here he drew a blank. Dyson had been drowned in a swimming accident three months after the memo had been written to the Foreign Office; and Simpson had later been murdered by the Gestapo in Slovakia.

When Anna got back that evening, her satchel was bulging with files and photostats, and she was lugging a string-bag full of books taken out of the LSE library. She went to work almost at once, sorting the papers into piles on her desk, and stacking the books on a nearby shelf.

She had managed to talk to two professors at the School who both knew something about wartime economy, and after sparring around for a bit, she had asked them direct how they thought the Nazis had got their oil. Both men were evasive : it was obviously a subject to which they had never applied their full academic skills, and they were forced to improvise. They trotted out the same answers as Logan, Robak and Shanklin : reserves built up before the war; captured supplies in Occupied Europe; natural sources in Russia and Rumania; synthetic fuel.

'Tom, I'm going to take each one of those factors and destroy it, systematically, rationally, by means of hard facts and statistics − and not just random ones, but ones that check and double-check.'

Hawn then described to her his own day's findings.

He felt reasonably satisfied. He already had a number of plausible leads. Toby Shanklin − wartime secret agent and ABCO executive in the Caribbean; de Vere Frisby, ditto secret agent, killed in mysterious circumstances (relevant file missing) by Shanklin and German double-agent, Rice. Furthermore, both Shanklin and Frisby had spent periods of the war in Istanbul and Vera Cruz − both highly sensitive and strategic sea-ports, one commanding the Eastern Mediterranean, the other the Gulf of Mexico and the Atlantic.

Anna put the dinner on, then afterwards began working through a complex table of oil consumption statistics for Western Europe in 1939.

When Hawn had first arrived in Fleet Street, the Economics Correspondent had been an elderly colonel who had spent the Second World War in an obscure Whitehall ministry called MI14, which dealt with Economic Warfare. He was a quiet Scotsman named MacIntyre : and on one occasion early in Hawn's career the old man had gently corrected a serious error in his copy − a slip which would probably have led to the sack.

After that MacIntyre assumed an almost paternal role, and gave him innumerable pieces of advice, as well as much practical information. Hawn had never been adept at economics, and whenever one of his stories touched on this bleak subject, it was to Colonel Angus MacIntyre that he turned.

The man had retired from the paper three years ago; and after a brief correspondence, Hawn lost touch with him. The last he heard was that MacIntyre had gone to earth in a small riverside house in Teddington; he was widowed, childless, and probably bored. Hawn knew that the old man was also loyal and decent; and he felt sure that if he approached him tactfully, and put his thesis to him as cogently as possible, MacIntyre would at least listen with sympathy. Above all, Hawn knew that he could trust him.

He found the man's number in the book. The familiar Scots voice answered: 'Tommy, my lad! So what are you doing wi' yourself?'

'I'd like to come and see you, Mac. To discuss a few things with you. Draw on your wisdom.'

'Any time, laddie. When can I expect you?'

'Would this afternoon be too soon?'

'Never too soon. You know Teddington? Fielding's Lane, and I'm second on the right after the post office – last house.'

'I'll be seeing you, Mac.'

Hawn left his flat shortly after lunch, driving through a thin rain. After Shepherd's Bush, he cut south towards Hammersmith and the river. He was a swift driver, but an observant one. His ancient Citroën was fitted with both side and wing mirrors, so that it was difficult for any speed-hog to creep up on his inside without being seen.

It was just beyond the scramble after the Hammersmith roundabout, as he was turning under the legs of the flyover, that he first suspected that he was being followed. It was a grey Ford Escort which had been behind him now since before Shepherd's Bush. Just the driver, and the usual radio aerial.

Hawn put on speed over Hammersmith Bridge, then opened up fast once he reached Barnes Common. The Ford had kept its distance at first, and now began to drop back. Hawn shot the lights on amber at Roehampton Lane, and on the long stretch to Richmond he knew that the Ford had lost him. But he had taken the precaution of scribbling the car's number down on the back of his A to Z.

Five minutes later, in the snarled one-way system at Richmond, he spotted a second Ford – a white one this time, again only the driver, and an ordinary aerial. It stayed three cars behind, manoeuvring skilfully.

Hawn's training as a journalist had taught him most of the tricks of following cars, and of being followed. Usually it had been tailing film stars and top celebrities to and from London Airport, and if necessary, shaking off the opposition. The techniques he had learnt had never been very subtle. You just kept the car behind in sight, then pulled up as close as you could when it looked as though some lights were going to change.

But this time he had a feeling that things were different.

At the turning to Richmond Bridge he slowed down, noting that the white Ford did the same. Most of the traffic had filtered right, and Hawn was now on the narrow winding road along the river. The Ford was directly behind him, but had been able to drop back. There was little room for overtaking here. He came up behind a heavy lorry, and slowed still further. This time the car behind closed in enough for him again to note its number.

Then a couple of miles on, just before the main road to Teddington and Kingston, the Ford disappeared. Hawn felt almost a sense of anticlimax. He had passed the sign to Teddington, and was reaching for his map to find Fielding's Lane, when he saw a third car in his mirror. Another damn Ford – a yellow one this time, with a black roof, two aerials and two men inside. Christ, he thought, they're not going to start any rough stuff here, in a nice riverside spot like Teddington?

These two behind were taking it easy. They weren't even playing the game. They made no attempt to pass him when he slowed right down to consult the map again. And they gave him plenty of time to note their number.

He passed the locks, a mock-Tudor tea-house, then the post office, and turned in the lane : but not before he had had time to see the yellow Ford cruise past.

He stopped at the last house and got out. It was the sort of place that he would have expected old MacIntyre to choose for his bachelor retirement.

The man was gaunt, with yellow cheeks stretched taut across his long face; but his eyes were still bright. He clasped Hawn's shoulders with two strong bony hands. 'Tommy, me old lad! Come on in.' He was wearing a knitted fisherman's hat, gumboots, and a very old tweed jacket. 'Sorry I was so long – must get a bell fitted. I was out at the back with my tomatoes. I don't suppose a worldly young man like you would be interested in anything like tomatoes?'

'I eat them sometimes,' Hawn said, as his host led him down a dark hall, into a small untidy room full of books. There was a log-fire and it was warm.

MacIntyre nodded. 'Not much fresh air in here. I have to have the fire going to keep my bones dry. Most o' the time I spend out in the greenhouse.'

'I hope you haven't turned into one of those dodgers who go in for giant marrow competitions?'

'Don't be daft, man. Tomatoes are my speciality. But last summer I did manage to get some grapes going – though I'm more of a man for the grain, if y'know what I mean?' He winked and picked an old black pipe out of a rack and began filling it from a plastic pouch. 'You won't say nay to a wee drop of the Glen to celebrate?'

Hawn sat down in a lop-sided armchair with a broken spring prodding his left buttock. For all his age and frailty, MacIntyre's movements were surprisingly deliberate, despite his slight limp. He reached into a cupboard and brought out a triangular bottle half full of clear liquid, and two big tumblers.

'Steady on,' said Hawn. 'I'm driving.'

'Och, it does a man some good to take a few risks. I wish I could.' He sat down opposite, close to the fire, and pulled at his pipe with a wet crackling sound.

'Mac, I was followed here. By three cars.'

The old man sipped his drink, sucked his pipe. 'You're not a sentimental man, are you, Tommy? You didn't come down here just to keep an old man happy for a few hours. You're either in trouble, or you need advice. Well, let's have it. I've got all the time in the world – until the Great Reaper comes for me.'

'Do you mind if I start back-to-front? How are your connections with the police, Mac?'

'Friendly. Just the local lads, of course. Nothing grand.'

'Can you get me the owners of those three cars that followed me here? They all had "T" registration.' He handed him his A to Z which he had brought in.

'Shouldn't be too much trouble. I'll call them now. But three cars – that's an awful big detail. What we used to call a "Grand Slam". You really do seem to be attracting the big battalions.' He got up and went into the hall; and was back in a couple of minutes. He sat down and got his pipe going again. 'You have me intrigued, Tommy. Just relax and enjoy your drink and tell me all about it. I don't suppose there's much help I can be, at my age, but I'll give you what I can.'

Over the next forty minutes, and generous refills of malt whisky, Hawn recounted every detail, every impression, from Venice to Kew and the London Library. Mac interrupted only to elucidate the odd point. At the end he took out a crumpled tissue, screwed it up tight and began to clean lumps of black dottle out of the stem of his pipe. He tossed the tissue in the fire, drank from his glass, and said, 'You've been very concise, Tommy. Very methodical. You always were. But what you're trying to do is look for King John's treasure in the Wash. It's been tried. Everybody's tried it. Nobody's found it.'

'Nobody's tried to fathom the mystery of Hitler's fuel supplies.'

'True, true. But you need evidence. It's no good telling me that a file is missing from the PRO. Or that a big-wig like Shanklin may have killed an embarrassing Intelligence officer called Frisby. That was cleared through the FO, if your information is correct. From then on it's rather like trying to unravel a ball of string. Or peel an onion.'

'Am I right in assuming that part of MI14's job was to evaluate German fuel supplies?'

'It was.'

'And did you never have suspicions about where the Germans were getting their oil – particularly in the last year of the war, after Rumania fell?'

'Laddie, we didn't deal with suspicions and theories. We dealt with facts. Trouble was, in war you don't get too few facts – you get too many. Too much information, from too many sources. Statistics galore – and you know what they say about statistics? Lies, damn lies, and so on.'

The phone rang in the hall, and this time MacIntyre was gone about five minutes. He came back, rubbing his hands together with a smooth dry sound. 'All three hired from a place in Wandsworth called Hamilton Motors. They can check on the drivers, but only if you put in a complaint.'

'I'll check myself. I don't want the police involved – at least, not at this stage.'

There was a pause, broken only by the wheeze of Mac's pipe. 'Tommy, you're groping in the dark. You've already tangled with Shanklin, and he's not a man who fools around. On the other hand he put you on to this chappie, French. Now that's a mite odd of him, if he's got something to hide. You might almost say that Shanklin was trying to help you.'

'Well, that's his business. As for French, the clue seems to lie somewhere with that man Rice. Do you know anything about him?'

'Not much more than you do, laddie. He disappeared from Central America at the end of the war, when the War Crimes Tribunal got on to him in Germany in 1945. As you know, he was a top scientist, as well as a double-agent. But I do have one name that might help you. A certain Hans Dieter Mönch – Herr Doktor, of course. An important administrator in the Ministry of War Production, working on the petro-chemical side. Synthetic fuels. He was a full Party member and the Yanks got him on a number of technical charges. He served altogether two years, then went down to live in Spain. As far as I know he's still living there.'

He poured more whisky. 'But there were one or two wee mysteries about Doktor Mönch that were near cleared up. We were getting all kinds of informants and turncoats coming to us at that time with the wildest tales. One was that Mönch had been working for a secret project – so secret that it was kept well away from Nazi top-brass, and that Mönch was answerable only to Himmler direct. The suspicion at the time was that it concerned one of those fancy rocket projects, which would have tied in with Rice. Another was that it was part of the German A-Bomb. The trouble was, we never discovered one damn document relating to Mönch's activities. Now that was a wee bit bizarre, because the Germans hoard documents like squirrels. Half their war criminals went to the gallows because of the evidence they left behind them. And Mönch was born a professional bureaucrat.'

'Meaning that Mönch hid these documents?'

'Mönch, or Rice, perhaps. Rice had disappeared, remember. If you could find Rice, you might get yourself a nice little story.'

'Do you know where Mönch is supposed to be in Spain?'

'Last known to be running a little farm in a town called Soria, between Pamplona and Madrid. He's an old man now – he's paid for his sins. He might help you. You could but try. But I'm leading you on, laddie. And it's all speculation. I'd hate to be wasting your time.'

'Those three cars that followed me here weren't speculation, Mac. Nor is that missing file at the PRO. And the fact that Shanklin and Frisby were in both Istanbul and Vera Cruz is something I don't accept as a coincidence. Supposing we assume that those two ports might have been used for clandestine oil shipments from the West to Germany? What do you know about Istanbul in the war, Mac?'

'Och, I didna' have the luck to be there during the war – and being a young man brought up in the kirk, maybe it's as well I wasn't!' He advanced on Hawn with the rapidly emptying bottle; Hawn held up his hand. 'What's happened to ye, laddie? You used to be quite a promising drinker.'

'Not when I'm working. We were talking about Istanbul, Mac – during the war.'

'Bright and dirty, and full of sin. The Turks were sitting on the fence, being wooed by both sides. In the Great War they'd opted for the Germans and paid heavily for it. We were desperate to get them in. So desperate, I even heard a wee tale about Sir Winston wanting to bribe them with gold from our reserves. But the Treasury boys put a quick end to that, so I'm told.'

'Come to the point, Mac. Did you have any dealing with Turkey during the war – with Istanbul in particular?'

'Only from a desk in Whitehall. No sin there, laddie. Not even a sniff of it.'

'I gather the British were pretty thick on the ground in Turkey – as well as the Germans? And a lot of double-dealing went on, just like it did in Lisbon and the Caribbean?'

'Stands to reason. So you take money from one side and sell to the other. What's the worst that can happen to you? Maybe one side gets sore enough to put a knife in your back one dark night, but usually it's up to the Turkish authorities. And what do they care – as long as the nightclubs are full and everyone's paying in hard cash? I used to hear that information was almost as cheap as the lassies.'

'Who ran the Turkish operation – from our end?'

'Cairo, officially, through POE – Political Operations Executive. But of course, they were answerable to London.'

'Mac, if stuff had been getting to the Germans illegally through Istanbul – say, the odd tanker across to the Danube – would you, in MI14, have heard about it?'

The old man jiggled his pipe and rubbed his knees and stared at the ceiling. 'Long, long ago I signed a piece of bumf called the Official Secrets Act, and they still haven't torn it up. But I'm an old man now. I'm not even burdened with the awful responsibility of Fleet Street, and carrying the Gospel every morning to every breakfast table in the land. Yes, Tommy. Stuff got through. Tankers from the

Gulf, switching cargoes, false Bills of Lading, putting in for phoney refits before going down to Alex or up to Naples when the "Hanging Garden" fell.' He grinned : 'That was the name we gave Italy, because no one ever knew which side she was on.'

'If you knew, why didn't you do anything about it?'

'Without evidence? In a neutral country which was as corrupt as an old cadaver? And if we'd started arresting Turkish nationals, it would have just driven Turkey closer to the Germans.'

'How do you know some of our people weren't involved?'

The old man gave him a sly smile along the stem of his pipe. 'If I did, I can't prove it. Not then – not now.'

'You can't even give me a lead?'

'Well' – he was fiddling with his pipe again, spilling tobacco from his pouch and picking it off his bony knees – 'I might be able to give you a name. Man called Salak. Imin Salak. He'll be getting on now – if someone hasn't already knifed him and tossed him in the Bosphorus. But he was a young man then, very bright, very highly thought of by our side. He was a wrestler by profession – last I heard, he still was. Runs a chemist shop in the Kumkapi District – apparently used to be one of the most picturesque parts of Istanbul, but also pretty seedy, o'course.

'Sounds as though you still keep in touch with him?'

'Only gossip at the club. He still draws a pension from us. Though the mandarins aren't too happy about it, as he's supposed to be tied up in the rackets. Drugs.' He pulled a face : 'Nasty stuff.'

'What was his exact function during the war?'

'Officially, a middle-man for the Istanbul Port Authority. His job was to vet the masters' credentials and check on the cargoes. He's supposed to have had amazing contacts, both above board and in the underworld. He was also entrusted to recruit agents and spies among the local dock people. If there was any funny business going on, Salak was your man. He shouldn't be too difficult to track down. Wrestling's one of the most popular sports in Turkey, and wrestlers stick together like an old boys' fraternity.'

There was a pause. The room had become thick with Mac's pipe smoke, and with the smell of malt.

'Let's go back to the Caribbean for a moment,' Hawn said. 'It was that man Robak who put the idea forward. Supposing someone – Rice, for instance, and others – fixed up a deal by which a few tankers crossed the Atlantic, lost the convoy, and made it round to the north of Norway, then down the German-controlled coast to Sweden? Would it have been possible?'

'Aye, I guess it would.'

'What about the Royal Navy?'

'The Senior Service, you mean? That magic phrase.' He stroked the edge of his jaw. 'The Navy lads had their hands full – what with trying to protect our lifeline across the Atlantic, and hunting down U-boats. They didn't have the time to stop every stray ship they didn't like the look of, including the odd tanker. Besides, even if they did, there wasn't a lot they could do – providing the Bills of Lading appeared to be in order.'

'They must have had some instructions from the Admiralty? Supposing they spotted a tanker round Iceland, obviously heading for Norwegian and Swedish waters? They boarded her and found she had papers made out to some dubious Swiss bank dealing with someone in Sweden? What did they do? Sink the tanker?'

'Laddie boy, even a captain in the Royal Navy doesn't go round sinking unarmed neutral vessels just because he doesn't like the look of their papers.'

'The captains still must have had some degree of discretion. How subtle would you say the average Royal Navy captain is?'

'Not too subtle – especially where paperwork's concerned, and that's all in a foreign language. You must remember that as neutral countries, places like Sweden and Switzerland were perfectly entitled to import oil, and anything else they wanted, for their own domestic consumption.'

'How did the Swiss manage it? Directly through Germany?'

'Officially they used the pipeline up from Genoa – the

78

first of its kind ever built. The Swedes, of course, imported directly from the States – although the American authorities were not at all happy about the arrangement.'

'What was the position with U-boats?' said Hawn. 'How did they know how to distinguish a rogue tanker from just another ship which had lost its convoy?'

MacIntyre got up and put a log on the fire. 'Well, that's where the skulduggery would have come in. If your theory is correct – and I'm not saying it either is or is not – the Nazis would have had agents in the Caribbean, probably working inside the oil companies, notifying the German Admiralty, who in turn would have passed the information on to the U-boat commanders.' He paused, busy packing his pipe; this time he took five matches to get it alight.

He went on : 'Forget the Caribbean angle for the moment, laddie. If you've come to me for advice, I'm telling you to look to Turkey. It's nearer and cheaper to get to. Besides, the Caribbean's sewn up – the Yanks have seen to that. If there were any dirty traces left after the war, you can be sure they've been kicked over by now. But Turkey's another story. It's a wild country – always has been. Talk to Salak. Only if he decides to tell you anything, he'll want to be paid. And from what I've heard of him, he's expensive.

'But first, why don't you try Doktor Mönch? Still nearer, and he's probably much cheaper. As I told you, Mönch was tied up in some very hush-hush business with Nazi war production. He may not be prepared to give you details – for fear of reprisals – but he might provide you with a useful overall picture.'

He poured them each the last of the malt. 'And one last thing, Tommy. A piece of advice you haven't asked for. Advice from an old man. You're stepping into dark waters. You've almost certainly stepped already on some mighty sensitive toes. These multi-national oil companies have a great deal of money, a great deal of power. They make most crime syndicates look like corner sweet-shops.'

'Mac, are you trying to warn me off?'

'No, just trying to salve my conscience. I wouldn't like

you to get into any kind of trouble, Tom – not on my account.'

'You think if I go through with this, I might be putting myself in some danger?'

Mac said, 'A few years ago a couple o' lads in Italy tried to pull a fast one on ABCO. They chartered a tanker full of high-grade crude and made a swap in mid-ocean for low-grade stuff. Then they tried to cash in on the difference. I say "tried", because they'd hardly started negotiations when their car was in a head-on collision with a road tanker outside Rome. Both were killed outright. And the funny part of it was, the tanker belonged to one of the rival companies. You can draw whatever moral you choose from that.'

He banged out his pipe in the hearth and stood up. 'Keep in touch, laddie. I'll be thinking of you.' He insisted on seeing Hawn to the front door : but no suspicious cars waited in the lane.

Hawn drove back carefully, and checked in his mirror every few seconds : but this time there was nothing to arouse his suspicions. His street behind Notting Hill Gate was quiet in the late summer evening.

His flat was still double-locked and empty. Anna had been due home nearly an hour ago. She was a punctual girl – sometimes irritatingly so – and was never late without warning him in advance. He realized that she might have tried to ring him that afternoon, and had got no reply; he had not given her Mac's number and had stayed longer than he had expected.

He had a hot bath, to freshen up and sweat some of the malt out of his system; then lay down on the bed, still wrapped in a damp towel, and fell asleep. The names of Doktor Mönch and a wrestling drug peddler called Salak had receded into a haze of alcohol and pipe-smoke : the memories of an old man who lived alone, growing tomatoes.

It was more than an hour later when he woke. He heard the lock turn, then footsteps. Anna stood in the main room in her monk's habit, holding her satchel-like bag. 'Tom.'

She looked at him defiantly; she was rather white. 'They've stolen my string-bag. The one with my books and notes in it.'

He blinked at her. 'Who have?'

'You tell me.' She went over and poured herself a drink. 'It was while I was in the library. They went to the old man who looks after the coats and personal belongings. They said it was a bomb-scare and they wanted to look at all bags and parcels. They took mine, to examine it. He said he couldn't stop them.'

'Who were they? I mean, what did they look like?'

'He said they were well-dressed, well-spoken. Might have been police, but he didn't think they were ordinary police. Special Branch, or Terrorist Squad, I suppose.'

'Have you told the police?'

'Yes. They just asked me a lot of silly questions.'

'What was in the bag, Anna?'

'Oh God. Practically everything. I mean, most of my notes brought up to date. All the petroleum import and export figures for the neutrals during the whole war, against the same for oil exporting countries for the same period, month by month. Sounds pretty simple, but it's been a bloody headache. At least a month's work up the spout. But that's not the point. I know where to begin again – but so do they. They know exactly what I'm on to, and how far I've got.'

Hawn told her about the three cars following him to Mac's that afternoon. She listened impassively, then went into the bathroom and returned almost at once.

'Tom, someone's been in the flat. They've turned it over – thoroughly.'

'How do you know? It looks all right to me.'

'My toilet things – they've been moved. Not much, but enough.' She went quickly over to her desk on which were arranged tidy piles of books with paper-markers in them, documents, photostats, the rest of her typewritten notes. 'They've been through these, too.'

Hawn went to the bookcase. He had a large collection of books, amassed since his student days, and he took pride in arranging them in selected categories. He noticed almost immediately that among his hard-cover editions of Orwell's *Collected Essays and Letters,* Volumes I and II were in the wrong order. 'Funny sort of break-in. The locks haven't been broken – no damage, nothing taken, that I can see. Usually they piss on the carpets.'

'Tom, when did you get back?'

'Over an hour ago.'

'And when did you leave here?'

'After lunch.'

'They must have been watching the flat, then. But who? Not the police?'

'Then who?'

'ABCO.'

'Oh my God.' She drank some whisky very fast. 'You don't mean they've got on to us this soon?'

'I wouldn't have thought so – until what's happened this afternoon. At least, I'd have expected them to hold their hand a little longer. And what about the stuff on your desk? I haven't read any of it yet.'

'Mostly German fuel reserves and their commerce with Rumania. All very technical, and some of it quite useful.'

'These boys this afternoon were technical. They knew how to pick two security locks, and they also knew what they were looking for. Sweden – Turkey – Rumania – Switzerland – and comparative oil import figures for all of them. Anna, all this might just be a roundabout way of scaring us off. Now, you tidy up, then we'll go and have dinner.'

He was still partly sceptical, but still not discounting a hidden 'mike' or the latest in the 'dirty tricks' department. He waited until they were out in the street, before making his proposition. 'Tomorrow I'm wiring Pol for business expenses, and we'll take a little holiday in Spain. How are you fixed with the LSE?'

'I've got two weeks' holiday.'

'Then we'll be spending them in an obscure little town in the middle of the Castilian Plain. A town called Soria.'

He sent the wire that night to Pol's PO number in Annecy,

then booked two open return tickets for himself and Anna, and for his old Citroën, on the Southampton ferry to Le Havre – which would be almost deserted at this season, and would give him plenty of scope to see if they were being followed.

There were also two other things to be done. First, in the morning, he rang New Scotland Yard and asked for extension 429 – Chief Superintendent Muncaster, a man with whom he had long been on close professional terms. Muncaster was in conference, but someone said he would ring back. From Hawn's experience of police work, that might mean any time before midnight. He decided to fill in the time with a trip south of the river, to Wandsworth.

Hamilton Motors were in a cul-de-sac behind a railway bridge. From the outside the place looked as respectable as any establishment can with a forecourt full of freshly painted second-hand cars for sale. A notice over the door announced that they also dealt in hired cars.

Hawn picked his way through pools of oily mud to a door marked OFFICE – WALK IN, WHEN OPEN. It was open. A youth with long plaited hair, in stained overalls, sat reading *Melody Maker*. A transistor bellowed, unseen. There was a cluttered desk, one telephone, several chairs arranged along the wall. Hawn glanced back round the car-park, but saw no sign of the three Fords which had followed him yesterday.

He pushed his way in and shouted at the youth above the music : 'Where's the boss?' The youth called over his shoulder, 'Bunnie – business !' – then returned to his magazine.

An inner door opened and a youngish man with small flat features and curly blond hair came in. He wore a white shirt with blue stripes and his worsted jacket had too much padding in the shoulders. In his breast pocket was a blue silk handkerchief that matched his blue socks. He smiled at Hawn, with teeth the same colour as his hair. 'Morning, sir. What can I do for you ?'

'I understand you had three cars out on hire yesterday – two blue Escorts and a yellow Cortina. I'd just like to know who took them out.'

The man's smile persisted; he looked tough and relaxed. 'Our records are confidential – unless you've got a warrant.'

Hawn showed his Press card. 'It's all right – I don't want to look through your VAT fiddles. I just want to know the name of the man, or men, who hired those three cars from you yesterday.' He handed him a list of the three registration numbers.

The blond man looked at them. 'You say you're a reporter? For what?'

Hawn took out his Scotland Yard Press pass, with two ten-pound notes folded inside. The man looked at them as though they were a couple of postcards; then still holding them, he turned to the youth in overalls and said, 'Go on, Jerry, scram. You've got that Merc to get ready by this evening.'

When the door had closed, he put the two notes in his pocket and handed Hawn back his pass. 'You're lucky I run this place. Otherwise I could get myself into a load of trouble.' He shook his curly head. 'Ah, you never know who's going to make trouble for you these days. I'm asked to do a special turn for someone – three cars in good condition hired for one day, full comprehensive insurance – *five* hundred paid in readies, but no licences. Now, I don't believe in miracles, Mr Hawn, but Christ – if this happened to me every day I'd be a bleeding millionaire.'

Hawn looked at him. 'And that's all you know?'

'Scout's honour. Why should I lie? I could say it was a delegation from the Liberal Party and you wouldn't know no better.'

'Three cars, one obviously equipped with UHF, all hired together, and presumably returned together, and you don't know anything about it?'

The man shifted his feet slightly apart, but otherwise made no movement. 'I'll let you into a little secret of the trade, Mr Hawn. I specialize in second-hand jobs. Now I know a bit about the Press – I know that when someone gives you a good tip-off, you don't reveal the source. Same with me. I'm discreet. If a bloke comes to me and wants three cars, for a good fee, I don't ask for his birth certificate.'

'I'd like you to be my source,' said Hawn, 'in total confidence. The people who came to you yesterday were pros. They were as good at a relay tail-job as the police. The only mistake they made was that I spotted them. You still don't want to tell me who they are?'

The man stood with padded shoulders squared, hands curling at his sides. 'I think you'd better go, Mr Hawn.'

Hawn took out a third ten-pound note. 'Not until I've seen your books.'

'Sorry, chum, my books aren't in order.'

Hawn still held out the note, but the man made no attempt to take it.

'Christ, you must have money to burn, mate. Am I going to feature in the *Sunday Mirror* or something?'

'This is private, confidential.'

'Like fuck it is.'

'I just want to look at the three cars that tailed me yesterday. Any objections?'

'I have. They're all out on hire. Besides, I don't like snoopers. Now put your money away and get out of here.'

'I think you're getting me confused with the police,' Hawn said. 'There might be something in this for you. Who do I ask for if I ring?'

'Bunnie.'

'See you at the Playboy Club,' Hawn said, and opened the door.

The blond man watched him into his Citroën DS. He had plenty of time to memorize the number; and in his mirror Hawn saw him return to his office and lift the telephone.

Chief Superintendent Muncaster phoned back just after lunch. Hawn, without mentioning his theories or the extent of his investigations, told him straight out about the three events of yesterday afternoon.

Muncaster was a sly, taciturn man who never used a syllable that was not necessary. 'Three cars from a garage in Wandsworth? And the owner won't talk?'

'Only that he was paid over the odds and they didn't

identify themselves. What about the business at the LSE and the "break-in" last night at my flat?'

'What's your girl's name?' Hawn told him. 'Did she describe the two men?'

'Vaguely. Professionals.'

'You say your flat was gone over, only because she has a nose for these things, and because two of your books were in the wrong order? That's not evidence, Hawn. Nor are three Fords in London traffic. Still, I'll look into it. Call you back.'

'When?'

'When I'm ready.' He hung up.

Early that evening Norman French rang, calling from a pay-phone. His voice was faint, but betrayed that ingratiating self-confidence of one who does not expect to be refused. 'Tom, I've booked a table for us both at the Trattoo. Tonight, eight o'clock. I think you'll be interested.'

'In what?'

'I'd prefer to discuss it at dinner. Just the two of us.'

'Eight o'clock, the Trattoo.'

Anna had still not returned; Hawn left her a note to say he'd be late and that she was not to keep dinner for him.

Just after eight he parked his car near the restaurant in Abingdon Road. French had not arrived. The table he had booked was in the far corner downstairs, under an umbrella of potted plants. It was the most secluded spot in the restaurant. French was a fastidious man, and a careful one.

By nine o'clock he had still not appeared. Hawn allowed himself a fourth drink. By 9.30 he rang the Eden House Hotel. It was some time before the landlady answered. Hawn gave his name, then – remembering just in time French's alias – asked for Mr Hudson. The landlady informed him that Mr Hudson had already retired, and did not wish to be disturbed.

'But I was supposed to meet him for dinner tonight – he invited me himself. For eight o'clock. I'd be very grateful if you went up and told him I'm still waiting.'

'Mr Hudson has retired,' she repeated.

'Would you kindly go up and ask Mr Hudson to come to the phone?'

After a long pause she said. 'Mr Hudson must be asleep.' Then : 'Are you one of the gentlemen who called earlier?'

'What gentlemen?'

'I'm afraid we do not discuss Mr Hudson's personal affairs with strangers.' She terminated the conversation.

Hawn had a plate of spaghetti, half a bottle of wine, then drove round to Sussex Gardens. He suspected that the woman was covering up for French, who had obviously had a more important visitor, and had no scruples about dumping Hawn without even the courtesy of a telephone call.

He arrived at the hotel shortly before ten. It was one of those gloomy terrace mansions which had been given a skimpy cosmetic of cream paint and its name in red neon script, to attract second-class tourists and foreign students. There was a permeating smell of damp earth, old cooking and the ancient grime of Paddington Station.

The landlady was unhelpful. She repeated that Mr Hudson did not wish to be disturbed. Hawn became aggressive. Ten o'clock was too early for a man to go to bed, unless he had female company. Certainly Mr Hudson had no female company! she retorted. In which case, Hawn required to see him immediately.

She tried the house-phone, then put it down, shaking her head. Hawn said, 'If you can't take me up and open the door, I'll call the police.' She led him up.

The room was on the third floor. It was unlocked : a small room, cheaply partitioned, with a basin, TV, a side-table with an electric kettle, sachets of sugar and instant coffee; also a Baby Belling cooker which had recently been used.

French was in bed. The bedclothes had been pulled down to his waist and his feet stuck out at the end. The pillow was soaked thick and wet, like a huge skinned liver sausage. His head, with its short furry-black hair, was propped up against the pillow. In his left hand was a half-smoked cigarette which had slightly singed the sheet. There was still a red pinch at the top of his nose, left by his tinted glasses which lay on the bedside table, next to his cigarettes. His eyes showed like dull fish-slits.

In his throat was a long wide gap, drained and glistening pink, and Hawn could see the severed vocal-chords sprouting up like rings of spaghetti. Having recently enjoyed a good first course, he vomited it into the wastepaper basket.

The landlady was screaming.

Then he went and washed his face in the basin and looked round to see if French had had any drink. A half bottle of gin lay behind his shoe-cleaning equipment. Hawn drank most of it, while the woman went on screaming. Then he went downstairs and dialled 999, called the Yard and asked for Muncaster, urgent.

The police arrived in two Pandas and a Jaguar. There were too many of them. They kept starting to ask Hawn questions, then being interrupted when a call came through. Hawn's fingerprints were on the inside and outside door handles, round the basin, possibly on the wastepaper basket.

The slow, pedantic ritual began. Thirty-five minutes later, when the photographers and forensic men had arrived, Muncaster appeared.

The Chief Superintendent had a long nose and very little hair. His manner was quiet but abrupt. 'All right, Hawn, you found the body. That makes you a witness. Now, there's a little pub up the road called The Falcon. It's about closing time, but I know the manager. Then you can tell me what you're doing in Sussex Gardens.'

The last customers had left half-an-hour ago and the barman had finished washing the glasses and locked up. Hawn had told his story from Venice to his 999 call, omitting nothing.

Detective Chief Superintendent Cyril Muncaster sat drawing wet rings on the table top. 'Hawn, there's one thing that good policemen and good journalists have in common. We deal in facts. Not theories, fantasies. Facts. Evidence. Proof.'

'You've already got those two sneak-thieves yesterday at the L.S.E. And what about the hired cars?'

'We've given Mr "Bunnie" Regan a rap over the knuckles

for that. But he won't go down for murder. He rented the cars to a foreigner – strong accent, thought he was German. We're circulating a description, but it might fit half the male master-race.' He sipped the dregs of his glass. 'Now you say that you last saw French alive three days ago, and you hadn't seen him before that for nearly two years? You say he gave you some useful info. about ABCO? And you paid him for it?'

Hawn said nothing.

'But you've absolutely no idea what French wanted to talk to you about this evening? And don't hold out on me, or my God I'll make your life so bloody miserable you'll want to emigrate.'

'I only know he said it was something important – something he couldn't talk about over the phone. What about those two guests he had earlier? They're the obvious ones, aren't they?'

'Yes, we've got a good description of them from the lady downstairs. Smartly dressed – again, foreigners. She wasn't sure about the accent. They were obviously known to French – he was probably expecting them. You noticed that he was smoking a cigarette when they killed him? No sign of a struggle. Messy, but it had the advantage of cutting the vocal-chords so quickly that there wouldn't have been time for him to scream. Then they went through the room. The forensic boys have got a lot of sets of prints, but I doubt we'll have them on record. Foreigners, professionals – you know.'

He stared into his glass. 'For the moment, Hawn, I'm treating your problems and this murder as two separate cases. Now, do you know if Norman French had any enemies?'

'He wasn't a paticularly lovable character. He knew a lot of people, but I don't think many of them were friends.'

'I didn't ask if he could win a popularity contest. Did he have any enemies?'

'There was an incident about six months ago. French had come back from the States where he'd been working for ABCO, and had apparently been involved in some dirty work and got the sack. But he was living it up – more or less on his new American wife's money. I went to a party at their place, and just as I was leaving I overheard a row going on between French and an American, who was drunk. At least, the row was on the American's side. French was just trying to keep his end up. The American was accusing him of every kind of swindle, and shouting that he had ruined several people. I think he said something like, "Nobody skims cream off us and gets away with it". He's called Don Robak – the one I told you about whom I met in Venice. Senior European executive with ABCO.'

'We'll put a call out for him,' Muncaster said : but his face portrayed nothing.

Hawn continued : 'There's one thing you haven't asked me about. French's connection with Toby Shanklin. Shanklin, remember, first suggested I went to French.'

'I haven't forgotten,' Muncaster said moodily. 'I understood that Shanklin was just trying to be helpful? But I'll be frank with you – Shanklin's an important man, he has important friends. I'm not going to put my career at stake by dragging him into a murder case unless I've got damn good evidence.'

'Shanklin's somehow tied up in all this – I'm certain of it. All right, I don't have the facts, or the proof. But I've got a hunch. Don't policemen work on hunches too?'

'I'll bear it in mind,' Muncaster said, standing up. 'I'll walk you back to your car.'

There was an ambulance in the street outside the hotel. A crowd was being held back fifty feet away. A huge 'mobile' in white helmet and breeches placed a leather gauntlet into the middle of Hawn's chest and said, 'And where do you think you're going?'

'Piss off,' Muncaster said. Two men in white coats had come out of the hotel, their pink rubber gloves smeared red. Hawn finally got his Citroën out, after one of the Pandas had had to be moved, and drove back to the flat. Anna was asleep, and he did not wake her.

# CHAPTER THREE

## *Mönch*

*A secret ceases to be a secret if it is once confided – it is like a dollar bill, once broken, it is never a dollar again.*

HENRY WHEELER SHAW

They took three leisurely days to reach San Sebastian, where they spent a day on the beach, braced by the chill Atlantic and the fresh September breezes. Hawn needed time to rest, to think. Doktor Hans Dieter Mönch may have been an old man, but he had survived more than thirty years since the war, and another few days wasn't likely to make much difference. Besides, French's death had given the whole scheme of things a deeper dimension.

They spent another two days driving over the Pyrenees and down through the wooded foothills to Pamplona, then due south across the bleak brown plain towards Madrid. The towns were grey and shuttered and the people had a grey shuttered look. In the evenings a sharp wind blew across the plain and the men crowded the bars, chewed *tapas* on little sticks and drank purple wine and a thin frothy beer.

Soria was recommended in the guide-books on the strength of a ruined convent and a couple of Government-run tourist hotels on two jutting rocks overlooking the narrow town below. Hawn had booked into one of them. A suit of armour stood half-way up the stairs, and the bar in the basement had a juke-box and one of those machines on which you can play tennis with yourself. He and Anna seemed to be the only guests.

On their first evening they drove down into the town and strolled up the main street. It smelt ripe but not fresh: there was donkey manure on the streets: the meat in the shops was covered with nesting flies : and in the bars there was sawdust and much drinking and no women. The men eyed Anna in silence. It was not a friendly town.

Hawn's Spanish was poor, but Anna could manage a rather literate version which she had learnt at university; however, it required a tactful boldness on her part in order to get into conversation with the men, all of whom seemed to regard her presence with interested contempt. She made the point that she was looking for an old German gentleman who had lived in the town for many years and had been *un doctor*. This was frequently interpreted as *un medico* – that they were ill and wanted a doctor. Hawn would intervene with *doctor profesor*. The men were not helpful.

They had come to the end of the street and it was growing dark. The bar was long and narrow, like a cattle-stall, with scarcely space to squeeze past between the drinkers at the counter. A black bull's head eyed them evilly from the far wall. Hawn found a space at the bar and ordered them both Fundador; they had already had a few drinks and he was beginning to feel easier, more confident. When the barman put their glasses down, Hawn repeated their ritual of questions. The man looked at Hawn empty-eyed, muttered something and moved on. Hawn tried the man on his left, but received only a shrug. He was finishing his thimble of brandy, wondering whether to have another, when someone nudged him in the ribs.

The man was holding up a glass of wine which had stained his lips black, and toasted them both in Spanish; then, without consulting either of them, he ordered wine for them both. As he did so, he kept kicking the bar softly with his canvas espadrille, like a nervous tic. He was very old, small, frail, in blue dungarees and a workman's shirt, and his face was tanned to the colour of brown paper – except for his nose which appeared to have suffered some accident. It was thin, bent sideways, and veined with white scar tissue.

'Mönch?' He pronounced the name with the long Spanish vowel. 'You are interested?'

Hawn said that he was.

'You are English?'

'We are.'

'And why would Señor Mönch want to meet with English visitors?'

Hawn bought them all more wine. It had a thick rusty taste, but was not bad after the first three sips. Their new companion drank his like water. Anna put in, 'We have a special reason for seeing Doktor Mönch. It is a personal matter.'

The old man gave a crooked smile, his bent nose curved like a question-mark over his mouth. 'You speak good Spanish, Señora. How is your German? Herr Mönch is German, you know.'

'I know. Is he known here as Señor Mönch?'

The old man made a sound in his throat like burnt toast being scraped. 'You talk about Señor Mönch. You ask the Guardia about Señor Mönch and they have never heard of him. You ask me about Mönch. You are excellently informed. What do you want to know of him?'

Anna went on in Spanish: 'We have a proposition to make to him. My friend here is a journalist. It will be in Señor Mönch's interest to see us.'

The man lifted his white nose from his glass and excused himself. Hawn watched him go into the telephone booth at the end of the bar. He was there for ten minutes. When he came back, he said, 'In half-an-hour. Señor Mönch agrees to meet you. Here is the address.'

They had two more drinks together, then parted with pumping handshakes. He was the only man to have addressed Anna since arriving in the town.

Out in the street Hawn looked at the piece of paper the old man had given him. In careful block capitals, in pencil, was written: SENOR ALBERTO MILLAO, CALLE FONCADA 2. Anna said 'Would you prefer to go alone?'

'Certainly not. Seeing you may make him more at ease. Just at long as you don't blow your stack if he starts trotting out the odd National Socialist sentiment.'

Calle Foncada was a twisting track with a few small houses set back among olive trees. They found Number Two

93

near the end : a single-storey white house with a shallow-tiled roof behind a high iron gate. When the engine stopped, they could hear chickens, and a dog began to bark ferociously.

The gate was padlocked, but there was a bell-pull. They heard it clanging distantly inside the house. The barking grew louder; then presently an old peasant in a beret came out and unlocked the gate without a word, led them to the door, unlocked it, then showed them into a dark tiled passage with stone walls. The air was stale and cold. He opened a door at the end and stood back, allowing them to pass into what appeared to be some kind of old-fashioned parlour. He closed the door and left them.

The room was furnished in rustic Spanish style : thick wooden furniture, white-washed walls, uneven tiled floor. There were no signed photographs of Adolf Hitler, no SS insignia : just a couple of framed prints of Spanish knights-in-armour, and some earthenware jugs and vases on a side-table.

The dog was still barking, until someone shouted at it, and it went into a low growl. It sounded like a big dog. It was the only German thing about the house. They waited.

Five minutes later, the door was opened again by the peasant. He beckoned to them, and they followed him out, back down the passage to a heavy mahogany door. A clock began chiming somewhere. The peasant knocked and turned the handle. Hawn and Anna walked past him.

It was an unusual room for such a house. They both had the sense of entering some ecclesiastical library. Except for a Gothic stained-glass window, hideously blood-shot and jaundiced in the evening sun, the walls were covered in uniform leather volumes behind glass cases. In one of the armchairs sat the frail old man with the white crooked nose, whom they had met half-an-hour ago in the bar. He was dressed in the same dungarees and espadrilles.

He grinned at them both with his stained teeth. 'You are the first English visitors I have had in ten years. My English is not very perfect. Would you prefer that I spoke Spanish?'

'My Spanish is not good,' Hawn said. 'And Miss Admiral

here does not speak German.'

Anna said, 'You go ahead. Don't worry about me.'

'We can speak German,' Hawn said.

'So you know German?'

'I studied for a year at Heidelberg.'

The old face brightened. 'Ach, Heidelberg! What a fine city. So you know all the old drinking songs? "Ich habe mein Herz in Heidelberg verloren, auf einer lauen Sommernacht . . . !" How sweet, how sentimental. I am an old man now, and like all old men I live on my memories.' (What memories? Hawn wondered.) 'But stop, we have not yet been formally introduced! It is most incorrect of me to talk to you so, without the proper formalities.'

Hawn duly introduced Anna and himself, and Mönch got up and fetched them three glasses of good Spanish brandy. He was not an obviously wealthy man, but what money he did have he had certainly lavished on this room. Hawn tried to read some of the titles in the bookcases, but most of the bindings were so old that the lettering had faded. He did read one title, however: *The Christian Man in the Modern World*.

Mönch toasted them both. 'Herr Hawn, I understood your lady-friend here said that you are a journalist? That is correct? So I must presume that this meeting is a professional one. Now let me be honest. I have lived here for a long time, and I have lived in peace, without problems. As you will no doubt know, I spent two years after the war in an American prison. Not because I was a war criminal – I had not murdered Jewish babies and burnt synagogues – but because I had been a functionary of the State. The Americans were not very discriminating in those days.

'However, during my duties for the Reich, I was privy to certain secrets. I served, as you may know, in a department under the Ministry of War Production. There are many things I know which I have never told, and which have never been told. But I hear that the young generation of Europeans have become very interested in the history of the Third Reich. I presume, therefore, that you have come to interview me in order to further enlighten that generation?'

'More or less. It would depend, Herr Doktor, on what you have to say.'

'That I appreciate. But you too must appreciate that I am a very old man now, I am sick, and I have little in this world besides this house, my books and my chickens. And God the Father, through the Blessed Saviour, the Lord Buddah. You are not, by any remote chance, Herr Hawn, a Buddhist?'

'No.'

'No, quite.' The old man nodded. 'It is most indelicate of me to mention the subject. But if I recount my memories to you I must expect some reward.'

'Certainly – I wouldn't presume on your hospitality for nothing. But of course, it will depend on the material.'

'You will not be disappointed,' Mönch said, with a rapine grin. 'For instance, you may know that Hitler was something of a mystic. He was against the Established Church, which he saw as a spiritual irrelevance to his Modern Germany. But he was not altogether against Christ. Christ had been murdered by the Jews, the apostles of Satan. But although Hitler had much wisdom, despite his mistakes, there was one thing he did not know. Christ was a Buddhist.

'I surprise you? But the evidence is not only strong, it is conclusive! It is only the arrogance and fanaticism of Christianity which prevents the truth being known. I ask you, what was Our Lord doing between the ages of twelve and thirty? History does not tell us. History is silent. The Church is silent.' He was leaning forward, squeezing his brandy glass so tightly that Hawn feared it might break in his hands. 'During those lost twenty-one years, Christ was studying the teachings of the mighty Buddha! He travelled widely, and he listened to many wise tongues. Christ was the reincarnation of Buddha.'

Hawn nodded with a patient despair. He was listening not to a dangerous ex-war criminal, but to a sad senile man whose mind had wandered into the fantasies of religion. He hadn't the heart to point out that until recently Buddhism had been an exclusively oriental religion, and that the first Westerner to penetrate the Far East had been Marco

Polo. He said : 'With great respect, Herr Doktor, I have come to discuss more material matters. Matters concerning your job with the Ministry of War Production.'

Mönch held up his hand. 'I understand. But first you, too, must understand. I have already told you that I have lived here a long time without problems. However, I do take precautions. The situation here in Spain has changed much since the death of the Caudillo. We German exiles are not quite as welcome as we used to be. So I cannot rely for my security in the normal state of things. You understand me?'

'Do you still consider yourself in danger after so long?'

The little man shrugged his thin shoulders. 'It is always possible. There is a tiresome Jew in Vienna called Wiesenthal. You have no doubt heard of him? He makes it his life's work to hunt down former National Socialists and bring them to what he calls "justice".'

'I thought the Wiesenthal Office was only interested in the big fish. I'm sorry, I didn't mean to be disrespectful, but from what I have heard, you would hardly qualify for Wiesenthal's attentions.'

'That is a strange compliment, Herr Hawn. Perhaps you underestimate Wiesenthal. Or perhaps you underestimate me. Maybe I am a big fish – or used to be. I know all the dossiers describe me as an important functionary in war production. That is not all the truth. There were many aspects to that production. For instance, there was much slave-labour. I was not personally responsible – it was merely the system – and the Americans could not prove my guilt. But there are others – not just the Jew in Vienna or his masters in that gangster-state, Israel. There are others who might be even less scrupulous. That is why I have to be very careful with visitors.

'But you look too young to be of the dangerous generation. Besides, you are English – neither of you are Jewish;' although he shot a quick glance at Anna, at her straight profile and reddish hair – 'and you both have honest faces. I am prepared to trust you. Now what is it you want to know?'

Hawn told him. He told him the heart of his theory, then

elaborated – without names – on the various incidents that had occurred since he had returned from Venice. Mönch waited until he had finished, then poured more brandy.

'What is it you want me to give you, Herr Hawn?'

'Herr Doktor, I know it may sound an outrageous idea. But as I've told you, things have made me believe that it could be true – or at least, have a large amount of truth in it. But I need proof. Information, and, if possible, corroboration.'

When Mönch said nothing, Hawn added : 'Did you ever hear of a Doktor Alan Oskar Reiss?' The old man's face was blank. 'An Anglo-German scientist who worked in Germany during the war, was trained as a double-agent, pretended to defect to America through Mexico where he got a job with ABCO – before he disappeared in 1945.'

Mönch was silent. When he did speak, it was not to answer Hawn's question.

'How did you hear about me?'

'A friend who used to be a Colonel with British Economic Intelligence. He interrogated you in 1946. A Scotsman called MacIntyre.'

The German laid a finger along the edge of his bone-white nose and slowly began to rub it. It made a dry sound like someone rubbing very thin paper. Hawn found it obscene.

Mönch said, 'I do not remember. I must have been interrogated by a hundred people. You British were best. Far more civilized than the Americans. It is a pity that you have become so degenerate in recent years.' He sipped some brandy. 'What are your motives, Herr Hawn?'

'The exposure, and possibly the destruction, of an overpowerful, multi-national organization which knows no morals, owes allegiance to no government, no principles, and has no motives except those of profit.'

Mönch gave a slow laugh. 'Are you a revolutionary? Don't be afraid to answer. I have always believed that the modern generation of Anarchist revolutionaries are not so very different in their philosophy and ideology from the early National Socialists. They certainly have the same

passions. The people I abhor are these intellectual liber-
tarians, these Jewish internationalists. What you call multi-
nationalists.'

'ABCO is certainly not run by Jews,' Hawn said, with
some discomfort.

Mönch smiled. 'How do you know? It is partly controlled
by the Americans, is it not? Wherever there are powerful
American organizations, there are Jews. The Jews may not
control America, but they are certainly the single most
influential ethnic group in the country.'

'Doktor Mönch, I must make one thing perfectly clear. I
have absolutely no intention of waging a private anti-
Semitic vendetta. If there happen to be Jews on the Board
of ABCO, then it is entirely fortuitous and of no interest
to me. It also happens to contradict my entire theory. If
ABCO had been controlled by the Jews during the war,
they would hardly have been keen to trade with your
people.'

'Lieber Herr! You are naïve. Or perhaps you are just
too young. Let me tell you a story. It was told to me by
someone very senior in our Ministry of War Production. I
can vouch for its authenticity. At the beginning of August,
1944 – just after 20 July had failed, and about a week
before the Rumanian oil-fields were taken – the leading
bankers and industrialists of the Reich held a meeting in
Switzerland. It was never reported and it has never been
officially acknowledged. At this meeting were all the leading
bankers and industrialists from the Allied nations, particularly from the United States. The Germans were represented
principally by Krupp, von Thyssen and Flick. I can tell
you that half the American delegation were Jews, and there
were at least two Jews from Britain and three from France.
Yes – Occupied France!

'Krupp was in the chair. He did not waste words. He
opened the proceedings by saying "Gentlemen, I'm afraid
we've backed a loser. Our horse is not going to finish the
race." No minutes were taken of that meeting, and it only
lasted a couple of hours. But its purpose was clear. The
bankers – the Jews, the Internationalists, the Multi-

nationalists – were already preparing to carve up their empire in Europe. While hundreds of thousands of brave men were dying all over Europe – millions of civilians dying in bombing raids – these commercial bandits were prepared to sit down in a quiet, nice house in neutral Switzerland and work out their share of the post-war profits. Does this story disgust you?'

'It doesn't surprise me. Does it disgust you?'

'Nothing disgusts me any more, Herr Hawn. I am too old to be a moralist. My pleasures are few. What I value most is tranquillity, peace – virtues I have learnt through the wisdom of the Lord Buddha and transmitted through the blood of Christ. I am no longer a man of war, nor a man of the flesh. But I must survive – that is the first rule of Nature, and applies to the highest as well as the lowest. Even Buddha did not say that one can exist on the fruits of the spirit alone. I need money, Herr Hawn. The information you want, and which I can give you, is not cheap. It could well compromise me – as it could you. I require ten thousand Swiss francs, in one-hundred notes. That is approximately, at the current rate of exchange, £3,300, or just over US $6,550.'

Hawn thought that for an old recluse who kept chickens in the wilds of Spain, he was remarkably well informed, particularly in fiscal matters. No doubt he had a radio, besides a telephone. He said :

'Swiss francs may be difficult. I don't know how Spanish banks operate with foreign exchange, but it will be quicker and easier to go to Madrid for the money. Dollars would be the simplest. Shall we say a round figure of six thousand?'

The German nodded and refilled their glasses. 'Prosit! The money will be ready when?'

'I shall wire for it tomorrow morning. How soon will you be able to let me have the information? And in what form?'

'I give you two affidavits. They will contain names and dates, secret meetings, shipping lanes, Bills of Lading, and certain other details which can be checked for their authenticity. But what you are after – the really important information – will be contained in the kind of details that no outsider, not even the most astute historian, would either know or be able to invent.'

'In what form will you give me this information?'

'I cannot provide you with original documents, or even copies. But my memory is excellent, even at my age. I was trained to have a good memory – it was part of my administrative duties to memorize data that could not be committed to the files.'

'And you can let me have these affidavits when I produce the money?'

'That would be a reasonable arrangement. Of course, it will all depend on us trusting each other. I should add that even in this solitary place, I take certain precautions.' He rose to his feet. 'Here is my card, with my telephone number. Remember, I am always Señor Alberto Millao.'

Hawn told him where they were staying; then, just as they were about to take their leave, he said, 'By the way, Herr Doktor, my friend in London told me of a rumour he had heard after the war – about certain aspects of what we have been discussing. He said that a collection of files and secret documents disappeared at the end of the war. They were not destroyed, and they were not captured by the Allies. Does that mean anything to you?'

'Herr Hawn, I would remind you that we have an agreement. I am selling you confidential information for a specified sum of money. I am not prepared to disclose any part of that information until our agreement has been ratified.' He came across the room and escorted them outside to the front door; then, instead of shaking hands, in the German fashion, he gave a little bow with his fingertips pressed together in the traditional Eastern gesture of greeting and farewell.

In the car Hawn had his first opportunity to give Anna a rough translation of his discussion with Mönch. She did not seem over-enthusiastic. 'Tom, that's a lot of money to pay over to a complete stranger, blind. How can we know that the stuff he gives us isn't a load of rubbish?'

'We don't. We're taking a chance – but it's not our money we're chancing, it's Pol's. Mönch may have been a bastard in his time, but now he's just an old, lonely exile, and a religious crank to boot. People who follow Buddha don't usually make petty crooks.'

'Talking of Pol,' she said, as they turned up the road towards the hotel, 'he's going to want something for his money, too.'

'It's up to him to come and get it.'

Two days later Hawn drove to Madrid and drew out the six thousand dollars which had been wired from France. He was back in Soria by three in the afternoon, stopped the Citroën outside the iron gate, rang, and listened to the dog's fury until he was let in again by the servant who showed him to the same bare white room. This time he had to wait nearly half-an-hour.

When the man finally reappeared Hawn was led out of the back of the house, into a stifling little garden, lush and well-kept, with a stench of geraniums and chicken-droppings. Mönch was seated alone at a little iron table, drinking coffee. He was in white ducks, two-tone shoes, and an open shirt with short sleeves. One of his thin arms was ribbed with white scars, like strings of gristle. He nodded Hawn towards the only other chair. No smile, no greeting, hardly even a trace of recognition.

Hawn took out the sealed envelope containing the money, in one-hundred dollar bills. He pushed it across to Mönch. The old man did not touch it.

'Herr Hawn, I regret that the price has increased. Ten thousand dollars. Not a cent less.'

Hawn sought in vain for the appropriate German obscenity. Instead, he left the envelope lying there. 'We made an agreement.'

'Unhappily, mein lieber Herr, there have been certain developments in the last forty-eight hours. You know we mentioned the Wiesenthal Office when we last met. Well, unfortunately it is not the only gang of self-appointed moralists who have chosen to track down former servants of the Third Reich – it is just that they are the most notorious, and the most successful.'

He sipped his coffee, without offering any to Hawn. 'For some time now I and my friends here in Spain have heard reports of another organization – this time French. They call themselves Jacques – after the initials JAC – Justice pour les Anciens Combattants. They are old Resistance men – fanatical, embittered, above all soured by the knowledge that they lost the war – and with far less courage and honour than we did. Their aim is simple. Revenge. They do not think that the present governments in Western Europe do enough to persecute those of us who are left.

'Last night, after you had gone, I received a telephone call from an old comrade. He warned me that a senior member of Jacques had arrived in Logroño, a little town about fifty kilometres from here, half-way to Pamplona.' He put down his coffee cup, half-drunk, and pushed it away from him; but still did not touch the envelope. 'Herr Hawn, I find this distasteful, but I must ask you to formally identify yourself. The night before last I did not ask for your credentials, or those of your companion, because I had no reason to fear intruders or imposters.

'I am not a coward,' he added quickly. 'I accept the divine law of Buddha, and will gladly accept my fate. But I would be lacking in my spiritual duties if I were to neglect even the simplest precautions. May I see your passport, Herr Hawn?'

Hawn still had it with him, as he had needed it at the bank in Madrid. He took it out and tossed it across the table between them. Mönch sat examining it with more than usual interest, turning the pages slowly, holding some of them at an angle so that he could better read the entry and exit stamps. 'You have travelled very widely. That is not exceptional, of course, for a journalist. North Africa, the sub-continent of Asia, Indo-China? It is all excellent cover.' (He used the military expression, *Tarnung*.) Finally he snapped the passport shut and placed it beside the envelope. 'I am already checking where you last stayed before coming to Soria. If it happened to be Logroño – even by chance – I am afraid that the consequences for you will be serious.'

Hawn had loosened his shirt, and in the heat of the little garden had begun to sweat. 'I am delighted you are taking the trouble. The Spanish authorities will confirm that I and my companion stayed two nights ago at the Hotel Tres Reyes Nobles in Pamplona. They did not register my companion, Fräulein Anna Admiral, who also has a British passport. But you will be able to confirm her identity here at the Hotel Parador Antonio Machado.'

Mönch watched him in silence. Hawn wiped some sweat off his eyelids. 'Herr Doktor, our discussions yesterday were a ploy, were they not? You had no intention of selling me any information. You were testing me. Testing me to find out if I had any connection with this organization, Jacques?' But while he spoke with sincerity, an uncomfortable worm of suspicion was beginning to stir in his mind. He was thinking of Pol.

'You don't have to believe me, Herr Doktor. But I've never heard of Jacques. The only time I've been in Logroño was when we stopped for a couple of beers on our way down from Pamplona four days ago.' He reached out and collected his passport and the still unopened envelope. 'Why do you now want ten thousand?'

'Because I must get away. To disappear, if only temporarily. I am not a rich man and I need the funds. I am also, as I said, no coward. Nor am I a fool. It would take a fool to lay himself open to the justice of a bunch of French gangsters.' He paused, and his foot began to kick the leg of the table.

'Herr Hawn, I wish to renegotiate our agreement. I will accept the six thousand dollars as an advance payment. You in turn will receive, at the Poste Restante of the American Express in Madrid, the documents you required – within less than a week. You will also receive an address to which you will forward the next four thousand dollars.'

'All of a sudden you seem to be trusting me an awful lot – considering that I might have something to do with these Frenchmen?'

Mönch gave a crafty smile. 'Do not be naïve, lieber Herr. You mentioned to me the other night that you had heard a rumour about certain secret documents being hidden after the war. It is just possible that I can help you in this matter. But the price will be those four thousand extra dollars. Is this new arrangement agreeable to you?'

'It still requires a great deal of mutual trust.'

'Herr Hawn, you have far more reason to trust me than I have to trust you. For a start, you know where I live. You can disappear – I cannot. You know of the existence of Jacques – either because I have just told you about it, or because you belong to it yourself. I have no more proof of your identity than that your passport claims you are a journalist and that you have travelled extensively. The English are no longer great travellers. They prefer their concrete palaces on Majorca and the Costa del Sol.

'You have sought me out – found out where I was living – from a former British Intelligence Officer. Then you offer me money for information which is more than thirty years old. You say you are pursuing an ideal – the destruction of an immoral, multi-national oil company.' His fingers fluttered for a moment in the air. 'I do not question idealists – I was one myself. But you ask me, on such evidence, to trust you? And when I agree to trust you, you question my own sincerity.' He leant forward with a slight creak of his chair, which might have been the joints of his old bones.

'I am near the end of my life, Herr Hawn. It is my ambition to die in bed. But I have no ambition to cheat strangers out of a few thousand dollars. You will give me the money, and I guarantee that you receive your information.'

Hawn surrendered. He passed him back the envelope and watched the old man carefully count the sixty notes. Mönch fastidiously folded them into the breast pocket of his open-necked shirt. Hawn stood up.

'The American Express, then. I shan't ask for a receipt, Herr Doktor. And if you have trouble with this organization, Jacques, that's your problem, not mine.'

Doktor Hans Dieter Mönch stood up and this time shook

Hawn's hand; his grip was surprisingly strong. As the servant showed Hawn out, the dog began to bark again. Hawn wondered if it was the only protection that Mönch had.

The key to their room was gone, and there was no one at the reception desk. Hawn went up the two flights of wooden stairs, past the suit of armour on the landing, and along to door number 17.

The room smelled of a perfume that Anna never used. Her eyes were bright and she looked flushed. There was a half-empty bottle of export whisky and three glasses on the table in the centre of the room.

Hawn stepped past her and looked at the figure sitting on the edge of the bed. 'What are you doing here, Monsieur Pol?'

The Frenchman heaved his massive shoulders contentedly. 'I think, without too much reminding, that you will know what I am doing. Did you not visit a certain house in the Calle Foncada two nights ago? And again this morning?'

Hawn looked at the smiling, sweating face, like a huge Easter-egg with beard and kiss-curl painted on. Pol looked absurd – yet it was this very absurdity that made him impressive. No buffoon or confidence trickster could afford to appear so comical.

Hawn turned to Anna : 'How long has he been up here?'

'About half-an-hour. You look in a bad mood.'

'I've just handed over six thousand dollars in exchange for a promise. Without a receipt.' He looked at Pol : 'That might interest you, since it was your money. But first – how did you get on to us?'

The fat man drew a big yellow silk bandanna from his pocket and mopped his brow and cheeks. 'You have not made things difficult for me, mon cher. Merely a matter of checking with the right authorities as to where you were stopping the night.'

'And how did you know we were coming to Spain, if that isn't an indiscreet question?'

Pol tapped a finger to his soft red lips. 'Mon cher, in French we have an old proverb – "There are never indiscreet questions, only indiscreet answers." But I regret – your last question was indiscreet.'

'But why track us down here? When I am on a job, I like to do it in my own time, in my own way. I was doing well until you turned up. It may be a coincidence, but the old German gentleman who lives in Calle Foncada was all ready to co-operate, until he got wind that you – or at least, some of your Resistance colleagues – had turned up in the area. Now he's preparing to bolt. What's more, he's upped the ante and has only agreed to send me the information in a week.

'What are you playing at, Pol? Are we investigating the past activities of ABCO, or are we helping to pursue some private vendetta against a senile old man who runs a chicken-farm?'

'The good Doctor Mengele also happens to run a chicken-farm – somewhere in Bolivia, I believe. The senile old man who lives up on the Calle Foncada bought that farm with the money of the innocent and the dead. From the systematic proceeds of genocide.' There was a soft hatred in Pol's voice which Hawn had not heard before.

He said lamely : 'I thought he was an administrator with the German Ministry of War Production. I know there was some talk of his being involved with slave labour, but that his real job was just as a run-of-the-mill bureaucrat?'

Pol interrupted him : 'It was your so-called run-of-the-mill bureaucrats – those grubby little *ronds-de-cuir*, with their pens and papers and files – who made the war possible. Just as much as did the Generals and street bully-boys. In a way, Mönch and his kind were even more important, more lethal. Just as Hitler and his Wehrmacht drove the Nazi war-machine, so the good Doktor Professor Mönch and his friends oiled its wheels – quite literally.'

Hawn said : 'You're not here to destroy a major multi-national oil company – you're just using me and Mademoiselle Admiral to help you hunt down some wretched old religious crack-pot who may, or may not, have been vital to Hitler's war effort. The one irony is, he's the only one so far who's benefited – by six thousand dollars of your money.'

Pol stuck a thumb in his mouth; he was silent for a moment. 'Monsieur – Mademoiselle – you are quite right. My motives are somewhat personal. You will excuse me if I bring up a subject that may be a trifle embarrassing for you both. You, Monsieur Hawn – look back for a moment to the day, or night, when you first gained your manhood. Your first girl – at the university, or in a back street while you were doing military service.' He turned to Anna, his lips parted to show two large white teeth. Her answering expression was puzzled rather than embarrassed.

'You, ma chère – you look back too, and remember. Your first love. Your first dazzling experience. Perhaps it was exciting, unexpected, unsatisfactory, even absurd. But you will not have forgotten it.' He took a long drink of whisky. 'My friends, it is my misfortune that I look back to the day when I *lost* my manhood. 29 July 1944, to be precise. In a prison cell in Lyon where I was being asked those rather awkward questions which I did not answer. But my interrogators did not even bequeath me the dignity of being able to die for my country. I was merely robbed of my *couillons* – which was probably no great loss to the flower of French womanhood. And for my silence Old Long-Nose de Gaulle pinned a little medal on my chest. But he could neither restore to me my virility, nor wipe out my hatred for the people who had destroyed it. That is why a certain Doktor Mönch and all his living colleagues are of such intimate interest to me.'

Anna spoke : 'But it wasn't that old man on the hill who interrogated you, was it?'

'Not personally, ma chère.' Pol smiled indulgently. 'They used specialists for that kind of work. People like Mönch were more important – and like all pen-pushers, they didn't like to dirty their own hands.' He patted his vast thighs. 'But this is all academic. Let us get down to the business of day – only not here. Here we are merely in danger of drinking too much whisky and attracting attention. Let us meet tonight for dinner. I suggest we drive to a pleasant little spot fifty kilometres from here. It has a bar, which is un-prepossessing, and a restaurant which is almost invariably empty and which serves suckling pig and a very pleasing wine. It is called La Busia, on the road to Logroño. We meet there, upstairs, at nine o'clock.'

Without waiting for their agreement, he hauled himself to his feet, drained his whisky and waddled across the floor. Hawn opened the door for him. When he was gone, Hawn said : 'So he just walked in, like the man from the Pru?'

She nodded. 'But no briefcase. Just the bottle of whisky.'

'Didn't he have any explanation?'

'He said he would wait for you. Tom, are we being set up?'

'We're certainly being paid, and that implies a price. But one thing we can't hold against Pol – he's being honest with us, or as reasonably honest as a man like that can ever be. He's using us to sniff out his quarry. What he then proposes to do about it is something we don't yet know. But what I do know is that Mönch is obviously scared of him. And at this stage, the last thing we want is Pol, or one of his friends, getting rid of that wretched old German before he's able to earn his six thousand dollars.

'Pol told us in Venice that he was following the same path as us – that he wants to expose the Western oil companies who traded with the Nazis. Now I'm not so sure. Mönch talked about an organization called Jacques. We can assume that Pol is part of that organization – that perhaps he even runs it. In which case our paths are not the same – although he's still picking up the bills. Angel, that fat man could lead us into a lot of trouble. Interesting trouble. The point is, will he be able to get us out of it?'

It was dark and crowded inside, with a smell of tar and old sherry. There were hams hanging from hooks in the ceiling, their cured skins the colour of dull red mahogany. Men were playing dominoes and reading the sports pages of the evening editions. Nobody paid any attention to the two of them as they made their way up a twisting iron staircase to the restaurant. It was more like the dining-room in a private house : the furniture was heavy, pitch-black, the lighting dim. A pair of swords hung crossed on the wall. The room was empty except for Charles Pol.

As in Venice, their host ate with his fingers. He had three helpings of suckling pig, and ordered copious wine, while the conversation remained evasive, prosaic. He did not invite questions, and skilfully avoided answering them when they were put to him. Anna drank a lot, probably because she was nervous. Pol clapped his hands, and a little boy, pale and dark-eyed, hurried in with cheese and coffee, and a local liqueur that tasted of olives.

Pol wiped his fingers on the tablecloth. 'Now, my dear Monsieur Hawn, we have eaten well. We have drunk good wine. We are no doubt in the mood for confidences. Let us talk of the German, Mönch. Why has he decided to flee? Using my money to facilitate his escape?'

To Hawn the question seemed rhetorical. 'Because we both think that you're a member of an organization called "Justice pour les Anciens Combattants".'

Pol giggled, as he carved himself a slice of goat's cheese. 'Mon cher, if I am a member of a secret or illegal organization, I do not discuss it, even with my friends. The important thing is, Doktor Mönch has flown – or rather, he hired a taxi this afternoon and drove towards Madrid. I must give the man credit – after so many years, his intelligence network is remarkably good. But then of course, the Nazis were first-rate professionals.'

'Monsieur Pol, do you have any reason to believe that Mönch was a Nazi – as opposed to someone who served them?'

'He was a long-standing Party member.' Pol sucked at a finger that was like a freshly-peeled shrimp. 'Have no illusions about Hans Dieter Mönch. He was a very superior Nazi. If handled properly, he could be of immense use to us.'

'He's no use to us if we chase him away the moment we've found him.'

Pol ignored the objection. 'Have you considered the possibility that Mönch, having taken the money, will invent the information?'

'Then why hasn't he done so before?'

'Because no one has ever asked him to. Mönch is one of those war criminals who lack what we might call "political sex appeal". He has no glamour, no status, like Albert Speer. Nobody would be normally interested in his memories. And if he decided to cover them with a *maquillage* of incriminating facts against ABCO and other Western companies during the war, the manuscript would almost certainly be thrown back in his face. No reputable – even disreputable – publisher would touch it. And even if he did find some fly-by-night journal of scandal to print the stuff, they would not pay him the sort of money that would make it worth his while.

'Mönch and his kind want a quiet life. They have just enough money to live comfortably and in reasonable safety. Why should they rock their own boat? Why should they stand up and shout things to the world that most people would prefer to leave unheard? Above all, why should they make new enemies at their stage of life?'

Anna broke in: 'So you think we've thrown your six thousand dollars into the Nazi Pension Fund?'

'Not necessarily, ma petite. You forget that Mönch is frightened – frightened of a French organization called Jacques. If I were Mönch, and I had been presented with six thousand dollars, by a stranger, in return for a few hours' work, I think I would oblige that stranger. Then, if I found that Jacques was getting close to my doorstep, I might try to do a deal. I might come up with a list of names – eminent names, and not just the names of Frenchmen. Veterans, even heroes, who made their money out of the Second World War.

'That is another reason why Mönch and his friends have not been so quick to divulge all they know. It is a form of insurance. Their best and only insurance.' He sat back and belched luxuriously. 'No. My guess is that you will find a letter waiting for you in Madrid.'

'And what happens to Mönch?'

'The fate of Doktor Mönch no longer concerns you.'

'And when I get this letter, and the information in it, how do I contact you?'

'*I* will contact *you*. Do not be embarrassed or annoyed – but I must make it my business to know where you are. I cannot allow you to contact me. I am conspicuous enough. I must permit myself some privacy.' He turned and smacked his little hands together, and the boy came trotting in. Pol asked for the bill; after he had settled it, he tossed the boy a five-hundred peseta note.

'The Herr Doktor is already proving a most expensive investment,' he said. 'Let us hope he is worth it.'


Hawn and Anna spent the next five days meandering around the wide plain of Castile, with its barren red earth and broken windmills and paltry furrows of cultivation.

The interlude since Soria, and the encounter with Doktor Hans Dieter Mönch, followed by their reunion with the mercurial, gluttonous Pol, had distanced events enough to give them a disquieting sense of unreality.

To his dismay, Hawn had come to realize that the only event that could be taken as both absolutely serious and relevant was the murder of Norman French. He had twice been able to buy English newspapers, and saw that although French's death was still mentioned, there were no clues, no suspects. This had at first whetted the sub-editors' appetites, but later, with nothing to report, the story had slid lower down the inside pages; and Hawn saw – both with relief and some curiosity – that his own name had been left out of all the reports. Perhaps the one thing all the newspapers wished to avoid was billing an ex-journalist who might at that very moment be snatching the exclusive.

He was up early on Monday morning, before Anna; and without waking her, and armed with his passport, arrived outside the American Express a few minutes before nine o'clock, to join the lines of brittle, bright-eyed American divorcees wating to collect their alimony – a dole-queue of sexual disaster.

Only today he found the pavement empty, the doors

locked. It was a national holiday to commemorate some saint. Hawn cursed the saint and had a coffee, then a few beers, followed by a medicinal Fundador; and returned to the hotel in time to find Anna getting dressed.

He repeated the routine next morning, but this time Anna joined him. They reached the Poste Restante desk and Hawn showed his passport. The clerk checked, but there was nothing for Señor Hawn, Mr Hawn, Herr Hawn.

They returned at noon, just before the place closed; and again at 4.30 when it re-opened; and still there was nothing.

That evening they drove out to Segovia and got drunk at dinner.

Next morning, both rather raw-eyed, with Anna wearing dark glasses, they once again joined the grim queue inside the baroque building on the Plaza de las Corces. When they reached the desk, Hawn again handed over his passport; the clerk checked the rows of pigeon-holes, came back and said, as usual, 'Nada'. Hawn made him check again; while he was doing it, he himself took a bleary look around the hall, looking for anyone who might be watching. There was an elderly man reading a newspaper, but he seemed almost too much like a private detective to be one. Both Mönch and Pol would use professionals.

The clerk came back, looking bored, and said again, 'Nada, Señor.'

Hawn thanked him and turned, unwilling to attract further attention. Anna said : 'Ask him to look under "E".'

' "E"?'

'That's right.'

'Mönch knows my name well enough.'

A pair of women behind them were growing impatient. Anna ignored them; instead, she asked the clerk herself to look under E. The man came back to her a moment later with a bulky envelope on which was written, THOMAS HAWN ESQUIRE, and marked PRIVADO.

Hawn kissed her with extravagance, then they walked quickly out, failing to notice that the man with the newspaper had not moved. When they were in the street he kissed her again, messily on the lips, setting her sunglasses askew on her nose, and squeezing both her buttocks. 'Careful!' she said: 'In Franco's time we'd have been arrested.'

A drunk was watching them, propped against the wall and trying to light a cigarette. Hawn, on an impulse, gave him a box of matches. Mönch's letter made an uncomfortable bulge in his inside pocket.

'I want to go back and screw you,' he said happily.

'But first, let's go and get a drink and see what's inside that envelope.'

It was a stout manila envelope, well-sealed and reinforced with Sellotape. Inside were eleven sheets of quarto bank paper, each covered with single-spaced typing on what had obviously been a cheap and badly maintained machine. It was entirely in German, with a great many errors and corrections – crossings-out, letters elided and words clumsily inserted above others. It was clear that whoever had written it had not been a professional typist, and that this was almost certainly a first and only draft. Whether the author' had kept a carbon was another matter.

Hawn looked warily round the café and bar. It was still too early for the pre-lunch crowds, and their table was reasonably isolated.

Anna said, 'Is your German up to it?'

'It'll have to be. I'm not going round to the German Consulate to get it translated.'

The first two pages were highly technical and contained a number of commercial names, of which I G Farben and Fischer-Tropsch Werke GmbH featured most prominently. The word 'Braunkohle' cropped up several times : 'brown coal', which confused him, until Anna guessed that it meant 'lignite', the main substance used in the production of synthetic fuel.

The gist of the first few pages was not sensational : by the end of 1943 the fuel crisis had become critical and Himmler had established a secret department within the Ministry of War Production with the sole purpose of producing two million tonnes of crude oil a week.

When he had read this out to her, Anna said : 'But that's impossible ! I've seen the figures myself – they were down to 1.7 million tonnes.'

'Were those official statistics? German statistics?'

'No – American. At least, Anglo-American. Post-war figures that were brought out by the Allied Commission – I looked them up in the Petroleum Library.'

A waiter had turned on a television set behind the bar, and a few people in the café had moved over to watch it. One was a smartly dressed man in dark glasses, carrying a bull-fighting gazette rolled up under his arm.

Hawn said, 'Of course, Mönch doesn't say here that they were actually producing two million a week, just that they were aiming at that as a "provisional target".'

'Well, unless Mönch is lying, they were being crazily optimistic. I won't bore you now with comparative figures, but that sort of production and consumption – even for a highly industrialized state at war – is colossal. What date does Mönch say it was?'

Hawn referred back through the notes. 'End of 1943. Then it seems they had what Mönch calls a "highly secret meeting", in somewhere called Neustrelitz, near the Polish border. Here it becomes very confused. Mönch starts talking about someone or something called Bettina.'

Anna was looking at the TV screen which was showing a re-run of a bull-fight parade. She said, 'All I know about Bettina is that she was Beethoven's mistress.'

'That would figure. Very sentimental people, the Germans – very musical. They had a full-time orchestra playing Strauss and Mozart at the gates of Auschwitz, twelve hours a day.' He drank some beer and read on. 'Yes, I thought so. Bettina's a code-word.' He turned the page, where the typing had become faded, as though the ribbon had come to an end.

Hawn persevered, slowly deciphering the cumbersome German phrases and convoluted sentences, rendered more difficult by Mönch's pedantic style. He turned a page and there was a roar of excitement from behind the bar. A bull had appeared on the screen, dodging, lurching about, while the first toreadors taunted him with little skipping pirouettes. The man in dark glasses had unfolded his gazette and was watching intently.

Hawn said, 'Now we're getting somewhere! Salak. Imin Salak. Bettina's operations move into the Turkish Strategic Zone – Salak is recruited by Bettina's agents, totally apart from the Abwehr or the RSHA, the Political Police, which included the Gestapo.'

Anna stopped him. 'You're going too fast for me. What's the particular significance?'

There was another roar, followed by a chorus of whistles and boos as the picadors lumbered on to the screen, astride their wretched horses, watched by everyone in the bar except Hawn and Anna.

He said, 'Salak was a name MacIntyre gave me just before we left. A wrestler in Istanbul, known member of the local underworld, and recruited as a top British agent. The significance is obvious. Now if Mönch had trotted out Doktor Alan Reiss's name, it might have meant nothing, as he'd already heard it from us. But Mönch could not have possibly known about Salak, except from his own experiences. Nor does he say here that Salak was a British agent. Perhaps he didn't know – or more likely, he regarded him as a loyal German agent doing a good job double-crossing the British.'

With some difficulty he attracted the waiter's attention and ordered more beer, careful to keep Mönch's notes concealed. 'The rest is a bit diffuse. Salak was working for "Bettina" in Istanbul. Mönch also says that two top British agents were operating in Central America, ensuring the safe transportation of fuel across the Atlantic. Presumably the old fox is holding those two names up his sleeve, waiting to barter them for the balance of four thousand dollars.'

'How does it end?'

'Just a note that Reichsminister Himmler, in the name of the Führer and of the whole German People, expressed his deepest gratitude to the operatives of "Bettina", but on account of the extreme secrecy and delicacy of the operation, no formal or official recognition could be granted.

'That's Mönch's way of signing off and telling us what a wonderful person he was. There's no signature, no date.' He paused, then folded the pages up and returned them to the envelope, which he slipped under the table as the barman arrived with their drinks. When the man had gone, Hawn leant further over and tucked the envelope into Anna's bag, which was hanging under the table from her chair. 'Angel, when I'm half-way through this beer, I want you to get up and go to the loo. When you get back, the drinks will have been paid for and I'll be gone. You stay and finish your drink, look a bit impatient, then go up to the barman and ask if he's seen me.'

'Trouble?'

'I think we're being followed. We're certainly being watched. I'm not particularly worried – I just want to find out how good he is. Ask the barman to get you a taxi and tell him to take you to the Ritz. When you get into the taxi, say you've changed your mind and give him the address of our hotel.'

Five minutes later Hawn was walking briskly down the Ventura de la Vega. He bought a packet of cigarettes, an airmail edition of the *Daily Telegraph*, crossed the street twice, and stopped in a bodega for a quick brandy and a glimpse to see how the late Norman French's death was rating in the British Press. His name had disappeared. The smart man with the dark glasses was leafing through a copy of *Olé* on the news-stand across the street.

When Hawn got back to the hotel he called Anna up on the house-phone. 'Angel, ring down to the desk and ask for some writing paper and an envelope. Then stick Mönch's stuff inside and address it to yourself at the LSE – not the flat, remember. They might just have someone tampering with the mail.'

'I'll do better than that – ' her voice was crackling, distant – 'I'll send it to my brother in Harrogate.'

'But better not post it yourself. The porter can do it for you. Then go to the Ritz. I'll join you there, one way or another, in about half-an-hour.'

'Are we still being followed?'

'I am. You didn't see anyone?'

'I didn't get much chance. The taxi-driver was like a madman.'

'Good. If there's only one of them, he's probably decided to follow me. So champagne at the Ritz – in half-an-hour. And make sure you give the porter enough for the right postage.'

'Any more paternal advice? What sort of disguise should I wear? Or should I create a diversion by going out into the street in my knickers and nothing else?'

'Just look out for bag-snatchers,' Hawn said, and hung up.

He went outside, into the Puerta del Sol, where he had a couple of coffees and wrote half-a-dozen postcards to fictitious addresses. He saw Anna leave the hotel, and after a moment get into a taxi. The *aficionado* in dark glasses was having his shoes shined in a café a couple of doors away.

Hawn paid, and strolled back to the hotel. As he asked for his key the receptionist handed him an envelope, addressed to M. Thomas Hawn. The sealed flap bore the blue insignia of the Ritz Hotel. Inside, on Ritz notepaper, in a big childish scrawl, was the message in French: 'Meet me here at 12.45. Lunch. With my best compliments, Charles.'

Hawn had a confused sense of a time-lag. It was now nearly 12.30. Anna would be at the hotel in five minutes. If he hurried, he would just make it by 12.45. He had told Anna to go to the Ritz because it was the only big hotel he knew in Madrid – at least, the only big civilized one. It was also spacious and quiet, and an easy place to spot strangers.

He thanked the receptionist and walked out again into the bright autumn sunlight. The man in dark glasses was looking into a shop window and blowing his nose on a clean white handkerchief. Hawn went up and stood beside him and looked into the window. It was a leather shop – mostly women's shoes, belts, handbags. The prices seemed even higher than Bond Street. He took a step sideways and said, in his best Spanish, 'Will you share a taxi with me to the Ritz?'

The man looked at him with empty black lenses. The bull-fight gazette was again rolled up under his arm. With his free hand he reached inside his dark flannel jacket, pulled out a wallet and snapped it open. Hawn looked at the card behind the celluloid window. 'Polizia de Securidad, Señor Hawn,' he added, in English, with a heavy accent, 'you will accompany me please.'

Anna had seen Monsieur Pol almost as soon as she entered the main foyer of the Ritz. He had greeted her with a little cooing cry, stumbling awkwardly to his feet and pulling out a gilt-backed chair for her. He had a bottle of champagne in an ice-bucket, its neck wrapped in a white napkin, and three glasses. He poured her a glass and said : 'So the good Doktor was not so lazy after all?'

'It was *you* following us?'

Pol spread his hands. 'I regret, ma chère mademoiselle, but I had a man watching the American Express. A simple precaution. I wanted to protect you from any difficulties,' he added ambiguously.

She wanted to ask him what difficulties, then changed her mind. 'Tom will be here soon.'

'He has the documents?'

'No.' She looked quickly around the elaborate room.

'Then you have them?'

'No, I do not.'

There was a pause. Pol sat very still, without expression, except that he had begun to sweat rather more than usual. The hotel was pleasantly air-conditioned. 'Mademoiselle, I ask you not to play the comedy with me.'

'This is no comedy, Monsieur Pol. We're the ones who've been doing all the work, taking all the risks.'

'With my money.'

'Tom said we were being followed, so we took a few simple precautions.' She went on to give him a brief description of their subterfuge, including the posting of the letter.

Pol watched her, his fat comic face turned solemn, thoughtful. 'They were following Monsieur Hawn, you say? They were not following you.'

'Perhaps you know more about that than I do, Monsieur Pol?'

He ignored this. 'You arrived here without trouble. If you did not trust me with the original documents, you could have made a photocopy of them. There is a machine here in the hotel.'

'I didn't know that. The most important thing is that the documents should be safe.'

Pol sighed; mopped his face with his silk bandanna; then wearily poured two glasses of champagne. Anna did not really want any : she had drunk enough already that morning.

'Monsieur Hawn speaks German, does he not? He will have read the documents?'

'If you were having us watched, you would know that.'

'Yes, of course.' He gave her a sad smile : though she now detected a tiny gleam of anger in his eyes. She guessed that he could be dangerous when he became angry. 'As I told you, I had you watched at the American Express,' he said at last. 'But I did not have you followed here. Why should I? We trust each other, do we not?'

'Then why did you bother to have us watched at all? Did you think we were going to take the documents and use them for our own profit? They would be very interesting to a lot of people.'

'Only if they were handled correctly, by the correct people. They would need authenticating. That is something that you and Monsieur Hawn cannot do alone. That is why you need me.'

Anna had left her champagne untouched. She said, 'You still haven't told me why – if you trust us so much – you had us watched this morning. And all the other mornings, presumably.'

Pol reached again for his bandanna; the sweat was glistening on the tip of his goatee-beard and he was breathing heavily; he drank his glass of champagne. 'You must forgive me, Mademoiselle – but an old dog never forgets its tricks. My life is very complicated – I never know when friends will turn enemies, when trusted colleagues will turn traitors. You ask me to make exceptions – but in this game you can only make one exception too many, and you are lost.'

'Then who was following us today?'

He shook his head and a drip of sweat fell into his massive lap. 'You and Monsieur Hawn have decided to combat the largest, the richest, the most powerful industrial organization in the world. To have received their attention this morning in an unsuccessful attempt to divest you of those documents is surely no trivial matter. You were lucky. We all were.' He looked at his watch. It was almost 1.15. 'Now what has happened to our friend, Monsieur Hawn? I was hoping to offer him lunch, and I'm getting hungry.'

As he spoke, one of the huissiers arrived at his elbow, whispered something to him and passed him a note. Pol frowned, nodded to Anna, and said, 'Mademoiselle, a small problem. Your beloved is enjoying the hospitality of the Spanish Security Police – Special Section. They deal with counter-espionage and external threats to the State.'

She stared at him. 'Does he want to speak to me?'

'There will be plenty of time for him to speak to you. Let me speak to him first. I can be of more help.'

Pol was gone for nearly twenty minutes. Anna prided herself on being a practical girl who was good in crisis : but it was with immense relief that she saw Pol's huge figure waddling back towards her. He sat down on the little gilt chair, which Anna was surprised could sustain his weight.

'Eh bien, ma chère, our friend has some problems. It appears that someone with considerable influence has denounced him to the authorities, claiming that he is in possession of classified documents of interest to the State. Fortunately for him – as you told me – he has already got rid of those documents. The Security Police are therefore somewhat embarrassed by his presence. To release him would be an affront to his denunciators, who, as I said, are men of influence. The authorities have therefore devised a simple compromise. They have ordered his extradition. Regrettably, that will also apply to you.'

She stared at him. 'Both of us? But when? How?'

'My child, you have a car parked here in Madrid near your hotel. The authorities are allowing you twenty-four hours to drive to the French border at Irun-Hendaye. When you arrive there, you will check with the Civil Guard. If you fail to comply, the consequences could be serious for you – as well as embarrassing for me. I should add that it was after some persuasion from myself that the authorities agreed to take the more lenient line and allow you to drive back, instead of putting you on the next plane and making you pay your own fares. As well as impounding your car, of course.'

'I'm sure we're both very grateful to you, Monsieur Pol!'

The Frenchman spread his hands across his belly. 'You forget that I have my own interests in this affair. Six thousand American dollars' worth, for a start.'

Anna said, 'There is something you forget. Or perhaps you don't know? Monsieur Hawn agreed with Mönch to pay him another four thousand dollars, in exchange for a second set of documents.'

'Eh bien?' Pol stroked his little beard. 'To what address? The same?'

Anna nodded. 'With us gone, you won't be able to get it. And Mönch won't give you anything without the money.'

'Do not concern yourself, ma chère. There are ways – there are always ways. As long as I know that he will contact Monsieur Hawn at the American Express.'

Anna, with slight misgiving, then described the misunderstanding over the indexing of Hawn's name. Pol merely nodded; he seemed content.

'Who denounced us?' she added.

'Ah! You ask me to speculate. The America-Britannic Consortium have a 90 per cent franchise here in Spain. One telephone call from one of their executives, objecting to the presence of a couple of foreign nationals on Spanish soil – need I go on?' He looked again at his watch. 'Mademoiselle, I hesitate to ask a favour – but would you consent to lunch alone with me? I am starving!'

# CHAPTER FOUR

# Digging

*When you have excluded the impossible, whatever remains, however improbable, must be the truth.*

SIR ARTHUR CONAN DOYLE

They returned to London, to a damp flat and the usual pile of bills, circulars, final reminders. But nothing from the Police or the Courts, summoning Hawn to appear at the inquest on Norman French. He knew that in a murder case these things took time : but he was surprised to hear nothing from Muncaster – no news, no explanation for the break-in at the flat, or for the incident involving Hamilton Motors.

By now Hawn was dramatizing his precautions : he had rigged up a thread across the door of the flat; left a smear of Anna's lipstick on the inside of the Citroën driver's door; and never walked or drove anywhere without checking, every few seconds, who was behind him. His efforts yielded nothing but the very vaguest suspicions, which he could not substantiate.

On the first day back he dropped Muncaster a note to the Yard, marked 'Confidential', but containing nothing more potent than the news that he was back. The Chief Superintendent replied two days later with a bland note saying that he would be in touch if anything cropped up. The only thing that cropped up was the inquest on Norman French. Verdict : Murder by Person or Persons Unknown. Apart from Muncaster, the first two policemen on the scene, and the forensic team, the landlady was the only lay witness. Hawn considered it odd, even irregular, that he had not been called. It was not like Muncaster to bend the rules, particularly in a murder case, unless someone was bending

124

them from above – and from very high above.

For Hawn's part, he decided to lie low and await Pol's further instructions – which he knew must come. There was also the small matter of Mönch's second instalment, which would presumably have reached the Amex in Madrid by now, enclosing the old man's hideaway so that the balance of four thousand dollars could be forwarded to him.

It had occurred to Hawn, with varying conviction, that Pol himself had arranged their deportation simply in order to get his hands on this second document – and above all, on Mönch's whereabouts.

But the difficulty of ascertaining Pol's actions was that it was almost impossible to deduce his true motives. It was not that Hawn had found him implausible, even a liar – these would have been simple defects on which to judge him; it was that the Frenchman was so throughly improbable. He was also tied up – on his own confession, and in some obscure way – with ABCO. But then, that might mean anything. The late Norman French had worked for ABCO. So had Shanklin and Doctor Alan Rice, and a certain Rupert de Vere Frisby, of the FO.

While they awaited Pol's call, Hawn and Anna sank back into the hack-work of research. But it was now with a difference. What had begun as the vaguest theory had congealed, over the last three weeks, into a clear but complex conspiracy buried by more than thirty years, and covering half the globe : and which must, at all costs, be brought to light.

On his first return to the Public Record Office, Hawn struck lucky. He was going through the confidential files of the Political Operations Executive (POE) in Cairo which had controlled, among many activities, operations in Turkey.

Imin Salak was mentioned briefly and with enthusiasm – or as much enthusiasm as the dead prose of a secret memo is capable. Salak had been a dependable man who enjoyed the confidence of the Istanbul underworld, as well as having been virtually immune to the attentions of the police. The only drawback to his character had been greed. Salak required to be paid highly for his services, and was not satisfied with the local currency.

There were several tedious memos relating to Foreign Exchange Control, in which the Treasury made the usual bleating noises of disapproval. Cairo and POE Turkey won the day – though one memo, from a Special Operator connected with the Consulate in Istanbul, added this note : 'We must never lose sight of the possibility that a man who sells his services so highly, to the highest bidder, may transfer his allegiances elsewhere, if we are outbid. Whilst I have no reason to questions S's loyalty, I must emphasize that that loyalty is primarily to himself.' The author of this memo was the Consulate's Information Officer, Rupert de Vere Frisby.

In September 1943 a second memo was sent from Istanbul to the Head of London Special Operations Executive by a Major Robert Dugdale : CONFIDENTIAL/POE/236/9WOLP.

Am becoming concerned Operative Frisby. Very keen, good Turkish, but playing too close to the wicket. Keeping dangerous company. His contacts excellent, but drinks and gambles to excess, and in lowest places. Is attracting attention. Toby S has turned up – a true cowboy who treats Istanbul like a playground. Bad influence on de Vere. S's pet protégé, Salak, is also concerning me. He plays poker for high stakes with S and de Vere, and both come to me with complaints that they need money. We have paid out rather more than ten thousand plus (T L) in less than a week. De Vere promises to repay it, but the Turk could become troublesome. There is too much skulduggery going on in this city, as it is. T S promises to behave himself, though I strongly suggest that if the situation continues, de Vere should be transferred. He is too open to blackmail. I also suspect that he has information which he is not divulging to higher authority. Memo ends.

The reply had come five days later : CONFIDENTIAL/POE/942/9DARG.

Contents of 236/9wolp noted. Suggest if your concern continues, Operative should be transferred. T S's loyalty cannot be questioned without definite proof. But keep careful tabs on the Turk. Must leave you to be the best judge of this. Am meanwhile arranging for de Vere to take a working vacation in Cairo where he will be subjected to vetting. Memo ends.

The next reference to Rupert de Vere Frisby was that he had been posted to the Consular Service in Vera Cruz, Mexico. There was no trace of his 'vacation in Cairo', and of what he might, or might not, have told his masters in the Political Operations Executive.

But there was a further file on Imin Salak. It was dated early 1944, after Frisby's departure, and written by a certain D. S. Frobisher, Commercial Attaché to the Istanbul Consulate :

TOP SECRET. POE CAIRO. LE/942/WOLP.

This is to confirm that I am authorized to pay Imin Salak, a Turkish National, Resident of Istanbul, an increase of two hundred pounds sterling (£200) per month for his services to the British Government. His only rpt only contact is to be Major T. Shanklin. Any additional payments must be sanctioned by POE. The agent's duties are to keep detailed observation of all vessels entering and leaving Istanbul. Ends.

Hawn ran a further check. Major Dugdale had been transferred himself three months earlier to France. So Salak seemed to have won the day – with the help of Toby Shanklin.

Anna had extended her holiday from the London School of Economics and was spending most of her waking hours working through piles of photostated documents, files from the LSE and the Petroleum Institute Library, and reference books from the British Museum.

Hawn had meanwhile restricted himself to reading all the standard books on the Second World War – trying to find anything that gave a clear indication of how the Germans had solved their fuel problem.

He was struck at once by two things. Firstly, the subject of oil was rarely mentioned, except in passing, and never as a major factor in the conduct of the war. The second was that the two men whom he would have expected to have been most concerned with this subject did not merely ignore it – they made light of it. The first was Albert Speer; the second, Adolf Hitler.

Speer's memoirs were so detailed, so disarmingly frank, that Hawn was left with the strong impression that the former Minister of War Production was not covering up – it was simply that there were things he had not known about, but which, being a vain man, he was not prepared to admit. And if Mönch had been telling the truth, and a secret operation had been set up, independent of Speer's Ministry, and under the code name 'Bettina', Speer might well not have heard of it.

But what of Hitler? Of all the books through which Hawn laboured the one author who diverted him most was Hitler, in his *Table Talk 1941-43*. This proved a fascinating and bizarre chronicle. Almost every night, and often deep into the morning – in the spartan comfort of Berschesgaden, or the grey claustrophobia of the bunker – the Führer would hold forth. His select captive audience would range from the most powerful and deadly men in his empire, to long-suffering generals back from the Front, or hapless visitors like the head of the Danish SS Viking Division.

Hitler spared none of them. He talked about anything, everything, which captured his whim. To the Danish lapdog he talked at length about the 'brutal and savage nature of women'; then his views on English public schools and the British monarchy – the former of which he deplored, and the latter admired – to his copious views on music. 'The English like music,' he announced : 'unfortunately music does not like the English.' At which his obedient guests fell about with laughter.

But perhaps the worst affliction of these dinners was the fact that no one was allowed to drink or smoke; and battle-weary veterans would constantly excuse themselves to go to the lavatory for a quick puff and a pull at their hip-flasks.

Hawn was left with the impression that Hitler was not mad, and certainly not stupid: he was just one of those unfortunate people who know a little bit about a great many things, and felt an obsession to express himself on every one. Whether it was power, money, nationality, history, empire, aristocracy, architecture, cinema, literature, drama, sex, discipline, animals, pornography, philosophy, race, royalty, religion – Adolf Hitler had views on all of them, very firm views, and views which he expounded at length and with passion.

But – recalling the proverbial dog in the night, in the Sherlock Holmes story – there was one subject upon which he hardly touched at all during these three years when his 'Table Talk' was being so meticulously recorded. That subject was oil. At no point did he express any serious concern about a fuel crisis – let alone that it was the single most crucial fact in his waging of the Second World War.

When he did mention oil, his comments were either blithely sanguine, bordering even on the frivolous, or wildly theoretical. He had the modern ecologists' passion for discovering new forms of fuel – not out of necessity, but because he regarded the automobile as a smelly, dirty object. At the same time he had grandiose ideas for exploiting oil under the rain-forests of South America; and even, at a lunch in July 1942, expressed enthusiasm for prospecting for it beneath the woods round his beloved Vienna.

The nearest he came to expressing any concern on the subject was his admiration for the Soviets who had

cut out the monopolies and private interests ... As a result, they are now in a position to prospect throughout their territory for oil with the assistance of very large-scale maps ... There is no limit to what we could have extracted from the sources in the vicinity of Vienna, if the State had undertaken the necessary exploitation in time. This, added to the oil-wells of the Caucasus and Rumania, would have saved us all from anxiety.

His one other reference to fuel was again in 1942 when he said :

In future mobilization will no longer be a problem of transport for us. We still have the problem of petrol, but that we'll solve.

He did not say how – which, Hawn reflected, was a pity.

It was the first week in October, and they had still heard nothing from Pol. It was the week-end. The libraries and Record Office were closed. They had a large lunch, made love until it was almost dark, then brewed up a pot of strong coffee, lacing the cups with brandy, and began a detailed post mortem on their researches – which might accurately be described as more dead than alive.

'The trouble is,' Anna said, 'it's all negative. Negative proof, if you like. Nothing to prove that our theory isn't feasible, or untrue. But nothing to prove *definitely* that it's true.'

'Nevertheless, there was still a dead body in a Paddington bed-sitter. And Mönch's memoranda.' (Anna had got the documents back from her brother, which Hawn had translated and had copied, with the original deposited in his bank.) 'Then there's the tie-up with Salak and Shanklin, and Shanklin and Frisby and that man Rice. It would be enough to get my editor putting ten of his best men on the job.'

'Let's just look at the facts first,' Anna said. 'What do we have on the credit side? We have no evidence – in any of the files that we've gone through or books we've read – that contradicts our theory. All right?

'Secondly – there are firm, corroborated statistics that German consumption of oil actually *increased* as the war went on. I can give you chapter and verse for all this if you want it.

'Three – one of the commonest arguments we've heard to dispose of our theory is that the Germans had accumulated vast oil reserves before the war, and went on to capture more huge reserves in the Occupied countries. The facts, however, are that when Hitler invaded Poland, he had only *three months' reserves*. And in France – where he captured most oil – the supplies were barely enough for *two months*. Also, we mustn't forget that in this first year of the war, the scale of Hitler's mechanized machine was vastly inferior to that of the later years.

'Four – contrary to popular belief, he did not receive a great deal of oil from Russia, either during the Nazi-Soviet Pact, or after his invasion of Russia in June 1941. The Russian oil industry was very underdeveloped, and after the invasion what there was of it was being constantly sabotaged.

'Five – and this is the really crucial factor, the linch-pin on which our theory stands or falls. Ploesti, Rumania. Officially, from the beginning of the war, Rumania was Germany's main source of crude oil. But, Tom, here the statistics are very odd.' She turned to a page with columns of handwritten figures; he groaned sardonically and she held up her hand. 'I know – lies, damned lies, and statistics. The trouble is – from ABCO's point of view – these statistics don't add up. They not only contradict each other – they contradict history.

'Unfortunately, I've had to do a certain amount of improvisation – inspired guesswork, as our critics and enemies would no doubt call it. Anyway, pay attention, because this is vital. In 1943 the Germans were refining approximately *23 per cent* of Rumanian oil. We know that Ploesti didn't have many refineries of its own, so I think we can make an intelligent guess that total German fuel imports from Rumania would have been about *30 per cent*.

'And we know that after the Allies invaded Southern Italy and captured the airfield at Bari, Ploesti and the other smaller Rumanian fields were being bombed round the clock. I haven't been able to find any exact figures to confirm how quickly production dropped off, except that by August 1944 – when the Russians overran Rumania – the figure of exports of crude to Germany was down to about *10 per cent*. A miserable bloody 10 per cent! And yet Germany went on fighting.

'Now, as I told you in Madrid, the average weekly German fuel consumption in 1943 was down to *1.7* million tonnes – and the German and Allied figures more or less agree here. And according to Mönch's memorandum, under "Operation Bettina" they were aiming at a target of *two million* a week.

'Yet by December 1944 – at the time of the Ardennes Offensive – they were still, apparently, producing *two-thirds* refined oil, as compared to any other month of that year. All right – it was still a long way short of Bettina's target, but it was still more than four months after Rumania had been captured by the Russians. So where were they importing it from?'

'They still had their quasi-legal sources,' Hawn said, 'via the neutrals. What Robak was flying a kite about, at my meeting with him in the Gritti. And they could have been feeding off reserves from Rumania.'

'All right, I'll take your second point first. Contrary to what that ass Logan says, we now know that at the outbreak of war they had very short reserves – presumably because they were so cock-a-hoop about winning. But later – and there are plenty of odd sources for this – it appears that Hitler actually issued an edict forbidding the hoarding of supplies of any kind – from food to vital raw materials, which of course included oil. He considered it tantamount to pessimism, defeatism, which in his unholy mind meant treason. That would explain why so many of his staff, including Speer, were doing their nuts complaining to him about the shortage of materials, while he just fobbed them off by saying that everything would be all right. But then, of course, he knew about "Operation Bettina" and they didn't.

'In short, he still thought he could counter-attack and win the war. But he needed oil for that, Tom. He needed one hell of a lot of it, and he went on importing it and refining it right up to the end – although the official German statistics for some reason stop early in 1945.

'Now, as for the neutrals, he certainly managed to get some through the friendly ones, like Spain, via Vichy

France – as well as lovely Switzerland and Sweden.'

Hawn nodded. 'Yes – Robak flew that kite for me too.'

'But what proportion would that have been in pure percentages? And we're not talking about a few hundred thousand odd barrels. We're talking of several hundred million tonnes. Of crude, not synthetic.'

'Now – point six. The question of synthetic fuel. That, we're all told, was their great stand-by.' She began to read from another sheet of notes : ' "Of the total German fuel consumption between 1943 and May 1945, *49 per cent* was synthetic, due to the process known as hydrogenation." That's a quote from an Allied Commission report, by the way. And we also know now from our friend Pol that the synthetic stuff was only suitable for aircraft and light vehicles. We also know that by 1944 Goering had to ground two-thirds of his Luftwaffe, when it was most needed against Allied bombing attacks, because of lack of fuel.

'So *49 per cent* couldn't have been very much. On the other hand, we have that figure of *30 per cent* from Rumania, dwindling to a miserable *10 per cent* – of both crude and refined, which was somehow enough to keep the mighty German armour alive and rolling. However you juggle the figures, Tom, they come out the same. A discrepancy as wide as the Grand Canyon.

'Oh, and I almost forget. Right up to the end, in 1945, Hitler was still prepared to allow Werner von Braun as much high-grade fuel as he wanted for his rockets, mainly the V2, and the experimental V3 that was supposed to hit New York.'

'I shouldn't pay too much attention to Hitler's judgement. In those last months he was hepped up to the eyeballs and as mad as a March hare.' Hawn sat up. 'Let's take those figures first. Say, from 1943 to the end. Forty-nine per cent synthetic. Thirty-five per cent, if we're going to be really generous – generous to ABCO and their accomplices, I mean – for Rumania, dropping to around 15 per cent, if we count the peripheral fields in Hungary, Poland, and Silesia. Then perhaps 5 per cent from reserves or captured supplies. And another 5 per cent from the neutrals, through their "laundering" service.'

'That's an absolute maximum – and more than bloody generous to ABCO.'

'Angel, we're not only prosecuting. We're defence, judge and jury. And if we start paring the figures down just to suit our theory, they'll hang us up by our balls.'

She grinned. 'Speak for yourself. But I take your point. Your absolute maximum leaves a discrepancy of *6 per cent*. Rising to *26 per cent* after the bombing of Ploesti started. And up to *36 per cent* when Rumania was swallowed up.'

'Now wait a minute, angel. That figure isn't necessarily a discrepancy. It's simply a net reduction of total German oil supplies.'

'It's more than that, Tom. It's an almost total elimination of all their crude oil. Yet they were getting it from somewhere. I'd say as judge and jury, we've got a copper-bottomed *prima facie* case. I'd say more. If those figures of yours were a bank statement of credits and debits, it would be about time to call in the Fraud Squad.'

She sat forward with her hands pressed together. 'All damned lies and statistics. We're not going to prove anything – let alone convince anybody – with a lot of figures. People will say the figures are wrong, that the Germans falsified them, that they're not complete – all kinds of legalistic bunkum.

'We've got to *prove* that the Germans got it from ABCO. They obviously did – in huge quantities, and pretty regularly. But we've still got to make a case. A case for the prosecution. And a case that ABCO – with all its power and money and well-dressed henchmen – isn't going to be able to break or fix.'

'And you don't think we'll be able to do that by ourselves? That we'll have to go on sitting on our hands waiting for Pol – to know what's in that second instalment from Mönch? D'you think Pol will let on?'

'It depends if he thinks we can still be of any use to him.'

'You're pretty cynical about Pol, aren't you?'

'If you mean, do I trust him? – no! The moment we start trusting a man like that, we're finished.'

# CHAPTER FIVE

# The Turk

*Give a thief enough rope and he'll steal it.*     ANON

Two days later a letter arrived from France, date-stamped Chamonix. Pol was writing on hotel notepaper. Considering his flamboyance, the contents of the letter were impersonal and peremptory. He wanted to meet them both in three days' time at the Hotel Lotti in Paris at 8.00 p.m.

Anna's extended holiday had finished, and she had just started work again at the LSE. It was with some difficulty that she managed to persuade them to grant her another week's leave – though Hawn had an idea that one week would not be enough.

The post next day enclosed two first-class tickets, one way, from London to Paris. Hawn did not like the one way, since he could scarcely credit Pol with meanness : but also he could hardly argue.

At London Airport there was a bill-board for the evening paper :

POTATO CANCER SCARE

Ah, we live dangerously, he thought; and bought the paper which he read over the champagne during the flight. It was in the Stop Press :

FORMER NAZI WAR CRIMINAL FOUND HANGED

Monsaraz, Portugal. Former Nazi official, Dr Hans Dieter Mönch, was found hanged here in his hotel room. Local Police are treating it as suicide.

He and Anna had spent too long having their senses lulled by the dead drudge of statistics. Now they were alert again, awake to the full potential menace of Pol and their one-way ticket from him to the Lotti Hotel.

The fat man was already at the bar when they walked in. He greeted them voluptuously, but was careful not to disturb himself from his stool lest he could not get back on again. 'Excellent, mes chers! Now, Monsieur Hawn, I shall be able to offer you that meal which the Spanish authorities so rudely denied you.'

They ate in a little restaurant on the Ile de France behind Notre Dame. It was unpretentious, and half the tables were empty. The proprietor was a gaunt man with a bad leg and a fat wife. He greeted Pol by kissing him on both cheeks. Hawn guessed that they were either confederates in crime or old Resistance comrades.

'This is not a famous place,' Pol explained, tucking in his bib : 'but it is probably the best restaurant in Paris.'

Hawn waited until the wine had been poured and Pol had ordered the first course. 'So what happened to Mönch?'

The Frenchman gave a grandiose shrug that caused his chair to creak. 'Ah, the poor Doktor. He had cancer, you know – cancer of the bone. He had not long to live.'

'Did you, and your friends in Jacques, do it?'

'Mon cher Monsieur Hawn, that is scarcely a polite suggestion. And I was so looking forward to an agreeable dinner with you both. I am sure Mademoiselle Admiral would not like it spoilt for her.'

Anna looked him in the eye. 'I'd be happier if I knew what happened to Mönch.'

Pol spread out his napkin and sighed. 'Mönch was a very wicked man, my friends. He worked close to Himmler – he was a confidant of his. He employed slave-labour – and we all know what that meant.'

'Did you collect his second affidavit?'

'I did. And you have the first, of course?'

'Of course.'

Pol sat smiling brightly at them both. Hawn added, 'First, why the one-way tickets?'

'Ah, a mere bagatelle. Just that I do not expect you to be returning direct from Paris. But we can discuss your travel arrangements later. First, the document.'

'And yours,' Hawn said.

Pol gave his girlish giggle : 'Ah, Monsieur Hawn, you are so suspicious !'

'You'd think me an idiot if I wasn't.'

The Frenchman wobbled with laughter; then reached inside his voluminous jacket and produced a folded wad of typescript, identical in appearance to the first – only this time there were only six pages. In return, Hawn handed him the photostat of Mönch's original documents, which Pol read while he ate. He ate busily, washing almost every mouthful down with a glass of wine. He read them a second time, then folded them away inside his jacket.

Hawn had meanwhile worked his way through Mönch's second missive. There were not two names – only one. Reiss. Mönch confirmed that the man had been a top double-agent in both Istanbul and the Caribbean, that he had worked for 'Operation Bettina' throughout, and that this was an organization so secret that it was known only to Himmler and his immediate entourage.

The last three pages consisted of loose technical verbiage, mostly German industrial firms – several of them still in existence – on which 'Bettina' had fed for its information, its know-how and transportation facilities. Mönch was not specific about anything. The implication might be there, but there was no direct link with ABCO, or with any Western agency, diplomatic or commercial.

Hawn said, 'And you paid four thousand dollars for this?'

'My friend, I am not so naïve. I am aware that these documents are not important in themselves. But Mönch also enclosed his address. I was anxious to make contact with him. Not personally. Through friends.'

'The friends being members of Jacques?'

Pol's smile became less benign. 'Mon cher, Jacques is a highly exclusive organization. You happened to hear about it only from Mönch. That was not your fault. But do not think, as a journalist, that you have the privilege to mention Jacques so lightly whenever you feel like it.' He ordered more wine and there was a moment's uncomfortable pause.

'Why did you ask us out here?' said Hawn.

'Because I think you can be useful to me. I also like you – and that is more than I can say for most of my fellow creatures. I want to continue to work with you. But first, let us share our resources. You have shown me Mönch's original documents. I am particularly interested by his references to "Bettina". In my own researches I have come across this name before, but have never known what it signified.

'Mönch's information is far from complete, and it leaves much guessing. But I happen to know, from private sources, that he held a unique position in the Third Reich – one that enjoyed the confidence of the Nazi leadership on one side, and gave him easy access to the British and Americans on the other – that is to say, agents working for the British and Americans. But only in the most intense secrecy.'

Anna interrupted him. 'From what I know, the Nazis *always* worked in the greatest secrecy. Even the extermination of the Jews was kept secret from most Germans. There are no records, for instance, of the Wannsee Conference when they decided on the Final Solution for the Jews.'

'The Jews were another question,' said Pol. 'Hitler's gang knew that once they embarked on the murder of an entire people, they were putting themselves beyond the pale. Given the Nazi ideology, the Final Solution was the obvious consequence, of course. But they also knew that if they lost the war, the world would never forgive them. At Nuremberg Goering is reputed to have said, "If it hadn't been for Auschwitz, none of us would be in the dock now." '

'All right,' said Hawn, 'but the guilt of murdering six million Jews is rather different from importing a few million tonnes of crude oil from your adversaries. So why the intense secrecy?'

'Because for the first time in the history of the oil business, the big international companies were not entirely their own masters. There were plenty of crooks about in the Second World War, on both sides, but on the whole Churchill and Roosevelt played a straight game. And if they had even suspected that their underlings were trading in oil with the enemy, heads would have rolled, perhaps even literally. The Nazis needed that oil. And they needed to protect the people who were supplying it to them.'

'But do we have proof of all this?' Hawn said.

Pol grinned. 'Proof, mon cher, is a relative thing. It depends on whom you want to convince. No, I do not need sufficient proof to satisfy an international court of law. All I need is enough proof to satisfy myself and – how shall I put it? – my friends.'

'Then you take justice into your own hands?'

'Justice? What is that? Give me an example of justice that has emerged from any war? But these are academic arguments. We're wasting time, and, worse, we're wasting this excellent food!' He ate for a moment in silence. 'But you surely have something to tell me?'

Hawn paraphrased his researches into Salak and the unhappy de Vere Frisby – though he was careful at this point not to mention Shanklin : Shanklin was too near home for comfort – while Anna followed with a neat résumé of her researches to date.

'I'm afraid it's not much to show for a month's work,' Hawn said. 'At least, hardly enough for you to unleash your dogs of justice once again.'

'Not at all, mon cher! On the contrary, what you have both recounted interests me greatly. For a start, it establishes a definite link between Turkey and the Caribbean. That is the one link that has so far evaded me.

'Now, I have been doing a little work of my own. I have a friend who was in Istanbul during the war. He has also heard of this man Salak. The gentleman appears to have been a formidable character – no wonder your SOE used him. Or rather, shared him with the Germans ! But most important of all, the man is still alive.' He put his hand inside his jacket and hauled out a long plain envelope which he handed across to Hawn.

Inside were again two first-class air tickets, this time open-return, Paris to Istanbul. They were booked in his and Anna's full names – departure time 9.30 next morning from Orly. There were also 100,000 francs in 500-franc notes – more than a thousand pounds.

Hawn was not immune to the seductive sight and feel of

so much cash, so suddenly, gratuitously offered. He felt his judgement and resolution weakening. He looked at Anna, and she looked back at him, bright-eyed, curious. He said to Pol : 'What's the brief? Track down this man Salak, so your boys can catch up and deal with him?'

'Mon cher, even for a journalist you have sometimes a most indelicate way of expressing yourself. I want information from Salak. I want you to help me to get it. I want you to bribe him – buy him. And if you need more funds, you know where to get them.'

'Why don't you do it yourself?' said Anna.

'Because, as I have told you before, I am sadly too conspicuous – too many people know me – and my reputation is wide, and not always so pure.' He wiped some sauce off his beard. 'But you are the ideal pair – a professional journalist and his researcher mistress' – he nodded to Anna – 'if you will pardon the expression.'

Hawn sat sipping his liqueur. 'My friend in London told me only that Salak used to be a wrestler and has a shop in a district called Kumkapi. Can you give us any other details about him?'

'That is really all you need to know. Kumkapi is a very low area, in the south of the city. But Salak prefers to be the big fish in a small dirty pond. Also, wrestling in Turkey is like boxing in New York. Just find a café or bar where wrestlers congregate.

'One word of warning. Salak is rumoured to be still a powerful and influential man – in his own domain. Be careful how you approach him. You may not find him as amenable or as vulnerable as Doktor Mönch. And one other thing. Keep out of trouble with the Turkish police – they are not gentle.'

'And how do we get in touch with you?'

'When you get to Istanbul, book into the Pera Palace. It is one of the most civilized hotels in the Middle East – once rivalled only by the St Georges in Beirut, which unhappily is now a ruin. I will contact you in my own time.'

He turned, as though to call for the bill; then paused. 'I have not been quite frank with you. When Mönch sent us this second document, he also enclosed his address – as I told you.' He rummaged in his mighty trouser pocket – an effort which caused him to sweat – and finally produced a folded sheet of hotel note-paper. Across the back, in that old-fashioned Germanic script, made almost illegible by a wobbly hand, were traced two lines. It took Hawn several minutes to decipher them – and he only succeeded because they were two of the most famous lines of verse in German literature.

Die Vöglein schweigen im Walde beim See.
Warte nur – bald rühst du auch.

Hawn looked at him. 'Maybe Mönch's last words – before he hanged himself? Although the newspapers say he didn't leave a note.'

'He enclosed it with his address.' There was a note of impatience in Pol's voice. 'What does it mean?'

'It's Goethe. It has to be. No one else is ever quoted in German. Only the quote isn't correct. It should read, "The little birds are silent in the wood – just wait, and soon you will be silent too." In this version Mönch says, "The little birds are silent in the wood *by the lake* ... " ' He looked at the big sweating face above its food-stained bib ... ' "Just wait, and soon you will be silent too." The final testament of an old man close to death? Or just a warning? You and your boys were too impatient with Mönch. If you had given him a little more time, and handled him correctly, he might have told us everything.'

'Such as?'

'Such as where the complete files on "Operation Bettina" were hidden. In a lake, by a wood, maybe.'

'Keep that piece of paper, Monsieur Hawn. Or rather, memorize it. It could be useful.' He paused. 'How typical of the Nazis! Goethe and Beethoven. What romantics to drag such names into their filthy business.'

They landed at Yesilkoy Airport, Istanbul, on a cool grey afternoon. Customs and Immigration formalities were swift and casual. Hawn changed 20,000 francs into Turkish lire, bought a street-map of the city, and fought with a scrum of taxi-drivers; the winner was a solid man with a ferocious black moustache like a scouring-brush. During the thirty-minute drive into the city, he kept to the fast lane of the dual carriageway, his foot flat down, his hand on the horn, giving way to no one. If a car had been following them, the driver would have had to have been either exceptionally skilful or downright reckless.

They passed small white houses with tiny allotments, spreading into wooden slums that clustered round the feet of grey tower-blocks, many of them unfinished, reaching down to the edge of the Sea of Marmara. The city beyond presented a wide undulating panorama, humped and spiked with mosques and minarets – magnificent and filthy, built layer upon layer upon the decaying stones and clogged effluence of many civilizations, from Byzantium and Constantinople to the opulent barbarity of the Ottoman Empire – now raddled by the corruption of a modern Western city, of high-rise hotels, multi-storey car parks, boutiques, discos, supermarkets, constipated traffic.

Istanbul is the only city in the world which stands on two continents. The main half, on the eastern extremity of Europe, is divided from the other by the Golden Horn, which is shaped more like a fat snake, its dark waters churned and thrashed by crowds of dilapidated river-craft fighting to find a berth, or to scramble through the narrow gap in the Galata Bridge – an ancient pontoon structure whose central sections open twice a day to let shipping squeeze out into the Bosphorus. Across this famous channel of water lies Istanbul's eastern half – Usküdar, formerly Scutari, which is part of Asia.

The traffic in the city was appalling, but did not seem to deter their driver. They crossed the Golden Horn by the more recent Atatürk Bridge, into the commercial district where whole areas had been cleared to make way for modern office-blocks whose angular shapes almost overshadowed the bulging, archaic mosques below.

They climbed steeply, through a fog of exhaust fumes, and drew up finally at the steps of a modest building with a blue glass dome. The driver charged them treble the sum on the clock; Hawn refused to pay; the driver yelled at him; Hawn offered him a third; the driver accepted, grinned hugely and wrung his hand.

Once inside, Hawn could see why the Pera Palace Hotel was no longer the watering-place of the rich and fashionable. Instead of air-conditioning, there were big swinging fans from the ceilings that stirred the tepid air; the tall mirrors round the walls were mottled brown; the staff, in their white mess-tunics and red tarbouches, looked as though they needed dusting down, and the potted plants wanted watering. The walls were veined marble and black teak, under chandeliers looking like clusters of gilded orchids. Flaking cherubs stared sadly down at them from above the reception desk.

Hawn had the impression that the hotel was far from full. In the lobby the few guests to be seen were either plump, prosperous-looking Turks or ageing foreigners of distinguished and academic appearance, like old-fashioned archaeologists.

The room was spacious, heavily-draped, with wide windows overlooking the steep sprawl down to the Bosphorus, with the minarets sticking up like sharpened pencils. The bathroom was enormous, tiled in marble, with elaborate plumbing which might have been part of an ancient steam-engine.

At four o'clock, downstairs, the tarbouched retainers were moving discreetly among the tables, serving tea and tiny cups of muddy black coffee. Hawn gave his usual quick glance round to see if there was anyone to arouse his suspicion. Then they went outside.

They had been warned that it was almost impossible to get a taxi, so they walked. The streets were not imposing – grey, grubby, deafening, the pavements moving with dogged, silent crowds, their button-black eyes registering no expression. Seen close to, even the mosques lost their magic : huge hunks of Oriental Gothic which reminded Hawn of Victorian railway stations in London. There were many money-changers and souvenir shops bristling with hideous over-priced artefacts of bogus pedigree.

After half-an-hour, their eyes stinging with dust and fumes, they returned to the melancholy charm of the Pera Palace.

Here they asked Reception if they could arrange for a chauffeur-driven car. A more than usually alert man at the desk said it would be done at once. The result was a brand-new Mercedes with no meter and a driver who smiled a lot and was obviously keen to show off his English, which was rapid and colloquial, with an American accent. Hawn told him that they wanted to go across to the Kumkapi District.

The driver said, 'Kumkapi no good. Full of bad men. Dirty, it smells. You must go to Suleymaniye Mosque. And the Mosque of Rustum Pasa. You have already seen the Topkapi and the Blue Mosque?'

It took Hawn several minutes to convince him that they were determined to go to Kumkapi. Hawn's final explanation seemed a ludicrous one, especially with Anna sitting beside him. 'We are interested in wrestling. Do you understand, "wrestling"?'

The man turned and showed his white teeth. 'Very good sport. Football, wrestling. Very good!' Then he shook his head, as they narrowly missed the car in front. 'But you see no wrestling in Kumkapi.'

'No? But many wrestlers come from there? There are many bars and cafés where wrestlers go? Yes?'

'They are not good places. The good wrestlers do not go there. Only the older ones, the bums.' He laughed and repeated, 'Bums!' – with a sideways glance in his driving mirror at Anna.

'Take us to one of those cafés,' Hawn said. 'We'll give you a bonus.'

It took them almost an hour to get back across the river, into an area of shabby crooked streets full of tiny wooden shops like cupboards, and the occasional covered bazaar. They came to a small square with a brick mosque and seedy shops, most of them selling meat. On the steps of the mosque sat a row of long-haired European youths and their girls, their faces pinched and vacant.

The driver stopped, pointed ahead; he seemed disappoint-ed and did not smile. 'There is wrestlers' café. But not a good place.'

After a long haggle, they agreed on a price for him to wait.

The square smelt of charcoal, coffee and charred meat; the shops were hung with bulbous lumps of greasy white goat's meat. There was only the one café, full of grim-looking men sitting over empty cups. Hawn and Anna went inside and ordered coffee.

It was now that they encountered the most awkward and obtrusive aspect of Turkish life. They had only been there for a couple of minutes when two glasses of a yellowish liquid appeared on their table. A man of savage aspect, sitting at the next table, and dressed in boots and a khaki vest, shouted at them : '*Akadash!*'

Hawn had taken the precaution of bringing an elementary English-Turkish dictionary. The man shouted at them again – '*Akadash!*' – and made a gesture as though drinking.

Hawn smiled politely at him and, presuming it was some kind of white wine, swigged the glass in front of him and nearly choked, his throat burned raw.

'Raki!' the man shouted.

Hawn smiled again, bitterly, and took another sip. Then he consulted his dictionary. '*Akadash*' meant 'Good friend'. He repeated it back to the man, offering him a tentative toast.

He and Anna finished the two drinks and called the waiter – a stout man in a dirty white apron – and ordered one raki, gesturing to their host. The man at the next table howled something, obviously furious. A moment later two more rakis appeared in front of them both.

'American?' the Turk demanded.

'English,' Hawn said.

'Ah, Eenglish.' He turned and bawled at some men at another table. One of them came across. He was stout and bow-legged, very unshaven, wearing a blue tracksuit. With-out being invited, he sat down at their table.

'I speak very good English,' he said, and called to the waiter for more raki.

Hawn was beginning to find this aggressive hospitality both tiresome and a little disquieting. He was thinking more of Anna than himself, and how they were going to get away without fuss; but so far none of the men appeared to have taken any interest in her at all.

'How long you in Istanbul?' the stranger said. His breath reeked. Then, without waiting for an answer, added: 'You have American cigarettes?'

Hawn explained that Anna and he did not smoke.

'You want to buy American cigarettes?' the man said. 'Good price. Fifty Turkish lire, two hundred Lucky Strike.'

Hawn decided this was his cue. He said, 'What is your name?'

'They call me Baka.'

'Well listen, Baka, *akadash*. We have to go back to the hotel now. But tomorrow we will come back and I will give you some good American cigarettes. You give me raki – I give you cigarettes.'

There was a lot of shaking hands and kissing on the cheeks – though none of them attempted to kiss Anna. They at last got out of the café and returned to the car.

'One thing I will say for all that,' Hawn said, when they were inside. 'After the first glass, that raki's not bad stuff.'

'Why didn't you ask about Salak?' she said: and Hawn nudged her violently, noticing the driver's eyes watching them in the mirror.

'We walk before we run,' he muttered, then tried to distract the driver by kissing her with passion.

She straightened up. 'I don't know about you, but I could do with a long cold drink.' Back at the Pera Palace they ordered a bottle of Krug, non-vintage. It was the best the hotel could provide.

As they had come back in, Hawn thought the keen-looking receptionist had eyed them both with more than usual interest. Perhaps it was because, beside the rest of the clientele, they were young and good-looking. Perhaps.

Next day they decided to keep away from Kumkapi. It was one thing for a couple of foreigners to sample the city's low

146

life on a casual visit; it was another for them to make a habit of it.

Hawn was an idle and indifferent sightseer; but Anna, with her precise academic nature, felt that if she did not always enjoy it, she must at least do it.

They spent the morning making the statutory round of the Blue Mosque, the Sancta Sophia, the Hippodrome and the gloomy vaults of the Roman cisterns, through endless palaces and dungeons and fortresses, all blood-soaked in history, and now peopled by gawping, shuffling tourists and their rapacious guides.

Exhausted, Hawn and Anna lunched away from the main street, Taksim, in a foul expensive restaurant where the only delicacies were the cheese and thick black coffee. In the afternoon they visited two palaces and three more mosques, and in one of the bazaars, after some exhilarating bargaining, he bought Anna a heavy silver bracelet.

The only jarring incident of the day had been the obsequious intrusion of a fellow tourist – a middle-aged Austrian, alone, bespectacled, bald, and armed with a guidebook in which he made notes on the flyleaf in pencil.

He had joined them in the Sancta Sophia, and at first had been quite useful in explaining some of the special architectural features of the church; and as they tramped between the colonnades of the Mosque of Suleymaniye, he padded along beside them like some lost dog from the Great Bazaar. His name was Otto Dietrich, he was an accountant from Vienna, and had recently been widowed.

Hawn's first instinct was to be suspicious of him: yet the man was such a stupendous bore that Hawn's only reaction was one of exasperation, tempered with a grudging sense of pity for the man. He realized that such creatures were one of the penalties of tourism, and of sightseeing in particular.

He and Anna made several attempts to rid themselves of him: but Otto Dietrich was no ordinary bore: he was both persistent and skilful. They only managed to shake him off finally at the entrance of the Pera Palace, where Dietrich's farewell was accompanied by the threat that he would telephone or call round in the next few days. He kissed Anna's hand and said, with awful sincerity, 'I have so enjoyed myself today! I have not enjoyed myself so much for a long time. Thank you both so very much!'

That evening, feeling free at last, Hawn went out and bought yesterday's *Herald Tribune*. There was no further mention of Mönch's supposed suicide. The Herr Doktor had disappeared as thoroughly as Norman French.

Next morning they took the precaution of telling Reception that if anyone called for them, they had gone for a day's excursion up the Bosphorus.

They decided to leave their second visit to Kumkapi until after siesta. Hawn bought a pack of two hundred king-size American cigarettes, and this time the hotel ordered for them a different car, with a different driver – an older man who seemed to speak no English. He also had little feel for the traffic, and they were soon caught up in the same laborious crawl back over the river into the wooden slums of the south-western area of the city.

When they at last arrived, Hawn told the driver to wait in one of the narrow side-streets off the square. The man obeyed impassively. Hawn and Anna got out and walked.

Nothing had changed. The hippies sat like hungry crows at the foot of the mosque and fat green flies moved leisurely among the hanging meat. They came to the café. Hawn was relieved to see that their ferocious host of two days ago was not there. They found a table outside, and when the waiter came they ordered two rakis; then Hawn said casually, 'Baka?' with a wave towards the inside of the café.

The waiter muttered and moved off. When he returned with the two drinks, he was accompanied by a tall man in a surprisingly smart oyster-white suit, who bowed and sat down.

'You want to talk to Baka?'

Hawn laid the carton of cigarettes on the table. 'Two days ago I promised to give these to Baka.' He smiled. 'Baka is *akadash*.'

'*Akadash*,' the man repeated, without smiling. 'You English friend of Baka.' It was a statement, not a question.

'We met here two days ago. We had some drinks together. I promised him cigarettes.'

The man gave Hawn a slow stare. 'Baka not here.'

'Where is he?'

The man clasped his wrists together, as though in handcuffs. 'Kemeret. Very bad place.'

'Kemeret?' Hawn frowned.

The waiter arrived and placed a cup of coffee in front of the man. He sipped it delicately, licking the brown scum off his lips. 'Kemeret is Istanbul Prison,' he said at last.

Hawn stared at him. The man had a cruel face that betrayed no change of expression. 'What happened? What did Baka do?'

'Contraband. Cigarettes.' He looked threateningly down at the carton on the table. 'You no friend of Baka. Baka do business with English. Americans. Now he is in Kemeret.'

Hawn was aware that the whole café was now watching them. Their faces were as empty as that of the man at their table; there was also a sullen air of hostility.

'I give you my word,' Hawn said, 'that I have never done any business with Baka. I met him for the first time the day before yesterday.'

The man did not seem to be listening. He said, 'Drink your raki. Then you come with me.'

'Are you police?'

The man laughed; it was a harsh sound, like a dog barking. Then he put his head back and shouted something, and the whole café laughed.

'You finish your raki,' he said to Hawn, without looking at Anna; 'then you come with me.'

Hawn's hand closed round Anna's under the table; he could feel her trembling. 'Just don't worry – I'll handle this. They're not going to risk any rough stuff with foreigners. They're just being careful. A lot of stupid tourists come here and get caught up in the drug racket. So they want to make sure of us – probably taking us to their boss, where we can explain everything.' He spoke with a good deal more coolness than he felt.

Anna stood up, very pale. They were not asked to pay for

their drinks. The man in the white suit led the way out, and two stocky men in overalls ambled after them. They crossed the square, into a dingy side-street slippery with donkey droppings: out into a wider street where there were pavements, people walking, cars honking along, bumper to bumper.

They came to a shop with an illuminated green cross above the door, over the word *Eczane*, and a red neon sign which read COLGATE. Inside was a sharp stench of disinfectant and cheap perfume. It was a well-stocked modern pharmacist's. Two girls in white coats were serving behind the counter. The Turk said something to them, and one of them nodded to the back of the shop. Hawn and Anna followed him, down a narrow passage lined to the ceiling with dark bottles and phials. Hawn was still carrying the carton of cigarettes, not knowing whether it would count in their favour or against them.

The two stocky men had stopped inside the shop. The Turk led the way up a dark wooden staircase, down a passage lit by a single naked bulb. There were no windows. He came to a door and knocked, then murmured something in which Hawn thought he detected the name, 'Baka'. A voice from inside shouted back, and the Turk opened the door. He stood aside and beckoned to Hawn and Anna.

They walked past him into what might have been the set for some lavish production of 'Scheherazade'. It was a long dim room with dark-stained panelling, blood-red damask curtains, and huge embroidered cushions arranged around the walls. Ornate lamps were suspended by chains from the ceiling and the floor was covered with a handsome carpet. There were two windows, small and heavily glazed, admitting little light and affording no view. A grandfather clock ticked noisily away in the corner, next to an antique desk.

Plumped down on one of the great cushions was a man in blue-striped pyjamas. Hawn could see that he was well over six feet tall. His head was the size of a football, and as bald as a stone – lumpy and pitted and cracked like the head of a very old, unlovely statue. His eyes were small and creased up, black and crafty.

But the thing about him that Hawn noticed most were his feet. They were bare – big feet with the soles horribly scarred, like corrugated brown paper, presumably as a result of the traditional Turkish torture of the bastinado.

He was smoking a Western-style pipe and reading a local newspaper. He took the pipe from his mouth and gestured Anna and Hawn towards one of the cushions; then, still holding the newspaper, he said something to the man in the white suit. The Turk replied at some length. The huge man in pyjamas lay listening, looking faintly bored. Finally, he replied, briefly, and the Turk in the white suit bowed low and withdrew, closing the door without a sound.

The huge man looked across at Hawn and Anna in silence. He took a pull at his pipe, found that it had gone out, knocked the ash into a brass bowl by his leg, and said in English, 'What are your names?' His voice was low and mellifluent, his English well-educated, with almost no accent.

Hawn told him. The man took his time answering.

'I hope I am doing you both an injustice,' he said at last, 'but recently I've been having a lot of trouble with foreign visitors. Mostly Americans. I don't want to bore you with the details of my work, except to say that a degree of discretion is required. Recently several of my employees have been in trouble with the police through dealings with foreigners. I understand that two days ago you visited a certain café where you made the acquaintance of a man who calls himself Baka?'

Hawn nodded. 'It was an entirely accidental meeting. We were introduced to him by a complete stranger who insisted on buying us drinks.'

'When did you arrive in Istanbul?'

Hawn hesitated. 'Two days ago.'

'The very same day you visited the café?' The man's black eyes did not shift from Hawn's. 'Don't you think that's rather an odd thing for two tourists to do, on their first day in Istanbul? Our city has so many magnificent sights – yet you two choose to visit the poorest, the filthiest district in the city. It is not even as though you were seeking out the low life – prostitutes and belly-dancers. You would find those off Taksim. Instead, you choose Kumkapi.'

'I am not a conventional tourist.' Hawn spoke with forced pride. 'You seem to be talking about those bus-loads of camera-covered morons who trek through the bazaars and round the Blue Mosque like herds of cattle. We're interested in the real Istanbul. And I don't care if it is poor and stinking. It exists.'

The man on the cushion gave a broken-toothed smile. 'I congratulate you, my dear sir, on your eloquence. Unfortunately there is one small matter which rather spoils it. You are staying at the Pera Palace, are you not?' He smiled again. 'Do not look so surprised. You see, the day before yesterday you hired a car from there. You asked the driver specifically to take you to a certain café in Kumkapi. A café frequented by ex-wrestlers. You see, the driver of that car is a friend of mine. He thought your behaviour was odd, and he reported it to me.'

'Why?'

'Please, my dear sir. Do not take me for a fool. I have already explained that my work requires discretion. I do not like foreigners who spy on me. I do not like foreigners who talk to one of my employees, and discuss contraband in cigarettes, and then next day that employee is taken away by the police.'

'You're mistaken. I had no illicit dealings with this man Baka at all. The fact that he has been arrested is a total coincidence.'

'Is it a coincidence that on your first day in Istanbul you insisted on visiting the café where most of my employees spend their free time?'

'We were looking for somewhere with atmosphere. As I said, somewhere well off the tourist beat.'

The big man began to fill his pipe from a porcelain bowl. 'Mr Hawn, why have you come to Istanbul?'

'For a holiday.'

He slowly shook his head. 'I'm going to be gentle with you. Usually people like you are found in a back-street so badly injured that they spend the next six months in hospital.

There is a lot of robbery – what you call "mugging" – in Istanbul. You would not find yourself attracting much attention from the police. And our hospitals are not very good.

'However, I will give you a chance. And besides, you have such a charming lady-friend – I should not like to see her harmed. I will ask you again. What are you doing in Istanbul? Or shall I put it another way? What were you hoping to do?'

Anna had been sitting silently beside Hawn, pale, her hands pressed together in her lap. Her voice now broke in with soft measured fury:

'Just who the hell do you think you are? You're behaving like some cheap gangster out of a 1930s B-movie. We come to Istanbul as tourists and happen to visit a café where we're bought a few drinks by a stranger, and introduced to another stranger whom we agree to meet again, and just because he's been arrested, your "heavies" pick us up and march us round to this shop and up into this ridiculous room. Who do you think you are? Sydney Greenstreet?'

The man, who had lain listening impassively, looked puzzled. 'Greenstreet?'

'Never mind. He was an actor. And a lot better one than you are. You say you spoke to the chauffeur who drove us to the café. Did he tell you that we specifically wanted to go somewhere where wrestlers meet?'

'You are interested in wrestling?'

'We thought the place might have atmosphere. But we've explained all this already. Now will you call your bodyguard outside and let us go.'

The man began to light his pipe. The only sound in the room was the heavy ticking of the grandfather clock. He looked up at last with his cracked smile.

'I congratulate you, too, young lady, on your little speech. Unfortunately much of what you have said is true. We Turks so often behave like the films. The cinema is very popular here – more popular even than wrestling. People think of Turkey as an exotic, even romantic country. But apart from a few mosques and palaces that have been turned into museums, and the traditional dancing put on for the tourists, we are at heart a coarse primitive people.

'I myself had the advantage of being educated at your excellent Trinity College, Cambridge. People tell me I speak like a true English gentleman – though I hardly look like one. I am not a gentleman. I am an uncivilized Turk, and my methods of business are also uncivilized. It is useless to lose your temper with me. I do not even mind being abused, providing you do not insult the memory of my father or my mother.'

He settled back into his cushion and drew on his pipe. 'But we are straying from the point. I asked you what you were hoping to do in Istanbul, and you persist in telling me that you are innocent tourists. It may interest you to know that after your chauffeur had reported back to me. I checked with the Pera Palace Hotel. I discovered that you, Mr Hawn, are described in your passport as a journalist. While you, Miss Admiral, are a researcher. Might I inquire into what you research?'

'Economics.' Her voice was still stiff with anger.

'And Mr Hawn is perhaps a journalist who specializes also in economics?'

'I'm on a sabbatical, writing a book about medieval Italy. Does that satisfy you?'

'Mr Hawn, I am never satisfied until I am sure. I have only your word for what you say.'

Anna broke in: 'Well, you'll just have to be satisfied! If you think you can kidnap us, then intimidate us, you're wrong. At least they might have taught you some manners at Cambridge.'

The big man held up his hand. He sounded bored. 'Please, please, no more histrionics. Unless absolutely necessary, I like to think of myself as a peaceful man. Now I tell you what I propose to do. I am going to give you two simple choices. Either you tell me what you are doing in Istanbul – in the interests of "journalistic research". Or I shall insist that you leave the city on the first available plane. And don't think it will help you by going to the police. They would probably prefer not to believe your story – but even if they did, I have influence in high places, and I could no doubt persuade them that it was in the national interest that you were both declared personae non gratae. I will give you two minutes to make up your minds.'

Hawn decided, reluctantly, that they had little to lose now by being frank. Pol had warned them to treat their assignment circumspectly: although Pol had perhaps not bargained for quite these circumstances.

Hawn spoke with care: 'We've come to meet a man called Imin Salak. By all accounts, a very brave man. We're writing a book about the wartime activities of the Special Operations Executive, and part of the book involves British espionage and counter-espionage in Turkey. An old friend of mine – a veteran of British wartime Intelligence – recommended that we try to talk to Salak.'

The man's black eyes watched him, without blinking. 'You are foolish not to have mentioned this before. Salak is a very proud man – proud of his war exploits, which have never been chronicled. He will be delighted to have a book written about him. Why did you not tell me this at once?'

'If your methods hadn't been so heavy-handed,' said Hawn, 'we might have done.'

The man raised both hands as though in prayer. 'That is the uncivilized Turk in me. As Miss Admiral so truly said, they taught me no manners at Cambridge. Besides, I have my business interests to protect – and in my business one sometimes becomes unnecessarily suspicious.' He stood up, with a smooth swift movement, and walked across the room to a telephone on the desk. He walked very straight, on his scarred bare feet, like a soldier.

The conversation lasted nearly five minutes; then he hung up and shouted something, and the door was opened by the man in the white suit. The big man gave him an order and he withdrew; he turned now to the others.

'My car will be here in a couple of minutes. And I have arranged for your new driver to be paid off.' He smiled. 'There is at least one way in which I am civilized. I believe in organization. My organization is probably the best in Istanbul. It is certainly superior to the Government's. Now, if you will excuse me for a moment, I will dress.'

He reappeared a few minutes later, from behind one of the damask curtains, wearing cavalry-twill jodhpurs, soft black calf leather boots and a tunic buttoned to the neck. He looked like a cross between an ageing bandit and a high-class chauffeur.

The others followed him back down the dark stairs, through the chemist's shop and out into the street, where a large old-fashioned American car stood, shining black, with a shark-mouthed radiator grill, high chromium fins and smoked windows. They all three got into the back. The man in the white suit was driving.

They headed north, out of the narrow shanty town and across the bridge into Galata, stopping at last outside a big neon-lit café with steel-framed chairs and plastic-topped tables at which groups of men sat playing dominoes, backgammon and noisy card games. The walls were decorated with Pirelli calendars and posters for the latest American films. There were no women. Hawn wondered whether the men in Turkey worked at all.

The driver stayed outside with the car. The big man led the way in, to a far corner where two men were playing rummy. They were both elderly – one with a mass of white hair and a great white moustache, the other balding, and of a dark hooked Semitic aspect. Unlike most Turks whom Hawn had seen, he was closely shaven, and again unlike most Turks, he wore a collar and tie under a tight-fitting business suit. His black shoes shone like mirrors, and he wore a pair of gold-rimmed bifocals behind which his eyes were two opaque marbles.

The big man drew up chairs and made the introductions. For the first time he disclosed his own name to Hawn and Anna : 'I am Selim Pasha Esquire. And this is Effendi Mustafa Gebel.' He did not introduce, and totally ignored, the white-haired man.

'Mustafa is my lawyer,' Selim Pasha explained. 'He looks after my business interests and advises me on matters of delicacy. You may talk freely – he speaks English.'

The man called Mustafa Gebel inclined his head and

kissed Anna's hand. 'Delighted. You are enjoying your stay in Istanbul?'

'It's certainly been eventful,' Hawn said; he stared between the two men, at the poster behind them from which Julie Andrews pranced joyously out at them, followed by her band of happy children. He wondered how long the way to Imin Salak was – if indeed there was a way – or whether these introductions were merely part of an elaborate oriental ritual of prevarication.

The man with white hair got up, grunted something, and walked away. Mustafa Gebel began stacking the cards. Hawn noticed that although he was a small man next to Selim Pasha, he had surprisingly large shoulders and hands, and that he wore a spectacular diamond ring.

He looked at Hawn from under his bifocals. 'Selim tells me that you are interested in meeting a certain important man in Istanbul? That you wish to interview him in connection with his memoirs? I must tell you at once that it will depend much on what you want him to tell you.'

'How do you mean – depends?'

'The gentleman in question knows many secrets. Secrets that have never been revealed. He will expect to be paid for his services.'

Hawn looked, frowning, at Selim Pasha. He had decided that a little innocent bluffing would not be wasted at this point. 'But you said he'd be delighted to have his exploits written up. You said nothing about money.'

The big man shrugged and said nothing. Mustafa Gebel folded his thick brown fingers together and gazed between Hawn and Anna.

'It is I who talk about money,' he said softly. 'No secret is free – not even after more than thirty years.'

'Are you negotiating for him?'

'No. I am simply preparing the way for negotiations. I would not like you to be disappointed.'

'I prefer to negotiate directly with the seller. I'll put the questions to him, he can name his price, then we can argue.'

Mustafa Gebel inclined his vulpine face across the table and pursed his thin, moist lips. 'You would save us all much trouble and inconvenience, Mr Hawn, if you told me now the kind of questions you want to ask.'

Anna, who had so far been completely ignored by both Turks, said, 'What's so special about this man that he has to be protected like this? We've heard he's important. He's presumably also intelligent. So why can't he do his own negotiating?'

Mustafa gave a peevish smile. 'Miss Admiral, you are right – the gentleman is most intelligent. But he does not have experience of journalists. And journalists, as we all know, not only make news, they make scandal.'

'What scandal does this man have to hide?' she asked.

Mustafa Gebel smiled again, a patient smile this time. 'All great men have scandals to hide. During the war the gentleman was in a very difficult and delicate situation. You know that, or you would not be here trying to interview him.'

At this point Hawn broke in: 'All right. What do you want? A broad résumé of what we're after, or a detailed list of questions we're going to ask him?'

Selim Pasha had sat all this time huge and rigid in his chair, watching the three of them with small sly eyes. He had spoken not one word.

'A résumé would be sufficient,' Mustafa said.

'And if you're satisfied, when do we meet him?'

'It can be arranged for this evening. At least, the preliminary meeting.'

Hawn said, 'I need a drink.'

Without turning, Mustafa snapped his fingers, and immediately a waiter appeared beside them. 'You would like whisky? Do not be afraid, it is not the usual stuff you find in Istanbul – contraband stuff. I shall make sure that you receive the best.'

The waiter brought two glasses, with ice and water. Neither of the Turks seemed to be drinking.

Hawn drank half of his neat; then said: 'Miss Admiral and I are following up a theory about the last war. To be brief, we think the Germans were being supplied with fuel by Western oil companies. We think that some of that fuel passed through Istanbul. A very good and reliable contact of mine in London recommended that your gentleman friend might provide us with some useful information about this.'

Mustafa Gebel began to speak, quietly, rapidly in Turkish. When he had finished, Selim Pasha shrugged and nodded. Hawn drank the rest of his whisky and waited.

The lawyer had pressed his fingertips together and spoke, without looking at Hawn, 'You have a tape-recorder?'

'No.'

'Do not all journalists have tape-recorders?'

'Not all. I'm old-fashioned. I believe in taking notes. Besides, if your friend has to be so protected, he won't want all his secrets committed to tape.'

'Instead, he will have to trust to your memory and your discretion?'

'Mr Gebel, I consider myself an experienced and reputable journalist. Remember that I will also have to trust your friend, and accept that he is not just telling me fantasies and lies.'

'Our friend does not lie.' Mustafa Gebel glanced across at the great ravaged face of Selim Pasha. He said something, and again Selim nodded. Mustafa turned back to Hawn. 'I agree in principle that you may meet our friend. But I must warn you. If you in any manner attempt to trick or deceive him, your body will be found in the Bosphorus. Also that of your charming friend here, Miss Admiral. I know it is a melodramatic threat, but remember, Istanbul is not London. We are trusting your honour, and in Turkey, if a man abuses that honour, he pays the ultimate price.'

'You make yourself admirably clear. So when is the meeting?'

'You will be collected at your hotel at eight o'clock. In the meantime you are to communicate with no one. We have reliable contacts at the Pera Palace, and if you disobey, we shall know.'

He stood up, and each man ceremoniously took their leave of them, while Mustafa Gebel explained that he and Selim Pasha were staying behind, as they had business to discuss. The car would drive Hawn and Anna back to the hotel. Selim Pasha gave him a bone-cracking handshake.

'You will accept my apologies for this afternoon. But you must also keep it as a confidence. I don't want tiresome inquiries from the British Consulate.'

'They're the last people I'd go to,' Hawn said, and they parted with more handshakes but no smiles.

At precisely 7.49 p.m. by Hawn's watch, the man in the oyster-white suit appeared in the lobby of the Pera Palace. Hawn and Anna followed him out to the same American limousine. Hawn asked him where they were going, but he did not answer. Since he spoke some English, they decided it was wiser not to discuss matters further – they had worked out their strategy for the evening while waiting at the hotel – and for most of the next hour they rode in silence.

Hawn guessed that they were driving north, since the darkness on their right indicated that they were following the coast of the Bosphorus. The city lights began to fade, the traffic thinned, and they were soon speeding along a wide highway into the black night. Hawn watched the speedometer needle, which was touching the 120 kmh mark, and saw that they had driven nearly 50 miles, when a cluster of lights came towards them and the driver slowed into a gravel siding.

He gestured his two passengers to get out.

They seemed to be in a small fishing village, with a fresh tang of salt in the air. There were a couple of open-air cafés and a huddle of small white houses. On their right, moored at the end of a wooden jetty, was a handsome sixty-foot motor yacht, ablaze with light. The driver began to lead them down the jetty.

They were a few feet from the gang-plank, when the sleek black-suited figure of the lawyer, Mustafa Gebel, appeared on deck. He had a welcoming, proprietorial air: he was proud of his vessel, as he had good reason to be. It was painted gleaming white and every inch of metal had been polished until it gave off a dazzling glint under the lights. Hawn noticed that he was wearing blue rubber-soled plimsolls.

After greeting them both, he added apologetically, 'I must

ask you to remove your shoes. I will give you others to wear. The deck, you understand.'

As soon as they stepped aboard, Hawn understood. The deck was of teak planking scrubbed almost white, like scraped bone. They ducked down into a saloon that was like a long narrow drawing-room, all dark mahogany and shining brass: velvet curtains across the port-holes, a well-stocked cocktail cabinet in the shape of a glass-fronted bookcase, and banquettes along the walls of button-backed suede.

On one of these sat the huge figure of Selim Pasha. Even in the comparative spaciousness of the yacht he looked quite out of proportion. And he was alone.

The driver had disappeared. Mustafa Gebel closed the door and moved to the cocktail cabinet. 'You choose – we have it. Whisky, gin, champagne on ice, martinis?'

He fixed the drinks himself. There seemed to be no one else on board. As a seasoned member of the Fleet Street round, Hawn always felt a faint mistrust of people who did not drink. Again, Selim Pasha and Mustafa Gebel were not drinking.

By now they were all seated – Hawn and Anna wearing plastic flip-flops, and Selim Pasha in outsize bedroom slippers. The two Turks sat opposite them, at far ends of the banquette.

Hawn took a sip of his whisky. 'All right, the polite charade is over. I've come all this way and I want results. Where is Imin Salak?'

Selim Pasha's face broke into its ugly grin. 'I am Imin Salak. Welcome aboard.'

Hawn asked for another whisky; Mustafa fetched it. 'How did the British recruit you?'

'In those days they recruited anyone. Anyone who spoke English and knew his way around. I had then, as now, special contacts, special sources. I knew many people. Even as a young man,' he added immodestly, 'I had much influence.'

'And you worked solely for the British?'

Imin Salak laughed, and Mustafa Gebel responded with a dutiful smile. 'Don't take me for a fool, Mr Hawn. As a young man I made mistakes, but I was never stupid. Or perhaps you know little about Istanbul during the war?'

'I was still having my nappies changed. Enlighten me.'

Salak paused. Now that the interview had begun, he seemed to be enjoying himself. 'In Turkey during the war we had no loyalties, no special interests. In 1917, in the First War, we offered to join you British in exchange for money. Your Foreign Office refused. They considered such a transaction immoral. In the Second War we found ourselves being wooed by every side – we were like the most beautiful girl at a party who arrives without an escort.'

'So you worked for the Germans too?'

'When they paid me. And I made sure they paid me well. I also made sure that I didn't make the same mistakes as that valet to your idiot ambassador in Ankara. Ah, that was a joke! The fellow stole every British secret – even the minutes of the Tehran Conference – and sold them to the Germans. Except that the Germans didn't believe the stuff. They also paid him in forged pound notes. I was paid in gold.'

'Did you find it easy to operate?'

'Easy? What's easy? Playing with children, maybe? No, it was not easy. It was not too difficult. It was all a matter of tact and judgement, and above all of knowing the right people.'

'What about your Security Police? Neutral countries in a war tend to be very touchy about espionage, in case they tip the scales too far to one side.'

'Security?' Salak laughed again. 'What sort of security do you think there was when Bay Faik Oztrak, who was Minister of the Interior, was dining with the Germans twice a week? Even Ismet Inönü, who was President of the Republic, had a German mistress. And she wasn't just a tourist or a whore.'

'Let me ask you a direct and simple question, Mr Salak. Do you believe that my theory about the illicit oil trade is true?'

'I not only believe it. I know it.'

'Was it generally known?'

'Generally – that is a vague word. No, it was a dead secret. But a secret shared by many people in high places.'

'When did it begin?'

'Oh, the first arrangements were made as early as 1938. But it was not until 1942 that the real work began. And by 1944 Istanbul had virtually become a German supply-base.'

'How was it worked?'

'It was simple. Your oil tankers came from Arabia through Suez, and sometimes – when the port of Alexandria was too full to take them – they came up to Istanbul to take on supplies, and sometimes change crews. It was not unknown for them to change cargoes too. But the bulk of the oil came up in small tankers on private charter – usually to a Swiss or Swedish concern – carrying fuel which was supposed to be intended for Turkish internal consumption. The amounts were excessive, and your Government constantly complained to ours. But Faik Oztrak and his friends – they were our Government at the time – were able to play games with the British, knowing how keen you were that Turkey should join the war on the Allies' side.'

'We must have been pretty naïve!'

'Some of you were naïve. Some not. It wasn't just Oztrak and certain other members of the Turkish Government who were privy to the secret. There were British officials involved as well.'

'Do you know who these officials were?'

'Ah. Now, Mr Hawn, everything I have just said is merely the meat of good café gossip. But do not presume too much of me. The real information will cost you money. What exactly do you want?'

'Everything you know. Names, dates, facts, and proof – above all, proof to back it up.'

Salak took out his pipe, but made no effort to light it; then spoke, in the refined English accent which jarred so grotesquely with his appearance: 'The information will cost you a quarter of a million Turkish lire. I would prefer a harder currency, but I am rather low in funds at the moment, and the money will come in very useful.'

Hawn made a rapid calculation: at the current rate of exchange, the man was asking for nearly five thousand pounds. It was not the sum that troubled Hawn, since it was not his money – it was Pol's. On the other hand, he did not know how high the Frenchman was prepared to bid – presumably happy to leave that to Hawn's judgement and discretion.

He decided to play for time. 'Mr Salak, I'd like to make one thing quite clear. Miss Admiral here and I have done a great deal of work on this story, and have already gathered a great deal of information – including names. If the stuff you sell us turns out to be trivial or inaccurate, we shall know.'

If Salak took this to be some kind of clumsy, ineffectual threat, he showed no sign of it. 'I shall expect the money before the banks close the day after tomorrow.'

Hawn decided to fall back on what initiative was left him. 'Before we finish this discussion, I want to be sure that you know what you're talking about. I mean no offence, but I only know you by reputation – and very long-distance at that. Let's have some more of your café gossip, and see if it ties in with what I already know.'

To his surprise, Salak nodded vigorously. 'I agree. I do so as a gesture of trust. There is no point in doing business together unless we trust each other.'

Hawn thought of remarking that the British had trusted Salak in the war – trusted him as their exclusive agent, while the Germans had also trusted him, to more advantage. But Salak gave the impression not only of being a man with whom it would be unwise to argue: it would be doubly unwise to dispute his good faith. He left Salak to continue:

'If you know anything about shipping, you will understand that the process was really remarkably simple. For every ten tankers that docked in Istanbul, there was usually one captain who could be bribed. The crews would be changed, the flag changed, even the name of the ship painted out during the night. After that it was a matter of supplying the captain with false papers and new Bills of Lading. The

Germans, as you know, were expert forgers. In Istanbul they had one of their best teams on the job.

'The new destination of the cargo was put down as another neutral country – usually Spain, but sometimes, to vary the procedure, we used Genoa, with its pipeline up to Switzerland. The British didn't at all like us using an Axis port, but there wasn't much they could do about it, since the Swiss were being so very co-operative.'

'Those bloody Swiss!' Anna cried : 'I bet they got a handsome cut from the Germans. All they're interested in is money.'

Salak nodded, with his hideous smile: 'They are not an attractive people. I rather like the comment by your Oscar Wilde – that they all look like waiters, including the mountains.'

They all laughed; the initial tension in the room had begun to dissipate.

Salak went on: 'Then after the Allied invasion of Italy in 1943 things became more difficult. After the invasion, the Germans moved into Italy in force, and Genoa was blockaded. The Swiss had to get their fuel through Sweden, via Germany. That was another source, but it was not in my territory so I do not know the details.

'The southern Italian ports – Bari, Salerno, Naples – had fallen to the Allies. The only one left was Trieste, but by late 1943 it was being crippled practically every night by Allied bombers. Then the Germans – and their Western accomplices – hit on a rather ingenious idea. They decided to use Venice. Not so extraordinary, when you think about it. But the Allies did not think about it – for them Venice was just another old Italian city, popular with tourists.

'They forgot that it had once been the greatest port in the world. It has a shallow lagoon but there is a modern harbour at Mestre, and when the bigger tankers couldn't get into the port, the Germans devised pipelines out to sea to pump the oil ashore. With Trieste bombed impotent, the British Navy concentrated few of their efforts in the Adriatic, so there was little difficulty of passage.

'But Venice had one other supreme advantage. The Allies,

with touching aestheticism, had made it a policy not to bomb historic Italian cities. So as far as we were concerned, Venice became an open port.'

'When you say "we", you mean the Germans?'

'Mr Hawn, do not try to trap me with semantic tricks. I was the citizen of a neutral country, remember. In the world's market-place, open to the highest bidder.'

'Did you have no special sympathies about which way the war was going?'

'Listen, good sir – the human animal has been going to war for thousands of years. You might as well ask me whether I supported the Romans or the Carthaginians. As a child I had seen my country humiliated after the First War – emasculated, with our great Ottoman Empire destroyed by the greed of the British and French. In the last war my only interest was that Turkey should survive – and that included me.

'But that must be sufficient. The rest will have to wait until your banker's order arrives. I do not ask from where, or from whom.' He stood up.

At the door up to the deck Hawn turned. 'Mr Salak, are you familiar with German?'

'I have a practical knowledge of it.'

'Have you read much German poetry? Goethe, for instance?'

'Sir, you flatter me. No, I have not read Goethe.'

Hawn paused. 'Mr Salak, someone died, or was killed, a few days ago, after leaving a note – two lines of Goethe's poetry. Now, you probably know that there's a rumour that all the files relating to this oil-smuggling disappeared at the end of the war. They were hidden. Would you perhaps know where?'

Salak smiled. 'When I have my quarter of a million lire, Mr Hawn, I will tell you all manner of things. Now, my driver is ready to take you back into Istanbul.'

At the head of the gangway, as though by way of a pre-arranged ceremony, Mustafa returned their shoes.

As before, they said little on the drive back. It was only when they were in the hotel that Anna turned to Hawn:

'You're not honestly thinking of paying that big crooked bastard a quarter of a million lire – however much that is? Just to buy a lot of tittle-tattle we won't be able to check out anyway, and perhaps a few names thrown in? – mostly of people who are probably dead now, and the others will just sue us for every penny we've got!'

'Why should we worry? We're not punting with our own money, remember. We're not even our own masters. Pol calls the tune. Pol wanted us to track down Salak and find out what he knows. And he's prepared to pay the bill at the end of it.'

Up in their room Hawn lay down on the bed and lifted the telephone. He remembered that they had not eaten yet, and were hungry. The hotel restaurant was closed, so he ordered sandwiches, and, for good measure, a bottle of whisky. He felt they both deserved it.

'But Salak's so horrible,' Anna persisted. 'I think he's perhaps the ugliest, most sinister man I've ever met. Did you notice how he hardly ever looked at me? He didn't even speak to me, until I tried to bawl him out, and then he just treated me like an hysterical child. He's obviously a misogynist.'

'Salak's as queer as a three-legged snake. Like a lot of Turks. Disciples of Sodom and de Sade.' He smiled at her from the bed. She was pacing the room like a hungry cat.

'Have you considered,' she said, 'that if he thinks we've already unearthed something really compromising about him, he may turn really nasty? As he said, Istanbul isn't London. He may just be playing us along, pretending to want that quarter of a million.'

'He'll take the money if it's offered him – after all, why shouldn't he? And he'll give us something in return. I don't know much about the Turkish character, but I know they're a very proud people, and they put great store on honouring their word. Salak said as much. If we don't try and cross him, I don't think he'll cross us – or worse.'

There was a knock on the door, and the whisky and sandwiches were brought in. When he had poured a glass for each of them, Anna said: 'Tom, what is all this stuff about poetry by Goethe?'

' "Little birds are silent in the wood by the lake – soon you will be silent too." Mönch didn't strike me as a particularly humorous man – or frivolous. He wrote those lines for a purpose – to tell us something. A lake by some woods where birds no longer sing. Sounds German enough, doesn't it? And a quiet lake would be a good place to dump a box of documents.'

'And you propose dragging every lake in Europe?'

'The trouble with you, angel, you're too practical. We get a lead – a bloody obscure one, I agree – but I just thought I'd try it on Salak to see his reaction. He might come up with something – you never know.

'Now, let's continue this discussion in bed, before we've drunk too much.'

'I want to drink. I want to drink myself silly.' But she was already pulling her dress up over her head.

Next morning he walked up to the American Express offices, in the shopping arcade under the Intercontinental Hotel, on Taksim Square. Anna, in a rare moment of vanity, had gone to try and get her hair done. They were to meet back at the hotel at twelve.

Hawn sent a terse telegram to the enigmatic PO number in Annecy, demanding the immediate transfer of twelve thousand US dollars, to be cabled immediately to his name and passport number, c/o Amex, Istanbul. The sum was rather more than he had agreed with Salak, but he suspected that if things went well the old scoundrel might need the odd 'sweetener'.

He arrived back at the Pera Palace just after midday. Since his key was not on the rack, he assumed that Anna had already returned. He also noticed that the keen-eyed receptionist gave him a courtly nod, but avoided looking at him, almost as if embarrassed.

Hawn clanked up in the ancient lift, walked down the spacious mellow corridor and reached their room. The door was locked. He knocked, then called Anna's name. There was a pause; then the door was opened, but only a few inches. Anna stood facing him; she looked taut and pale. Behind her, in one of the armchairs, was the Austrian arch-bore Otto Dietrich. He nodded to Hawn, composed, benign.

Hawn looked at him in silence. 'Hello, Otto. You should have warned us you were coming.'

'I was perfectly prepared to wait.'

Hawn looked across at Anna. 'Did you invite him in?'

'He invited himself in. About a quarter of an hour ago. He'd been waiting down in the lobby.' Her voice was not quite steady.

Hawn turned back to Dietrich. 'So just what the hell are you doing here? I give you exactly two minutes to explain, or I shall call downstairs and have you thrown out.'

'I must advise you to leave the telephone alone. Nobody wants trouble. All I want is to talk to you, Mr Hawn. Or, to be more exact, I have a friend who wants to talk to you. Would you agree to accompany me to the Hilton?'

'Supposing I'm busy?'

'Then I would suggest that you postpone what business you have.'

'Is that an order?'

The Austrian folded his hands in his lap, like two plump napkins. 'I had hoped that that would not be necessary. My friend is most interested to meet you. I would advise that you accept his invitation.'

'If he's that keen, why didn't he come here with you? Sorry, Otto, I'm going to call reception. Unless you prefer to leave of your own accord?'

Otto Dietrich's dull bespectacled face had a pained expression. 'Mr Hawn, please. Please try to be more co-operative.'

'Not until I know what this is all about. Who is this friend of yours?'

'I would prefer that you met him first. I have to maintain a certain discretion.'

Hawn looked again at Anna. 'What do you think, angel?'

Her voice was small and hushed: 'Tom, get rid of him.'

'Has he threatened you?'

'I don't like him. Get him out of here. Please!'

Dietrich made a little clucking noise with his tongue. 'Mr Hawn, the young lady is not being very polite. The other day, during our most pleasant excursion, I had thought you such a charming pair.'

'Otto, I'm touched. I'm also puzzled. As I said, what's so special about your friend that he couldn't have sent a note over, or just telephoned – instead of sending an unlikely chaperon like you?'

The Austrian nodded. 'Perhaps he should have done. But then he could not have been sure that you would have accepted. And my friend is most insistent. He has a very tight schedule. He wants to see you today – now, at once.'

'Supposing we say no?'

'I do hope you will not. I so dislike scenes.'

Hawn nodded towards Anna. 'Does your friend want to see Miss Admiral as well?'

'He wishes to see you both.'

Hawn stood thinking for a moment, then turned to Anna: 'Let's see what this gentleman wants. The Hilton's a civilized place. The worst than can happen to us is to get pitched out of a window on the seventeenth floor.'

Dietrich smiled and stood up. 'I am so happy that you are being sensible. I have a car waiting downstairs. Taxis are impossible in Istanbul.'

They left, with Dietrich walking several paces behind them. In the lobby the receptionist pretended not to notice them. Hawn wondered how soon Salak would hear of this encounter.

It was a fifteen minute drive up the edge of the Bosphorus, where the Hilton stood like a freshly polished headstone with a commanding view of the city. They entered in the same formation, although Hawn sensed that Dietrich had become less at ease: when the lift did not arrive at once, he grew uncharacteristically irritable.

They rode up to the twelfth floor. Dietrich knocked gently at a door at the end of the corridor. It was opened by a man in a grey flannel suit and a short executive haircut. He held the door open, without a word.

It was a large, two-roomed suite, with the appearance more of an office: telex, several telephones, recording machine, a lot of papers and documents littered about on tables and desks. In an armchair in the centre of the room sat the American, Don Robak; his thatch of grey-blond hair looked even more rumpled than last time. He was in his shirtsleeves and smelt of aftershave. He did not rise or shake hands.

'Sit down, Mr Hawn, Miss Admiral. We've all met before, haven't we?'

Hawn and Anna sat down opposite him.

'But I didn't think we'd meet again so soon, Mr Hawn.'

'It's a small world, Mr Robak – from the Gritti, Venice to the Hilton, Istanbul. Where next, one wonders. The Hotel of the Heavenly Flowers, Peking?'

'I'll come to the point. I'm a busy man. I don't like wasting my time or anyone else's. When we met in Venice you were talking about some crazy idea about ABCO having traded with the Nazis. I didn't take you entirely seriously. I don't have much respect for newspapermen – in my experience they're either lazy or drunk, or both, and even when they do get hold of a good story, they usually screw it up. But you seem to be rather more persistent. You obviously not only believe this theory of yours, but you're prepared to invest time and money in following it up.

'Now ABCO's a big organization and it can look after itself. But like all big organizations it has an image to protect. We get a certain amount of stick from time to time – usually from the eco-mob, when there's a spillage – and lately we've had to lie down and stick our tongues up a few Arab arses, but on the whole we keep our noses clean.

'But that doesn't mean that we can afford to have guys like you running round Europe spreading dirty stories about us. Unsubstantiated stories. Vicious, baseless lies. 'Course, if you tried to print anything, we'd have our lawyers on to you before the ink was dry. But by that time some of the dirt might have smudged off. You follow me?'

Hawn took his time answering : 'I think I get the general

drift of things. You're warning me off. But you're doing it in a pretty clumsy way. When we met at the Gritti, you pretty well laughed in my face and told me to get proof. Now, when I'm getting proof, you have me tailed by Otto here – who, by the way, is much too old for that sort of thing, surely? You may be warning me off, Robak. But you're also whetting my appetite.'

Robak's smooth square face showed about as much expression as the hotel furniture. 'Hawn, I don't often make mistakes. But it seems I made a mistake about you. Back in Venice I was interested to hear just how hard your theory was, and I decided it was pretty damn soft. I didn't think you'd go through with it. I was wrong.'

'How much do you know that I know?'

'That's why I have asked you up here. I want to find out. I know you've contacted a man called Salak. I don't know how you got on to him, but it must mean that you've been doing some pretty deep digging.'

'It wasn't so difficult.'

There was a pause. Robak put a cigarette in his mouth, without lighting it. 'Salak's a tricky and expensive man to deal with. He wouldn't talk to you for nothing. This must be costing you money. Who's backing you?'

'That's none of your business.'

'The hell it's not. When you start investing in a smear campaign against ABCO, it's all my business. You're not a rich man, are you? I never met a newspaperman who was.'

'I borrowed some money from a friend. Not an investment, just a loan,' Hawn lied. 'If Salak turns out to be that expensive, I'll just have to cut my losses and go back to London.'

'What's Salak already told you?'

Hawn thought for a moment: Robak was certainly no man's fool, and with the resources of ABCO behind him he could no doubt call on a highly sophisticated intelligence network. It was just a question of how much he already knew. Hawn's experience had taught him that in a touchy situation like this it was always better to tell as much of the truth as possible; and even the most experienced interrogator knows that every question he asks gives away what he doesn't know.

'He said he worked for both the British and Germans during the war. And that there was a certain amount of dirty play with tankers calling into Istanbul from the Middle East. It seems his job was fixing false Bills of Lading and bribing the captains. He didn't give me any details, and he didn't mention ABCO.'

'How much did he charge you for this information?'

'Nothing. He seemed to treat it as though it were common knowledge.'

There was a long silence. Robak took the unlit cigarette from his mouth, tossed it away, shook out another, which this time he lit. 'All crap. The same sort of crap you were shooting me at the Gritti. But I'll give you a useful tip. Salak's a hard and dangerous man. He swings a lot o' lead in this city – on both sides of the fence. People who cross him don't usually get the chance to apologize.

'And I'll give you another tip. The America-Britannic Consortium doesn't like being crossed either. Our methods are rather more subtle – and they're usually a good deal more effective. If you can persuade Salak – if you haven't done so already – to give you facts and figures, you might find us on your back. And when that happens, you're in trouble. Both of you. Keep out of this, Hawn.' He looked at Anna. 'Keep out of it, if only for her sake. You're a couple of kids playing with a rattler. Not a toy,' he added, smiling : 'The kind that bites.'

'Are you ordering us out of Istanbul?'

'That would be the most sensible thing for you to do.'

'And supposing we want to stay and see the sights?'

'I understood you saw most of the sights the other day with Herr Dietrich here? But just as you like. Only remember this. If you contact, or make any attempt to contact Salak, I shall know about it. He may have a pretty good organization here, but so have I.'

Otto Dietrich yawned. Hawn glanced at him, then back at Robak. 'I must say, it's the first time I've heard of a senior oil executive running his own Secret Service. Do the stockholders know about this?'

'You're green, Hawn. We have a lot of interests and a lot of secrets to protect. We not only have to protect ourselves against our business rivals – we have OPEC and the whole darned Middle East and Iranian fuck-up to contend with. But now we also get people like you. Or does that make you sound too important? Well, let's just say that people like you are worms in the woodwork. If necessary they have to be got rid of.' He stood up. 'I've done you at least one favour, Hawn. I've given it to you straight. Just don't run yourself and your girl dead into the ground.'

He called something and the man in the grey flannel suit opened the door from outside. As they left, again Robak just nodded. The door closed and they were alone in the corridor.

'Not a very nice man,' Anna said, as they stood waiting for the lift. 'Did you take him seriously? Senior oil executives don't usually behave like that, do they?'

'I rather suspect some of them do.' The lift arrived; it was empty.

'He was trying to scare us, Anna. He's probably scared himself. He made a bad mistake in laying it on about Salak. He obviously knows that Salak is a fund of information, and he's terrified that he'll give it to us. Robak's just a cog in a huge organization, and it's my guess he's been delegated to kill this story. If he doesn't he's in for the chop.'

They reached the lobby. 'Tom, do you think he's bluffing?'

'Not altogether. Only he'll need a lot more to go on before he takes really drastic action. What worries me is the efficiency of his intelligence sources. He's obviously having us thoroughly covered while we're here, which is going to make it bloody difficult to contact Salak again without ABCO knowing.'

'You realize, of course, that we're in the classic squeeze – to use the poker expression? I've never asked you this before, angel. How brave are you?'

Her spoonful of crusty yoghourt stopped halfway to her mouth. 'I don't know. Not very, I don't think. I hope I've done all right so far?'

'So far the going's been fairly smooth – except for young French, which you weren't involved in, and which may have nothing to do with this business anyway – and that little trouble with the Spanish police.' He smiled. They were at a pavement-table outside a small restaurant near the Covered Bazaar. The crowds made it easy for them to be observed, which did not worry Hawn. He had chosen the place for this very reason.

'But now that we've run into Salak, the stakes have got rather higher. Salak's offered us a deal, and it's probably already too late to go back on it. But while Salak may have a strong arm, I doubt it extends far outside Istanbul – whereas ABCO's certainly does.'

She took another spoonful of yoghourt. An old-fashioned hippy with a guitar sat watching them both lazily from a nearby table. He was eating bread and honey. She said: 'You're not suggesting we run out, are you? Like Salak first threatened to do to us – put us on the next plane?'

'I haven't suggested anything. I was just presenting the facts. Because you're in this as deep as I am – don't forget that. You came in at the very beginning. And if I go down, you go down with me.

'The real point is, the story's so obviously true. The files, statistics, Shanklin and Frisby, Mönch and Salak – Sweden, Switzerland, Turkey, even Venice. It all hangs too well together. Otherwise why are ABCO getting so worried? Just what are they frightened of?'

The waiter had banged down two plates of blackened shish-kebab, and for a moment they sat picking at the meat in silence. The hippy strummed the first three notes of a tune, then seemed to give up. Across the street, at the corner of a blind alley, an old Negro sat against the wall: gaunt and blue-black, before him a shabby carpet on which were spread carved wooden artefacts – effigies, tribal trophies, symbols of the power of darkness? What assiduous tourist, Hawn wondered, would visit Istanbul to haggle over the obscure relics of Black Africa? For that matter, what lone journalist and his innocent girlfriend would travel here, to take on a known criminal like Salak and the whole might of ABCO?

'I think I know what they're scared of,' Anna said at last. 'We know the Nazis got their oil from the West. We know that ABCO was involved, and we've got a pretty good idea how it was done. But I'd give you good odds, Tom, that it wasn't just ABCO playing truant with the Nazis and finishing the war as rich men. I think it goes deeper than that – and a lot dirtier.'

Hawn had stopped eating. 'Could we be thinking along the same lines?'

'I think there may have been people high in the Allied Governments who were in on it. But we still have to prove it. In a box of documents, perhaps, hidden in a lonely lake? You're right, though, ABCO aren't worried just for themselves. As Robak said, they've got an image to protect – and they hire buffoons like Hamish Logan to protect it. But when things start getting hot for them, their methods become pretty unsophisticated. They believe in bullying people. That's how oil companies do business.'

'I should have thought the easiest way out for them would have been to try and buy us off.'

'Maybe they will. We might even finish up rich.'

Anna was thinking that they might just as easily finish up dead; but at this late stage she saw no point in saying so. She knew too well that once Tom Hawn had set his mind on something, he would go through with it, come hell or high water.


Having left Anna in the hotel, Hawn walked the short distance from the Pera Palace to the Intercontinental.

After waiting in a queue for ten minutes, he presented his passport at the bureau de change desk. It was received with instant reverence, even awe: a fussy little man in a black suit came out of the back and dealt with the transaction himself. It was not every day that an English tourist drew out a quarter of a million Turkish lire. By evening the news would be all round the Istanbul business community; Robak would know without having to leave his hotel suite.

Hawn returned again on foot, down the crowded street,

without hurrying, pausing every few minutes to glance into some shop window. By a quarter to five he was back at the Pera Palace. Anna was asleep. There had been no calls, no messages.

He let her sleep, and ordered a whisky. He drank it slowly, almost neat. He had a bath, put on a clean shirt, but deliberately wore the same trousers and jacket as before. It was out of idleness, rather than caution, or even cowardice, that at six o'clock he rang down to reception, asked for another whisky and for the times of the next planes out, to London or Paris. The last flight to London had already left, but there was one at eight to Paris, via Rome.

He was just asking the clerk to make a provisional booking for two seats, when the floor waiter arrived with his whisky. There was also an envelope, addressed to MISTER HAWN, in typed capitals. Inside, a sheet of plain buff paper, without heading or date. On it was typed: '1730 hours. Ferry Bogaz Iskelesi – Salacak Iskelesi.'

It took him a moment of studying the city map before he understood. He lifted the phone, cancelled his airline booking, woke Anna, and showed her the note, together with the map. Bogaz Iskelesi was the crossing point, at the end of the Galata Bridge, across the Bosphorus to Usküdar.

'There's no bloody way of warning Salak that Robak's on our tail. I've given them God knows how much opportunity to show themselves today, but I wasn't able to spot anyone – unless it was that hippy at lunch, or the African across the road, but they somehow didn't look as though they were on ABCO's payroll. But I still don't believe that at this stage Robak would be using team work. And Dietrich's blown his cover for a start.'

Anna yawned, still sleepy. 'I don't see what you're getting at.'

'Just that it's not far across the Bosphorus and I don't suppose the ferry is much more than a step-on step-off job. There'll be no cover there for anyone following us.'

'Perhaps that's why he's chosen it?'

'Perhaps. If Salak knew about Robak. But how could he?'

'He seems to know quite a lot about what goes on in

Istanbul.' She got up, wearing only her loose French knickers, and picked up her dress.

Hawn stared absently at the shape of her breasts as she leant down. 'If his idea is to meet us on the ferry and Robak is still tailing us, we're going to be in the shit. Salak could probably fix something for us – if only he knew.'

'Isn't there some way we can get a message to him?' She stood buttoning up her dress without putting on a bra. 'We could try going down to Kumkapi and finding that chemist shop.'

'There's not time. It takes nearly an hour to get there, and he'll have certainly left. Anyway, what about Robak? If he's still having us tailed, Salak's hardly going to thank us for leading them straight to his doorstep. That's no doubt why he's not made the rendezvous at his shop.'

'Which means you think he *does* know about Robak? Tom, you must make up your mind.'

'I'm trying to.' Hawn remembered the whisky which had come up with Salak's note, and took a grateful gulp of it. 'All I do know is that if we go through with this deal with Salak, we've got to play it by his rules. Otherwise, there's a plane at eight to Paris. We could still make it, if we hurried.'

'No. We talked this all over at lunch. We go on the ferry.'

A tepid rain was falling, and it was fast getting dark when the hotel car dropped them at the far end of the Galata Bridge, under the vaulted mass of the Yeni Camii Mosque. In the heavy stream of evening traffic it was impossible to know whether they had been followed or not.

There was a small crowd at the landing stage – local people, nearly all men, grubby-jowled, in shabby Western clothes, carrying bundles of luggage. Hawn and Anna were the only foreigners to buy tickets. The ferry itself was less decrepit than Hawn had expected: it was painted almost white, with a covered promenade deck and sundecks fore and aft, lined with sodden deckchairs. There was also an upholstered saloon and a bar.

They left punctually at 7.30. The Bosphorus was flat and calm under the asphalt sky. Hawn and Anna stood for a time on the promenade deck, watching the necklace of lights sliding away behind them; then the rain began to come down hard, splashing off the deck-boards and seeping into their shoes. They went inside to the bar, where a row of men were lined up drinking thimbles of black coffee.

Hawn ordered two rakis and carried them over to a table by the wall. On a bench opposite, a big man in an astrakhan hat and knee-high boots lay sprawled out with his face covered with a local newspaper, snoring above the pounding of the engines.

Hawn and Anna hardly spoke. There was between them a kind of tacit tension, a sense of uncertainty which inhibited conversation. No one approached them; no one forced their attentions upon them or bought them unsolicited drinks; and no one could sensibly arouse Hawn's suspicions, except perhaps the snoring man under the newspaper. But as the ferry began to draw into Usküdar, passing the tiny island with Leander's Tower, the man awoke and Hawn saw that he was clearly Turkish, with a heavy black moustache and bleary eyes. He was drunk.

It was still raining hard and quite dark now, as they tied to at the concrete jetty at Salacak Iskelesi. They both stayed where they were, waiting until most of the passengers had disembarked. They watched the big drunk haul himself up from the bench, his astrakhan hat askew, and cross the saloon in a shunting roll as though they were in a heavy sea. He disappeared with the rest of the passengers into the night.

Hawn and Anna were the last to leave, except for two old men and a tiny woman in black, bent almost double under a quilted rucksack. Outside there was no shelter from the rain, which had formed huge blistered pools all the way up the jetty to the little square with the massive rococo Fountain of Ahmed III, looking like a great pile of artistically-arranged bird droppings. Behind it loomed the dome and two minarets of a mosque, lost against the black sky.

A bus had collected most of the passengers. There was also a *dolmus*, or communal taxi, waiting to make up its full complement of five. Otherwise, apart from the small crowd waiting to board the ferry back to Istanbul, the place was deserted, with almost no lights. No private cars, no glare of approaching headlamps. A shed stood in one corner, which might be a café. Hawn and Anna turned up their collars and ran towards it.

Four tables were arranged along a bar wall under a single unshaded light. There was music from somewhere – a woman's shrill plaintive wail, muffled by the drumming of rain on the iron roof. Eventually a man appeared from the back, wiping his hands on his apron. Hawn ordered two rakis; there was nothing else to drink, except coffee.

Anna said at last, 'It's not like Salak to be late, is it? He gave the impression of being so efficient.'

There was a dull boom from outside, signalling that the ferry was about to leave. When the proprietor returned with their drinks, Hawn asked him, slowly and deliberately, when the last ferry was due to leave. No good, the man spoke no English. After a moment, he made a sign to them and disappeared again into the back of the café. He returned a couple of minutes later, followed by the big shuffling figure of the drunk who had been on the ferry.

The man was no longer wearing his astrakhan hat. His hair was cropped short and square, growing in a straight line across his low forehead. He gave a short bow, jerked out a chair and slumped down between them; then snapped his fingers at the proprietor, who nodded and withdrew. 'I speak English,' he said, looking at Hawn with a leaky squint. He tapped Hawn's glass. 'You drink raki, huh? Very good.'

'When does the last ferry leave for Istanbul?'

'No more ferry from Iskelesi. You must go to Usküdar Iskelesi.'

'I thought this was Usküdar,' Hawn said, and reached for his map of Istanbul. The man leant forward and peered at it as if it were some puzzle, and finally laid a black-rimmed thumb-nail on the edge of the map, showing the main port of Usküdar about a kilometre away.

'When does that ferry leave?'

The man turned, as the proprietor brought him a tumbler of the yellowish raki. He swallowed half of it, put it down on the map and leant forward on both elbows, breathing heavily. Hawn waited, then repeated the question. The man's eyes rose slowly, focusing with difficulty. Then he laughed. 'Why you come to Üsküdar? You want hotel?'

Hawn kept his voice steady, patient: 'We want to return to Istanbul. Is it possible to find a taxi?'

The big man sat very still; then he groped in his trouser pocket, produced a khaki handkerchief and noisily blew his nose. 'Why you not stay in Üsküdar? Tomorrow the sun. Beautiful place, Üsküdar.' He leant back and very deliberately spat a huge gob onto the floor between his feet. Hawn was aware of Anna sitting beside him, watching the man with uneasy disapproval.

Hawn wanted to consult her, but could not be sure how good the drunk's English really was. Again, the man seemed an unlikely candidate for one of Salak's henchmen – but then Salak might believe in doing business in unlikely ways. And if this *was* Salak's man, he would set the pace.

The pace he set was to finish his raki and yell for another. The only consolation was that he did not insist that they both join him. He drank three tumblers, one after the other, then grunted something, pushed back his chair, began to stand up, fell with a crash on his stomach, and lay still.

'We leave him where he is,' Hawn said. 'But we can't very well stay here. There must be a hotel somewhere.'

'I'd sooner we tried to go back to Istanbul. I don't like this place.' The man on the floor had begun to snore with a noise like a bath running out. 'It's not like our friend not to keep an appointment – especially when there's nearly five thousand pounds at stake. You're quite sure we took the right ferry?'

They studied the map again, which showed several dotted red lines curving out from the Galata bridge, across the Bosphorus, to join the Asian mainland at several points along the coast of Asia.

Hawn had unfolded the note in his pocket. 'Salacak Iskelesi – it's written here, and it was written up at the end of the jetty.'

'That *dolmus* should be back soon. Can't we take it to the main port?'

Hawn paused. 'This whole thing could be a set-up. Or a test to find out if we'll go through with it or not – and perhaps to see if we're followed.'

'Do you think we've been followed?' she said; and they both glanced down at the man on the floor.

'As I told you, I haven't spotted anyone all day. But that's only because I've been looking out for Westerners. I just assumed they wouldn't use a Turk. Because I was assuming that they were ABCO people.'

'But who else would follow us? Salak's men?' Hawn cut her short with a quick gesture, got up, went to the door and stared out at the spears of rain, returned to the table and swallowed the rest of his raki. 'If only there was somewhere else we could wait. It's like being in a rabbit-hutch, waiting for the snakes.'

At that moment they heard the clatter of a very old diesel motor. He sprang back to the door and saw the headlamps of a car swinging into the square. It was the *dolmus*. It drew up outside the café with a great splash, and the driver came in, wearing leggings and a dripping leather jacket. He shouted something, and the proprietor hurried from the back, stepping over the drunk, and handed the driver a glass of brandy. Hawn stood up and began to negotiate.

The driver said he was finished for the night and demanded an exorbitant sum to drive them to the Üsküdar port. Hawn was in no mood to argue about money. When he agreed to the sum, the man looked faintly disappointed, even contemptuous, as though he had challenged Hawn to an honourable contest and had been rebuffed.

Hawn paid for the rakis and they left. The drunk had not moved. Five minutes later they arrived at a well-lit square which led to the port, where there were already several boats waiting. One of them was the ferry for Istanbul.

Here, again, they saw no one who was obviously suspicious; a few minutes later the engine started. Hawn was relieved; it was not every day that he embarked on a blind date in a strange city, carrying the equivalent of nearly five thousand pounds in his pocket.

Despite the crowd of passengers and the persistent rain, they somehow managed to get a taxi outside the Galata landing-stage, and ten minutes later were back at the Pera Palace Hotel.

They had both had several strong drinks during the crossing, and Hawn was now inspired with a sense of reckless release, as well as an angry determination which was reinforced on learning that there were no messages at the desk.

They were both very wet, and Anna was for going up and having a bath and changing; but Hawn said, 'I want to get this thing sorted out – tonight. Right now. If Effendi Salak Esquire wants to play games with us, I want to know why.'

He knew that Salak had contacts in the hotel, but decided that things had now gone too far for it to be worthwhile being cautious or cunning. He asked the receptionist for a list of chemist shops in the Kumkapi district.

The clerk returned a moment later, showing no interest or surprise. There was an all-night pharmacy on the Ordu Caddesi, near Beyazit; and another in the heart of Kumkapi, at 13 Türkeli Caddesi. It was clear from the map, and the maze of streets in the Kumkapi area, that the latter must be the one. He asked the clerk what time the shop closed.

'Ten o'clock, sir.'

It was now 9.35. Hawn said, 'Get us a car – immediately. And I'll pay the driver double if he gets us to the Türkeli Caddesi by ten.'

The clerk looked doubtful. He lifted a phone, murmured something, and hung up. 'The car will be here at once, sir. But I do not guarantee that you will reach the Türkeli Caddesi by ten o'clock.'

'I don't know quite what we're trying to achieve,' Anna said, as they waited by the entrance. 'And even if we make it, we don't know that Salak will be there. Why don't we leave it until tomorrow, when we'll have more time? Why tonight?'

'Because I'm in the mood tonight.'

The driver was one they had not seen before – a smart young man driving a brand-new BMW. He made no comment when Hawn gave the address and spelt out the conditions; but as soon as they had pulled from the curb, Hawn knew that they had an excellent driver.

The traffic had thinned and the rain had almost stopped now. For the first ten minutes they made good time, as far as the Atatürk Bridge, dominated by the grim, green bronze statue of the founder of modern Turkey. And when they turned off the Atatürk Boulevard, they still had twelve minutes in hand.

Next they plunged into the narrow crowded labyrinth of Kumkapi, the horn bellowing impotently at the wobbling rumps of overladen mules and fat sauntering women with great loads on their heads. For several minutes they were stuck without moving at all. Hawn sat with his hands pressed together, his heart pounding with an enervated rage directed half at the impoverished crowds outside, half at that great granite-faced gangster, Imin Salak.

But an even more powerful emotion was one of compelling curiosity. Why should a mature old brigand like Salak turn his broken nose up at a quarter of a million lire? For it was quite possible that if his influence in the city was as wide as he claimed, he might well have heard that Hawn had drawn the money that very afternoon. And then, what was the explanation of that note, sending them on a futile expedition to Usküdar? It made no sense.

It was eight minutes past ten when they crawled into Türkeli Caddesi. The light was still on behind the green cross above Number 13. Hawn leapt out and tried the door, which was locked. There was a light on at the back of the shop. As Anna got out behind him, he banged on the glass door, then found the bell-push and gave a long ring.

A girl in a white coat came out of the back, peered at him, and waved him to go away. He signalled to her furiously, his finger still on the bell-push, and again pounded against the door. She came out at last, approaching slowly across the darkened shop; then stood behind the door examining them both through the glass with a hostile expression. Finally she turned the key and eased the door open.

Hawn had his shoulder against the glass, pushed her abruptly back and dragged Anna in after him. The girl was shouting at them as he hurried with Anna across the shop, down the narrow corridor lined with bottles, and reached the unlit staircase where he wasted a few seconds finding the switch.

At any moment he expected either Salak or the man in the white suit to bar his way. He still had Anna by the hand, squeezing it tightly, as he stumbled up the stairs into the long wooden corridor, which was pitch-dark except for a dim sliver of light under Salak's door.

He had taken only a couple of steps inside when Anna began to scream.

Salak stared down at them both with bulging, bloodshot eyes. His enormous face was distended, shapeless, the colour of an over-ripe plum, and his tongue lolled lewdly out, swollen and black. He was wearing yellow socks and no shoes, and his feet dangled a couple of feet above the floor. The wire noose had cut deep into his throat; his huge body dangled from one of the brazier-like lamps which hung by chains from the ceiling. There was a nasty smell in the room, and Hawn guessed, disgustedly, that at the moment of death the man had lost control of his sphincter.

Anna was still screaming, and there were noisy footsteps outside: then more screams as the girl from the shop appeared in the doorway.

Hawn, cold with shock, began to notice things. Salak's tight black suit was hitched up about his groin, where both his belt and fly-buttons were undone. On the floor below him, next to the pile of cushions, lay a car battery with two wires trailing off the terminals, each with a crocodile-clip at both ends. Spread around were four little brass cups, containing dregs of coffee, and two ashtrays stuffed with cigarette butts. There was no sign of Salak's pipe.

Further away, on the desk by the grandfather clock, were several sheets of paper and a gold pen. Salak, before dying, had evidently written something, or been about to write it.

What puzzled Hawn, after the initial shock, was the lack of disorder in the room. Salak had been a comparatively old man, but he must have been immensely strong: yet there was no trace of a struggle. Besides the neatness of the cups and ashtrays, the cushions still lay casually round the walls, some plumped up, others creased from people sitting in them. Had Salak been one of them – drinking coffee with his murderers, suspecting nothing? And how many had there been? Three, four – perhaps half a dozen? A whole gang of them – enough to hold the great wrestler down, and apply the electrodes to his genitals until he agreed to what they wanted? Then they had taken him, without a fight, pronounced sentence on him, and hanged him. It had been an execution, not a murder.

Only a few seconds had passed since they had entered the room. The girl from the shop was now crying uncontrollably. Hawn grabbed her by the wrist and smacked her twice, hard, across both cheeks. She gasped, then began to whimper. He said, 'Do you speak English?'

She jabbered inarticulately, trying to fight free of his grip.

'You speak English?' he said, and began to shake her.

'*Yok, yok*!' she cried; and Anna said, 'Leave her. She's hysterical.'

'She let in the killers. At least, she must have seen them. I want to know how many there were. And whether they were friends or accomplices of Salak.'

'For Christ's sake, Tom, leave that to the police. We don't want to get involved.'

'We're bloody involved already! The hotel clerk and the driver will both testify that we came here tonight looking for Salak and the police will want to know why. Anyway, let's get out of here!'

He had released the girl's wrist, and stood taking a last look at the big bloated body hanging in the middle of the room; then led the way back down the corridor to the stairs. The girl stumbled between them, sobbing and wailing in Turkish. Hawn walked back down the narrow passage, between the rows of bottles and phials, and out into the darkened shop. Two men were waiting for them. Badly-fitting suits, dark overcoats. He didn't have to be told what they were – it was a type you could smell half across the room.

One of them, a stout square-shouldered man, stepped forward and flashed a celluloid holder from his overcoat pocket. It was too dark to read the lettering. The man grunted, 'Police. You come, please.'

The second man, who was clearly the senior of the two – thin-faced, with grey cropped hair – stepped over and opened the door. He had a stiff military bearing, yet he moved swiftly, without appearing to hurry. It was then that something reacted in Hawn's metabolism: the combination of accumulated tension, too many rakis, the gruesome spectacle upstairs – all concentrated into a ball of mindless energy, like a bolt of electricity. He stepped back and grabbed one of the thick bottles on the shelves in the passage.

It was of brown glass with a glass stopper, and an ancient label on which was written some medical code. Even as he did so, the lucid part of his brain told him to go quietly – co-operate, tell everything, then endure the bureaucratic ritual of Istanbul police enquiries, with the sad hope that HM's Consulate would somehow intervene.

What he did instead was not just an act of panic, but of mild madness – the act of a rational man whose qualities of reasoning and self-control had totally jammed, as though seized by a cerebral cramp.

He drew the glass stopper and hurled the bottle at the first policeman. Instantly the shop was filled with the burning smell of ammonia aromatica. It hit the man just below the throat and crashed heavily on to the floor. The man stumbled back, choking, spluttering. At the same time Hawn saw the second man move. He moved fast, like a dancer. Hawn retreated a step back down the passage, grabbed blindly at another bottle. He was vaguely aware that Anna was shouting at him, but his mind was so closed that he could not understand a word she said.

The bottle hit the second man on the shoulder, and the next moment his thin face was splashed with dark indigo. Most of his overcoat, his trousers and shoes, had also turned a deep purplish blue. He hit Hawn somewhere on the neck, with a dull jarring pain that seemed to paralyse his whole body. Then the first man moved in, solid, square, his fists like big hairy hams. But they did not immediately knock him unconscious.

In an act of pitiful loyalty, Anna kicked one of the men and hit the other with her satchel-like handbag, several times, like a petulant child. They pushed her up against the counter and struck her twice, low down in the belly, and even in the darkened room Hawn saw her face go paper-white, as she crumpled on to her knees and began to vomit.

Hawn did not remember leaving the shop, or getting into the car outside. His first clear realization was driving down an open dual-carriageway, very fast, under strips of flood-lighting that flared into the car every few seconds. The thin man was driving – still stained an ineradicable blue – while Hawn and Anna sat squeezed up against the big policeman who, despite the fact that all the windows had been opened, gave off the pungent fumes of ammonia.

Hawn experienced a dangerous moment on the edge of hysteria. He wondered how their colleagues would receive them both – one dyed blue as if with woad, the other exuding his poisonous stench. Then he was aware that Anna was talking to him: 'Where are they taking us?'

'To jail. Or Police Headquarters.' He spoke as though it was of no real importance. He had seen a film once – about a young American who'd been picked up at Istanbul Airport carrying drugs. He had been driven to the main prison, which Hawn seemed to remember was somewhere outside the city.

With the return of full consciousness came a cold aching hangover – all aggression and self-confidence dissipated, leaving him dull, utterly apathetic. He noticed the girl from the shop sitting in the front passenger seat, and wondered what sort of witness she would make. And would they believe her – always supposing that they wanted to believe her? Salak had friends in the police, and they would want the case solved quickly. The girl alone could establish that Salak was dead when Hawn and Anna arrived.

And what had happened to their driver from the hotel? Would he come forward and corroborate the exact time that he had dropped his passengers at the chemist's? Hawn doubted it. He didn't suppose that the Turkish Police Force was the kind of outfit which invited the ready co-operation of the public.

He wondered, too, why Salak had been wearing no shoes. But he didn't suppose it was a detail which would worry anyone very much.

They were passing the airport now; Hawn stared out at the dark runways, at the swivelling light on the control-tower, and felt a weary despair. The idea of escape had not seriously occurred to him. They'd shoot them both down like dogs, and that would be the end of it. No awkward, un-answered questions, no rigged evidence at the trial. Perhaps that was the way they intended it, anyway.

Anna was quietly crying beside him. He experienced a moment of warped irritation that gave way almost at once to impotent rage. He yelled at the big plain-clothes man: 'Where are you taking us, you bastard?'

The man stared at him in the dark and said nothing.

'*Bastard!*' Hawn yelled again, but there was still not a flicker of reaction.

They had been driving for nearly forty minutes now, and were well outside the city: the floodlighting finished, but the road was still broad and fast, almost empty.

Hawn tried again to remember that film about the luck-less young American who had been driven straight to jail. He was sure the jail was nearer the city, not further away. And yet the further they drove, the more he felt the tiny flutter of hope. The car at least offered them a transitory hiatus between certainties – between the dangling corpse of Salak, and the clanging door of a stinking Turkish prison cell.

Now they were slowing down. The driver dipped the car's headlights; it was very dark. They pulled on to the soft verge and stopped; then the driver turned to the Turkish girl beside him and muttered something, at the same time leaning across her and opening the door on her side. She began to speak, very quickly, loudly, until the driver seized her by the arm and pushed her out. She was still dressed in her white coat, her face distraught and tear-stained, as she picked herself up from the grassy verge, shouting and weeping. The driver pulled the door closed and eased the car back on to the road.

Hawn was at first too confused to react. In any case, he knew it would be futile to seek an explanation – even if the two policemen spoke enough English, which he now doubted.

They drove for perhaps another ten miles, when the headlamps picked out the rear reflectors of a stationary car, parked in a lay-by a few hundred yards ahead. The driver slowed down again, but this time he flashed his lights three times, on high beam.

Hawn was sitting very straight, beginning to sweat, despite the cold damp slip-stream flowing through the car. He felt Anna reach for a handkerchief and wipe her eyes. The driver was pulling into the lay-by behind the other car. Hawn could just make out, under the dipped headlights, a wide dark-coloured American sedan, with what looked like smoked windows. It had a Geneva number plate.

The driver switched off the engine, and there was a moment of total silence. Then the door on the driver's side of the sedan opened. A man got out and came walking towards them. He was a big man, oddly, hilariously familiar: a man in an astrakhan hat and knee-high boots. Only this time he was sober.

When he had almost reached them, the policeman in the back opened the door and got out; and in the dead stillness Hawn heard them murmuring to each other. Then the man in the astrakhan hat leant down and said, in heavily accented French, 'You will both accompany me.' There was no trace of recognition in his voice or face, let alone a flicker of humour.

Hawn climbed out and helped Anna, who was still suffering from shock and pain. Outside, the man in the astrakhan hat nodded towards the American car. As Hawn passed the driver who had brought them from Istanbul, he tried to catch his eye : but the man sat rigid behind the wheel, the window closed, the blue stain showing livid under the headlamps, covering his grey-cropped hair and narrow military

face like a monstrous birthmark. His eyes stared ahead.
Almost a scholarly face, Hawn thought.

Together the three of them began to walk towards the
sedan. The air, after the lingering fumes of ammonia, was
fresh and cold and smelt of eucalyptus.

The man reached the car, opened the rear door and gestured them to get in. Anna entered first, with Hawn close
behind. It was very warm inside with a cloying stench of
perfume. Then, from an enormous shape in the corner,
came a peal of girlish laughter.

'Welcome, my friends! I hope you did not have too bad
a journey?'

Pol was plunged in a vicuna coat, holding a hip flask which
he offered them both. He was in good spirits. 'No doubt you
both require an explanation?' he said cheerfully.

Hawn was trying to think of an appropriate reply when
Anna said, 'I want to go to the lavatory.' Together they
waited while she got out and walked away under the eucalyptus trees. Hawn turned on Pol: 'They beat her up – you
know that? Your gorillas – your hand-chosen help. Is that
their idea of a bonus – beating up a girl? Or is that what
you call looking after us? Unique protection, *à la Charles
Pol.*'

'Mon cher,' the fat man laid a hand on Hawn's shoulder;
'do not be unreasonable. You undertook these inquiries of
your own free will. You were warned that there would be
risks, dangers, and you have encountered both. You cannot
now turn and blame me. What have I done? I have snatched
you from the scene of a very ugly murder in which you
might well have been implicated. And what chance do you
think you would have stood with them? How do you think
they would have received your little story – or rather, your
many stories? You should thank me, my friend.' And again
he offered Hawn the hip flask, while the man in the astrakhan
hat climbed into the driving seat.

Hawn drank deeply; it was brandy and tasted like the
best. 'We're not out of it yet, you know. We're still in Turkey.'

'The frontier is less than an hour away. Before dawn we

will be in Salonika. There your problems will be over.'

Hawn remembered that he still had his passport, from his visit to the American Express that afternoon; but he wasn't so sure about Anna. He had the impression that she hadn't collected her passport since leaving it at the hotel desk on that first morning, five days ago. He waited anxiously, peering out under the dark trees: through the smoked glass it was like looking into an unlit fish-tank. He did not see her until she had opened the door: her movements were stiff, as though suffering from cramp. He waited until she had tucked herself in beside him, then said, 'Have you got your passport?'

'It's back at the hotel.'

Pol answered, his voice soft and soothing through the warm dark car: 'Do not concern yourselves. Everything has been arranged.'

'What about the hotel – and our luggage?'

'That, too, is taken care of.' He patted Hawn's arm. 'You must trust me.' Then he gave what sounded like an order, in a heavy patois which Hawn did not understand. The headlamps flared on, the engine started with a powerful hum, as the car drew out into the road. Pol relaxed, and rubbed his fat little hands together. 'Our chauffeur is Monsieur Serge Rassini. I believe you have both already made his acquaintance? He is a native of Corsica, but has the advantage of looking like a Turk. He behaves like a Turk, too.'

'And who were our gallant "police" escort from Istanbul?'

'Ah, there you were privileged, mon cher! One of the gentlemen, until recently, was the most wanted man in France, until he turned informer. Now I protect him, like a son. The other – your driver – was a Lieutenant-Colonel of the Dixième Régiment Parachutiste. One of Massu's men, until I took him under my wing.'

Hawn felt warmed by the brandy, lulled by the swift smooth motion of the car. 'Why did you kill Salak?'

'Salak received the justice which he deserved,' Pol said, with gravity. 'His crimes were immense and he was lucky to have lived so long without receiving a bill for them. He paid tonight, in full.'

'You tortured him first,' Hawn said. 'Was that also part of the payment?'

'Salak had certain information which I wanted. Information which you want, too. But while you were prepared to pay *him*, and accept what you received in good faith, I preferred a simpler approach. I wanted to make sure that our friend Salak was telling the truth. The whole truth.' He patted the side of his vicuna coat; the heater was on and he had begun to sweat. 'I have it here – five pages, all beautifully hand-written by Monsieur Imin Salak himself.'

'Are we allowed to see these pages?'

'But certainly! When we get to Salonika – and you will have had your roles explained to you.'

'What was our role in Istanbul? To sniff out Salak, so that your boys could move in and deal with him in your own refined way?'

'You both have been invaluable,' Pol said, and passed the hip flask to Anna.

'How many men have you had working on us?' Hawn said.

'Enough. Enough to ensure that I knew your every movement in Istanbul from the moment you arrived. You see, my men have not only been chosen because they look conveniently Turkish – one of them even has Turkish blood – but because they are top operatives in the French underworld – mostly in the Marseille area – together with some senior ex-officers from the Secret Army, left over after Algeria. They do their job better than most policemen, I assure you!'

Hawn closed his eyes and nodded in the darkness. So Pol's elect troop of idealists, of Resistance heroes pledged to avenge their maimed and murdered comrades, were after all no more than a bunch of off-the-peg heavies and hitmen from the sump of the Riviera and the waterfront of Ajaccio, together with a 'respectable' corps of soured turncoats from two disastrous colonial wars, who still saw it as their abject duty to kill at a mere nod of command.

'Did you write the note from Salak – telling us to take the Usküdar ferry this evening?'

'Let us say that Salak wrote it, under my instructions.'

'So what was the point of sending us all the way to Üsküdar in that pissing rain?'

'Two points. I wanted to be absolutely sure that Salak had agreed to make a deal with you. If he hadn't, you wouldn't have gone on the trip so readily. But I had another, more important reason. You forget your little visit to a certain American gentleman who has been staying at the Istanbul Hilton. We know that you were brought to see him earlier today – under a certain duress, n'est-ce pas?'

'Go on,' Hawn said wearily. 'I suppose you've got the interview on tape?'

'That was not necessary, mon cher. You instead will provide me with the full account of your conversation with Monsieur Robak. No – my purpose in sending you to Üsküdar was to see how efficient this Monsieur Robak is. For it might amuse you to know that his employee, a certain Otto Dietrich, is also a full-time member of the BND – the Federal German Security Service.

'Now, you may well ask, what is a senior executive of the America-Britannic Consortium doing in the company of the West German secret police? And in Istanbul, of all places? I cannot give you the precise answer, although I can draw inferences. ABCO is anxious to cover its tracks in Turkey. And it follows that the organization will be even more anxious to cover them in Germany – for it is in Germany that the real truth lies. The truth that was buried there some time at the beginning of May 1945 – the complete documentation of a world-wide conspiracy, known as "Operation Bettina".

'However, I digress. In the event, you were not followed by Robak's men to Üsküdar. There is even a chance that they do not yet know of Salak's death. And that will be useful – it will give us time to breathe, to make plans.'

'Always assuming that we get over the frontier,' said Hawn. 'There was our driver from the hotel, remember. Then the girl from the shop whom your gorillas threw out of the car a few miles back. What sort of story do you think they're both going to tell the police? And Anna here hasn't even got a passport.'

Pol cooed happily in the dark, and fumbled under his mighty coat, from which he produced a pair of slim dark blue documents; then gave an order and the driver switched on the interior light. The two passports were neither new nor old. They had both been issued a year ago, in the married name of MARZIOU. Hawn's described him as JEAN-PAUL LAURENT MARZIOU, PROFESSION : PROFESSEUR D'ECOLE, NE 1938, REIMS. Anna was now YVETTE, NEE NALBE, and described as *Maitresse de Maison*.

The only items which were obviously new were the photographs. Hawn guessed that these had been taken with a zoom-lens some time in the last four days – probably while they were sightseeing, or sitting in a pavement café. The background had been shaded out, and the rest was bad enough to make a convincing passport photograph. Equally convincing was the recent messy stamp from Turkish Immigration at Yesilkoy Airport. There were also a number of other stamps from European Immigration, including one from Dover and another at Heathrow. Hawn realized that it was the first time he had ever seen a British entry-stamp.

Pol was sucking the tip of his thumb, watching them both with amusement. 'A beautiful job, *hein*? It was done by one of the most expert forgers in the Resistance. If he could deceive the Gestapo for five years, you can be sure he has no problem in deceiving the Turkish authorities.'

Hawn weighed the passport in his hand: it gave him an uncomfortable sense of distorted reality – like glimpsing the back of one's own head in a complex of mirrors. It would take time to get used to Monsieur Marziou, and his young wife, Yvette – to shedding a whole identity, and slipping into a new one, like changing one's clothes.

'And how long do we remain Monsieur and Madame Marziou?'

'As long as it remains convenient for you. And for me.' Pol patted Hawn's knee. 'You see how easily things can be arranged! You must not concern yourself so much, mon cher. Anyway, we will be at the frontier in a few minutes.'

They reached the border town of Edirne at 12.40 a.m. – just

two-and-a-half hours after Hawn and Anna had made their dreadful discovery above the chemist's shop.

It was a dark muddy town where the main road into Greece had been deliberately allowed to peter out into a pot-holed track, churned up by the endless procession of juggernauts rolling between Europe and the Middle East. There was a great row of them now, pulled up on the side of the road in front of two sheds which housed the Customs and Police. The big American sedan was the only private car.

A man in a dark uniform, in black gaiters and boots, with a machine-pistol, beckoned them forward. He looked casually at the number-plate, as the driver rolled down his window.

The rest of the police were busy negotiating bribes with the juggernaut drivers, and appeared to have little interest in a Swiss-registered car with French occupants. A second man with a machine-pistol glanced at the four French passports, hesitated, then glanced at the window of the shed, to where a man sat with his boots on the desk, his peaked cap pulled down over his eyes. The man outside shouted something and laughed. Inside the shed the man raised a hand, without otherwise stirring. The man outside turned, handed the passports back, and saluted.

The Greek frontier post was half a mile across desolate, uncultivated fields. Hawn watched the lights creep towards them; Anna sat very still beside him, her eyes staring out in front. Then Pol began to laugh. He was still laughing, when the Greek officials peered in through the smoked windows, and waved them on across the plain of Thrace.

Yugoslav Airlines Flight 268, from Salonika to Belgrade, was due to board in ten minutes. Pol had ordered another three ouzos. He was in an excellent mood – despite the paucity of Greek cooking – and his high spirits were infectious.

Hawn regarded this next stage of their odyssey with extreme misgiving. Until now, he and Anna had continued to operate as ostensibly free agents, even though their movements had been monitored by Pol, even manipulated by him.

But from now on they would be entirely Pol's creatures – their new clothes, new wallets, new luggage, air tickets to Belgrade and on to Frankfurt and Tempelhof, Berlin – all were ordained by Pol, as intractably as were their names and personal details written into their new passports.

Pol had been watching him carefully, obviously sensing his malaise. 'You are not happy, my friend?'

'You know I'm not. If I knew more – if I just knew where this information of Salak's is going to lead us.'

Pol spread his short arms expansively. 'But that is the whole point – the very thing we are hoping to discover! I cannot tell you what I do not know.'

The final call was going out, when Pol took his leave of them. 'Au revoir, mes amis. Until tomorrow night – at the Kempinski. And don't be late.'

'If we are,' Hawn said, 'it won't be our fault.'


The sharp grey sunshine cut through the copper-glazed windows of the restaurant café, which spread out across half the pavement of the Kurfürstendamm. Outside, the snow had stopped; traffic moved slowly, quietly.

Hawn and Anna had found a table from where they could see right up the Ku-damm to the Memorial Church, sticking up from the glaring neon like a burnt thumb. Next to them, at the same table, sat two stout women in plastic raincoats with fur collars, drinking mugs of chocolate. Hawn and Anna were having an early lunch, of white Bockwurst, beer and black coffee.

'Look, Tom! Over there!' Hawn was in time to see two tiny creatures disappear giggling into the back of the café. They both had frizzy ash-white hair, green mascara, blood-red lipstick, and each wore tall leather boots and steel-studded black leather bum-freezers. 'They must be girls?' Anna said.

Hawn stared. 'They can't be more than twelve years old?'

'I'd say nearer ten.'

Hawn finished his beer, called for the bill, and glanced back up the Ku-damm. A huge sign winked on and off against the heavy sky : 'BERLIN BLEIBT IMMER NOCH BERLIN !' Berlin Forever Remains Berlin.

Outside it was freezing, and for a moment they had to grab on to each other to avoid slipping on the packed slush. Hawn took his usual quick glance both ways. The BND would have at least one man, perhaps even a car; and Pol would probably have someone too – if only because Pol was a careful bastard, and liked to make sure that his hirelings and protégés did as they were told.

The crowds were dense and resolute, booted and fur-lined: the Berliners walked fast, he had noticed, with a dog-ged sense of purpose, as though each of them feared being late. A yellow truck crawled down the edge of the street, spraying sand on the frozen surface. They began to walk arm in arm up the street, reached their hotel and pushed through a heavy curtain, into the warm lobby mewing and tinkling with Muzak; a girl's sharp metal voice sounded from the bar. It was nearly three o'clock. Hawn stretched and winced. His neck and ribs still ached after the handiwork of Pol's 'most dangerous man in Europe', and he had slept badly; though Anna seemed to have recovered.

'I'm going to get a couple of hours' sleep. I'm done in.'

'Do you mind if I go out for a walk? I thought I might look at the city.'

'I'd rather you stayed here. If you go anywhere, I'd prefer to be with you.'

She smiled, crinkling up her eyes. 'Determined to play the knight in shining armour?'

'Just a sensible precaution. In Istanbul they decided to warn only me. Next time they may decide to do it the other way round – lean on you instead. Perhaps pick you up and hold you, just to make sure I behave myself.'

'Tom, love.' She turned and faced him in the middle of the lobby, putting both hands on his shoulders. 'Haven't you realized yet that whatever we decide to do, we're committed? You've just spelt it out yourself. Because even if ABCO let us go – on the assumption that we don't yet know quite enough to really damage them – there's always fat Charlie Pol. And you can be certain he'll look after me – make sure I'm not kidnapped.' She looked up at him, with a small crooked smile. 'Tom, what interests me is – why doesn't

ABCO, with its entire reputation at stake, just rub us out? Two French tourists murdered in Berlin – *poof!* – killed in a car accident, run over in the street. It'll take a bit of time to unravel the business of our real identity, but with ABCO's influence with the German police, I don't suppose anyone'll make too much fuss about that.'

He began to yawn, and clamped his jaws shut. 'You're asking me why we're still alive? Because ABCO don't yet know enough. They know we're on to something, and they must know we're not alone – that we've got powerful interests backing us and covering up for us, as well as murdering the vital witnesses, like Mönch and Salak, as soon as they cease to be useful. But as far as ABCO know, we're just the pathfinders – the pawns. Pol's pawns. And ABCO are no doubt far more interested in Pol than they are in us. For the moment they may be happy to let us run free – just to see how far the line leads, and how well they've covered their tracks and where the loose links are. It's when we come to the end of the line that we'll be in real danger.' The lift doors opened.

# CHAPTER SIX

# Go – between

*The only way to make sure that crime doesn't pay is to have
the government take it over and run it.*   ERNEST BEVIN

'All right, you go for your walk. If you don't come back . . .'
He shrugged dramatically. 'Well, if you don't come back,
I'll just go and meet Pol at the Kempinski at six and hope he
can set his organization on to finding you.' He stepped back
towards her. 'Anna, forget the walk. Come to bed.'

'No. You're far too tired. You look like a death's head –
you must get some sleep before we meet Pol.'

He took hold of her and kissed her on the lips and on the
forehead and behind her ear. 'Oh shit,' he whispered, 'I
hope this isn't the last time I do this. I don't want to lose
you, Anna. I don't want to lose you to anyone – least of all
to those bastards in ABCO.'

'You won't lose me,' she said, breaking free of him. 'I
can look after myself. Anyway, you're probably just as vulnerable in the hotel.'

'Thanks for the tip.' He watched her walk away and disappear through the revolving doors.

He woke suddenly, from a dreamless sleep. He couldn't think
where he was. The darkened chandelier, the dim shape of the
twenty-four-inch television set, the half-curtained windows
against the twilight which was already full of blinking
neon and the moving beams of traffic.

He must have dozed off again, because when he next
looked at his watch it was 5.32. He leapt up, turned on the
bedside light and glanced around. Anna was not there.

His first reaction was confusion. He didn't know whether

to be furious or scared. There was no time to take a shower; he doused his head in cold water, grabbed his trousers and shirt, and in the middle of pulling them on, rang down to the desk. There had been no messages for him, no word from Madame Marziou.

He now began to dress more slowly, feeling his rage turning against himself. It was his fault for letting her go on her little walkabout. She didn't even have a street-map – unless she'd had the sense to buy one on the way out. And she would be followed – that much was certain. They had both known it, when they had parted downstairs.

He must have been crazy to let her go! Or just dull with lack of sleep. Out there, alone, Anna would be as vulnerable as a child. A single bullet from a cruising car, or a manipulated skid against a blank wall. Or perhaps, after all, they would just want to hold her as a bargaining counter. It would be easy enough to have a car creep up beside her in the snow, the front door open, boxing her in with the rear door, then dragging her into the back. They were professionals – from whichever side they came – while Anna, for all her subdued ideological fervour, was an utter innocent.

Hawn preferred to think that if he had been with her it might have been different. Either they wouldn't have risked it, or he'd have spotted them in time and he would have been able to drag her into some doorway or down an alley where they couldn't follow.

But the hell with it, he hadn't been there. He'd been in bed asleep. He'd let her go on her own, and now there was less than fifteen minutes left before they were due to meet Pol at the Hotel Kempinski. It was only a couple of minutes' walk up the street, so he decided to wait in the lobby until 5.57.

He put on his boots and sweater, with his French raincoat over his arm; made sure he had his passport and new wallet, containing several hundred marks – Pol's most recent gift of pocket-money, in exchange for the vast sum in Turkish lire which Hawn had returned to him – and slipped out into the corridor. Both lifts were engaged, one coming up, the other going down. He waited next to the one coming up. His watch said 5.49. He had checked it that morning against the clock on the Pan-Am building, and again down in the lobby.

They were only on the fifth floor, but the lift seemed to take an interminable time. He felt his adrenalin beginning to rise again, and at the last moment stepped back to the right of the lift, pressing himself against the wall, his raincoat over his left arm, while his right hand groped in his pocket, wedging several one-mark pieces between his fingers, just below the knuckles. He heard the lift hum to a halt, the doors slide open, and a tall blond man stepped out carrying a black attaché case. He looked behind him, smiled and gave a little bow. 'Verzeihen Sie mir, gnädige Frau!' Anna stepped past him, with a little smile. She did not see Hawn until he had grabbed her wrist.

He waited until the man was out of earshot before he pulled her close to him. 'And just where the hell have you been?'

He saw she was flushed and slightly out of breath. He heard the lift doors begin to close, and jammed them with his foot. 'Get in. You can explain on the way down.' He pushed the ground-floor button.

'I'm terribly sorry, Tom. I went to the Tutankhamen Exhibition at the Charlottenburg Palace. Then I couldn't get a taxi, and I got on the wrong tram. I had to walk most of the way back.'

'You certainly managed to cut it pretty fine!' The hand in his pocket belatedly released the coins between his fingers. 'Got your passport?'

'Yes. I'm not making that mistake again.'

The lift stopped. They got out and began to walk towards the entrance. The lobby was surprisingly empty: it was the cocktail hour, the obligatory watering-time for all West Berliners, and only a few tourists and businessmen were busy at the desk. The receptionists ignored them both.

Hawn pushed Anna through the revolving door, and began to follow: then at the last moment stepped smartly back and bumped into a man behind him. He swung round, half inside the door, and pulled the man in after him; and kicked out with all his strength. Anna was in the street and the door had stopped moving. In the closed space there was a scream and the man stumbled and began to sink down on to the felt carpet.

He was wearing a fur hat and a long coat with a fur collar. The coat had protected his groin, so Hawn had gone for his kneecap. He brought both fists up, smashed one into the middle of the man's face, while he brought the other down in a chopping blow just behind his ear. The man slouched on to his knees, his gloved hands half covering his face, and Hawn felt a pang of shame as he remembered his victim had been wearing glasses. They now lay crunched on the carpet under Hawn's feet.

Blood was seeping down the leather fingers of the man's gloves, his fur hat had slid off his balding head and he had begun whimpering. Hawn checked quickly that there was no one near, grabbed the man under the arms and hauled him back onto his feet.

'Sorry, Otto. But I'm surprised at you. At least, I'm surprised at your organization. Using the same man twice, on a job like this. Surely they're not that short-staffed?'

'Ach, meine Nase!' The man gulped and peered at Hawn through his weeping eyes. His gloves were wet with blood and mucus, and drops of blood were falling on the floor.

'It was an accident, Herr Dietrich. You banged into the door. You have to be careful where you're going.' As he spoke, Hawn retrieved the broken spectacles and dragged the man into the street. One of his legs hung limp on the slushy pavement. Anna stood a few yards away, watching, perplexed. A few passers-by glanced at them, a few hesitated, but Hawn was now holding Dietrich up and seemed to be soothing him. 'A little accident – nothing serious,' Hawn told them.

An old woman stopped and said, 'Oh, the poor man – should I call a doctor?'

'He'll be all right – he just bumped his nose.' Hawn nodded reassuringly.

Otto Dietrich made no effort to contradict him; the last thing a BND man would want was to be the centre of a sordid punch-up with his quarry in broad daylight.

'What are you after, Otto? Working for your own people this time? Or still running errands for Mr Robak and his friends?'

'*Ach*, my leg!' the Austrian gasped. 'You have ruined my leg!'

'Tell me what you're doing here. Quick! Or I'll ruin your other leg.'

'I am under no obligation to answer your questions,' Otto Dietrich said, with a certain dignity, as he tried to wipe his burst nose with the back of his glove. 'Find me a taxi.'

Hawn propped him against the wall, and with one hand managed to get the man's broken spectacles back on his face; but at the last moment one of the lenses fell out. 'Anna,' he called, 'try and get a taxi. If you can't, get the hotel to call one. But hurry!' He turned to Dietrich and said softly, 'You won't hold this against me, will you, Otto? All in a day's work. When do you next report to Herr Robak?'

'I am now with my official duties,' the Austrian said, as the other lens dropped out of his spectacles.

'Do your official duties include reporting to Robak? Come on, let's have it!' Hawn's free hand had crept up to Dietrich's face and his thumb reached the place where the man's nostrils had been. 'Do you want me to give your nose a friendly little squeeze? Or perhaps my foot might slip and kick your knee again. Just a little tap to jog your memory.' He raised his left foot and let it dangle.

The man was breathing heavily, like an asthmatic. 'No, please. You are mistaken. I had certain duties in Istanbul for Mr Robak. Here, I am again official, with the police.'

'Listen, Otto,' – Hawn was now whispering to him – 'if you make any complaint about this incident, the story about you and Robak and Istanbul will be in every German newspaper tomorrow morning. I might even tie you in with the murder of Imin Salak – which I am sure you know all about. German readers will, no doubt, be interested to know the extent of the activities of their Secret Service.' He broke off, as Anna came running up:

'I've got a taxi – it's waiting at the corner.'

'Right. Give me a hand with him.'

Together the three of them made an ungainly trio as they dragged the limping, hobbling BND man along the pavement to the waiting taxi. Anna had retrieved his hat and put it back on his bald head, then found a tissue to wipe some of the mess from his face. Hawn pushed him into the taxi and left him to give the address: then stepped back and looked at his watch. It was 6.17. He took Anna's arm and began to run with her up the street.

The interior of the Hotel Kempinski was instantly expensive and ultra-modern – large, warm, carpets soft and deep; not crowded, but busy – busy with the consuming effort of pleasure: the best cocktails teased up by Europe's top barmen, and enjoyed by men in thousand – D-mark suits and enamelled girls stiff with jewellery and deep-frozen expressions, as though fearful that their make-up might crack.

Pol was not in any of the armchairs in the foyer; nor was he in any of the several bars or the restaurant. Hawn left Anna in a corner and went to Reception, where the clerk handed him a little envelope with flowers at the corner, like a birthday greeting. Inside was a sheet of the hotel writing paper, with across it a rounded scrawl: 'I am enjoying a massage. Join me. C.'

Hawn found the sauna and massage parlours at the side of the main hall, near a row of muttering telex machines. He paid a plump handsome woman 15 D-marks, with five extra for the towels; undressed in a steel cubicle with a locker which opened with a key on a loop which he hung round his neck; locked his French passport inside, then passed down a slippery white corridor with a sweet, hygienic smell, somewhere between honey and wet wool. The woman pointed to a door at the far end.

From all round, through the steamy whiteness, came the chaotic rhythm of pounding and kneading and smacking of flesh. The cubicle at the end was locked. Hawn had to identify himself as Monsieur Marziou, before a blonde girl with long legs under a short white coat let him in.

Pol lay on his stomach on the marble slab. A steep wall of towel covered his mountainous buttocks, while the girl returned briskly to the hopeless task of working away at his shoulders and back, both gleaming like sides of ham. He had the appearance of a grossly inflated baby on whom someone had maliciously painted a whirligig of hair and a short pointed beard. His crimson lips were parted, his eyes closed, and sweat crawled down every runnel of fat, as if from a melting snowman.

'Charles?'

'You are very late. You had my instructions.'

'I can explain.'

Pol gave a belly-chuckle. He said something to the girl, who nodded and climbed off him – looking rather relieved, Hawn thought. 'Lock the door,' Pol said, when she had gone. He waited until Hawn was lying beside him, then opened one eye and blinked painfully through the sweat. 'We will speak in French, but keep your voice down. This is a very cosmopolitan city.' As he spoke, he rolled over on to his side, supporting his huge head on his elbow, while his breasts hung down in two soft pendants of flesh with a deep cleavage between them, from which there was a steady trickle on to the tiles below. 'So, mon cher Monsieur Marziou! What have you to report?'

Hawn told him about his meeting with Dietrich. Pol listened, shaking with quiet laughter. 'I hope you were not too unkind to the poor old gentleman!'

'How the hell could Robak have got on to us that fast?'

'Ah, you are dealing with a large organization – one that is used to moving fast. The important thing is to move still faster! Which is what you will be doing later tonight. You both have your passports? Excellent! Then you will be ready to leave, when we have finished our little talk. I regret that I cannot give you dinner, but it is important that we are not seen together.'

'So where are you planning to send us next?'

'It depends. You are the one, mon cher, who goes forward and finds which doors are open and which are closed – who makes the first footprints. I merely follow, and try to make sure that no harm comes to you.'

Hawn took a deep breath, gasping for oxygen. The towel

wrapped round his waist was already soaking with his sweat. He eased himself up on to one elbow, so as to get a more commanding look at Pol.

The Frenchman shifted his belly with a sucking sound, like a stopper being pulled out of a bottle. 'Tonight I have arranged, on your last evening in West Berlin, that you should meet someone rather interesting. Rather superior to these policemen and gangsters who have been pestering you recently. Have you ever heard of a Doktor Wohl – Oskar Wohl?'

'Might be familiar,' Hawn said carefully; 'I can't place him off-hand.'

'He is what is known, in the terminology of East-West relations, as one of the 'Grey Men'. His precise status is difficult to define. By profession he is a qualified lawyer who practises in East Germany. He lives just outside the city boundaries, in a big luxurious house on the Grunau Lake. Runs the latest model of Mercedes, which he changes every year, and has apparently unlimited access to the West. He is a sort of unofficial Mister Fixit between the Russians and the Americans. If Moscow, or one of the Warsaw Pact countries, wants to feed some information to the West, or fly a kite to test Western reactions, they use Wohl.

'You remember in 1963, when there was a phoney story put round the world that Khruschev had resigned or been sacked? The story was said to have originated in Tokyo, of all places. In fact, it originated with the main Japanese agency here in Berlin. The Moscow caucus were just testing the water, before they finally gave old Nikita the boot a year later. The man who planted the story was Wohl.

'But his journalistic activities are something of a sideline. His main function — where he comes into the international eye – is as one of those East German lawyers who fixes up exchanges between Soviet spies being held in the West, and Western ones, so-called, being held by the Russians. Wohl's exact brief and methods of action are not quite clear. But his orders certainly come from the top in Moscow, and he also has access to the highest authorities in the West.

'Obviously he is accused of being an agent of Soviet Security. Some sources insist that he is a full colonel in the KGB. This he vigorously denies, and has even threatened to sue one of your English newspapers for saying so. He prefers to be thought of as an international lawyer with a special interest in East-West relations. In any case, you will shortly have the privilege of meeting the gentleman, when you will no doubt draw your own conclusions. He is not a particularly admirable man, although I hear he has great charm. In any event, you must trust him. You have no alternative.'

'I can always refuse to meet him.'

Pol dabbed at his goatee beard, which was pouring sweat like a tap. 'You are a newspaperman, Monsieur Hawn. You will not refuse. Besides, what harm can there be in meeting a legitimate German citizen on German soil? It is not something which should concern you.'

'It concerns me in so far as it concerns this whole story. What's he got to do with ABCO? Or with Mönch? Or Salak, perhaps?'

Pol had cocked his head and was grinning at him mischievously. 'Or with Doktor Alan Reiss, who has an important job with the German Democratic Republic's petrochemical industry? Born Alan Rice, of Anglo-German parents, and whose activities during the war are best not discussed. You know the name, of course?'

'Of course.' It was almost too casual, too obvious: and Pol's appearance, through the haze of steam, tended to render it absurd.

'So you see, mon cher! You see how the circle seems to be getting smaller? It is no coincidence. A grand conspiracy on this scale is very much like those merry-go-rounds one used to know as a child, where one had to try and step on to the revolving rim without being thrown off. It was very difficult, but once one had managed to get aboard and move towards the centre, it became easier. The trick, of course, was that the wheel was moving much more slowly at the centre. That is a rough but nonetheless accurate analogy for what we have both been doing – although each of us climbed aboard the wheel at opposite sides. But once we had learnt of the magic name, Doktor Reiss, then immediately the dimensions of the whole conspiracy shrank. You see, the success of "Operation Bettina" lay not only in its secrecy, but in its very compactness. It operated more like a club than a government agency.'

'It seems to have been a pretty big club – with half its members being Doktors. And once one started digging, an awful lot of people seemed to know about it. The first person to mention Reiss's name to me got his throat cut a few days later. A little matter that still hasn't been cleared up.

'Then there's a Monsieur Toby Shanklin – that high-flying trouble-shooter for ABCO who actually knew Rice in Central America in the last years of the war, and for whom all references, for some reason, have been either withheld or excised from the Public Record Office in London.

'Then we have Salak. I suppose Rice was one of the names on Salak's list?'

Pol shifted his immense weight and grunted, but made no reply.

'Salak,' Hawn continued, 'seems to have been a pretty easy lead. My old journalist colleague from wartime Intelligence put me on to him. He also put me on to Mönch, and Mönch knew about Salak, too. As I said, it all seems a bit too obvious – almost as though someone had left us a paperchase to follow.'

Pol was watching him through sleepy eyes. 'I am not sure, mon cher, that I fully understand what you are implying.'

'Let me put it another way. All these people I've met have been pretty accessible. They've been accessible for a long time. What I find odd is why no one had got on to them earlier. In short, why hasn't the whole story been blown wide open years ago?'

Carefully, and with skill, Pol manoeuvred himself over on to his back, keeping the towel tucked tightly around him to cover whatever pitiful obscenity sprouted from his groin. He settled his great head on his arms.

'Mon cher, as I said, it is all a matter of perspective – of the grand perspective. Rice was a scientist. Mönch was an administrator. Rice was technically a traitor, Mönch technically a war criminal. There is nothing interesting about that. There were hundreds of traitors, hundreds of thousands of war criminals. Some were caught, some were not. And the ones who got away usually preferred to keep to themselves. Few of them spill the beans – if they have any to spill – unless they have a special inducement to do so.

'In Mönch's case, there was a double incentive. You offered him money, with which he needed to make a quick getaway – and the second incentive was Jacques. Mönch may even have thought that by giving you information – assuming he thought you were connected with Jacques – he would be buying himself time, or what time was left to him. But of course, you had the supreme advantage – you had been blessed with your overall theory – a masterful inspiration, a flight of fancy, perhaps, but nothing more.

'However, I am straying from the point. You mentioned that unhappy Englishman, Monsieur French? There you had a stroke of luck – a stroke that may have cost the gentleman his life. He happened to know about Rice's activities in Central America during the war. He also knew about this man Shanklin. He may have known a lot more.'

'If they killed French, why haven't they killed me and Anna? Or even you?'

'Ah, that is one of the riddles that must be solved – although I have my theories.'

'Which are?'

Pol closed his eyes and belched. 'Mon cher, your conduct in this affair has so far been a model of tact and restraint. You have not posed awkward questions, and you have not obstinately sought answers to every problem. You have preferred to pursue events at their own pace, to wait and see how the story unfolds. So please, do not start asking me to divulge my theories – unless I choose to do so, of my own accord. Continue to see yourself as a soldier in the front line, with me as your commanding officer – you do not seek his answer to all your questions.

'However, I will put your mind at rest on one point. Salak. You are worried that you got on to him too easily. But you forget that Imin Salak was a big wheel in the Istanbul underworld. He was a big wheel during the war. The British made the mistake of trusting him, and he sold out to the

Germans. Istanbul in those days was like Lisbon – what one might call a social centre for high-life espionage. Anyone involved in Intelligence work in the Middle East – like your old journalist friend – would have heard of Salak. It would have been highly suspicious if he hadn't.

'The fact that he'd also heard of Mönch is because you exposed your theory to him and asked him specifically about the German fuel industry. Mönch had been a powerful man in that industry, and your friend – having specialized, as you say, in economic warfare – knew all about him, too. So you see, you do not have to worry about coincidences there. Again it is the matter of perspective. Unless you have the *theory* – the overall picture in your mind – that the Western powers, through ABCO, were supplying the Nazis with their fuel – the random names of Rice and Mönch and Salak have no particular significance. Have I put your mind at rest?'

'Not quite. Rice's presence in East Germany needs some explaining. Presumably he fled there after the war to avoid arrest by the British? And the Russians, not giving a damn about the British and their ideas of high treason, were only too happy to put him to work again as a top scientist? But how much do the Russians really know? And how much has Rice chosen to tell them? The Communists would surely love to expose the biggest Capitalist multi-national enterprise as a gang of master war criminals?'

'Yes, I have thought about that, too. But the Communists are very devious. They are also very pragmatic and consistent – when it suits their aims. One of the ironies of our time is that the Soviet Union, and the whole Eastern Bloc, depends a great deal on the stability, even prosperity, of the Western economy. Until now they have been short of oil – and it may well be that the hierarchy decided that it was not in their interests to try to topple the major Western oil consortium.

'Anyway, supposing Rice did tell them all? It would still have been one man's word against the collective voice of ABCO. It would also not only be a word emanating from behind the Iron Curtain, but that of a traitor who had worked for the Nazis, and one who was now lending his voice to the most crude Communist propaganda. Surely not a very edifying or convincing witness?'

'Which suggests that we don't have much hope of his talking to us?'

'That is something we shall see. It must depend on many possibilities which we cannot consider now. For it is time I gave you your instructions. Do you know Berlin? No – then listen carefully. But you must remember it – write nothing down.

'When you leave here you will walk up the Ku-damm, past the Gedäckniskirche to the Europa Centre opposite the Zoo. There you will take a number forty-seven tram up the Hardenbergstrasse to the Ernst-Reuter-Platz. There you will take the U-Bahn to the Charlottenburg station. As you leave the station, you will see on your right a bridge under the autobahn ringroad. You will pass under this bridge and the third street on your left is called Tiefengasse. Fifty metres down on the left is a bar called the "Chéri". Go in and order a drink. It should be nearly 8.15. At that time Wohl will introduce himself.'

'Wouldn't it be easier to get a taxi?'

'I have asked you to follow my instructions.'

'Do you anticipate that we will be followed?'

'Of course. It will be useless to evade them. At this stage they will have their best men on the job, probably using several cars, so a taxi would avail you nothing.'

'So what's the purpose of the tram and the U-Bahn? Or is the idea to give them the impression that I'm *trying* to lose them?'

Pol nodded. 'That is approximately the idea. You have reached a point in the game where you must act the part. If you take a taxi, and act as though you had nothing to fear, they would lose confidence in you – they would think that you were worse than an amateur – that you were an idiot. It is essential that they continue to think that they are dealing with someone reasonably serious. That is your insurance.'

Hawn climbed off the hot wet slab, feeling drained and parched and slightly giddy. 'I suppose there's no point in asking when I'll see you again?'

'You will see me when the time is right.' Pol raised a hand

like a pink flipper. 'Bonne chance. Et merde.'

A slow icy drizzle was falling as they climbed out of the U-Bahn station at Charlottenburg. A small crowd came out with them. Pol had been right – it would have been easy, even for one man, to have followed them: and almost impossible for Hawn to have spotted him. Most of the passengers on the train had looked like late commuters, mostly men, well-upholstered against the damp cold, reading the sports pages of the evening paper. There had been a big match in Cologne and the Berlin team had won.

The bridge was on their right, just as the Frenchman had said. Again, no reason why Pol should have lied. Hawn had to trust Pol, just as he had to trust the man Wohl. What really jarred with Hawn was that Anna had to trust them both too. Anna had been loyal, patient, almost unquestioning from the start; but like a pair of mountaineers roped together, Hawn knew that every step grew more treacherous, the drop more terrible. He was holding her end of the rope, while Pol held his. There was no going back now.

The passengers from the train had spread out into the gloom. A few cars threw up a spray of slush and sand. A tram came grinding and sparking round a corner; there was the distant shriek and rattle of the overhead S-Bahn. Hawn took Anna's hand and began to cross towards the bridge, through the puddles of dim light. He felt very exposed, very alone with her, as he walked under the concrete stanchions, hearing the dull roar of the autobahn ring-way passing above them. The street beyond was dark – wet cobbles stretching away like the skin of a reptile. Between the buildings, a glimpse of black ruins creeping down to the edge of the street like dead lava flows.

At the third street on their left they turned into Tiefengasse. An unsteady, blinking scrawl of red neon marked the Chéri Bar. Hawn paused for half a minute: but no one turned into the street behind them. He opened the iron-ribbed door and walked into a long room with a bar down one side, a row of wooden partitions along the other. Cheap cigar smoke swirled in a myriad of colours from a revolving ball of light in the middle of the ceiling. A jukebox was bawling out some German hit song, which had a distinctly martial beat – a crazy hybrid of pop and the parade-ground.

They found seats in one of the partitions where two men were just leaving. It had just gone 8.15. Anna asked for Schnapps. Hawn, still feeble from the steam bath, ordered a cold beer. He drank half of it straight down, and was just lowering the mug when a man stopped at their table.

'Monsieur, Madame Marziou? Vous permettez?' Before they could reply, he had removed his camel-hair coat and slid down between them at the end of the table. His smile was white, his French very correct. He held out his hand to Anna. There was a chunky gold signet ring on his index finger and a thin gold bracelet peeped from under his white cuff.

'Enchanté, I'm sure! The name's Wohl – Doktor Oskar Wohl.' He shook hands with each of them; his grip was strong and dry. Hawn noticed that his hair had two thick greying streaks folded back behind his ears, and that he was carrying no hat. Hawn guessed that a car had dropped him and was probably waiting outside. Doktor Wohl certainly was having no nonsense about pretending to be evading a 'tail'. People like him could afford to act in the open.

Wohl snapped his fingers and called for a whisky sour. 'Sorry I had to invite you to this joint. Fact is, all the decent places are a bit too public. Berlin's like a club – you can't move without bumping into somebody you know.' The switch from French into English had transformed him perfectly: he spoke with one of those American accents that no American has – what Hawn called the 'IBM accent'. He was the super-salesman, the transatlantic executive: relaxed, confident, full of hidden aggression. None of it showing now – smiling whitely over his whisky sour, toasting them both with his bright brown eyes.

Hawn said, 'You say Berlin's a club? Which half – East or West?'

Wohl laughed easily. 'I guess I should say, "touché"! No, I meant the West sector – what I call the Sin Sector.' He paused. 'Monsieur Marziou – can I call you something a little more relaxed? We don't have to play games here. And I hate

214

formality. What do I call you?'

'Call me Tom. And this is Anna.'

'Anna, Tom – I'm delighted.'

Anna had been studying him carefully. He was slightly below medium height, but strongly built, and he looked very fit, very tanned, but with that slight shade of orange tan which suggested the regular use of a sunlamp. His eyes were heavily-lidded, quick and shrewd.

But, most of all, Anna noticed his clothes. The tweed suit was a little too square at the shoulders, too narrow at the hips; the double-breasting an inch too wide, the check a few millimetres too large. His tie was a conservative blue, knotted a little too tightly, above a pin with a large paste pearl, and the points of his shirt-collar were too broad, too long. He wore no wedding ring.

He made conversation rapidly, changing his subject as deftly, effortlessly, as a card-sharp, never staying on one topic long enough to offend, or to arouse suspicion on controversy. He talked of life in London, Paris, Berlin – how he preferred Berlin because it had more 'zip, more fizz'. 'London and Paris are half-dead. Not what they used to be. Now you take Berlin – God, what a city. Crazy but fun!'

'You're talking about East Berlin, are you?' said Anna sternly.

Wohl held up his hand, and smiled. He obviously felt that his smile was his passport to social success. 'You ask me about East Berlin? OK, I'll tell you. Very sober. Very, very sober. Discipline and work. What do you feel about the Workers' State, Anna?'

'I've never been to one. But I don't like policemen who go around armed. And I like them even less when they're backed up by tanks – particularly when those tanks come from another country.'

'Ah c'mon, Anna, c'mon! That's an old disc from way back in the Cold War. Budapest, Prague – so you get a bit of trouble and the tanks come in to restore order. OK, so a few people get killed. But I can play that same disc to you – the flip-side. What about Chile, the Argentine, Iran, South Africa – and your own Ulster?'

'I'm a Socialist,' Anna said, reddening. 'I deplore what goes on in those countries. Anyway, I don't need an East German to tell me what to think.' She gulped her Schnapps and put her glass down with a bang.

Wohl leant out and patted her wrist. 'OK, Anna. I'm glad you're a Socialist. So am I. But we don't have to worry about old England going Communist, do we? Nothing revolutionary about England, eh? I think it was Stalin who said that England would never go Communist after he'd heard about the workers and the police playing a football match during your General Strike?

'Let me tell you both a little story. It demonstrates the English political character so beautifully. I once heard of a very old guy whose father had worked in the British Museum round about the time that Karl Marx used to go there. The son was asked if his father had ever talked about his patrons. He was asked about someone called Marx. The son said, "Oh yes, Mr Marx – the German gentleman with the beard who used to come in every day, year in, year out. A real regular. Then one day he stopped coming, and he was never heard of again."'

He was looking at them both eagerly: 'You get it, eh?' And he repeated the punchline. Hawn gave a polite laugh, and Anna smiled sourly. Wohl shook his head: 'No, there's nothing revolutionary about England. More the mentality of head in the sand, and to hell with the rest of the world.'

Hawn said: 'Have we come here just to discuss the night-life of Berlin and the degree of English revolutionary fervour?'

'No, Tom, of course not. Just a way of breaking the ice. Leave politics to the politicians. They get paid for it, after all. Let's talk about things that are of more immediate interest. Such as a French friend of yours called Pol. I gather he's a fairly recent friend?'

'I prefer to call him a business associate,' said Hawn. 'So you know him too?'

'Not personally. But I have friends who do. Pol is an interesting man. But you want to be careful of him – he's clever and he's dangerous. And he always plays alone. Anyone

216

who plays with him usually finishes up being used. You're both being used by him at this very moment. But I suppose you are aware of that?'

'I've got something to get out of this, too, you know,' Hawn said defensively.

'Sure, sure. But you still need protection. From what I understand, Pol will protect you just as long as it suits him, but no more.'

'Let me ask you something. How much do you know about this?'

'Enough. I make a point of never knowing more than I have to.'

'And how much is that?'

Wohl sipped his whisky sour. 'You and Anna are out to get some dirt on the America-Britannic Consortium. I have a contact in the GDR who may be able to help you. I don't know the details, because I haven't asked.'

'Let me get something absolutely straight, Doktor Wohl. You may talk about leaving politics to the politicians. But you come from a highly political part of the world and, from what I gathered from Pol, you have a practically unique position there. If we're to accompany you into what you call the German Democratic Republic, we want to know just where we stand.'

The East German lawyer spread his hands on the table, showing two inches of cuff. 'I am offering no guarantees. I can arrange for you both to be issued with temporary visas for the GDR at the city limits. I will also introduce you to the man you have come to meet. Whether he co-operates with you or not is entirely his affair.'

'That doesn't entirely answer my question. In your sort of work you must live in and out of the pockets of the East German Government. That includes their Security Police. And I'm not dumb enough to think that those boys make a move without consulting their bosses in Moscow. What you might call, "running a tight ship".'

Wohl raised his arm and called for another round of drinks. 'Hell, Tom, I'll say this for you. You're certainly direct! That's what comes of dealing with a journalist. But

I prefer the more diplomatic approach.'

'I prefer facts. Tell me straight. Does East German Security have a line on us both? If so, how much do they know?'

Wohl's face was working hard at being open and frank. He tried his smile, and Hawn could see the web of white wrinkles round his eyes that showed up against his false tan. He placed his hand on Hawn's arm. 'Tom, our Security will know about you if and when I tell them. They trust me. That's why you gotta trust me.' He took out a bronze-coloured packet of cigarettes which he offered to them both, and which they declined; then he tapped out an oval-shaped cigarette with a gold tip, produced a gold lighter as if by sleight of hand, and went through a smooth, elaborate ritual of lighting up, inhaling, resting his head back and letting the smoke curl out through his nostrils.

'I shall arrange for you to meet and talk with Doktor Reiss. This meeting will be entirely private. But it is possible that Doktor Reiss would prefer to communicate what he has told you to Security. He will do this more as a polite formality than as a duty. After that you will, of course, be free to leave the GDR.'

'With no questions asked? Come on, Wohl! Supposing Reiss tells your Security something they don't like?'

Wohl drew on his cigarette. 'Tom, you don't think that a man in Reiss's position — which is pretty high — would be fool enough to tell you something that would upset our authorities? Hell, your Government may have to stand to attention and salute every time the America-Britannic Consortium farts, but we don't have those problems. We don't owe ABCO a pfennig — and even if we did, we wouldn't pay them.'

'Now, I've got to make a short telephone call. It'll give you enough time to talk things over.' He finished his drink, slid out from behind the table and disappeared into the back of the bar.

'God, what an awful man,' Anna said. 'I'm not a nationalist, or even much of a patriot, but I don't like my country being run down by foreigners — particularly when I've only just met them.'

'Just a line in Communist small-talk. He also wanted to get

some idea of where we stood politically, if at all. Otherwise, you've got to hand it to the man. He's a hypocrite in the Olympic gold medal class, an ideologist gymnast, and a slick double-faced A-1 shit – and he's intelligent enough to know it.'

'He's ghastly.'

'He's got good dentures.'

'And he powders his nose – did you notice that?'

'Angel, he's going to finish that phone call in a minute. He left us to make up our minds. Which means whether to trust him, or to refuse to be led into East Germany – and out again, perhaps.'

'I don't trust him. How can you trust a man who plays for both sides so openly?'

'That's maybe the very reason why we should trust him. Wohl's racket is practically unique. He may sound and look like a con-man, but he certainly can't afford to be one.'

'You trust him because you want to trust him. Because you're frightened of backing out.'

'Lesser of two evils, my love. We've got ABCO behind us, the Communists in front. Which would you choose?'

'I'm going to have another Schnapps.'

'You've had enough.'

'I'm having another.'

At that moment Wohl returned. He stepped jauntily up to the table, rubbing his hands. 'All set! No problem, the car's outside. D'you have any baggage?'

'We weren't told to bring any.'

'That's OK. You got your passports? Fine! You need anything, you ask for it.' He began putting on his camel-hair coat, left some money on the table, and without waiting for the change led the way into the street where a beige Mercedes stood parked on the pavement, its colour exactly matching that of his coat. It had a five-digit registration number, which was not from West Berlin, or West Germany. Wohl motioned Anna into the passenger-seat beside him, Hawn into the back. Wohl was driving.

He drove with the confident arrogance of a man who likes cars, giving way to nobody, shooting red lights with a split-second margin of safety, using the automatic gears to brake, with a great deal of flashing of lights; but rarely touching the horn.

They sped along Bismarckstrasse, turning down by the Zoo, past the Europa Centre again, east through the garish shabby lights of Hallesches Tor, the pavements busy with pimps and tarts and drag-queens, acrobats and jugglers and tourists and tottering drunks, bouncers and bored policemen in cruising patrol-cars. A black man lounged in a doorway grinning under a lighted sign, SEXY SNAKEPIT. Wohl swerved and just missed a monkey walking on its hind legs, led by a girl in a stetson and cowboy boots.

'I guess you could say this is decadent?' Wohl grinned over his shoulder, only one hand on the wheel, scarcely touching it. 'But y'know, funny thing is, I find it all rather old-fashioned. All rather *déjà-vu. La nostalgie,* and so on.'

'Looks like any other big western capital,' Anna said with deadpan disdain: 'Rich, ugly and dirty. So much for your Socialism, Doktor Wohl.'

'Now don't go and misunderstand me, Anna! Maybe you'll see different if I explain about Berlin before the War. Before the Hitler time, when it was famous for what you call transvestites, yes? Well, I'll tell you something – something real crazy. The ultimate in degeneration. You know what I saw here in West Berlin a few weeks back? I saw a guy, a normal guy, get on stage and dress up as a girl – a beautiful girl. Fishnet stockings, lovely legs, sexy knickers, all his equipment tucked away and disguised, very clever, very effective. Gold lame bra, lots o'red hair and a hat like Sarah Bernhardt. Real nice. But wait! Here's this guy got up as a beautiful girl, and the next moment – without removing his makeup or hair – the guy dresses up as a guy again.' He turned his head slightly, smiling: 'You get it? A transvestite dressing up as a transvestite. Isn't that the ultimate in craziness?'

Hawn said, 'Almost as crazy as a fully-paid-up Party member driving around the fleshpots of the West in a brand new Mercedes, and setting up deals with shifty fat foreigners like Charles Pol, so we can all crap on one of the biggest oil companies in the world.'

'No, no, Tom, I don't rise so easy. Anyway, this car's coming up to nine months old. And hell, Brezhnev's got a dozen cars – including a Cadillac from his friend, ex-President Nixon. There's nothing wrong with a little style, providing it doesn't go to your head.'

Hawn saw no point in further comment. Trying to rile a man like Doktor Wohl over a matter of social conscience was about as effective as trying to spear an oyster with a fork. Wohl had heard it all before. In any case, he seemed to be only half listening.

They were past the bright lights now, driving up Zimmerstrasse towards the glow of arc-lamps. They bumped over a web of tram-lines and could see now the Wall – a long strip of breeze-block, flesh-coloured under the lights and freckled with furious graffiti, which included wobbly aerosol crosses and dates, each marking the spot where an escapee had been shot dead trying to climb over. The watch-towers, at every hundred metres, looked like toy signal-boxes, except for the moving search-light on the roof.

A West German policeman in a shiny black raincoat made a note of the car's number and checked their passports. A couple of American MPs sat in an open jeep, staring at nothing. 'Checkpoint Charlie' was a prefabricated shed with a single concrete lane for cars, ending at a red-and-white pole. A *Grepo* – an East German frontier guard – in smart field green, with an AK47 machine-pistol slung at his hip, peered in, saw Wohl and straightened up with a Prussian salute, then gestured Hawn and Anna to get out.

The shed was full of glaring blue neon. There were holiday posters of resorts on the Baltic, castles and lakes, the reconstructed main square of Dresden. A lot of reading matter was spread around – pamphlets with titles like *Art and Culture in the GDR, Socialism Rebuilds, Trade between the GDR and the Republic of North Korea*. On the bench beside Hawn were several copies of *Neues Deutchland*; he noticed that most of them were several days old.

They were called at last to the desk. A young officer, whose eyes were too old for his face, handed them two pink forms, and was about to embark on his little homily, in French this time, warning of the severe penalties for currency smuggling, when a voice shouted from inside the glass cabin.

Hawn did not understand what it said, but the young *Grepo* came to attention, took their passports away, returned a couple of minutes later, saluted and wished them a happy visit to the German Democratic Republic. They got back in the Mercedes – Anna in the back this time – the pole swung up, and they drove across towards Friedrichsplatz.

Hawn was at once aware of an antiseptic cleanliness, scented with the distinctive bitter-sweet smell of Russian petrol. The graffiti and noisy lights on the Western side had given way to red banners turned purple under the refracted glow of the arc-lamps, with white and yellow lettering that proclaimed the virtues of Peace, Work, Solidarity and Détente.

Wohl drove more slowly here, although there was far less traffic and the streets seemed wider and more orderly. 'This your first time in a Socialist country?'

'Only Libya and Chad,' said Hawn. 'Unless you count Islington and Merseyside.'

'You don't wanna turn your noses up at the GDR,' said Wohl. 'Everything you see around you was built up from nothing by the people themselves. We didn't have the luxury of American aid. The Soviet Union helped, of course, but they couldn't spare much. Most of it was done by the sweat of the people.' His manner had become noticeably slower, even solemn, like his driving.

He drove straight on down Karl-Marx-Allee – formerly Stalin-Allee – the dubious pride of the German Democratic Republic. The seven-storey blocks of white Soviet rococo were beginning to age, with the ugly charm of some gimcrack memorial to a bygone dynasty. The lavatory-tile bricks were leaking at the joints, the windows were too small, the pavements too wide; the expanse of grass verge down the centre looked like an abandoned fairway.

Wohl offered no comment; and the other two were silent. There was nothing very new you could say about Karl-Marx-Allee, except that it was one of the most depressing streets in the world. Instead, Wohl said, 'You pick up your visas at the Tierpark, at the end of here.'

After nearly two miles, the Allee grew dim and forlorn, as though either its builders or its inhabitants had lost interest in it. The frontier between the East Sector and East Germany proper was bristling with more flags and armed police. There was a row of heavy lorries lined up on the side of the road, but few cars. Wohl parked, told them both to stay where they were, and got out. Once again the Volkspolitzei – discourteously known as *Vopos* – evidently recognized the car and saluted.

Wohl stood chatting to some of the police. They seemed in no way to object to his camel-hair coat, which Hawn and Anna decided must be one of the most offensive objects ever to have been flaunted in the name of Socialism.

'So what do you think?' said Anna.

'It seems to be going fairly smoothly. They haven't arrested us yet. It's odd that they don't seem to need our passports. Or perhaps Wohl's the sort of man who can make up the rules as he goes along. You're not frightened, are you?'

'A bit. I think I'd be rather stupid not to be.'

'Well, there's one consolation. ABCO can't touch us here. We should be all right just as long as we play Wohl's game. I don't know what's in it for him, except that he must be acting on orders. And providing we play ball with him, I don't see what advantage there is – either from his point of view or the Communists' – to have us set up. After all, we are trying to break the biggest Western consortium. That's not the sort of charge that makes a Communist show-trial.'

'It's funny to hear you trusting the Communists.'

'Trusting them isn't the same thing as liking them. But the one thing about the Communists is that their motives are usually pretty straightforward, even if their methods aren't.'

Wohl returned, accompanied by an officer with whom he was talking rapidly. He stopped at the car and they shook hands. Wohl got in. He was holding two yellow cards, made out in their French names and impressively stamped. There were also two photographs, identical with the ones in their new passports. 'You see – everything arranged, hunky-dory!'

'How did you get these?' said Hawn, pointing to the photographs. 'From the Frenchman?'

'You guess correctly, sir. You got a lot to thank that Frenchman for – he looks after you two real good!'

A policeman waved them on, and they drove forward, up a steep ramp that curved round on to the autobahn, east to Oranienburg.

# CHAPTER SEVEN

# The Hunchback

*The wise guy is the sucker after all.*    DIAMOND JIM BRADY

After less than a quarter of an hour they left the autobahn, turning north up a bumpy, ill-kept main road, its surface cracked and broken by heavy lorries travelling between Rostock and Berlin. There was only the occasional car – usually an ugly, hump-backed Russian saloon, or a smaller mud-spattered Skoda.

They passed through the dreary suburbs of Oranienburg – the site of one of the original Nazi concentration camps, now containing the largest political prison in East Germany; then north, between black pine forests that grew right up to the margin of the road.

Wohl had hardly spoken since leaving the frontier. He was again driving carefully, slowing and pulling over for on-coming trucks, and negotiating the ruts and potholes so as not to damage the suspension of his beautiful Mercedes.

Anna slept, her head resting on Hawn's shoulder.

Forty minutes after leaving the border of Berlin, they reached a small town called Fürstenberg, a damp dark place lying in marshland amid small lakes. Wohl drew up outside a modern hotel just off the main square. A pitiful spray of red flags and bunting provided the only colour to the scene. The door was locked. An old man let them in, grumbling behind his spectacles, although it was not late.

Hawn and Anna were beginning to feel hungry. They asked Wohl about arranging some dinner, and he answered – a trifle impatiently, Hawn thought – that he would see to it in due course. Wohl's zest and humour, which had become so excrutiating back in West Berlin, had vanished; with the crossing of the border he seemed to have assumed an entirely new personality. Here in the East he was methodical, businesslike, as befitted a senior and privileged citizen of the German Democratic Republic. Even his transatlantic accent seemed to have assumed a distinctly Teutonic ring.

The hotel was built of breeze-block and pine. The pine was fresh and varnished yellow, and up in their small bedroom, with its two narrow twin beds, some of the boards were oozing sap at the joints, like bubbles of honey. It was very clean, very functional. The only decoration was a pale water-colour of mountains at sunset.

Wohl was waiting for them down in the dining room, sitting at a plastic-topped table patterned like wood. There was no bar, no other guests. As Hawn and Anna entered, a door at the other end opened and a white-haired woman peered suspiciously at the three of them, then disappeared again.

Wohl, with obvious reluctance, went through to the back to order something to eat. He returned and lit one of his gold-tipped cigarettes. 'They have cold sausage, salami and potato salad. And I ordered you both some beer.' He did not sit down again, but paused, then consulted his watch. 'I have to be back in Berlin tonight. So I'll be saying good-bye, or rather, au revoir.' He tried to turn on his smile, but this time it failed to work.

'Wait a minute,' Hawn said, trying to keep the anxiety out of his voice. 'You said you'd fix us up with some things for the night. We haven't even got toothbrushes.'

Wohl's eyes flickered oddly, avoiding them both. 'You are being sent some stuff round. They shouldn't be long. Enjoy your meal.'

'We'll be seeing you again?'

'Very possibly. You are in good hands. But for God's sake don't lose your passports and those visas. As for money, the hotel is all taken care of.' He waved and they watched him stride away towards the door, his expensive shoes making no sound on the concrete floor.

For some time Hawn sat staring at the glum framed photograph on the wall of Erich Honecker, Chairman of the

Council of State. He said at last, 'Well thanks a lot, Comrade Wohl. I suppose we can hardly blame the bastard. We certainly can't say that we didn't go with him of our own free will. As it is, without any East German money we can hardly move out of the hotel. And if we start fooling around with the Black Market, they'll have got us just where they probably want us – without having to rig the evidence. Still, they must be able to do better than that. I mean, the personal services of Doktor Oskar Wohl can't come all that cheap – in whatever kind of currency they pay him.'

'So what do we do?'

'Nothing. We wait. It's their move.'

Anna looked around. 'Do you suppose the hotel's bugged?'

'Probably. Fact tends to follow fiction in these sort of places. I don't suppose it matters much.'

'I mean, shouldn't we be speaking in French?'

'Oh Christ, angel. Do we have to act out the whole of Pol's script for the benefit of the East German Secret Police?'

'All right. Be serious for a moment. Did you notice how Wohl's manner changed when he got here?'

'I know. He seemed far too eager to get away just now. I can only think that he may have heard something at the border, when he collected our visas. Wohl's a big wheel over in the West, where he's his own master and can call all the shots. But here he's on home territory and has to toe the line.'

The white-haired woman slouched over to them with a couple of plates of cold food and two glasses of frothy beer. They began to eat, but with diminished appetites. Anna said, 'Maybe we could hitch a lift back to Berlin? I imagine those visas are in order?'

Hawn had them both in his pocket, folded inside his French passport. He examined them now for the first time. They looked genuine enough, valid from that day, for seven days. There seemed to be no restrictions on travel within East Germany; the only stipulation being that they return via the East Berlin crossing point.

'Wohl said he'd send us over some stuff tonight. Maybe that means he's passing us on to another contact – someone even more senior.' He drank his beer; it was thin and warm, and when the froth had settled the glass was barely half-full. 'I can make do for one night without a toothbrush,' he added, 'and I don't mind too much going unshaven. But what I'm going really to miss is something to read. I don't much fancy sitting here for a couple of days, trying to screw the odd beer out of that old bitch, and reading about the latest hydro-electric complex in Turkestan.'

'Well, what else can you think of doing in the middle of a dark, cold night, in East Germany?'

They drained their glasses, leaving the two cups of brown coffee which the old woman had placed, unsmiling, in front of them: walked out of the deserted dining room, up the pine staircase to their bare pine room. Anna undressed and had a shower in the narrow cubicle, while Hawn stripped off and got into one of the cheap lumpy beds. She was still slightly wet when she climbed in beside him, and for a moment they both almost toppled on to the floor. Anna began to giggle; and he held her close, caressed her, gently, skilfully, then raised himself on his hands and entered her. Her giggling became a soft mewing sound, growing louder. Vaguely Hawn wondered whether there were other guests, whether they could hear through the pine walls. He delayed for as long as possible, until she uttered a little shriek and he gave way to the moment of mindless delirium.

As he sank down on to her, kissing her mouth and eyes and hair, he was only dully conscious of sounds outside. A steady hammering, growing closer, louder. Heavy footsteps on the pine stairs, along the pine corridor. Boots – several pairs of them. Then the firm knocking on the door. He called in German, 'Who is it?'

'Sicherheitspolizei. Aufmachen!'

Hawn sprang up and dragged on his trousers, while Anna pulled the duvet up round her throat. Hawn went over and unlocked the door and opened it. Four men came in. Three of them wore the grey-green uniforms of the *Vopos,* and they were all carrying machine-pistols. The fourth man was older, squat and greying, in a sports jacket and open-necked shirt. 'Your papers,' he demanded. The three policemen, who were all very young, glanced at Anna, then looked away.

Hawn fetched their passports and visas. The plain-clothes man rifled through them several times. Hawn saw that he had big square finger-nails, bitten down to the quick. He finally snapped both passports shut and put them in the side-pocket of his jacket. 'You will please dress and accompany us,' he said in German.

'What is the meaning of this?' Hawn said, with forced indignation. 'We entered the GDR in the company of one of your leading lawyers, Herr Doktor Oskar Wohl. He obtained our visas, which are valid and correct.'

'You will explain all that to Headquarters. I leave you both to get dressed. One of my men will wait outside the room.' The four of them withdrew, and the door closed begind them.

Hawn took off his trousers again, put on his pants and vest, then sat down on the other bed and picked up his socks. 'Fuck. Fuck Wohl – fuck Pol – fuck the whole bloody lot of them!'

Anna, her face almost as white as the duvet, had sat up and was reaching for her clothes, which she had left scattered on the floor. 'Tom, what's happening?'

'What's happening, my love, is that we've just been arrested by the Security Police of the sweet German Democratic Republic.'

'But why?'

Hawn felt a stab of irritation. 'How the hell do I know? Either it's a mistake, or we've been set up. But why we've been set up, God knows. We're not going to be a lot of use to anyone in an East German clink.'

They finished dressing and opened the door. The young *Vopo* took up the rear and followed them down the stairs. 'I will say this for them,' Anna said, 'their timing was perfect.'

'That's about the only consolation we have.'

The other three were waiting in the passage. Without word or gesture they turned and marched towards the door, the plain-clothes man in the lead. Outside stood a small olive-green truck with no windows in the back. One of the *Vopos* opened the double rear doors and motioned Hawn and Anna to get inside. He and a second *Vopo* followed, while the other two got into the front.

As the engine started, a dim blue light came on. The interior of the truck was empty, except for the two steel benches along each side and a grill at the front end, opening into the cabin.

The two of them sat together on one of the benches, with one of the *Vopos* on one side, another opposite. Hawn turned to the one beside him: 'Where are we going?'

The boy shrugged. It was the second *Vopo* who answered: 'Security Headquarters, Oranienburg.'

'Do you know what the charges are?'

He was answered by the first *Vopo*. 'We are not permitted to talk to prisoners.'

Hawn squeezed Anna's hand, and they rode in silence.

The truck slowed down, took a sudden right turn and stopped. Above the throb of the diesel engine, the rhythm of marching feet. A bell rang; the truck drove forward again; stopped after about thirty yards. The rear doors clanged open and the inside was flooded with light. The third *Vopo*, from the cabin, motioned them to get out.

They were in a broad courtyard surrounded by grim five-storey walls in which few lights showed. Two platoons of *Vopos* were goose-stepping at the far end. The plain-clothes man led Hawn and Anna through an archway, down a bright corridor and up two flights of stairs. The three *Vopos* followed. They came to a polished wooden door with a black plaque marked PRIVAT in white lettering. The plain-clothes man knocked twice and entered.

It was a spare room full of cheap office furniture: grey steel filing-cabinet, plastic venetian blinds drawn across the window. The only luxury was a carpet. Like the rest of the building, the room was very bright, lit by two strips of neon, one of which fizzed and blinked at uneven intervals. On the wall, a photograph of Lenin.

The man behind the desk had haggard, heavy features behind horn-rimmed spectacles. Hard, questioning, suspicious: but not an altogether bad face, Hawn decided. He was dressed in a dark business suit and wore a wedding ring. A couple of small red and gold badges adorned his button-hole.

The plain-clothes man from the truck handed him the two passports and visas, then withdrew, followed by the *Vopos*. The man gestured Hawn and Anna towards two straight-backed chairs, then offered them a box of cigarettes. When they declined, he lit one himself, and Hawn saw that he had two fingers missing from his right hand.

'I am Colonel Kardich, of People's Security.' He spoke slowly in English, with a thick, awkward accent. 'First there are certain questions I must ask you. You entered the German Democratic Republic from West Berlin earlier this evening. You entered with Doktor Oskar Wohl. Wohl obtained your visas. Is that all correct?'

'Perfectly correct,' said Hawn.

'Can you think of any reason why you should have been detained?'

'None at all. We came as Doktor Wohl's guests. As such, we assumed we would receive a proper, decent welcome.'

A faint, apologetic smile crossed the man's severe features. 'You have already observed that I address you in English – not in French.' He leant out and gently drummed the three fingers of his right hand on the two passports. 'These documents are forged. You know that?'

Hawn was silent for a moment. He was fairly certain that the Grenzpolizei would not have spotted the forgery unless they had been told. 'How do you know?' he said at last.

'It is not important how I know. The fact is, they are forgeries. You are therefore in the German Democratic Republic with false documents. That is a serious crime.'

Hawn felt Anna flinch beside him. He put his hand out and touched her arm. 'You said you had several questions to ask us. That's only one. And you seem to know the answer. What about the others?'

'Who supplied you with these passports?'

Hawn paused only a fraction of a second. They had been betrayed, and must fend for themselves: it was too late to start clinging to old loyalties, if such things had ever existed.

Hawn saw no reason to lie. But it was quite another matter whether he would be believed. He said: 'A Frenchman – Charles Pol. Do you know him?'

'Please, I am asking the questions. Why did this man issue you with French passports when you could have travelled on your own?'

'It's a long story.'

'Very well. I am a patient man. Tell me the story.'

Colonel Kardich interrupted only once, near the beginning of Hawn's monologue, only to ask if they wanted coffee. They accepted. Kardich had smoked at least ten cigarettes, and drunk almost as many coffees, by the time Hawn was through.

'So you say you were issued these passports in order to escape a possible murder charge by the Istanbul Police? It seems that this man Pol is exceptionally . . .' he snapped his fingers for the word – '*findig?*'

'Ingenious,' Hawn suggested.

'Exactly! And you accepted his friendship without question?'

'We had no alternative. I don't know what your prisons are like, but I dare say they're better than Turkish ones.'

'I hope so. Though we are not proud of our prisons. They are an unpleasant necessity – as is my job.'

'Do you accept my story?'

'Do you ask me if I believe it?'

'If you put it that way.'

'At this stage I do not believe it or disbelieve it. First, I have still not asked you the most important question. What are your real names, where do you come from, and what are your professions?'

Hawn told him, and the man wrote the details down on a pad, holding the pen in a pathetic claw of three fingers. He sat back. 'Well, Mr Hawn, Miss Admiral. So, what to do with you? You cannot expect us to ignore this peccadillo, just because you, Mr Hawn, as a journalist, are interested in finding out the possible criminal activities of one of your leading oil companies.'

'*The* leading oil company.'

Kardich nodded. 'At this stage I am not going to proceed with formal charges against you, until I have made further investigations. However, you will be detained here while these investigations are made. We will make you as comfortable as possible.'

'Let me ask you a question, Colonel. Who shopped us? Wohl? Or Pol?'

Kardich gave a sterile grin. 'Even if I knew, Mr Hawn, I would not tell you.'

He must have pressed a bell under the desk, for the door opened and two *Vopos* – different ones this time – strutted in and saluted. 'These officers will accompany you to your quarters. I regret that our accommodation does not allow you to share a room. Are you hungry?'

'I think we'd like a drink.'

'I'll have some wine sent to you both. If you need anything, the guards will attend to you, in the day or the night.' He gave a dismissive gesture. Hawn and Anna stood up, and the two *Vopos* marched them to the door.

It was a spartan room: a camp-bed with a sheet and two military-style blankets; window of opaque glass high in the wall; lino floor, bare grey-brick walls, a table and chair. At the back, a windowless washroom and lavatory. No bath or shower, just a basin with a single cold tap, and no mirror. The lavatory-paper consisted of a wad of *Neues Deutschland* torn into small squares and skewered on to a nail. Both rooms were lit by naked bulbs in wire cages, which could be turned on and off by separate switches. The door was steel, locked, and fitted with a Judas eye.

Not so much a cell, Hawn thought, as the temporary billet of a military commander on manoeuvres. Nor was he denied the bare essentials of civilized living. Toothbrush and paste, shaving tackle, a cheap deodorant, hairbrush and pocket mirror, a pair of coarse striped pyjamas, even a change of socks and underwear – all supplied by courtesy of the People's Security Service. The one thing he still hankered after was reading matter. He asked if they had any Western Communist newspapers, and was brought a tabloid called *Soviet*

*Newsletter*, published in Prague. Apart from that, there was a bottle of tolerable Riesling.

He slept surprisingly well. Breakfast was lentil soup, hot Bockwurst and sauerkraut, together with the local coffee, which tasted of nutmeg.

Boredom set in soon after; and he tried to occupy his mind by running through all possible permutations of plot and counterplot, pondering on the various motives of Pol and Wohl, and why they should have betrayed them both. He went back even further, to Robak and Shanklin and French, even the absurd Hamish Logan, trying to decide whether the riddle lay with one of them. Was it possible that ABCO had so much manipulative power that it could influence the East German police? And what would the East Germans have to gain? A matter of forged passports might, as Colonel Kardich had stated, be a serious crime or a peccadillo: but even the East German Secret Police must be subtle enough to realize that they were not dealing with a pair of ordinary criminals?

Of course, the crux of the problem were those two damned French passports. Hawn had a decent scepticism regarding the powers of the British Foreign Service, and without British passports he saw his and Anna's difficulties becoming more than just temporary. Or was it possible that Pol had intended all that from the very start? There was at least one small point in their favour. Colonel Kardich had said they were not being charged, while investigations were being continued. What investigations?

At lunch he had another bottle of wine, on which he slept for a couple of hours. He then shaved in cold water, but felt grubby and listless. He was beginning to worry about Anna. He called the guard and asked to see her. The man shook his head and turned away. Hawn muttered after him the most complicated German obscenity he could remember from his student days, and the man stopped. A second guard appeared. 'You do not talk like that here,' he said. Both of them were fingering their AK47s.

'Bring the girl to me,' Hawn said. 'I only want to see her for a few minutes. If I don't get to see her, I will demand to see Colonel Kardich.'

There were mutterings beyond the door, then the sound of more boots as a third man arrived, though out of sight. Hawn guessed, from the way the other two saluted, that he was an officer.

He was a very tall man with a tired, sagging face, and wore soft leather boots and flared trousers under a loose grey-green smocked jacket, Soviet-style, with two shelves of red epaulettes. He seemed to be unarmed. He leant against the doorjamb and said, 'You make much noise, English.' His accent had the deep round Russian vowels.

Hawn said, 'Colonel Kardich has told me that I was not under arrest. I demand to see my friend – Miss Admiral.'

The Russian looked down at him with his blue-pouched eyes; his cheeks were creased and lightly pitted with acne scars. It was a face which managed to be both sad and cruel. 'The girl is correct. There is no problem.'

'I demand to see her! Get me Colonel Kardich.'

'The Colonel Kardich is not a domestic servant. I have authority here.'

'Then bring me the girl. For five minutes. I am claiming my rights as a free citizen in the German Democratic Republic.'

The man stared at him with blank eyes, then straightened up and turned, pulling the door shut with a bang. Hawn, in a burst of impotent fury, kicked it and hurt his toe. If this meant being detained pending investigations, he wondered what it would be like to be under full arrest.

The door was flung open again, and Anna walked in. She walked unsteadily, touching the wall for support, and her face had a slightly greasy pallor. 'Tom! I can't stand being shut up in that little room any more. What are they going to do to us? I can't sleep, I can't eat. I've been asking to see you too, but nobody took any notice. I suppose it's because I can't speak German.'

Two *Vopos* stood in the doorway. One of them was smirking. Hawn led her over to the bed and sat her down; then turned to the two guards. 'She stays here – with me.'

'Five minutes,' said one of them. The other, with the

smirk, began to smile openly. Hawn advanced towards him.

'Tell me what's so funny.'

The man shrugged, but said nothing. The second *Vopo* stepped forward. 'So the little lady is dissatisfied with her room? Where does she think she is – in a hotel?'

'A State hotel,' his companion said, and laughed. Hawn stepped up to him and hit him hard in the stomach, just above his belt; then he wheeled round and smashed his left fist into the other's eye.

Several things happened at once. Hawn kicked out and his shoe collided with a soft calf boot. A machine-pistol sprang up and its skeleton handle slammed against his cheek. He reeled back, bumping into Anna who had leapt up from the bed and now hurled herself between the two *Vopos*, her fingernails reaching for their faces. One of them chopped her down with a blow on the neck. Hawn tried to reach him, when his head seemed to explode in a bright flash. Fists were pummelling his face as though it were dough. He could taste the salty blood, but couldn't see anything. His head was bouncing off the lino floor, and Anna was screaming, but the screams seemed to be growing more distant; then an excruciating pain in his belly, followed by nothing.

He woke, staring at the concrete ceiling, at the wire-caged bulb which looked enormous. It looked like an enormous birdcage. He wondered why he couldn't see the birds. His face felt huge. He touched it, and it felt soft, like a toy balloon. He realized he could see with only one eye. There was a wet towel on his forehead. He moved his tongue against his lips and felt a brittle flaking, as though he were about to shed a skin. Then he passed out again.

The next time he opened his eye, he could just make out someone sitting at the foot of the bed. He tried to lift his head and gave a grunt of pain. A voice said, 'You are a very foolish man, Mr Hawn. You are lucky to be alive.'

A gruff, heavy voice. Not unfriendly. Solid man, square face, grey hair, horn-rimmed spectacles. Dark suit and tie. All dressed up for the occasion.

Hawn licked his fat flaking lips and said, in a voice slow and struggling, like a deaf-mute's, 'They insulted my girl.

They insulted Miss Admiral.' He managed to get his head up this time, despite the pain. The towel remained clinging round his head like a turban. 'Where is she?'

'She is back in her room,' said Colonel Kardich. 'She has been given a sedative.'

'How kind of you. You Communist bastard.'

'Mr Hawn, you are very lucky. There are not many countries in the world where you can attack a policeman and expect to get no more than a little blood on your nose. Your attack was unprovoked.'

'They insulted Miss Admiral,' Hawn said again, feebly. 'What are you going to do now? Charge me with assault?'

'We will forget about the assault. You are not only very foolish — you are very impatient. I wonder how you would behave if you had to spend twenty years in a prison cell.'

Hawn rested his head back and closed his eye. He was aching horribly from the neck up.

Colonel Kardich said, 'I have arranged for a doctor to come and arrange your wounds. You will not be pretty for several days, but you will survive. Your stupid action has come at an inconvenient time. I have arranged this afternoon for you to meet a most important person. He has flown here especially to see you.'

'Flown in from Moscow, eh?' Hawn said, without moving.

'In the meantime, I have given orders that if you make any further trouble, you are to be handcuffed to this bed. I repeat, you have been most fortunate.'

'Bloody fortunate. The German Democratic Republic welcomes you — arrest on arrival, interrogation, locked in a bare room, smashed up with rifle butts.' He paused, exhausted; and felt the bed stir as Colonel Kardich stood up. A moment later the door opened then clanged shut.

He and Anna met again in Colonel Kardich's room. This time two *Vopos* — ones they had not seen before — stood on either side of the door. Hawn's head was tightly bandaged and the blood had been wiped off, and his bloated lips and the side of his nose were now thick and sticky with some foul-smelling antiseptic jelly. His head still ached and there was a dull pain in his gut; but he could just walk straight and use his arms.

Kardich said: 'I have explained to Miss Admiral here that you will be meeting with a gentleman who has arrived especially at Oranienburg to see you both. He knows certain of the events in which you are involved, so he will know if you are lying, or when you ignore certain facts. So you will tell him everything. It is not my duty to question you further. So – do you have any further questions to put to me?'

'Our passports,' Hawn said. 'Do we get them back? And when will we be allowed to leave the country?'

'That will depend on the satisfactory outcome of the meeting that has been arranged for you.' He stood up. 'We will go now.'

The two *Vopos* led the way at a discreet distance, as though Hawn carried some contagious disease. Colonel Kardich walked behind. They left the building, crossed the corner of the parade-ground, through an arch where a red-and-white pole with an illuminated disc saying HALT! had been raised for them; and out into a grey street where it was already getting dark.

The Klub Hotel was three minutes' walk away: an anonymous block of dirty yellow concrete, brightened up with the statutory bunch of red flags and a slogan urging the German people to fight for peace.

The *Vopos* stopped outside on the steps. Kardich ushered the other two ahead of him. Despite Hawn's appearance, the clerk at the desk pretended to take no notice of them. They took the lift up to the fourth floor. The door was at the end of the corridor. Kardich knocked twice, and the door was immediately opened.

Hawn had difficulty focusing with his good eye. He could just make out a youngish man of medium height, with a plump, pale face and sleek black hair. He was casually but expensively dressed – rather too expensively for the ordinary East German, Hawn thought. But then what *was* the ordinary East German? Kardich? The *Vopos*? Doktor Oskar Wohl?

Kardich made no effort to introduce them. Instead, he turned to Hawn: 'I shall be downstairs. The guards will stay at the door. There is only the one entrance. The exit at the back through the kitchens has been locked. I mention this in case you are foolish enough to try to escape.' He nodded to them both, ignoring the guest whose room they were in, then turned back down the corridor.

The pale, sleek-haired man closed the door and beckoned the two of them across the room – a bland modern room, typical of any second-class European hotel. Television set in the corner; push-button radio over the bed; a Gauguin reproduction on one wall; and by the door, next to the long list of the hotel's rules and regulations, a map of the area – green, flat, with few towns or villages or roads, the whole area spattered with small lakes. A memory stirred in Hawn's battered mind: two lines by Johann Wolfgang van Goethe, with words added by the late Doktor Hans Dieter Mönch. 'The little birds are silent in the wood *by the lake* – Just wait, soon you will be silent too . . . '

Their host had sat down on the bed, after waving them both into the two armchairs. It was obvious that he had only just arrived; his single suitcase – a cheap grip-bag affair – stood unopened behind the door. He sat forward and gave Hawn a bright grin: 'My goodness, they seem to have given you a good walloping! What did you do? Hit one of those bloody *Vopos*?'

'That's exactly what I did.' Hawn's mind was now fully alert. The man had spoken English – fluent, rather guarded English with a very slight, unplaceable accent. Not recognizably German, and not quite English either. He went on:

'So you just arrived last night, eh? First time in the Workers' Paradise! They certainly must have left you with a lovely impression. But you really shouldn't go around hitting policemen. I'm not speaking up as the old bobby's spokesman – I just believe in giving them a wide berth.

'I once knew an Australian – news photographer based out in Beirut – biggest man I ever met. He was married to a South African girl, bust up with her, and she got custody of the three kids. Then this mad Ozzie bastard kidnapped them and tried to smuggle them out to what was then Bots-wanaland. He was picked up at the border by the police, and he put seven of 'em in hospital. And Afrikaans police are about as touchy as they come.'

'What happened to the Australian?' Hawn asked, though he was more interested in the man's voice and accent than in his story. It had been about half-way through that Hawn had got it: pure, straightforward, genteel North London Jewish. The explanation, of course, was simple: his family had escaped from Nazi Germany and settled in England; then the war over, they had returned, as faithful comrades, to that rump of Germany where others were building the Workers' State. It only surprised Hawn that the man had managed to keep his accent so intact. No doubt he had regular contacts with London – diplomatic, pseudo-diplomatic, or some other cover that Colonel Kardich and his friends had devised.

Perhaps Hawn's beating had left his appetite for life temporarily jaded: for he found that sitting face to face with a Communist secret agent – who had probably worked most of his adult life against Hawn's own country, and yet who was perhaps a few years younger than himself – not so much dramatic or intriguing, as rather embarrassing. He could think of nothing to say; nor was he much inclined to, since every syllable filled his mouth with the taste of antiseptic.

Their host, who had still not introduced himself or asked for their names, quickly broke the silence:

'Oh, the Australian? Well, they worked him over a bit, then they threw him out. I think they were scared of him. I say, I'm sorry, would you both like a drink?' He bounded off the bed and went towards his grip-bag. 'I've got some Scotch – bit of a rarity in these God-forsaken spots.' He paused. 'Only I don't think there'll be enough glasses.' He went into the bathroom and came out with a couple of tooth-mugs. 'Bugger – as I thought – only two.'

'We'll share one,' Hawn told him.

'I'm Sam, by the way,' the man said, bending down over the bed and opening his grip-bag: 'Sam Hanak.' Hawn noticed that his movements were leisurely, and that he was rather large around the hips. He certainly didn't look like a dangerous adversary. "'Fraid there's no soda,' he went on, taking out an unopened bottle of Scotch. 'Germans don't believe in soda. Have to be tap water.'

'We'll have it neat,' said Hawn, squinting carefully at the pale, plump features next to the bed. 'My name's Tom, and this is Anna.'

'Tom – Anna – one straight whisky coming up for the two of you!' Formal introductions were clearly no part of his game. 'And if you don't mind me saying so, Tom, you look as though you need it.' He filled their glass to the brim – 'Whoops! You can see I've never worked as a barman.'

'What *do* you work as?' Hawn said.

'Ah, that's a mighty question – a question that calls for mighty answers. Let us partake of the Demon Drink, before we bare our souls to each other. You'd better take the first sip – I'm spilling it.'

Hawn winced as the whisky seared his lips and bruised gums. He wiped the antiseptic off the glass and carried it over to Anna, his eyes watering with pain.

Sam Hanak had poured himself a more modest dose. 'Chin-chin! To happy days!'

'With two *Vopos* on the door, and a Colonel of the secret police waiting downstairs, Sam? Don't they make you nervous?'

'Nervous? My dear fellow, one must look upon the guardians of the State as the guardians of the People. The People are you and me.' He gave Hawn a sideways grin. 'Mustn't let a little punch-up sour one's broad philosophy of the world.'

'And what particular world is that?'

'There is only one world. We fight and squabble, and sometimes we even try and kill each other. Jolly silly. We're all citizens together.'

'And what country are you a citizen of, Sam?'

Hanak had stopped in the middle of the room, his glass half raised to his lips. A light flush had spread across his smooth cheeks. 'Do I detect the tiniest ring of hostility in that question? Or is it just the brutal instincts of the questing journalist?'

'It was a simple enough question. And you should be able to give me a simple enough answer.'

'Then I shall answer you. I am a citizen of the world. No, I jest. I will give you the correct answer, but first I am obliged to ask you some questions. You see, those passports of yours are a bloody nuisance. I mean, you were taking enough liberties coming here in the first place – considering the sort of game you're playing. But when you barge in with false documents, you're not only making it perishing difficult for yourselves – you're making it pretty bloody difficult for the authorities here.'

'Now listen to me, Herr Hanak.' Hawn was sitting forward, gripping what was left of the whisky in both hands, feeling the acids and adrenalin beginning to stir through his sluggish blood. 'I've still got a bit of kick left in me. And if you think you can answer my questions with a little pep-talk about how we've upset the authorities here, and what a nuisance we've been and so on, I don't mind reserving that kick for you.

'What the hell are you up to? Who's playing you along? Kardich? The Central Committee of the East German Workers' Party? Or someone else? Do you know somebody called Wohl? Acts like a playboy and calls himself an international lawyer? Yes, you know him. You're in his class, just about. Nice and breezy and anonymous.

'But first you'll tell me how you knew our passports were forged. Or rather, how Kardich knew. We picked up our visas at the border, with Wohl as our escort. At what point did they decide we were impostors?'

'You mean, the East Germans?' The young Jew sipped his whisky and stared out of the window. 'Somebody was obviously telling tales out of school. Who gave you these passports?' he added, turning back to them.

'Ask Colonel Kardich. We told him.' Hawn was now feeling mean and very angry; but Hanak either did not, or pretended not to, notice. His voice was still pleasant, with a dreadful mateyness:

'Tell me.'

Hawn had difficulty suppressing his temper. He gulped

at his drink and passed the glass to Anna. 'A Frenchman by the name of Charles Pol.'

'Ah, yes. Old Charlie Pol. I could have bet my last shirt that he'd get in on an act like this.'

'You know him?'

'Oh yes. I know him. A really naughty boy. Plays it mostly for kicks, too – that's the funny thing. He's made a fortune, in one way or another – most of them not quite legal. But it isn't really the money that interests him. Charlie Pol is an old-fashioned adventurer – a buccaneer, freebooter, pirate. He makes his own rules and he expects everyone else to play by them. Otherwise, he owes allegiance and loyalty to no one.'

'And whose rules are *you* playing by, Hanak?'

The man was pacing the room, making wide gestures as he spoke, and seemed not to hear the question. He paused by Anna's chair. 'Your whisky's a bit low, my dear. Let me refresh it!' This time he was rather clumsy, spilling some of the drink on the bed as he refilled the glass.

The whisky had anaesthetized Hawn's mouth and stimulated his gut; and although the aggression it aroused still lingered, he found himself fascinated by Herr Sam Hanak: by the glib, breezy prattle of the better class of London car salesman or bouncy hairdresser – with none of the sad, morbid introspection of most Central European Jews, nor the hard phlegmatic anonymity of the prototype Communist agent. It occurred to Hawn that since Hanak knew Pol, he might only know Pol's side of the story – something which the East Germans must be finding both confusing and a potential embarrassment. Murdering retired Nazi war criminals was a game they had long given up, if they had ever played it. But it was also a game of which they could not openly disapprove. Was Hanak's job just to ease Hawn and Anna back to the West, without too many questions asked and answers given?

Sam Hanak tasted his second whisky. 'What were we talking about? Ah yes, that Frenchman. You asked me how I met him. In a restaurant in Geneva, as a matter of fact. Pol had just been bankrupted by the Canton of Vaux –

which is the most frightfully degrading thing. I mean, no-body goes to Switzerland and gets bankrupted. Like going to a top brothel and flopping on the job.' He turned to Anna, with a little bow: 'If you'll forgive my coarseness?'

'I didn't ask you where you met him,' Hawn said. 'I asked you whose rules you were playing by.'

'Oh I'm only a sort of linesman chap. I keep the score and make sure the ball stays in play.'

'Herr Hanak, I think we've both been fairly patient with you so far. And we're certainly grateful for your hospitality. But it's about time you stopped poncing about and started being honest with us. Colonel Kardich told me that a very important person was coming to meet us – and Kardich doesn't seem the sort of man who exaggerates. So I'll accept that you're important. High-ranking Party member? Security? – although you could have fooled me.

'But what is it, Hanak, that makes *us* so important to you? Do you want to use us, or get rid of us? Or do you want to dandle us on your lap until it's time to expose us as dangerous Western agents, then put us away for twenty years? We'd like to know.'

Sam Hanak smiled pleasantly. 'You ask what's going to happen to you? I shall be quite honest – I don't know. I don't know that it's even been decided. I don't even know what it's all about. When one is put on to an operation like this, it is usual practice to be told only what is essential. What is essential about you is that you have been hired by Charles Pol – and that you have been working under his aegis for the last two months. The question is – what does Charles Pol want of you? Perhaps you could answer that for me?'

There was a slow pause. Hanak went on: 'You ask what it's all about. I can only tell you what I know. It's about politics. International politics. Big power games – but without anything parochial, like East-West tantrums. Super-politics. Super-national politics. At which point I should substitute politics with big business.' He had stood up and was watching Hawn with his bright dark eyes.

244

'Oil,' said Hawn. 'The Anglo-Britannic Consortium. Right?'

'Spot on, old chap. Oil's a funny thing. It gets everywhere, sticks to everything. It flows under the sea, underground, over frontiers, above ideologies – it can make governments, it can break them. It breaks friendships, too.'

'We're not friends,' said Hawn. 'We're not even allies or colleagues. We're here because we were brought here, under armed guard. We'll go away under guard.'

The Jew gave them a sad smile. 'You're wrong. You're staying tonight in this hotel, in the next room. The one condition is that you do not leave that room. Your things have been sent over from Headquarters and you can ring down for supper. Then tomorrow, at eight o'clock, we are going for a little drive.'

'Just the three of us? No escort?'

'Just the three of us.'

'Where to?'

'Not far. But please, don't press me. You see, my position is rather like that of a surgeon preparing to undertake a difficult operation. I prefer to discuss the case when it is all over.'

Anna spoke for the first time; her voice was weary, uninterested: 'I suppose that means you're performing the operation on us? Oh God, how is it that we always finish up getting used? First Pol. Then that creep, Doktor Wohl. Now you – whoever you are.'

Hanak was blushing again. 'That's me – the mystery man. Now, how about a last drink?'


They were woken by the 7.15 alarm call. Hawn had a headache that was not entirely due to the attentions of the two *Vopos*; and his mouth had a sour, furry taste flavoured with antiseptic and the aftermath of whisky.

They had a breakfast of omelettes and sausages and the brown bitter coffee. As Hanak had promised, their few belongings had been returned to them, with the exception of their passports and visas.

At 7.50 they knocked on Hanak's door. A voice called out in German, and Hawn replied quietly in English. The door opened. Hanak stood in front of them, wearing only a vest and a pair of Y-fronts. His body was white and completely hairless. 'Enter, my friends. Excuse my attire. Just trying to keep trim.'

He closed the door, dropped down on all fours, did six vigorous press-ups, then jumped up again, slightly flushed, 'I'll just nip into some clothes and we'll go down. The car's waiting.' He dressed without embarrassment, this time in a tweed shooting-jacket with leather shoulders and button-down pockets, matching plus-fours, and thick steel-toed boots, like skiing boots. He clumped into the bathroom, and returned a moment later with his hair combed and wet; then swallowed the remains of a cup of coffee by the bed.

Hawn had noticed, more from the way the man moved than from his shape, that there was something heavy under the shooting-jacket. Hanak was armed. Nothing very surprising about that: but it was a detail worth knowing.

The corridor outside was empty, also the lift: and in the lobby, just an old woman with a mop and pail and a sleepy-looking clerk behind the desk. No sign of any *Vopos* outside the entrance.

At the kerb stood a black Skoda saloon. It was empty. Hanak went round and opened the driver's door, which was unlocked. He gestured Anna to get in beside him, and Hawn in the back. The keys were in the ignition. People didn't steal cars in the German Democratic Republic.

They drove down the deserted street, in the opposite direction from Security Headquarters: into a broad grey avenue fringed with skeleton trees, pavements already busy with crowds hurrying to work: trolleys pasted with slogans swaying down the centre of the road between shoals of bicycles and belching trucks. There were few other cars.

Hanak was surprisingly silent. At the few attempts that Hawn and Anna made to find out where they were going, he either answered in a monosyllable or said nothing.

They drove on into straggling suburbs, past dilapidated factories bristling with red flags, but with chimneys mostly smokeless. The trolley-wires came to an end and they turned on to a narrow humped road with edges partially devoured by weeds. They met several trucks hogging the crown of the road, and Hanak had to pull over briskly on to the verge to avoid collision.

The dark pine-forests closed round them, casting a melancholy gloom under the pewter sky. The trees grew in almost perfect lines, tall and straight as ships' masts; while under them it was black as night.

They had been driving for half-an-hour when there was a break in the trees and Hawn saw a small lake, greenish-black like the forests, giving off no reflection. He felt a strange thrill, as Anna turned in her seat and gave him a questioning look. He leant forward and she whispered, above the noise of the engine. 'That German poem – the one Mönch sent us in Madrid?'

Hawn gave a quick nod, catching Hanak's eyes watching him in the driving mirror; then sat back, saying nothing. If Hanak wasn't going to tell them anything, why should they help Hanak? Wasn't it he who was now calling the shots?

They turned left, down an even narrower road, and passed a rusted red sign warning of deer. Hanak was driving slowly now, hunched forward over the wheel. The road was very straight, a long grey scar between the endless marching stalks of pine-trunks. Then, in the far distance, Hawn could just make out what looked like a hut, or perhaps a sentry-box. As they drew closer, he could see the sign on the roof: big yellow letters spelling HO IMBISS.

Hanak drew up on the opposite side from it and stopped, but did not switch off the engine. He looked at his watch. It was a few minutes before nine o'clock. Hawn leant forward. 'So we wait here?'

Hanak answered with a nod towards the hut across the road 'HO – *Handelsorganization*. State Trading Company.'

'All right if we get out and stretch our legs?' Hawn said. 'I need some fresh air.' He had already opened the door before Hanak replied:

'Don't go too far. Stay where I can see you.'

Hawn got out, and Anna followed, wrapping her French raincoat tightly round her. The air had a dank chill, full of the stifling odour of pine and rotting vegetation. Anna shivered. 'God, what a place! And Hanak's behaving so funnily. Not at all like last night. What do you think's happening?'

'That's what we've come to find out. You don't think they're going to make it easy for us, do you? Last night was just softening us up.'

'Well, they did a good job.'

Hawn led the way across to the hut. A pudding-faced woman in a black shawl sat behind a counter lined with metal bowls containing what looked like lard. On a shelf behind her was a row of soft drinks. She looked at Hawn and Anna as though they did not exist.

Behind them, the car's engine died. There was the distant cawing of a bird. Otherwise silence – total, unnatural. It was bitterly cold, and they returned to the car.

Hawn sank back into the rear seat. 'Lovely spot, Sam. What happens around here?'

'I believe it's a popular holiday resort in the summer. In winter there's hunting and fishing. The whole area is full of lakes. But it's usually empty round now, till the week-end.'

'How long do we have to wait?'

'Not long, I hope.' Not once did Hanak turn his head while he spoke.

Hawn sat forward, speaking close to the man's ear. 'Listen, Sam. We were pretty patient and easy-going last night – perhaps it was the booze, plus the friendly fists and boots of the People's Police. I didn't press you too hard. This morning I feel different. There are one or two more things I want to know. About you, for instance. You're not German, are you?'

'Why do you say that?'

'Well, if I met an Eskimo or a Papuan Indian, I'd say they weren't German either. I think you're English. London, born and bred.'

'Please yourself.'

'Come on, Sam. I'm not pleasing myself, nor are you. I thought you might be an English Communist who likes to play free and easy in East Germany. But the authorities in these countries tend not to trust English Communists – not

248

enough, at any rate, to have them practically pulling rank on a full Colonel of Security. I think you're here on a very special mission, with a very special status. Are you anything to do with ABCO?'

Hanak laughed. 'No, I am not.' This time he turned in his seat. 'Look, Tom, you got yourself into this thing. You went in with your eyes open – both of you. You've had plenty of opportunity to get out, but you carried right on. OK, that's your decision. But look at it from my point of view. This is a big game, and I'm one of the players. There is also a damn big pot in the middle of the table. And now, just as the final hand is about to be played, you ask to see my cards.' His soft lips smiled, but his eyes remained grave. 'Sorry, Hawn – I'm not showing you my cards.'

In the far distance, down the straight road, a dark blob had appeared. Hawn stiffened. Hanak and Anna had seen it too. It grew larger: an olive-green jeep with a canvas hood and two *Vopos* in the front.

It stopped exactly opposite them, in front of the hut. The *Vopo* in the passenger seat got out. He stared at the Skoda, then walked round to the back of the jeep. A second man appeared. He was tall, in a long black overcoat. He stood quite still for several seconds, then walked past the *Vopo* towards the Skoda, with a crooked loping movement. He was a hunchback.

The *Vopo* followed a few paces behind, opened the rear door of the Skoda. The man climbed awkwardly in, folding his legs up as though they were shanks of badly articulated machinery. He wore gold-rimmed spectacles which magnified his eyes out of all proportion. His hair was a shock of grey, with no parting, and his ears had a translucent look, mauve with the cold.

Hanak turned and said, 'I would like you to meet Doktor Reiss.'

Hawn looked the man in the eye and said, 'Shouldn't it be Alan Rice?'

The hunchback showed his teeth, long and yellow like well-polished wooden pegs. 'I haven't been called that in nearly thirty years!' His accent was clearly English, but slightly off-key: like one of those long-retired Englishmen who have lived for years in exile on some sunny slope.

Hanak said: 'Doktor Reiss knows why we are here.'

Reiss's bloodless lips stretched back again across his gums. 'I thought they'd have forgotten about it by now. Who dug it up?'

'Mr Hawn is an English journalist. Miss Admiral is a professional researcher.'

The hunchback nodded. 'I offer you both my congratulations. You must have both been very lucky and very tenacious. You must also have won the trust and co-operation of certain people who are not much given to friendly confidences.' He smiled again, at each of them; his breath had a sour bitter smell. Hawn wondered if he had been drinking.

Outside, the *Vopo* had got back into the jeep, and a moment later it started up. Hanak watched it until it was well past them, then turned again towards the back seat: 'Doktor Reiss, we still have to recover the documents – the full minutes and memoranda of every meeting concerned with "Operation Bettina".'

Rice drew his lips back even further; he looked like a man who had been dead for days. 'Why are you so sure that I know?'

Hanak spoke quietly, without once looking at Hawn and Anna: 'Because you were leading co-ordinating officer of the whole operation. You ran the Istanbul end, and later the Caribbean. And you have been interrogated by the authorities here and have told them where the documents were hidden. We know that it is somewhere in this area.'

Hawn interrupted: 'I'd like to ask Doctor Rice a question. Who was in charge of this operation on the other side – our side?'

Rice seemed not to have heard. He had taken out a handkerchief and soundlessly blew his nose. Hawn persisted:

'Was somebody called Shanklin involved? Major Toby Shanklin?'

Rice's reaction was swift and spiteful. 'What do you know about it all? It was too long ago – you were too young, you and this Jew here.'

Hawn said: 'I know that Shanklin was in Mexico and Venezuela with you. He was also with you one night when you killed a man in your car. I don't know who was driving, but the dead man was a Consular official called de Vere Frisby. He'd been in Istanbul earlier, and so had Shanklin.'

Rice made a whistling noise through his nostrils. 'I may have been driving – I can't remember now. Frisby was careless, stepped out under the wheels. He was also a nuisance. He'd started asking too many questions. In Mexico he got talking to one of the tanker masters, then he somehow got hold of some papers – top secret, German, from the German Embassy in Mexico City. I tell you, he was a nuisance.'

'Did you kill him?'

'The car did.'

'Did you murder him?'

'Murder? He was knocked down by a car. Read the official reports.'

'I have. At least one of them is missing from the files.'

'That's not my fault.'

'What about Shanklin? How much was he involved?'

'I was giving him a lift. His car had broken down.'

'I mean, how much was Shanklin involved in "Operation Bettina"?'

Another pause. 'He was suspicious. He'd become suspicious in Istanbul. He'd got himself posted to the Caribbean to try and find out more. Frisby could have told him – only he was killed first. Shanklin, I mean,' and he sniggered, as though he remembered something that amused him.

Hawn said, 'And what do you think's going to happen to you, Doctor Rice, when all this comes out?'

'Comes out?'

'Is published all over the world – at least, in the free press?'

'The free press!' Rice had again turned his skull-like features to Hawn and bared his dreadful teeth. 'My dear sir, I am a professional scientist. I am one of the three greatest scientists in the German Democratic Republic. Nothing will happen to me. I shall merely continue my work.'

'Let's get going,' Hanak said, with a note of impatience.

The road began to twist, the trees grew closer, darker, until it became twilight. Then it cleared. Ahead was a wide flat wasteland fringed with distant pines: an untidy pattern of lake and marshland, with road following the edge of the water for a few hundred yards, until it reached a wooden pier that ran out to a little island. At the end of this was a small café, shuttered and desolate, its terrace empty of tables, its yellow paint blistered and blotched with damp. On the roof was a red star with one of its points bent inwards like a rusty claw.

Doctor Rice told Hanak to stop at the end of the pier. For a moment none of the party moved, as though each were waiting for one of the others to lead the way. Hanak got out first. He opened Rice's door and held it back, while the hunchback climbed out and stood gaunt and lopsided against the dark wall of trees.

Hawn and Anna followed him. It was very still, very cold – a dank, bone-chilling cold that carried with it the corrupt whiff of stagnant water and dead waterlogged vegetation.

Hawn looked around: 'This another happy playground for the workers?'

Rice said, 'In the summer they sometimes have banquets in that café.'

Hanak turned. 'All right, Herr Doktor, show us the way.'

Rice pointed a long finger at the pier. 'That wasn't there before, you understand. Nor was the café. Just the island.'

'Lead the way.'

Rice loped on to the pier. Hanak let Hawn and Anna follow him, before taking up the rear, his big steel-tipped boots clomping on the spongy boards.

The pier was about fifty yards long. The water below was black and freezing; crusts of ice had collected round the wooden piles. The café stood at the near end of the island, which was perhaps a hundred yards long and thirty wide, tapering to a point.

They crossed the abandoned concrete terrace and began to follow a muddy path towards a clump of pines. At the far end two rocks jutted out of the water. Rice stopped and stood peering down between them, at a crevice half clogged

252

with moss. He raised his crooked shoulders and turned to Hanak. 'Down there,' he said, with a vague gesture towards the rocks.

'Get it.'

'It weighs at least fifty kilos! It'll take all three of us to get it up. It's made of lead.'

Hawn said, 'So you weren't just dumping the stuff? You were preserving it for posterity?'

'You know what the Germans are like,' Rice said: 'They love documents. They never destroy anything, if they can help it. As for this stuff, we never knew when it might come in useful.'

Hanak had stepped forward and stood examining the crevice. Hawn and Anna joined him. It took them several seconds to make it out : about three feet down, a stout piton, filthy with rust, had been driven into the rock at a steep angle. Hanging from it was a chain, its links at least half an inch thick, disappearing between the moss into the black water.

Anna said, 'You're going to need some sort of lever.' She glanced quickly round – at the silent water, the row of trees, the abandoned café behind them.

Hanak flopped down on his belly and poised himself forward until he was hanging over the mouth of the crevice. 'Just let's see how much slack there is.' He reached down, groped for the end of the chain and pulled. It came up slack – several feet of it. He then stood up and gave it a hard wrench, stumbled and sat down in front of Hawn. The icy chain was trailing limp and slimy between his fingers. They all stared at the severed link, dangling at the end of about four feet. It was crusted with algae and weeds, as well as rust, but by rubbing it in the mud they saw that it was a clean cut.

Hanak spoke first. 'A chain like that doesn't break. Somebody's been here before us.'

'The question is, just how long ago,' said Hawn. 'And it wasn't any casual picnicker playing around these rocks. It would take a heavy saw, even oxyacetylene, to cut through that chain.' He stood staring at the black frozen links lying coiled in the mud like the skeleton of a large snake. In the icy silence the only sound was the chatter of Rice's teeth.

Hawn looked at him; then at Anna and at Sam Hanak, and at the derelict café and at the path leading up to the pier, and at the trees across the still water. He sensed a numb anticlimax, a feeling of futility as though he were the victim of some obscure and protracted practical joke. Yet he was also puzzled. Hanak seemed puzzled too, as well as barely concealing his annoyance. Anna was looking at him for an explanation, but received none.

The only one who showed no emotion at all was Dr Alan Rice – except for feeling the cold. He looked like a man who had thin blood. Hawn turned to him:

'You knew somebody had been here before us, didn't you?'

'I knew nothing,' Rice replied, with chilling composure. 'I haven't been back to this place for over thirty years.'

'How can you be sure it's the same place?'

'The same place?'

Hawn said patiently, 'There are dozens of little lakes round here. This place has changed – you said so yourself. The café hadn't even been built when you were last here.' He took a step forward and his foot squelched in the mud; a twig snapped under his shoe. He was standing opposite Rice, facing out across the water.

Rice shrugged his misshapen shoulders. 'You saw the chain, didn't you?'

'I saw a bit of broken chain hanging on a nail. I bet half the islands and jetties round here have got chains or ropes at the end of them for mooring small craft in the summer.' He took another step forward, until he could smell the hunchback's breath. 'Whose orders are you acting on, Rice?' – but as he spoke there came a crack across the water. It sounded like branch splitting in the stillness, followed by a series of sharp echoes like whip-lashes dying slowly round them. He glanced out at the bank on their left, at the wall of trees where the noise seemed to have come from – but saw nothing.

In the same instant he felt Rice's sloping shoulder lurch

against him and the weight of the man's body collapse like a folding table. Hawn was just in time to grab him round the waist; then he looked into the man's face. The jaw-bone and most of one cheek had gone, leaving his eye hanging naked, glaring unseeing into Hawn's.

Hanak had yelled, 'Down!' He had already flung Anna flat in the mud.

Hawn was down on his knee, still supporting the inert body of Rice, as though it would be indecent to let it drop. It was Rice, dead, who had saved him.

Hawn now twisted round, holding the body in front and slightly above him, when he felt the impact of a second bullet drill between the man's shoulder-blades, straight into the hump-back, and exit through the collar-bone, brushing Hawn's sleeve with a draught of air, before spending itself against one of the small pines behind them where it sliced a scar in the bark.

Hawn, flat on the ground now, was edging towards Hanak and Anna under cover of the trees. He felt sick rather than frightened. The ground was spattered with slivers of bone and gristle, several teeth; and there was a great deal of blood about, soaked black into the mud.

He was near enough to touch Anna's hand, when he heard the third crack. This time the whine carried above the echoes. He knew it had been close, but he didn't know how close. You never did know. He had been shot at many times during his career, in jungle, desert, in cars, planes, helicopters. But it had always been an impersonal sensation : part of the random ritual of war.

This was different. There was a man, or perhaps men, out in those trees, and they weren't firing on vague orders from above : weren't firing to preserve some loose map reference or hold that edge of the lake. These were marksmen, shooting at him and Anna and Sam Hanak : and they were shooting single rounds with at least one high-velocity rifle, accurately, to kill.

Hawn realized again Rice's body remained his sole protection. He glanced quickly, desperately round. Whoever had set this up had done so with expertise. The paltry pines on the island could offer only the most temporary protection : enough for the enemy to adjust their sights, 'shoot their guns in'.

The path back to the café was open ground. One of them might make it, zigzagging, flat-out – then hole up in the café. But for how long, unarmed? The pier beyond, and the short stretch of road back to Hanak's car, would be death-traps. They might as well walk it, hands in their pockets, holding their heads up like clay pigeons.

The question was, how many of them were there? And *who* were they?

This was alien territory – beyond even the rules of Pol's game, with his clandestine bank accounts and band of mercenaries. True, Pol had arranged the meeting with the bumptious Dr Wohl – but then Wohl was merely a double-faced go-between, a privileged Party hireling.

Hawn was thinking fast, still lying flat, moving like a reptile towards the trees, wondering if he would feel the bullet, whether it would hurt him, or whether it would be just a blank nothing. Instead, he felt only the slimy chill of the mud. Time became concertinaed, meaningless. How many seconds now since the first shot? They had picked off Rice, and now were just firing at leisure. But who? And why?

The most plausible candidates, of course, were always ABCO; but Hawn doubted that even their arm could reach this far. For this was the other side, the enemy side, home of the spiritual and commercial adversaries of everything that ABCO represented, where the only writ was that of the Workers' State which operated on a very short lead from the Kremlin. Besides, ABCO had had plenty of opportunities to strike. Why should they choose this eleventh hour to risk a clumsy shoot-out in this distant, hostile domain?

He was in the shadow of the trees when the fourth bullet thumped into the mud a couple of inches from his left knee. He had decided, with a kind of reckless chivalry, that they would get him before they got Anna. Though his body would offer feeble protection, judging by the second

256

bullet that had passed straight through Rice and sliced into the tree behind.

Hawn thought, even one gun – a heavy automatic pistol – tilted the odds considerably. Now, if they could just get to the café . . . He remembered that Hanak's car was facing away from the trees. If they could only reach it, they would just have those few vital seconds to get the engine started. Enough for a bullet in the tyre, the petrol tank?

Hanak was lying on his side under the narrow tree-trunks, adjusting a long metal tube to the end of a pistol. Hawn thought at first that he was fixing a silencer, then realized that he was converting the gun into a small rifle. He had taken out a leather sling which he snapped round his shoulder and wrist to give himself extra leverage. 'Keep your eyes skinned on those trees – we may spot a muzzle-flash.'

'Who are they?' Anna said, in a small distant voice, as though she had not fully taken in what was happening.

'How the devil should I know? – except that there's at least one marksman out there with a very powerful rifle.' Hanak's voice was brisk, competent.

Then two sounds reached them simultaneously. The fifth bullet shrieked into the tree beside Hanak, grazing his left thumb; and at the same time, two quick rattling noises, like pebbles being shaken inside a tin can. Hawn recognized the sounds at once, horribly, excitingly familiar – bursts of automatic fire – and they were not being aimed at them. Then a third burst, followed by shouts, and a scream – shrill, like a woman's scream, carrying clearly across the water.

Hawn thought he could see movement in the trees opposite, but with only one good eye his vision was soon blurred. He heard a voice : 'No one move !'

More voices, shouts of command, tramping feet; then the growl of approaching vehicles. The three of them crouched rigidly behind the pines. The voices continued from the far bank, but less urgent now. Then, coming down the pier, the sound of boots. Hanak had hastily dismantled his gun and sling and put them away under his coat.

Whether it was the cold or the excitement, his pale cheeks were flushed pink.

Hawn said savagely, 'Well, Sam, how does this fit into your game? Or perhaps it wasn't part of your brief? They never brief you enough, do they? Always finish up by dropping you in the shit.'

Sam Hanak did not reply; he did not even look at Hawn. He was looking at the two *Vopos* who had appeared around the side of the café. They were followed by the short, bulky figure of Colonel Kardich. He was in uniform this time – epaulettes, smock-tunic, boots, belt and holster all polished like dark mirrors. The pair of *Vopos* had their guns aimed at the three of them. One of them said, '*Raus*!'

Anna was already coming out with her hands up. Hawn followed her, but without raising his hands, reaching instead to shield her from what was left of Doctor Rice. The *Vopos* had young hard faces, their eyes full of dull hostility. Kardich walked round them. 'Miss Admiral, you may put your hands down.' He stopped and glanced down at Rice, then moved the body gently with the toe of his boot, turning it enough to see what had happened to the scientist's face. He looked up at Hanak, then at Hawn.

'He was a valuable man, Doktor Reiss. One of the best of his kind.' His voice was flat, without emotion. 'Did you find what you were looking for?'

Hanak answered : 'You found it first, long ago. We should have known that Rice wouldn't have kept his secret that long.'

'You are very trusting, Herr Hanak. And a little naïve, I think, for a man in your position.'

The Jew stood studying his bleeding thumb, grazed by the bullet, then looked up at Kardich and smiled. 'You'd have done the same thing, Colonel. Only you had the advantage of operating on your home ground.'

Kardich blinked wearily at him. 'Follow me, all of you.'

They made their way round the café and along the pier. Two jeeps were drawn up a little way down the road, and opposite the trees where the shooting had come from stood a truck. A dozen men were moving around, several of them wearing steel helmets.

A couple of *Vopos* emerged from the trees opposite the island, lugging a bulky weight wrapped in an army blanket. One of them also carried, besides his Kalashnikov automatic, a sporting rifle with a telescopic lens. Kardich led the way until the two parties met. The Colonel signalled the *Vopos* to stop, said something, and they dropped their bundle like a heavy sack on the road. Kardich leant down and pulled back the end of the blanket. 'You know him?'

Anna shuddered and looked away. Hawn nodded. 'A Corsican – Serge Rassini. We first saw him in Turkey. He was pretending to be drunk.'

'He will not get drunk again,' Colonel Kardich said. The Corsican's face was splashed with mud, and there was a dark clotted mass at his throat. Kardich let go of the blanket and signalled to the two *Vopos* to carry on.

Behind them a massively laden stretcher was now being carried out from the trees. Kardich again led the way towards it.

They had thrown a blanket over this one, too, but it was hardly large enough to cover the body beneath, from which now came a shrill whimper – the same voice they had heard cry out from the woods.

The two bearers again stopped when they reached Colonel Kardich. He turned to Hawn and Anna. 'So this is your good friend – your comrade-in-arms, your protector and benefactor. The man who has just tried to have you killed.'

Pol's face was the colour of dirty water and his kiss-curl straggled over the dome of his forehead like the ends of a frayed rope. He peered up at Hawn with eyes miserable with pain. 'Ah, quelle jolie fin de partie!'

'Why did you do it?'

'It was necessary. An act of policy. I would like to explain, but I haven't the strength.'

Hawn gave him a tired grin and spoke without looking at Colonel Kardich; 'Die Vöglein schweigen im Walde – the woods by the lake, Charles. And soon you will be silent too.'

'Ah, not quite yet, I hope!' Pol giggled feebly. 'Mon cher,

there are good days and there are bad days. Voilà – this is a bad day. As you say, it seems that Doktor Mönch may have had the last laugh.'

Kardich said something in German and the two *Vopos* began to move away. 'Give me some cognac!' Pol cried, and closed his eyes.

'We have more waiting for you than cognac,' Kardich said, and turned to Hawn and Anna. 'You will both get into the first jeep, please.'

Hanak was already walking back towards the Skoda; then paused, and gave them both a sad smile. He was holding his wounded thumb, wrapped in a handkerchief.

As Hawn and Anna reached the first jeep, from inside they heard another squeal of pain. The last they saw of Pol were his tiny feet peeping out from between the canvas flaps at the back. Anna turned to Colonel Kardich. 'Is he badly hurt?'

'He will live.'

The car was a big black Russian saloon with a military driver and a plain-clothes man in the front, Hawn and Anna in the back. They drove fast, with the headlamps on high-beam. By noon they were past Oranienburg and on the autobahn heading west to Berlin. Except for a few whispered exchanges between Anna and Hawn, no one spoke. Anna was in a state of shock, her body shaken with spasms of shivering.

At the checkpoint into the East Sector they slowed down but did not stop. The plain-clothes man flashed a card and they drove through, down the dismal dirty-white reaches of Karl-Marx-Allee, looking now, in daylight, like two rows of vast pock-marked tombstones: across Alexanderplatz, and west into drab suburbs littered with workers' flats backed by great mounds of rubble half overgrown with scrub and weed.

They did not cross at Checkpoint Charlie, but at the more remote Glienicke Bridge. There they stopped, but only for a moment. Two *Vopos* surrounded the car and whipped the rear doors open. An officer appeared and pointed across the bridge. 'Go.'

It seemed a long lonely walk, across the murky, half-frozen waters of the Spee Canal. At the far side was a broad white line on the road; two American MPs sat in a jeep and glanced at them both, curiously. A taut-faced man in a black leather raincoat approached them. 'Mr Hawn. Miss Admiral.' He gestured towards a BMW parked a few yards on, with its engine running. A second man in a raincoat sat behind the wheel. They were again shown into the back, and again they drove off at speed.

Hawn tried to ask the first man what was happening, where they were going. The German replied, 'Please, I am not permitted to discuss matters.'

Twenty minutes later they drew up outside the international terminal of Tempelhof Airport, and were conducted to the British Airways counter. Here a youngish man with a clipped moustache and weak eyes stepped forward and said, 'Mr Hawn, Miss Admiral, my name's Wynn-Catlin – I'm with the British Consulate here.' He handed Hawn a plastic folder. 'These are your travel documents for entering the United Kingdom, and your tickets. Your plane leaves in just under half-an-hour.'

When Hawn looked round, the German had gone. He turned to Wynn-Catlin: 'Would it be too much to ask what's going on?'

The man looked at him, full of officious disdain. 'I'm afraid it would. You see, I haven't the faintest idea myself. I just know that you've lost your passports, and that it's our job to see you get back home.'

They landed at Heathrow at 2.15 local time. It was raining.

Customs and Immigration must have been tipped off; the formalities were swift and perfunctory. Hawn was half expecting, with a mixture of vanity and habit, to be greeted by reporters and cameras. Instead, there was just one man, in a chauffeur's uniform, carrying a card with 'Mr Hawn' printed on it. He told them he had a car waiting for them outside.

It was a dark blue Jaguar with a telephone between the

front seats. Hawn tried again : 'Where are we going?'

'To Mr Shanklin's place in Wiltshire, sir.' His accent was that of the perfect gentleman's gentleman.

'I'd prefer to go home. Number eighty-two, Pembridge Villas, please.'

'I'm sorry, sir. I have my instructions.'

'You'll do as I say, or I'll call the police.' But the car was already moving, gathering speed.

'Mr Shanklin gave me a message,' the chauffeur said, with no inflection in his voice. 'He told me to tell you that you are now in safe hands and that you have nothing more to worry about.'

'That's very nice of Mr Shanklin. Can I reach him on this telephone?'

'He won't be at home for another hour, sir.'

'I see. Supposing we jump out at the first red lights?'

'I wouldn't advise it, sir. Mr Shanklin is very strict about his instructions.'

Hawn sat back, holding Anna close to him, as they drove down the long underpass towards the M4.

# CHAPTER EIGHT

## Endgame

*Three may keep a secret, if two of them are dead.*

BENJAMIN FRANKLIN

It was a grey-stone farmhouse with a converted barn, standing on the brow of a hill behind a fringe of beech trees; and in a field beyond, a dilapidated windmill in the process of being restored. On the forecourt stood a muddy Range-Rover. The chauffeur nodded at it and said, 'Mr Shanklin's at home.'

The door was opened by a large woman with a long pleasant face, her hair tied in a bun. 'Mr Hawn, Miss Admiral! Welcome! I expect you're both exhausted? Have you seen a doctor? We've got a very good locum here – I'm sure he'd pop over and look at you.'

She led them down a passage lined with gumboots and overcoats and spades, into a high-beamed room with an inglenook in which a log-fire blazed between two brass lions. Apart from one or two pieces of expensive furniture, the room was spare and rustic, with a pleasant homely untidiness. On a table in a corner stood a handsome scale model of the windmill Hawn had seen outside.

The woman had led them towards the fire. 'Miserable weather, isn't it?' She rubbed her great hands together. 'It's a bit early for a drink, but would you like some tea?'

'I'd like a whisky,' said Hawn. 'Where's Mr Shanklin?'

'I expect he'll be down in a jiffy. He's probably having a bath. Now, you wanted a whisky? Would Miss Admiral like one, too?'

'Please.' Anna sat down in a very old chair and hunched her shoulders. The woman went over to a Welsh dresser to fetch the drinks. Hawn noticed that the only reading matter in the room was a shelf of leather-bound volumes, each containing three condensed popular novels, and several stout volumes of *Debrett's Peerage and Landed Gentry*.

The woman handed them their drinks, just as Shanklin came in. He wore no braces, and his shirt drooped out under a shabby cardigan that was too tight for his shoulders. He was carrying a shotgun.

'My dear Hawn! How very nice.' He paused. 'I don't think I've had the pleasure of meeting your young friend?'

They had both stiffened in their chairs. Shanklin glanced down at the gun, and laughed. 'Sorry, you mustn't mind the weaponry! You're in the country now, you know. I was just oiling it.' He propped the gun up carefully against the wall, then came forward and sat down. 'Mind you, I don't blame you for being jumpy. I would be, if I'd been through what you have.' He turned to Anna. 'But we still haven't been introduced.'

'Anna Admiral. I'm sure you've heard my name before.'

Shanklin gave a robust chuckle. 'Touché! I'm afraid in my job I get too much into the habit of standing on ceremony. Now, are you hungry? I expect you could do with something after that plastic muck they serve you on BA?'

'Later,' said Hawn. 'We haven't come down here just to enjoy your hospitality, Mr Shanklin. I want explanations – an explanation for everything.'

'Of course you do. The trouble is, where to begin? Perhaps I should ask you, where would you like me to begin?'

'Wouldn't the best place be the beginning?'

'Well of course!' Shanklin's voice had slid imperceptibly into that soothing tone that was at once intimate enough to be seductive. 'Indeed, what better place to begin at than the beginning? Trouble is, there are so many beginnings. Are your drinks all right?' He glanced round. 'Jane's left, has she?'

'Start with Venice,' Hawn said.

'Yes, Venice. As I think I recall, you were there on holiday – happened to bump into that unhappy fellow, Grotti Savoia, and then into Logan. Awful ass, Logan, but still, one mustn't be too unkind – fellow has the most ghastly job which he does very well. Through him, you met that fat Frenchie, Pol?

'At the same time, you had just had your inspired hunch – a wild pipe-dream glimpsed in the dark waters of the canals, eh? That the bogey-men of the America-Britannic Consortium had been fuelling Hitler's war-machine and reaping rich profits therefrom? Well, here we come to one of the few genuine coincidences of this whole bizarre saga – that at the same time as meeting that villain Pol, you should also have made the brief acquaintance of Mr Robak. Now unfortunately for you – for all of us, really – both these gentlemen took your pipe-dream seriously. You may ask why? Not, with respect, because you were the star reporter of Fleet Street. Men like Pol and Robak are not worried by journalists. They were worried by you for a simple reason. Because they knew your pipe-dream to be true.'

Without asking them, he fetched the whisky and refilled their glasses; then sat back and folded his mottled, hairy hands together. Hawn again observed that he was not drinking.

'At this point we must venture some speculation. Robak, who is not the subtlest of men, tried to warn you off. At the same time he contacted me. He seemed to be in a slight panic. He even hinted that if you made any positive moves to try and pursue investigations into your theory, then direct action would have to be taken against you. I told him not to be so primitive – to sit back and wait to see if anything happened. What happened was that you paid me a visit. At that point, I decided to play you along – like a fish on a line, if you'll forgive the metaphor.

'I put you on to Norman French, with whom I believe you'd already had dealings? French was a thoroughly horrid little man, but he'd chalked up one achievement to his name – he'd taken ABCO and a lot of its stockholders for a big ride. One of these was Robak. And while out in the Caribbean, French had also dug up a few skeletons from under the oil-rigs. I'll never be quite sure how much he knew, or how much he guessed. It was certainly nothing he could prove, or he'd have no doubt started to blackmail a few people – my good self among them, no doubt. But he put you on to Doctor Alan Rice, obviously knowing that Rice had been tied up in some sort of racket.

'You started to check on Rice. Don't worry, the Public Record Office *is* public, remember! I knew you were on to Rice and me and Frisby, and on to the Turkish end, with Salak. It wasn't a difficult trail to follow. To the average investigator, it wouldn't have meant much. But it just so happened that it fitted rather neatly into your theory.'

Hawn cut in: 'There's a missing file on your activities in the Caribbean.'

'There are several. Official secrets, hush-hush stuff. Those two Intelligence blokes who flew out to Mexico in '44 weren't at all happy about young Frisby's death – not at all happy, and they said so. Unfortunately it was thought best, in the national interest – which meant the interests of ABCO – that some of their reports should remain classified.

'Then, my dear Hawn, we find you going to your old chum, Angus MacIntyre. I'd been rather expecting you to do that – that is, if you were at all serious. And when you did, I confess I didn't like it. The old boy's a bit past it now, but he knows one hell of a lot. About the only thing he doesn't know is how to keep his mouth shut. He was always careful enough not to rush into print, but from an old friend like you I don't suppose he had many secrets. He put you on to Mönch, didn't he? And Salak?'

He rubbed his hands together, staring at the ceiling, the hair at the back of his balding head sticking out, making him look like an ageing bishop on the rampage.

'Now Mönch himself would not normally have worried me. He'd been a bureaucrat and an administrator, but strictly second-rank. He'd have only become dangerous if you knew exactly what questions to ask him. You did – at least, you knew some of them. The names of Rice and Salak would become clearer, more isolated. It would have been like the early stages of developing a film – the shapes would no longer be varying shadows, they would have been taking on definite outlines.

'But here I know what you're going to ask. What about Pol? Here you must understand that while you were carrying out your preliminary investigations, both Pol and I had you under increasing surveillance – but, unfortunately, independently of each other. Pol trusts no one, and only a fool would trust him. I tried to keep track of him, but he was too clever. When you went to Istanbul, for instance, I suspected that Pol was behind it.

'Now I have to be careful here – careful not to impute motives to Pol. As I said, the man's a total scoundrel, a rogue – even in a business like oil which breeds rogues. But fortunately I have some knowledge of Pol, and some insight into how he works. I'd made discreet inquiries at your newspaper, and found out that you were acting strictly freelance – a mixed blessing, since you would not have the resources of your paper behind you, but also because a little pressure applied in the right places would no doubt have dissuaded your editor and his executives from pursuing the story.

'I also ran a routine check at your bank, and found that your account is not in good shape. I even made similar inquiries about Miss Admiral here. At the last count she was fifty-two pounds in credit, and had two hundred pounds on deposit with a Building Society.'

Shanklin sank his head on to his chest and smiled at Anna from under his thick pale eyebrows. The deranged bishop turned gentle don: 'Hardly enough, my dear girl, to finance a round-trip to Istanbul – and staying at the old Pera Palace, too! Particularly since Imin Salak was not a man given to disposing of information gratis. It was then that I guessed that Pol was funding you.'

'Do you still not know what Pol's motives were?' said Hawn.

'Well, let's say, some of them – not all. Those motives were the same as mine.'

'You're not a member of Jacques? Or are you?'

Shanklin sat back and rubbed his hands together. 'The French Resistance and the SOE had a lot in common, I'll grant you. I'm tempted to answer in the affirmative – it would be rather a feather in my cap, at my age, even if it wasn't true. It isn't. Justice pour les Anciens Combattants is an obscure and distasteful organization whose aims are to eliminate former Nazis. Pol is *not* a member of that organization. He never has been. He has been using its name purely as a cover.'

'Then how the hell did your motives coincide with Pol's?'

'Simply, to protect ABCO. But in order fully to understand, it is also necessary to understand the full complexities of an organization like ABCO. Simplicity is something they do *not* understand, even on the most basic level. And in order to protect themselves, they devised at least two alternative scenarios. They could have eliminated you – which was the method preferred by certain executives, including Robak, who was delegated to do the hatchet-work. I was able to overrule that plan. It seemed to me unnecessarily crude, as well as risky. To have got rid of you would have meant getting rid of Miss Admiral too – and if anything went wrong, a lot of awkward questions might have been asked, leaving us in even worse trouble than when we'd started.'

'My goodness, Mr Shanklin,' Anna said, looking up from her glass of whisky, 'should I go down on my knees and kiss your hand?'

Shanklin looked serene. 'A most charming and worthy sentiment, my dear. But unnecessary. No, I persuaded my colleagues at ABCO to pursue a different course of action – one favoured, incidentally, by our Intelligence circles. I decided to let you both run free, financed by Pol, in order to find out just how far you would get. I wanted to find out just how strong, or how weak, ABCO's wartime secrets were. I reckoned – I hope, justly – that as a journalist of above-average ability, you'd prove an excellent probe. If you couldn't get at the full story – given your original inspiration, combined with the various helps and leads you had been given – then ABCO could be considered reasonably safe.

'However, I still had to reckon with Pol. As I was careful to say, while some of our motives were similar, his methods have been rather different.'

'He was in it for revenge,' said Hawn.

'That may have played a part, but only a small part. Pol's motive was still to protect ABCO – it was simply that his method of doing so was to eliminate, one by one, the main protagonists and potential witnesses in the "Bettina" conspiracy.'

'But why!' said Anna. 'Pol may be a rogue, but he's no worse than the rest of you. And one thing is certain – he hates ABCO's guts.'

Toby Shanklin looked down at her, chin on his chest, hands cupped together. 'With respect, my dear girl, the people Pol never hates are those who bring him money. And Pol has – or had – a thriving little petroleum enterprise going in France which he wanted to expand. He was negotiating a deal with ABCO when I met you both. One of the further prices for that deal was that Pol share a hand in snuffing out this "Bettina" business. His job was to liquidate every witness down the line. He simply used both of you, as two apparent innocents, to lead the way down that line. And you – and he – were very successful. Except that you all made your own mistake.

'You, Hawn, made the mistake of contacting me – on the prompting of the late lamented Prince Grotti Savoia. Admittedly, you would not have thought of getting on to Norman French, and without French your whole idea would probably have withered on the bough. No matter. I was alerted, and under the circumstances I knew what to do. But Pol's mistake was more mysterious. He killed Rice.

'Now here, apart from your fortuitous meeting with Pol and Robak in Venice, we come to the second and last real coincidence in this story. It was something which Pol should have checked out – or at least, which ABCO should have told him, if he hadn't insisted on working entirely on his own. Six months ago, ABCO signed a deal with the East

German Ministry of Trade to build a complex of petroleum-gas that will supply most of the Comecon countries. Because the deal is highly controversial, it has been kept secret. Rice was to be in charge of the German side of the deal.'

'Rice doesn't entirely make sense,' said Hawn. 'First I hear of him studying in a pre-war German University, with a British passport, then he's working with one of the Nazis' big industrial firms, and next he pops up as a so-called political refugee in the Caribbean, where he gets a top job working for ABCO. And it's about this time that you come into the picture. The files show that you knew Rice – knew him well enough to have been travelling in the same car with him when a certain young British diplomat was killed. Run over by you.'

'It was Rice's car, and he was driving. We must get that straight. As for the rest, I am not here to prove my innocence. Far from it. I simply want to get matters in perspective – so you don't go running around with any other funny ideas. All right?'

Anna sucked in her breath; otherwise there was silence. Shanklin stared into the fire. 'Rice was a scientist. One of the best. And as a petroleum expert, he understood the workings – the political workings – of the oil industry backwards. In the war that became almost as important to the Germans as his scientific knowledge. He was also half English and bilingual, and could therefore pass himself off as a refugee. He had started by helping to co-ordinate the Middle East operation, by way of Istanbul – making the right contacts through certain British diplomatic circles there and in Ankara – and went on to recruit his own men, the chief of whom was Salak. He did so well that the Germans decided to sacrifice his services as a scientist and ship him over to the Caribbean, when the Mediterranean was becoming too hot for the Germans. So Rice was put in charge of the Mexico-Venezuela end – and I'll hand it to him, he did it damn well.'

'Hardly a very alluring personality,' Hawn said, 'if I'm to judge from what I saw of him this morning. It *was* Rice that Pol killed this morning, I suppose, and not some grotesque decoy-duck put up for shooting practice by the *Vopos*?'

'No – it was Rice all right. That's why the East Germans are so annoyed.'

'So the East Germans are annoyed, are they? And what was their role in all this – apart from playing footsy with ABCO on some big petro-chemical deal? Hell, what was their moral stand? Rice's knowledge has presented them with conclusive evidence of a massive war crime by the West – a war crime committed by one of Communists' favourite pet aversions, a multi-national Capitalist corporation which is one of the very foundations of the bourgeois economy. Yet they sit back and let one of Pol's mercenaries pick off one of their plum scientists. Why?'

'My dear fellow, I'm surprised that you should be so naïve – that you are under the illusion that the Communists have any morality about anything. The Communists are, and always have been, supremely pragmatic beings. They operate from self-interest – a characteristic which I find rather encouraging. Personally, give me the self-seeking any time, rather than the self-righteous. And in the case of the East Germans, the moment one of our hated multi-nationals could be an advantage, they happily seize that advantage. As for war crimes, fortunately, as I have said, our fraternal friends in the East do not indulge in self-righteous recriminations, unless it is for a specific purpose.'

Hawn said : 'But you do admit that a war crime was committed by ABCO?'

'Look, what is a war crime? Auschwitz – Belsen? So, it's naughty to kill Jews. What about the bombing of Coventry, Hamburg, Dresden? Were they war crimes?'

'You sanctimonious shit!' Anna, sitting very straight and white-faced, had dashed her glass to the floor; and for a moment she seemed about to spring at Shanklin. 'You loathsome old hypocritical gangster – armchair gangster – gambling club-room gangster! You haven't got the guts to commit crimes yourself! Pol was a hypocrite and a gangster, but at least he took some part in what he was doing – was out there when the shooting started! But people like you ... ' She paused, about to cough with rage ... 'You have no conscience, no compassion, no morality. You're nothing but an ugly, greedy, wicked old man. And as long as ABCO pays your bills, you'll go on licking their arses!'

'Tut, tut, my dear lady – such language. I wouldn't have expected it.' He was peering at her from under his eyebrows, still the benevolent don rather than the wild bishop. 'But no matter, sticks and stones, sticks and stones.' He glanced at Hawn : 'I'm merely trying to put your minds at rest – by giving you some useful information, which is more than your friend Pol apparently did. If, however, you only wish to indulge in trivial abuse ... '

'All right, Shanklin. How did you get tied up in all this? Apart from having worked as a junior executive with ABCO before the war?'

'Well, I was drafted into SOE, which made me a lot more than a fly on the wall. Undercover work, with responsibility for the Middle East and the Balkans. Istanbul happened to be slap in the middle. And in Istanbul in those days you didn't just *hear* rumours – you could buy them on the street corner like lottery tickets. Some of the numbers came up, most of them didn't. And the people selling them were usually selling to both sides. There was even an occasion when the desk-wallahs in Cairo bought a piece of information already sold to the SOE in Sofia. Usual *Snafu* – situation normal, all fucked up. If you'll pardon the expression, Miss Admiral,' he added, with a snigger of sarcasm.

'But there was one rumour that wasn't sold – it was given to me by that young Englishman, de Vere Frisby, who held a junior post at the Istanbul Consulate, which was his cover for Intelligence operations. He was neurotic and drank too much – which in some ways helped his cover – and when he was sober, he wasn't at all a bad agent.

'It was from him that I first heard about Salak, who – as you no doubt know – was also working for us. We knew that oil was getting out of Istanbul and going astray, but because Turkey was doing a nice balancing act by remaining neutral, and because the Allies were desperate to get her in on our side and not to upset her, we had to be very careful how we acted. I put in a tentative report to POE, but it got mysteriously mislaid. At least, it never seems to have reached London – and if it did, somebody sat on it or flushed it down the toilet.'

'There's nothing in the Public Record Office.'

Shanklin crossed his legs. 'I'm sure there isn't. Anyway I got shot up in Yugoslavia, and at my own request was transferred to the Caribbean. I did more than that – I managed to get de Vere Frisby transferred with me, to Mexico. Frisby hadn't known about Rice by name, until he saw him face-to-face when Rice was working for ABCO in Vera Cruz. He recognized him at once as a German agent he'd known in Istanbul. Rice almost certainly recognized him, but unfortunately he was not only a good scientist – he was a good agent. He didn't let on and, stupidly, I didn't act on the spot. I made the mistake of sitting on Rice and following up further leads.'

'In what capacity?' said Hawn. 'Fearless undercover agent fighting for King and Country? Or as ABCO's faithful, well-paid lapdog?'

'Both. The two were the same. The interests of ABCO were part of the interests of Britain. The two were indivisible. They still are. You might both do well to remember that. Anyone who tries to hurt ABCO is trying to hurt this country. And when anyone does that – my God, they have me to answer to. And I'll smash them – I'll grind them underfoot. I've told you that before. And I mean it.'

Anna blurted out, her voice shuddering with fury : 'But wasn't ABCO doing everything it could to hurt this country by giving the Nazis oil?'

'They had very good reasons. But I'll come to those in a minute. Let's go back to Rice and Frisby in the Caribbean. I was, by now, pretty certain that elements in ABCO, and their agents, were shipping oil out under phoney Bills of Lading, even using false passports for the masters. Trouble was, there was no absolute proof. The only way we could have stopped it dead would have been to blockade the whole Caribbean and search every ship. That was out of the question – the oil was keeping our war effort alive, even if some of it happened to be keeping the enemy alive, too.

'Then I got my first piece of hard evidence against Rice. He'd been in contact with the German Embassy in Mexico City. And that was when I made my second mistake – I didn't arrest him there and then. Instead, I arranged for a meeting between him and Frisby – on some incidental pretext, I can't remember what. I went armed, in Rice's car. Rice was supposed to have the impression that I was on his side, ready to fix a deal. We arranged to meet outside the town, without witnesses – the sort of place where I could use some strong-arm stuff, if necessary.

'It was dark. I suspect Frisby had been drinking – though I can't be sure, because there was never an autopsy. He just stepped out into our lights as we approached, and Rice accelerated and ran him down, splitting his skull open. Rice said he thought it was a wild dog, but I knew damn well it was a lie. I was mad at the man, I can tell you. I filed official complaints, to the Mexican authorities and through ABCO, that Rice had driven with intent to kill, but both somehow managed to get bunged up in the works. Finally I made out an official report to London, and it seems London was worried enough to send out those two MI6 men. I told them what I thought, as well as what I suspected about Rice's activities, and why he wanted Frisby out of the way. I was even beginning to fear for my own life and took to going about armed, even sleeping with a gun under my bed.

'The trouble was, without Frisby I didn't have much of a case. Rice was grilled, but denied everything. Eventually the two officers went back to London. I don't think they were entirely happy, but whatever report they made, it conveniently disappeared. It was as though somebody up there was seeing that Rice led a charmed life! It always seemed that way, until this morning.

'Anyway, shortly after the agents flew back to London, ABCO – in the form of some of their top brass from New York – put a Big Brotherly hand on my shoulder and showed me the error of my ways. Rice's activities had to be tolerated, and my suspicions – not only in the interests of the Consortium, but also in the national public interest – had to be suppressed. In short, I was told to belt up.'

'And you went along with that?' said Hawn.

Toby Shanklin gave an impatient wave of his hand. 'I was a wild young man in those days. But not so wild, or green, to bite both hands that fed me. And I certainly wasn't going to finish up like de Vere Frisby, lying like a dead dog in a ditch.' He gave Hawn a hard, unambiguous stare. 'There was too much at stake – there still is. And nothing to be gained. Oil is our life-blood – quite as much today as it was during the war. And ABCO is still the heart that pumps that blood. We don't rock the boat, Hawn.

'I agree that there may have been a few bad boys about – some of them are now big boys with fat pensions and handles to their names. But we don't touch them – we absolutely must not touch them – or we not only upset the apple cart, we upset the whole rhythm of Western indus-trialized society.' He leant forward and stared grimly at each of them.

'And here I'm not talking about just a few retired ABCO executives in London and New York – or put out to pasture in Haslemere or Palm Springs. I'm not even talking about protecting ABCO's reputation. I'm talking about senior figures in the British Wartime Government. No, no,' he added hastily, holding up both hands this time : 'You don't catch me playing the dirty sneak. No tittle-tattle, no smear stories from me !'

Hawn spoke calmly. 'Civil servants, or politicians?'

'Both. The whole system was involved. And it wasn't just a matter of money – not for all of them, anyway. No – they were acting, as always, in the *national interest*. Be-cause, like all of us, they were shit-scared of the Russians.

'To really understand, you have to go back to the period – get the real flavour and tone of political thinking of the thirties and forties. Pretty muddled, pretty messy – and sometimes pretty daft. You see, with most of the intel-ligentsia still convinced that Soviet Russia was a haven over the hill, and with the Red Army seen as the great heroes of the day, the Communist menace was, if anything, even more potent than it is today. It was left to a handful of people at the top of the British and American Establishments to realize that Bolshevism had always been the true enemy. It was all right, of course, when the Russians and Germans were allies, and kissing each other in public – then the menace was clear enough, even to the stupidest soul. But after June 1941, when we woke up to find the Russian bear was on our side, a lot of people had to do a lot of rethinking.

'As early as 1943 it was becoming fairly obvious that the Nazis were beaten. It was just a matter of time. And time was the crucial factor. For every week, every day, the Russians were getting closer. And the Russians, remember – in most people's minds – were allowed to do no harm. Like the Blacks today, they were blessed with some sublime innocence, the mysterious gift of truth and all-seeing wisdom – as well as every other kind of poppycock and applecrap that you can name.

'And the only thing that could hold the Russians up, while the Western Allies captured as much of Europe as was left to them, was the mighty German Army. And without oil we know that the German Army would have been finished by the summer of 1944. A few months, even weeks later the Russians would have been eating chips in Boulogne. At least ABCO did their bit there.'

Hawn said : 'Are you repeating what the Big Boys told you to say back there in Mexico? Or do you really believe all this?'

'That's something I need not answer. Instead, let me ask you a question. How many hours did it take you to fly today from Berlin – from a hundred miles behind the Russian lines to London? Just over two hours – barely enough for a couple of drinks, a frozen lunch, and coffee. But that time and distance could have been a great deal shorter. It might not have existed at all. Just remember that.'

'Who killed Norman French?' said Hawn.

'I honestly don't know. But I can make a few intelligent

guesses – which is no more than the police have been able to do. Young French had made himself very unpopular with a lot of people. Mostly in America, and mostly in ABCO. But ABCO has a long arm, and an even longer memory. Normally they go after the big fish, not worms. Perhaps it was just unfortunate for French that he'd already got himself involved with your investigations.'

'Robak?'

'Robak – Schlobak.' Shanklin heaved his shoulders in a dismissive sigh; then got up, crossed the room and picked up the shotgun from where he had placed it against the wall. Deftly, in a single movement, he swung it up until it pointed at the wall above Hawn's head. Then, very deliberately, he cracked the gun open, and lowering it a few inches, squinted down each barrel. 'Don Robak was in Brazil, I understand. You've got contacts in the police. You can check.'

He blew hard, first down one barrel, then the other. 'Or it could have been any number of stockholders whom young Norman French had torn off, even ruined. There we are – clean as a whistle!' He replaced the gun and came back to his chair. He was smiling at them both indulgently: 'Anything else either of you want to know?'

'Who is Hanak?' Hawn said.

'Ah yes. Hanak. Rare bird. One in a million. Not out of the usual Secret Service mould – all Burton suits and rounds of bitter in the local in Horseferry Road. Oh no, Hanak's special. It was something of a privilege having him sent in to work with you. I hear he hurt his thumb, by the way?'

'Who the hell is he?' said Hawn.

'One of our brighter lads attached to the Ministry of Defence, as it is euphemistically put. Jewish, of course. Rather a nice irony there, I think – one that would appeal to your newshound's sense of the absurd. Only I forget, of course – you won't be able to write it, will you?'

'And who's going to stop me?'

'You will. Or rather, your self-restraint. Your wisdom and better judgement.'

'Inspired by your honeyed words, Shanklin? By your sweet reason, combined with your appreciation of recent history? Perhaps that's why you and Robak's boys never tried to buy us off? No, Anna and I are satisfied to leave the bribing – what I call petty ex's – to that evil genius, Pol. God let him rot in an East German jail.'

Shanklin nodded. 'That was the one mistake the East Germans made – they underrated Pol. They didn't trust him either, of course, or they wouldn't have sent a platoon of troops to the lake this morning. But they didn't expect him and his mercenary thugs to start a shoot-out and kill their star witness.'

Hawn stared at him. 'How the hell do you know about it so quickly?'

'Little machine called the telephone. Plus a telex to their Security in Alexanderplatz, East Berlin.'

'You and ABCO and Pol had the East Germans eating out of your hand. How come? They're nobody's saints – and they're certainly not blind kittens, either.'

'Menés par le bout du nez,' Shanklin said, with a rarified accent: " 'Led by the nose", as your chum Pol would have said.'

'Used!' Anna broke in bitterly. 'That's what we were – used by you and Robak and Pol – even by British Intelligence. And what the hell was in it for *them?*'

Hawn gave a savage laugh. 'That would be a good story – connivance between MI6 and the boys over the Wall. I wouldn't like to jump to any false conclusions there.'

Shanklin blew his nose. 'I can't answer every little question, you know. It all boils down really to a matter of priorities and common interests. When our interests and those of the East Germans happen to coincide, hoopla! – you almost hear wedding bells in the air. But seriously. You have to look at it not only from the East German point of view, but also from Whitehall's. The Communist Krauts are busy doing a deal with ABCO – ergo, ABCO suddenly has a lot of lead to swing behind the Iron Curtain. The East Germans are very anxious that their deal goes through. And – through a certain Colonel Kardich, of their Security

Police – they are persuaded to go along with ABCO's plan, whatever that is.

'And Kardich appears to have agreed, but on two conditions. Firstly – you and your girlfriend cannot be allowed to run around loose on their patch. Secondly, when the crunch comes with a meeting between you and Rice at the lake, the Commies want nothing officially to do with it. They insist that at this point the responsibility passes either to ABCO directly, or to the British or Americans.' He waved his hand :

'Happens all the time, though it never gets reported. You'd be surprised how much co-operation we get from the other side, and vice versa.'

'But I bet there was another reason,' said Anna. 'Our spooks in Whitehall felt it necessary to take a hand, not just to protect those so-called vital national interests that are tied up with ABCO, but because there are too many big-wigs still loose round Whitehall, not to mention the bloody Lords, who had a hand in the whole conspiracy from the beginning! And of course, the British Establishment can't afford to start having all its dirty linen – as well as its starched shirt-fronts – washed in front of the whole world.'

'Bravo!' Shanklin had sat up and was patting his hands together. 'In a nutshell, my dear! Couldn't have put it better myself – though I don't think I could have matched all your social venom.'

Hawn said : 'It still doesn't explain why the East Germans went so far as to put up their leading scientist as target practice for Pol and his friends. Particularly when you say that they didn't trust the man.'

'I said they underrated him. Like ABCO, they wanted the ends tied up. Rice had spoken his piece a long time ago, and they'd already retrieved their box of documents from the lake. Of course, there's no danger of the East Germans using them now – although they might come in useful, if ABCO ever wanted to become difficult. And no doubt future Communist historians will find them an entertaining source.'

'But why the hell were we two billed so big in all of this –

right until the end of the last reel, when Pol decided to change the script?'

'You were the bait, my dear fellow. Both of you. As I have explained, it was either a question of disposing of you – with all the untidy consequences – or of leaving you to follow the spur right to the dead end. The dead secret, if you like. Somebody had to do it, sooner or later. You were the chosen pair – or rather, you chose yourselves, and received our reluctant blessing.'

'And supposing I write it up as a story?'

'Based on whose evidence? Mine? Pol's? Colonel Kardich's, perhaps? Even young Hanak's?'

'There's that old dictum of the Duke of Wellington – "Publish and be damned".'

'You even try to publish, and you'll be damned. I mean that, Hawn. And you should believe me. Do me at least that courtesy. I'm the one who's acted as your advocate – spoke up for you both, pressed for the soft line – and, fortunately for you, won. I may not go on winning. So don't let me down. I don't give a bugger about you or this girl here – but I do care about what happens to ABCO and this country. You cross me and you make an enemy for life.'

There was a long pause. Hawn finished his Scotch. 'So where do we go from here?'

'Home. And don't try to be a hero. If there's anyone I dislike more than a fool, it's a failed hero. What would you hope to achieve? What newspaper do you think would even print your story? Mönch is dead, French is dead, Salak is dead, Pol is *hors de combat,* and I shall deny everything.' He stood up.

'So, if you're ready, my man will drive you back to London. You should be in time to have a good dinner at Odins. I'll ring and have them keep their best table for you – they know me pretty well. And don't worry about the bill.'

'Thank you,' said Hawn. 'We'd prefer somewhere a little quieter.'

Anna propped up the steel stepladder, climbed to the top

and reached for the file *Na* to *Ne*. She went back to her desk and turned the pages to 'National Enterprise Board': 'British Leyland – subsidiaries – Export Figures, June-October'. She took notes in her neat, sloping hand until a couple of minutes to five, when she returned the file and fetched her coat.

A quarter of a mile away, in the British Museum Reading Room, Hawn finished reading a lengthy thesis entitled 'The Religious and Socio-Economic Realities of the Renaissance Dynasty. Part 1 : Influence of the Medicis'.

He had parked his car on a yellow line in Coptic Street, and experienced a moment's exhilaration when he found that he had not collected a ticket.

He picked up Anna on a corner of Aldwych. Neither of them saw a very ordinary Ford keeping its distance behind them down the Strand. And when they reached the quiet of Pembridge Villas they took no notice of the car that parked a hundred yards ahead of them, under the trees.

THE END

## THE WORLD'S GREATEST THRILLER WRITERS - NOW AVAILABLE IN GRANADA PAPERBACKS

### Robert Ludlum

| | | |
|---|---|---|
| The Chancellor Manuscript | £1.50 | ☐ |
| The Gemini Contenders | £1.50 | ☐ |
| The Rhinemann Exchange | £1.50 | ☐ |
| The Matlock Paper | £1.50 | ☐ |
| The Osterman Weekend | £1.25 | ☐ |
| The Scarlatti Inheritance | £1.25 | ☐ |
| Ludlum Super-Thrillers Gift Set | £5.95 | ☐ |

### Ian Fleming

| | | |
|---|---|---|
| Dr No | 95p | ☐ |
| From Russia, with Love | 95p | ☐ |
| Diamonds are Forever | 95p | ☐ |
| On Her Majesty's Secret Service | 95p | ☐ |
| Goldfinger | £1.25 | ☐ |
| You Only Live Twice | 95p | ☐ |
| Live and Let Die | 95p | ☐ |
| The Man with the Golden Gun | 95p | ☐ |
| Octopussy | 75p | ☐ |
| Casino Royale | 75p | ☐ |
| Thunderball | 75p | ☐ |

### Alan Williams

| | | |
|---|---|---|
| The Widow's War | 95p | ☐ |
| Shah-Mak | 95p | ☐ |
| Gentleman Traitor | 60p | ☐ |
| The Beria Papers | 75p | ☐ |
| Barbouze | £1.25 | ☐ |
| Long Run South | 85p | ☐ |
| Snake Water | £1.25 | ☐ |
| The Purity League | 85p | ☐ |
| The Tale of the Lazy Dog | 85p | ☐ |

## THE WORLD'S GREATEST THRILLER WRITERS –
## NOW AVAILABLE IN GRANADA PAPERBACKS

### Len Deighton

### Peter Van Greenway

### Ted Allbeury

## THE WORLD'S GREATEST NOVELISTS
## NOW AVAILABLE IN GRANADA PAPERBACKS

**Simon Raven**

| | |
|---|---|
| Bring Forth The Body | 95p ☐ |
| The Survivors | 95p ☐ |
| Come Like Shadows | 95p ☐ |
| Sound the Retreat | 95p ☐ |
| Friends in Low Places | £1.25 ☐ |
| Fielding Gray | 95p ☐ |
| Doctors Wear Scarlet | 30p ☐ |

**Paul Scott**

| | |
|---|---|
| The Raj Quartet | |
| The Towers of Silence | £1.95 ☐ |
| The Day of the Scorpion | £1.95 ☐ |
| The Jewel in the Crown | £1.50 ☐ |
| A Division of the Spoils | £1.95 ☐ |
| The Bender | 75p ☐ |
| The Corrida at San Feliu | £1.25 ☐ |
| A Male Child | £1.50 ☐ |
| The Alien Sky | £1.25 ☐ |
| The Chinese Love Pavilion | 1.25 ☐ |

## MYSTERY AND SUSPENSE FROM COLIN WILSON

## BESTSELLERS AVAILABLE IN GRANADA PAPERBACKS

**Leslie Waller**

| | | |
|---|---|---|
| The Swiss Account | £1.25 | ☐ |
| The 'K' Assignment | 50p | ☐ |
| Number One | 85p | ☐ |
| A Change in the Wind | 40p | ☐ |
| The American | 75p | ☐ |
| The Family | £1.25 | ☐ |
| The Banker | £1.25 | ☐ |
| The Coast of Fear | 60p | ☐ |

**Patrick Mann**

| | | |
|---|---|---|
| The Vacancy | 60p | ☐ |
| Dog Day Afternoon | 60p | ☐ |

*All these books are available at your local bookshop or newsagent, or can be ordered direct from the publisher. Just tick the titles you want and fill in the form below.*

Name ...............................................................

Address ...........................................................

...................................................................

Write to Granada Cash Sales, PO Box 11, Falmouth, Cornwall TR10 9EN.

Please enclose remittance to the value of the cover price plus:

UK: 30p for the first book, 15p for the second book plus 12p per copy for each additional book ordered to a maximum charge of £1.29.

BFPO and EIRE: 30p for the first book, 15p for the second book plus 12p per copy for the next 7 books, thereafter 6p per book.

OVERSEAS: 50p for the first book and 15p for each additional book.

*Granada Publishing reserve the right to show new retail prices on covers, which may differ from those previously advertised in the text or elsewhere.*